LIGHTNING

AN 87TH PRECINCT NOVEL

ED McBAIN

AVON BOOKS NEW YORK

AVON BOOKS
A division of
The Hearst Corporation
1350 Avenue of the Americas
New York, New York 10019

Copyright © 1984 by HUI Corporation
Published by arrangement with Arbor House Publishing Company
Library of Congress Catalog Card Number: 84-3030
ISBN: 0-380-69974-5

First Avon Books Printing: July 1985

AVON TRADEMARK REG. U.S. PAT. OFF. AND IN OTHER COUNTRIES, MARCA REGISTRADA, HECHO EN CANADA.

Printed in Canada

UNV   10

This is for Ruth and Basil Levin

1

DETECTIVE RICHARD GENERO DID NOT LIKE to go out on night calls. The truth of the matter was that the nighttime city scared him. There were all sorts of things that could happen to a person in this city once the sun went down. Even if the person happened to be a cop, things could happen to him. He knew plenty of cops who'd had things happen to them at night. Somehow, the things that happened to cops happened to them more often at night than during the day. That was one of the sacred precepts he had learned about police work, and he had formulated a rule about it and the rule was *Never go out at night,* an impossible rule to observe if you didn't want your fellow police officers to think you were chickenshit.

Once, when Genero was still a patrolman, he was walking his beat one cold December night when he saw a light burning in a basement and, like a good cop, went down to investigate. He found a dead kid with a blue face and a rope around his neck. That was one of the things that had happened to him at night. Another time—well, that wasn't even *night*time, that was during the day; things could happen to cops even during the daytime. He'd been walking his beat, it was raining, he remembered, and he'd seen somebody running away from a bus stop, and when he'd picked up the bag the person had left behind on the sidewalk, it had a human *hand* in it! A person's *hand!* Cut off at the wrist and left on the sidewalk in an *airlines* bag! Boy, the things that could happen to cops, day *or* night. The way Genero figured it, you

1

weren't safe in this city no matter *what* time you went out in it.

He felt only a little safer with Carella by his side.

The two men had gone out at night because they were doing a followup on a crib burglary, and the victim worked as a night watchman at a construction site. It had taken Genero a long time to learn that a crib burglar wasn't somebody who went around stealing beds that babies slept in. A crib, in a burglar's vocabulary, was an apartment. A crib burglar was somebody who burglarized apartments, and that was usually done during the daytime, when most apartments were empty; the last thing a burglar wanted or needed was to walk in on some old lady who'd start screaming her head off. That was why burglars who went into office buildings went in at night, when everybody had gone home from work already, and usually they went in after the cleaning lady was finished, too. That was a safe rule for smart burglars to follow: *Always go in when nobody's there.*

The burglar in this particular case had gone into the apartment at two o'clock in the afternoon and was confidently unplugging the television set in the living room when all of a sudden a guy in his pajamas walked in from the bedroom and said, "What the hell are you doing here?" The guy turned out to be a night watchman who worked at night and slept during the day, and the burglar ran like hell. Carella and Genero were here at the construction site tonight to show the watchman some mug shots, even though a safe rule for smart cops to follow was *Never go out at night,* even if you went with Carella. Carella wasn't Superman. He wasn't even Batman.

Carella was either a little over or a little under six feet tall, Genero wasn't so good at estimating heights. He guessed Carella weighed about a hundred and eighty pounds, but he wasn't so good at weights, either. Carella had brown eyes, slanty like a Chink's, and he walked like a baseball player. His hair was only slightly lighter than his eyes, and he never wore a hat. Genero had been out with him in the worst rainstorms, and there was Carella marching around bareheaded, as if he didn't know you could catch a cold that way. Genero liked being partnered with Carella because he figured Carella was a man you could count on if something was about to happen. The very *thought* of something about to happen made Genero nervous, but he didn't think anything was going to happen tonight because it was already 3:00 A.M. when they finished showing the mug shots to the burglary victim, and he figured they'd head back to the squadroom, have a cup of coffee and some donuts, do some paperwork, and wait for the day shift to come in at a quarter to eight.

The night was almost balmy for October.

Genero came out of the construction site ahead of Carella because he thought he'd heard some rats scampering around when they were skirting the edge of the excavation, and if there was one thing he hated worse than spiders, it was rats. Especially at night. Even on a mild October night like this one. He breathed deeply of the autumn air, glad to be out of the fenced-in area with its great mounds of earth and its open gaping holes and steel girders lying around everywhere so a man could trip over them and break his head and get eaten by rats in the dark.

The construction site occupied one side of the entire street, and the other side was all abandoned buildings. In this neighborhood, a landlord got tired of paying taxes, he simply abandoned the building. The abandoned row of empty tenements faced the construction site, looking like soot-stained ghosts in the light of the moon. They gave Genero the creeps. He was willing to bet there were thousands of rats in those abandoned buildings, staring out at him from windows as black as eyeless sockets. He took a package of cigarettes from his jacket pocket—it was mild enough to be going around without an overcoat—and was starting to light one when he happened to look up the street.

Carella was just coming through the gate in the fence behind him.

What Genero thought he saw was a person hanging from a lamppost.

The person was attached to the end of a long thick rope.

The person hung twisting gently on the still October air.

The match burned Genero's fingers. He dropped it just as Carella saw the body at the end of the rope. Genero wanted to run. He did not like to be the one to discover dead bodies, or even *parts* of dead bodies; Genero had a large aversion to corpses. He blinked his eyes because he'd never seen a body hanging like this one except in Western movies, and he figured if he blinked it might go away. Even the boy in the basement hadn't been hanging like this one, hadn't been hanging at *all* when you got right down to it, had just been sort of leaning forward on the cot, the rope around his neck, the end of it tied to the barred basement window. When Genero opened his eyes again, Carella was running toward the lamppost, and the body was still hanging there, dangling there on the air, twisting, as if a posse had found a rustler and strung him up on the spot.

Only this wasn't Utah.

This was the big bad city.

"What the hell *is* this?" Monroe said. "The Wild West?"

He was looking up at the hanging body. His partner was looking up too, shading his eyes against the glow of the sodium vapor bulb at the end of the lamppost's arm. They had put sodium vapor bulbs in this part of the city only last month, on the theory that bright lights prevented crime. So here was a body hanging from a lamppost.

"This is the French Revolution," Monoghan said, "is what it is."

"The French Revolution was they cut off your head," Monroe said.

"They also hung you," Monoghan said.

The two men, despite the unusual fall weather, were both wearing overcoats. The overcoats were black. It was *de rigeur* for Homicide cops in this city to wear black. It was a custom. It was not a custom for Homicide cops to wear pearl gray fedoras, but both Monoghan and Monroe were wearing them, the snap brims neatly turned down. Genero was pleased to see that they were wearing hats. His mother had told him to always wear a hat, even on the hottest days, *especially* on the hottest days because then you wouldn't get sunstroke. Today hadn't been particularly hot, just unusually mild for October, but Genero was wearing a hat, anyway. You could never be too careful.

"You get lynchings up here, huh?" Monoghan said to Carella.

"Yeah, we get all kinds of shit up here," Carella said.

He was looking up at the dead body slowly twisting on the end of the rope. As always, but only for the briefest tick of an instant, he felt a sharp dagger of pain behind his eyes. *The waste,* he thought.

"You get the French Revolution up here," Monoghan said.

"You get the Wild West up here," Monroe said.

They both stood in the street, their hands in their coat pockets, looking up at the dead body.

"Nice white panties," Monoghan said, looking up under her skirt.

One of the dead girl's shoes had fallen to the pavement. A purple French-heeled shoe, the color of her blouse. Her skirt was the color of wheat, the color of her hair. Her panties, as Monroe had already observed, were white. She hung dangling above the detectives, slowly twisting at the end of the rope, a purple shoe on one foot.

"Looks how old, would you say?" Monoghan asked.

"Hard to tell from here," Monroe said.

"Let's cut her down," Monoghan said.

"No," Carella said. "Not till the M.E. gets here."

"And the P.U.," Genero said.

He was referring to the Photographic Unit. The men stood under the lamppost, looking up at the dead girl. A crowd had gathered. It was now 3:15 in the morning, but a crowd had gathered from nowhere, filtering in from the side streets onto this deserted street with its abandoned buildings and its construction site. Any hour of the day or night, there were people awake in this city. Genero thought it was a conspiracy, everybody being awake day or night. The four patrolmen, who'd responded in two separate r.m.p. cars when Carella called in the 10-29, were busily erecting barricades and trying to keep the crowd back. Somebody in the crowd thought it wasn't a real girl hanging there. He commented that it was a dummy or something. They were probably shooting a movie or something. A television show. They were always shooting movies or television shows in this city. It was a very photogenic city. The girl kept twisting at the end of the rope.

"How do you hang somebody on a city street," Monroe said, "without nobody seeing you?"

Carella was wondering the same thing.

"Maybe she hung *herself*," Monoghan said.

"So then where's the ladder or whatever?" Monroe said.

"Up here in the Eight-Seven," Monoghan said, "she coulda hung herself and somebody coulda *stole* the ladder later."

"Anyway, it's *hanged*," Monroe said.

"Whattya mean it's hanged?" Monoghan said.

"A person hangs himself, you say he got hanged. Not hung."

"Who told you that?"

"It's common knowledge."

"Hanged?"

"Right."

"That don't sound right. Hanged."

"It's right, though."

"You see a guy with a big dork," Monoghan said, "you don't say he's well-hanged, you say he's well-hung."

"That's a different thing entirely," Monroe said. "We're talking here about a different thing entirely."

"When you hang up your suit on a hanger, you don't say I *hanged* up my suit," Monoghan said. "You say I *hung* up my suit."

"That's also different," Monroe said.

"How is it different?"

"It's different because when you *hang* somebody then the person has been *hanged,* he has not been *hung.*"

Genero didn't know which one of them was right, but he was enjoying the conversation. Carella was walking around the lamppost, hatless, looking at the sidewalk and the street. Genero was wondering what Carella expected to find. There was just the usual shit in the gutter—cigarette butts, gum wrappers, crumpled paper cups, like that. The debris of the city.

"So what do we do here?" Monoghan asked. "Stand around all night waiting for the M.E.?" He looked at his watch. "What time did you call this in, Carella?"

"Three-oh-six," Carella said.

"And how many seconds?" Monroe asked, and Monoghan burst out laughing.

Genero looked at his watch. "Twelve minutes ago," he said.

"So where's the M.E.?" Monoghan said.

A man in the crowd stepped out boldly from behind the barricade when one of the patrolmen turned his back. He walked over to where the detectives were gathered in a knot under the lamppost. He had obviously been appointed spokesman for the spectators. He assumed the

polite, deferential air most citizens of this city affected
when they were asking information of policemen.

"Excuse me, sir," he said to Monoghan, "but can
you tell me what happened here?"

"Fuck off," Monoghan said politely.

"Get over there behind the barricade," Monroe said.

"Is the young lady dead?" the man said.

"No, she's learning how to fly," Monoghan said.

"She's wearing a safety rope and learning how to
fly," Monroe said.

"She'll be flapping her arms any minute," Monoghan
said.

"Get back there behind the barricade and you can
watch her," Monroe said.

The man looked up at the dead girl twisting at the end
of the rope. He did not think the girl was learning to fly.
But he went back behind the barricade anyway, and reported to the others what he'd just been told.

"You ever get anybody hung before?" Monoghan
asked Carella.

"Hanged," Monroe said.

"Few hanging suicides," Carella said. "Nothing like
this, though."

"A real hanging, you need a good drop," Monroe
said. "Most of your hanging suicides, they get up on a
chair, put the rope around their neck, and then jump off
the chair. You don't *hang* that way, you *suffocate*. You
need a good drop for a hanging."

"Why's that?" Genero asked. He was interested. His
mother had advised him to listen carefully all the time because that was the way you learned things.

" 'Cause what happens in a *real* hanging, the rope . . .
the knot up there . . .."

"Regular hangman's knot up there," Monoghan said,
looking up.

"The drop snaps the knot up against the back of the
guy's neck, and it breaks his neck, that's what happens.

But you need a good drop, six feet or more, otherwise the rope just suffocates the guy. You get a lot of amateurs trying to hang themselves, they just choke to death. Guy wants to kill himself, he ought to learn how to do it right.''

"I had a suicide once, he stabbed himself in the heart," Monoghan said.

"So?" Monroe said.

"I'm just saying."

"Well, you get all kinds," Genero said, trying to sound worldly and experienced.

"For sure, kid," Monoghan said, solemnly agreeing with him.

"Here's the M.E.," Monroe said.

"About time," Monoghan said, and looked at his watch again.

The assistant medical examiner was a man named Paul Blaney. He had been at an all-night poker game when he'd been summoned to the scene. He was angry because he'd been sitting with a full boat, kings over threes, when the phone rang. He'd insisted on playing out the hand before he'd left, and had lost the pot to four jacks. Blaney was a short man with a scraggly black mustache, eyes that looked violet in a certain light, and a bald head that looked very shiny under the sodium vapors. He greeted the men curtly, and then looked up at the hanging girl.

"So what am I supposed to do?" he said. "Climb up the lamppost?"

"I told you we shoulda cut her down," Monoghan said.

"We'd better wait for the lab boys," Carella said.

"What for?"

"They'll want to look at the rope."

"You ever get a case where there was fingerprints on a *rope?*" Monoghan said.

"No, but . . ."

"So let's cut her down."

Blaney looked uncertain. He glanced up at the dead girl. He looked at Carella.

"They may know what kind of knot it is," Carella said.

"It's a *hangman's* knot," Monoghan said. "Anybody can *see* it's a hangman's knot. Don't you ever go to the movies? Don't you ever watch television?"

"I meant the one around the post. The one tied around the post. The *other* end of the rope."

Blaney looked at his watch.

"I was playing poker," he said to no one.

The Mobile Crime Unit arrived some ten minutes later. By that time, there were three more radio motor patrol cars at the scene, and the ambulance had arrived from Mercy General. The crowd had swelled behind the barricades. Everybody was waiting for them to cut the dead girl down. They wanted to see if she was really dead or if this was a movie they were shooting here. None of the people in the crowd had ever seen a person hanging from a lamppost before. Most of them had never seen a person hanging *anywhere* before. The girl just kept hanging there, it sure looked as if she was real, and it also looked as if she was dead. The boys from the P.U. took pictures of the hanging girl and the area around the lamppost and the rope tied and knotted around the post. The lab technicians held a brief consultation with Carella, and it was thought advisable to preserve the knot as it was tied, rather than untying it to lower the girl; they would want to look over the knot more carefully at the lab. It was decided that they would cut the girl down, after all.

Monoghan walked around nodding righteously, his hands in his pockets; it was what he'd suggested all along. The Emergency Service truck had arrived by then, and a sergeant unhooked a ladder from the side of the truck and asked one of the lab technicians where he wanted the rope cut, and the technician indicated a place about midway between the hangman's knot behind the girl's neck and the knot where the rope had been fastened to the post. The Emergency Service cops spread a safety net under the hanging girl, and the sergeant went up the ladder and cut the rope with a bolt cutter.

The girl dropped into the net.

A cheer went up from the crowd behind the barricades.

Blaney examined the girl, pronounced her dead, and ventured the opinion that the cause of death—pending autopsy—was fracture of the cervical vertebrae.

It was a little after 4:00 A.M. when the ambulance carried her off to the morgue.

The first time was always easiest.

There was an element of complete surprise involved, none of these women ever thought anything like this would happen to them, even here in this city where surely they knew it was a common occurrence. All he had to do was ambush them, show them the knife, and they turned to jelly.

The other times were difficult, very difficult.

A lot of patience was involved.

Some of them wouldn't even budge from their apartments after the first time, so terrified were they of what had happened to them, so fearful that it might happen again. After a few weeks, though sometimes a month, they'd come outside again, usually accompanied by a husband or a boyfriend, and never at night, they were still afraid of going out at night. You had to be patient.

And you had to check the calendar.

Eventually, after that first time, they got over the trauma, and they ventured out into the nighttime city alone again, and he was waiting, of course, he was waiting for them, and the surprise was even more total this time, lightning couldn't strike *twice,* could it? Ah, but it could. And it did. And the second time, if they recognized him, and some of them did, they usually pleaded that he not do it to them again, they who would impose their will on *everyone* if they had their way, begging him not to impose *his* will on *them,* the irony of it. None of them knew he was watching the calendar, or that his attacks were precisely timed.

After the second time, they became trembling wrecks. Some of them moved to other neighborhoods, or left the city entirely. Others went on long vacations. Still others jumped out of their shoes if an automobile horn sounded three blocks away. They began to think of themselves as helpless victims of something inexplicably evil that had chosen them as targets out of all the women in this city. One of them hired a bodyguard. But the others—well, you get over things, you go on with your life. You spend a few hours out of your apartment in the daytime, never wandering too far from home, and eventually you extend your time outdoors and you expand the range of your excursions, and before long you were back to what you supposed was normal, though you were still fearful of the night, and always accompanied by friends or relatives after dark. Until, eventually, you began to think you were safe again, it was all behind you, and the first few times you went out alone at night and nothing happened to you, you figured it was all a thing of the past, it had happened twice, yes, but it could never in a million years happen again. But what you did not know was that he was watching the calendar, and it *would* happen again because he was very patient, he had all the time in the world.

The third time—one of them had fought him as if her very life depended on not being violated again. He had cut that one. Cut her on the face, and her screaming had stopped, and she had submitted to him, whimpering and bleeding. The third time—one of them had promised him extravagant sums of money if only he'd leave her alone. He had done to her what he wished to do, and then had come after her a week later, into her apartment this time, he knew she lived alone, and had done it to her a fourth time, she was the one he'd caught a total of four times. It became almost impossible to carry out the plan after the third time because by then they knew they weren't being chosen as random victims, they knew that somebody was after *them* specifically, and that if it had happened three times it could happen four or five or a dozen times, there was no stopping him from doing whatever he wanted whenever he chose.

All he had to do was keep patient.

Keep watching the calendar.

Keep ticking off the dates.

Only once had he been entirely successful the first time out.

He'd followed her afterward. He knew where she went. He knew he'd succeeded. He'd left her alone after that, except for watching her, and he knew for certain later that she'd been forced to do exactly what he'd planned for her to do all along, and there was such a sweet rush of triumph when he saw her again a month later, watching from a distance, and knew that his plan was viable and sound, and that it could succeed again and again.

The woman tonight was named Mary Hollings.

He had raped her twice.

He had raped her the first time in June. June tenth, to be exact, a Friday night, he had marked the date on his calendar. She'd been out late shopping, and she was carrying a department store shopping bag full of wrapped boxes when he yanked her off the sidewalk and into the alleyway. He'd shown her the knife, held it to her throat, and she'd submitted without a sound, the wrapped boxes lying scattered on the pavement beside the torn shopping bag. She was one of the few who refused to be cowed by the first experience. She was out on the street again, alone, at night, a week later. Cautious, yes, she was not a fool. But fighting her fear with a show of bravado, squarely facing what had happened, refusing to be domi-

nated by it, determined to live her life as she had before
he'd entered it.

He raped her again on the sixteenth day of September,
a Friday like the first time. He'd marked that on his calendar as well. He raped her not six blocks from where
he'd assaulted her the first time. She'd gone to a movie
with a girlfriend, the early show. The movie had let out at
nine-thirty, a quarter to ten. She had walked her girlfriend home, and was starting up the street toward the
bright lights on the Stem, when he grabbed her. Again,
she had not made a sound. But this time, she was terrified. This time, she was shaking all over when he
slashed her panties with the knife and did it to her.

September sixteenth was three weeks ago.

He'd watched her whenever he could during the past
three weeks. Noticed she never went anyplace alone during the daytime unless there were huge crowds around.
Never went out at *all* during the night unless she was with
a man, sometimes two men. He could tell, just from ob-
serving her, that she was still jumpy, even *with* escorts to
protect her, looked around all the time, crossed the street
if a man approached them from another direction, very
cautious, very careful, determined that this wouldn't
happen to her again.

Last Saturday, he'd followed her downtown to Police
Headquarters. He suspected she went there to give further details on what had happened to her twice already.
He followed her when she left there, and was surprised
when she walked into a gun shop, and showed the man
inside a piece of paper, and then began looking over pis-
tols he began producing from under the counter. She had
gone to Police Headquarters for a gun permit! She was
buying a gun! He smiled when she concluded the purchase. He knew she'd soon be on the street again, at
night again, alone again, a gun in her handbag this time,
thinking she was safe from him.

But he was wrong.

This past week, she hadn't budged from the apartment. The nighttime city had truly subjugated her, she would not dare to go out into it alone, even with an escort, even with a gun in her handbag. She was taking no chances. The calendar was ticking. The week was flying by and October seventh was coming up very fast. He knew that to get her again he would have to go into her apartment, the way he had done with the only one he'd caught four times.

Today was the seventh of October, the seventh had finally arrived; a good time, even if it was *barely* the seventh, only a quarter to five in the morning. Today would be her third outing. Once or twice more after that, and he'd have her, unless she decided to move to Outer Mongolia.

Today, he would get her in her own bed.

2

A POLICEWOMAN ACCOMPANIED MARY HOL-
lings to Mercy General, where not three hours earlier the
body of the unidentified hanging victim had been delivered to the morgue for autopsy. The policewoman's
name was Hester Fein. She was a stocky woman with the
height and girth of a short wrestler, twenty-eight years
old and still plagued by acne, a plain squat fire-hydrant of
a woman who—like many of her male colleagues—believed nobody got raped unless she was asking for it, especially not three times in five months; she had learned
back at the station house that this was the third time Mary
Hollings had been raped. Hester Fein's one great ambi-
tion in life was to carry a .357 Magnum, which the Police
Department in this city would not allow. She sometimes
thought of transferring to Houston, Texas. Out there,
they knew what kind of gun a police officer needed to
protect herself.

The plastic box was three and a half inches wide, six
and a half inches long, and an inch deep, with a lid that
was opened by twisting two small plastic knobs in opposite directions. Fastened over the top and side of the box,
in one of the corners, was a narrow tape printed with the
words "Integrity SEAL Slit To Open." Glued to the top
of the box was a label that identified the box and its contents as the JOHNSON RAPE EVIDENCE KIT. The nurse
asked Hester what the case number was. Hester told her,
and she filled in the appropriate space on the label. She
asked Mary Hollings what her name was, and then wrote
it down in the "Name of Subject" space. She asked Hes-

16

ter what the offense was. Flatly, Hester said, "Rape," though she didn't believe it for a minute. The nurse filled in the "Date of Incident" and "Time" spaces on the label. She signed her name as Search Officer and wrote in the location as Mercy General Hospital. She slit the seal on the kit with a scalpel.

The kit contained a wooden cervix scraper, a slide holder with two slides, a plastic comb, a pubic hair collection lifter, a white gummed envelope marked "A" Combings, a white gummed envelope marked "B" Standard, a Seminal Fluid Reagent Packet which was a plastic bag containing a white cotton pad and a blue reagent tab, an instruction booklet, and two red labels lettered in white with the words:

The nurse administering the tests was familiar with the instruction booklet. So was Mary Hollings.

Mary was trembling as she climbed up on the examination table and removed her torn panties. The nurse assured her that this wouldn't hurt her, and Mary said something incoherent in reply, and then put her feet in the stirrups and sighed deeply and forlornly. Using the wooden cervix scraper, the nurse took two vaginal smears and prepared the slides, allowing them to air-dry as warned on the slide holder, and then slipping them back into the small plastic container. She wrote Mary's name again in the "Subject" space on the slide holder, filled in the date, and then her own name in the "By"

space, and placed the holder in the open plastic kit box.
She stepped on the pedal of a trash can and dropped the
used wooden scraper into it.

"We'll want those panties," Hester said.

"What?" the nurse said.

"For evidence," Hester said.

"Well, that's your department," the nurse said.

"Damn straight," Hester said, and picked up the panties and put them in an evidence envelope. The panties
were black and edged with black lace, confirming Hester's surmise that nobody got raped unless she was asking
for it.

The printed lettering on the "Pubic Hair Collection"
envelope was purple. It called for the same information
as the label on the kit itself. The nurse filled it in, copying
from the label on the kit, and then opened the envelope
and held it under Mary's vagina. She passed the plastic
comb through Mary's pubic hair several times, allowing
any loose hairs to fall into the open envelope. She put the
comb into the same envelope with the hair, and then
sealed the envelope, and put it into the plastic kit box,
alongside the slide holder.

Since there still may have been some loose pubic hairs
remaining in Mary's pubic area, the nurse now took the
Pubic Hair Collection lifter, peeled the clear plastic protection shield from the narrow piece of adhesive, and patted the adhesive surface over the entire pubic area. She
closed the white plastic cover over the adhesive surface,
filled in the same information yet another time, and returned the lifter to the kit. She threw the clear plastic
shield into the trash can with the used wooden scraper.
Mary was still trembling. She seemed unable to stop
trembling.

"We'll need a sample of your pubic hair," the nurse
said. "Did you want to take it yourself, or shall I?"

Mary nodded.

"Which, dear?" the nurse said.

Mary shook her head.

"Shall I do it, dear?"

Mary nodded again.

The second "Pubic Hair Collection Envelope" was lettered in blue. It differed from the first envelope only in that one was lettered "A" and "Combings" and the other was lettered "B" and "Standard." They both called for the same case information which the nurse filled in before firmly grasping a fistful of hair in Mary's pubic area. It was important that the hairs not be cut; she quickly pulled some ten or twenty of them loose (Mary gave a short, sharp gasp) and then placed them in the envelope and sealed it.

"Almost finished," she said.

Mary nodded.

Hester Fein watched.

The nurse opened the plastic bag labeled "Seminal Fluid Reagent." She removed the small blue tab from the bag. She saturated the cotton pad with distilled water, wiped the wet cotton over and around Mary's genital area, and then said, "Do they want me to do the test here, or will they handle it at the lab?"

"Nobody told me," Hester said.

"Might as well do it and get it over with," the nurse said.

"Might as well," Hester said.

The nurse opened the blue tab by peeling it apart, exposing the activated acid phosphatase paper. She applied the paper to the wet cotton for several seconds. She removed the paper and looked at it.

"What will that tell you?" Hester asked.

"Presumptive presence of semen will cause an immediate color change in the paper."

"What color?" Hester asked.

"There it goes," the nurse said as the paper turned a dark purple that was the exact color of the printing on the acid phosphatase tab.

"So what does that mean?" Hester said.

"Positive for semen," the nurse said, and returned the cotton pad and the tab to the plastic bag. "They'll want to test further at the lab, but that's it for now. Thank you, dear," she said to Mary, "you were a very good patient."

Everything was back in the kit again. She closed the lid, picked up the two red police seals, peeled off the protective backing, said to Hester, "You see me sealing it," and then handed the sealed kit to her, and threw the instruction booklet into the trash can. "You can go now, dear," she said to Mary.

"Where?" Mary said.

"Back to the station house," Hester said. "We've got a detective from the Rape Squad coming up."

Mary sat up.

"I . . ."

She looked around, bewildered.

"Yes, dear?" the nurse said.

"My panties," she said. "Where are my panties?"

"I got them here for evidence," Hester said.

"I need my panties," Mary said.

Hester looked at the nurse. Reluctantly, she handed Mary the manila evidence envelope. As Mary put on the torn panties, Hester whispered to the nurse, "Talk about locking the barn door."

Mary seemed not to hear her.

The 87th Precinct squadroom was relatively quiet, but then again it was only eight in the morning when the detective from the Rape Squad arrived. The Graveyard Shift had already been relieved, and Genero had run home as quickly as he could, leaving Carella to type up the D.D. reports while the relieving detectives on the day tour drank their customary coffee before getting down to work.

The four relieving detectives were Cotton Hawes, Bert

Kling, Meyer Meyer and Arthur Brown, but Brown and Meyer had checked in only briefly and then had immediately gone out again to interview the victim of an armed robbery. Hawes and Kling were at Kling's desk—Kling behind it in a chair, Hawes half-sitting, half-leaning on one corner of it, both men drinking coffee in cardboard containers—when the Rape Squad detective arrived.

"Who do I see about Mary Hollings?" she asked.

Hawes turned toward the slatted rail divider. The woman standing there was perhaps thirty-four years old, a dark-eyed brunette wearing eyeglasses, a trenchcoat open over a blue dress, and blue medium-heeled shoes. A blue leather shoulder bag was riding on her hip, her right hand resting on it.

"This the rape?" Hawes asked.

The woman nodded and opened the gate in the railing. "I'm Annie Rawles," she said, and walked to where the two men were sitting. At his own desk, Carella looked up briefly and then continued typing. "Any more of that coffee around?" she asked.

"Cotton Hawes," Hawes said, extending his hand.

Annie took it in a firm grip, and looked directly into his eyes. He was six-two or six-three, she guessed, two hundred pounds more or less, blue-eyed and red-headed, with a white streak in the hair over his left temple, looked like he'd been hit by lightning or something. Hawes was thinking he wouldn't mind taking Annie Rawles to bed. He liked these slender ones with firm little tits and no hips. Idly, he wondered if she outranked him.

"Bert Kling," Kling said, and nodded.

Good-looking bunch of guys up here, Annie thought. The one who'd just introduced himself as Kling was almost as tall and as broad-shouldered as Hawes, with blond hair and eyes she guessed were hazel-colored or something, the open-faced look of a farm boy about him. Even the one who was hunched over a typewriter across

the room was handsome in a Chinese sort of way—but he
was wearing a wedding band on his left hand.

"You the ones who caught the squeal?" Annie said.

"O'Brien did, he's already gone," Hawes said.

"I'll get you that coffee," Kling said. "How do you
like it?"

"Light with one sugar."

Kling headed off toward the Clerical Office down the
hall. Carella was still typing.

"Where's the victim?" Annie asked.

"Policewoman took her to Mercy General," Hawes
said.

"Didn't we meet one time?" Annie asked.

"I don't think so," Hawes said, and smiled. "I'd remember."

"I thought we met up here one time. You get a lot of
rapes up here, don't you?"

"Our fair share," Hawes said.

"How many?" Annie asked.

"You mean a week? A month?"

"Annually," Annie said.

"I'd have to check the files."

"Citywide, we got about thirty-five hundred last
year," Annie said. "The national figure was close to
seventy-eight thousand."

Kling was back with her coffee.

"A friend of mine works out of Special Forces," he
said. "Does a lot of decoy stuff."

"Oh?" Annie said. "What's her name?"

"Eileen Burke."

"Oh, sure," Annie said, "I've seen her around. Tall
redhead? Green eyes?"

"That's her."

"Beautiful girl," Annie said, and Kling smiled.
"Good cop, too, I hear."

He'd called Eileen a "friend." Present-day euphemism for "lover," even when a cop used it. Scratch the blond, Annie thought.

The gate in the wooden divider opened, and Hester Fein led Mary Hollings into the squadroom. Hester looked around for O'Brien, saw that he was already gone, and seemed bewildered for a moment.

"Who gets this?" she asked, holding out the Rape Evidence kit.

"I'll take it," Annie said.

Hester looked at her.

"Detective First/Grade, Anne Rawles," Annie said. "Rape Squad."

She *does* outrank me, Hawes thought.

"I filled it in where I was supposed to," Hester said, and indicated the label on the kit. Under the heading CHAIN OF POSSESSION, there were three brief, identical information requests to be completed. After "Received From," Hester had written in Hillary Baskin, R.N. Mercy General. After "By," she had written in P.O. Hester Fein, and then her shield number. After "Date," she had written in October 7, and after "Time," she had written in 7:31 and circled the printed A.M. Annie filled in the identically requested information below, acknowledging *her* receipt of the kit.

"Anywhere I can talk to Miss Hollings privately?" she asked Hawes.

"Interrogation Room's down the hall," Hawes said. "I'll show you."

"Would you like some coffee, Miss Hollings?" Annie asked.

Mary shook her head. They both followed Hawes through the slatted rail divider and into the corridor outside. Hester hung around as if hoping either Kling or Carella would offer *her* some coffee, too. When neither of them did, she left.

In the Interrogation Room, Annie gently said, "I'll need some routine information first, if you don't mind."

Mary Hollings said nothing.

"May I have your full name, please?"

"Mary Hollings."

"No middle name?"

Mary shook her head.

"Your address, please?"

"1840 Laramie Crescent."

"Apartment number?"

"12C."

"Your age, please?"

"Thirty-seven."

"Single? Married? Divorced?"

"Divorced."

"Your height, please?"

"Five-seven."

"Weight?"

"A hundred and twenty-four."

Annie looked up.

"Red hair," she said, jotting it down on the report form, "eyes blue." She put an X in the *White* box on the form, scanned the rest of the sheet perfunctorily, and -then looked up again. "Can you tell me what happened, Miss Hollings?"

"The same man," Mary said.

"What?" Annie said.

"The same man. The same one as the other two times."

Annie looked at her.

"This is the *third* time you've been raped?" she asked, surprised.

Mary nodded.

"And it was the *same* man each time?"

Mary nodded again.

"You *recognized* him as the same man?"

"Yes."

"Do you *know* this man?"

"No."

"But you're sure he was the same man?"

"Yes."

"Can you give me a description of him?" Annie said, and took a pad from her pocket.

"I did this already," Mary said. *"Twice."*

Anger was beginning to set in. Annie recognized the anger, she had seen it a hundred times before. First the shock tinted with lingering fear, and then the anger. Compounded now because it had happened to Mary Hollings twice before.

"I can get a description from the files then," Annie said. "Were the last two occurrences in this precinct?"

"Yes, in this precinct."

"Then I won't bother you for a description again, I'm sure the files . . ."

"Yes," Mary said.

"Would you like to tell me what happened?" she asked.

Mary said nothing.

"Miss Hollings?"

She still said nothing.

"I'd like to help you," Annie said gently.

Mary nodded.

"Can you tell me where and when this happened?"

"In my apartment," Mary said.

"He came into your apartment?"

"Yes."

"Do you know how he got in?"

"No."

"Was the door locked?"

"Yes."

"Is there a fire escape?"

"Yes."

"Could he have come in through the fire escape window?"

"I don't know *how* he got in. I was asleep."

"And this was at 1840 Laramie Crescent, apartment 12C?"

"Yes."

"Is there a doorman there?"

"No."

"Any other form of security?"

"No."

"Did he take anything from the apartment?"

"No." Mary paused. "He was after *me*."

"You say you were asleep . . ."

"Yes."

"Can you tell me what you were wearing?"

"What difference does that make?"

"We'll need the clothes you were wearing when he . . ."

"I was wearing a long granny nightgown and panties." She paused. "Ever since the first time, I . . . I wear panties to bed."

"The first two occurrences . . . did they also happen in your apartment?"

"No. On the street."

"Then this is the first time he's been to your apartment?"

"Yes."

"And you're sure he's the same man?"

"I'm sure."

"Could we have the panties and nightgown you were wearing? The lab will want to . . ."

"I have the panties on."

"Now, do you mean?"

"Yes."

"The same ones you were wearing when he attacked you?"

"Yes. I just . . . I threw on a dress . . . I put on my shoes . . ."

"When was this?"

"As soon as he left."

"Can you tell me what time that was?"

"Just before I called the police."

"Yes, and what time was that, Miss Hollings?"

"A little before seven o'clock."

"What time did he come into the apartment, would you remember?"

"It must have been a little after five."

"Then he was with you almost two hours."

"Yes." She nodded. "Yes."

"When were you first aware of his presence, Miss Hollings?"

"I heard a noise, I opened my eyes . . . and he was there. He was on me before I could . . ."

She closed her eyes. She shook her head.

Annie knew that the next questions she asked would be difficult ones, she knew that most victims bridled at these questions. But the new state Penal Law defined first-degree rape as "Being a male engaging in sexual intercourse with a female: 1. By forcible compulsion, OR 2. Who is incapable of consent by reason of being physically helpless, OR 3. Who is less than eleven years old," and the questions had to be asked.

The new definition was in no way an improvement over the old one, which previously defined a rapist as "A person who perpetrates an act of sexual intercourse with a female not his wife, against her will or without her consent." Both the old and the new laws made it perfectly okay to rape your own wife, since a related provision of the new law defined "female" as "any female person who is not married to the actor." The old law had specified "When her resistance is forcibly overcome, or when her resistance is prevented by fear of great bodily harm, which she has reasonable cause to believe will be inflicted upon her." A related provision of the new law defined "forcible compulsion" as "physical force that overcomes earnest resistance; or a threat, express or implied, that places a person in fear of immediate death or

serious physical injury." In either law, the burden of
proof fell upon the victim. Meanwhile, close to seventy-
eight thousand rapes were reported committed in this nation last year, and hard-working detectives like Annie
Rawles had to ask hard questions of women who'd just
been violated.

She took a deep breath.

"When you say he was 'on' you . . ."

"He was on the bed, he was on top of me."

"Lying on top of you, do you mean?"

"No. S-s-straddling me."

"You heard a noise that awakened you . . ."

"Yes."

". . . and found him on top of you, straddling you.

"Yes."

"What did you do?"

"I reached . . . I *tried* to reach . . . for the n-n-
nighttable. I have a gun in the drawer of my nighttable, I
tried to g-g-get to it."

"Do you have a permit for the gun?"

"Yes."

"You tried to get the gun . . ."

"Yes. But he grabbed my wrist."

"Which wrist?"

"The right wrist."

"Was your left hand free?"

"Yes."

"Did you try to defend yourself with your left   ?"

"No."

"You didn't strike out at him or   . ?"

"No. He had a *knife!*"

Okay, Annie thought. A knife. Forcible compulsion if
ever there was.

"What kind of knife?" she asked at once.

"The same knife he had the last two times."

"Yes, what kind, please?"

"A switchblade knife."

"Can you tell me how long the blade was?"

"I don't *know* how long the goddamn blade was, it was a *knife!*" Mary said, flaring.

"Did he threaten you with the knife?"

"He said he would cut me if I made a sound."

"Were those his exact words?"

"If I screamed, if I made a sound, I don't know exactly what he said."

Threat, express or implied, Annie thought, fear of immediate death or serious physical injury.

"What happened then?" she asked.

"He . . . lifted my gown."

"Were you struggling?"

"He had the tip of the knife at my throat."

"Held the knife to your throat?"

"Yes. Until . . ."

"Yes."

"He . . . when my . . . my gown was up . . . he . . . he put the knife between my legs. He said he would stick the knife in my . . . my . . . my . . . *in* me if I . . . if I so m-m-much as s-s-said a word. He . . . he . . . tore my panties with the knife . . . cut them with the knife . . . and . . . and . . . then he . . . he . . . d-d-did it to me."

Annie took another deep breath.

"He was there for two hours, you say."

"He k-k-kept doing it to me, *doing* it to me."

"Did he say anything at all during that time? Anything that would lead to indentifi . . ."

"No."

"Didn't accidentally mention his name . . ."

"No."

"Or where he was from, or . . ."

"No."

"Nothing at all?"

"Nothing. Not wh-while he was . . . was . . ."

"He was *raping* you, Miss Hollings," Annie said.

"It's okay to say the word. The son of a bitch was *raping* you."

"Yes," Mary said.

"And he said nothing?"

"Not while he was . . . raping me."

"Miss Hollings, I have to ask this next question. Did he force you to engage in any *deviate* sexual intercourse?"

She was quoting from the Penal Law defining First-Degree Sodomy, another Class-B felony, punishable by a maximum term of twenty-five years in prison. If they ever caught him and could convict him on both rape *and* sodomy, he'd spend the rest of his life behind . . .

"No," Mary said.

Annie nodded. Simple First-Degree Rape. Twenty-five years if he got the max. Three years if he got a lenient judge. Out on the streets again in a year if he behaved himself in prison.

"B-before he left," Mary said, "he . . ."

"Yes?"

"He . . . he said . . ."

"What did he say, Miss Hollings?"

"He . . ."

Mary covered her face with her hands.

"What did he say, please?"

"He s-s-said . . . 'I'll be back.' "

Annie looked at her.

"He was smiling," Mary said.

3

THE PADDED MAILING BAG ARRIVED BY PARcel post on Tuesday morning, October 11. It was addressed to the 87th Precinct, and was accepted at the muster desk by Sergeant Dave Murchison, together with the rest of that morning's mail. Murchison looked at the bag suspiciously, and then held it to his ear to listen for any ticking. In today's world, you never knew whether there was a bomb in a package with no return address on it.

He didn't hear any ticking, which didn't mean a damn thing. Nowadays, you could fashion homemade explosive devices that didn't tick at all. He wondered if he should alert the Bomb Squad; he'd feel like a horse's ass if they came all the way up here and discovered there was a box of chocolates or something inside the bag. Murchison had been a cop for a long time, though, and he knew that one of the first laws of survival in the Police Department was to cover your flanks. He picked up the phone and immediately buzzed Captain Frick's office.

There were a hundred and eighty-six uniformed policemen and sixteen plainclothes detectives working out of the Eight-Seven, and Captain Frick was in command of all of them. Most of them believed that Frick was beyond the age of retirement, if not chronologically, then at least mentally. Some of them went so far as to say that Frick was *non compos mentis* and incapable of tying his own shoelaces in the morning, no less making decisions that could very easily affect the very real life-or-death situations these men confronted daily on the precinct

31

streets. Frick had white hair. His hair had been white forever. He felt it complemented the blue of his uniform. He could not imagine holding down a job that would compel him to wear anything but the blue uniform that so splendidly complemented his dignified white hair. The gold braid, too; he liked the gold braid on his uniform. He liked being a cop. He did not like being told by a desk sergeant that a suspicious looking package had just arrived in the morning mail.

"What do you mean, suspicious?" he asked Murchison.

"No return address on it," Murchison said.

"Where's it postmarked?" Frick asked.

"Calm's Point."

"That's not this precinct," Frick said.

"No, sir, it's not."

"Send it back," Frick said. "I want no part of it."

"Send it back where, sir?" Murchison asked.

"To Calm's Point."

"Where in Calm's Point? There's no return address on it."

"Send it back to the post office," Frick said. "Let them worry about it."

"Suppose it blows up?" Murchison said.

"Why would it blow up?"

"Suppose there's a bomb in it? Suppose we send it back to the post office, and it blows up and kills a hundred postal clerks? How would we look *then?"* Murchison asked.

"So what do you want to do?" Frick asked. He was looking at his shoes and thinking he needed a shine. On his lunch hour, he'd go for a shine at the barber shop on Culver and Sixth.

"That's what I'm asking *you,"* Murchison said. "What to do."

Responsibilities, Frick thought, always responsibilities. Cover your flanks, he thought. In case there's flak from upstairs rank later on. You never knew when departmental heat would come. It struck like lightning.

"What is your recommendation, Sergeant?" he asked.

"I am asking for *your* recommendation, sir," Murchison said.

"Would you suggest we call the Bomb Squad?" Frick asked.

"Is that what you suggest, sir?" Murchison said.

"This would seem a routine matter," Frick said. "I'm sure you are capable of handling it."

"Yes, sir, in what way should I handle it, sir?"

Both men were extremely expert at covering their flanks. It seemed as if they had reached an impasse. Frick was wondering how he could vaguely word an order that wouldn't *sound* like an order. Murchison was sitting there hoping Frick would not tell *him* to open the damn package. Even if there wasn't a bomb in it, you opened these padded mailing bags and all sorts of crud that looked like chopped asbestos fell out onto your desk and your clean blue pants. He did not want to open that bag. He sat there wondering how he could maneuver Frick into giving him definite instructions that would take the damn thing off the muster desk before it exploded in his face.

"Do as you see fit," Frick said.

"Yes, sir, I'll send it to your office," Murchison said.

"No!" Frick said at once. "Don't send any damn bomb to my office!"

"Where *shall* I send it?" Murchison said.

"I told you. Back to the post office."

"Yes, sir, is that your order, sir? If it later explodes at the post office?"

"It won't explode if the Bomb Squad looks at it *first*," Frick said, and realized an instant later that he'd been outflanked.

"Thank you, sir," Murchison said, "I'll call the Bomb Squad."

Frick hung up thinking that if there was no bomb in that package, the Bomb Squad boys would be telling jokes about it for months—chicken-hearted 87th Precinct calls the Bomb Squad when it gets a package without a return address on it. He almost wished there *was* a bomb in that damn bag. He almost wished it would explode before the Bomb Squad got here.

There was no bomb inside the bag.

The Bomb Squad boys were laughing when they left the station house. Shaking his head, Frick watched them from his upstairs window and hoped he didn't run into any departmental rank within the next few weeks.

There was a woman's pocketbook inside the mailing bag.

The pocketbook contained a small packet of Kleenex tissues, a rat-tailed comb, a compact, a package of Wrigley's Spearmint chewing gum, a checkbook, a small spiral-bound notebook, a ball point pen, a tube of lipstick, a pair of sunglasses, and a wallet. No keys. The detectives thought that was odd. No keys. The wallet contained four ten dollar bills, a five dollar bill, and two singles. The wallet also contained a Ramsey University student I.D. card giving the girl's address here in the city. The girl's name, as typed on the I.D. card, was Marcia Schaffer. A photograph was sealed between the protective plastic layers of the card.

The girl was smiling in the photograph.

She was not smiling in the photographs the P.U. had taken at the scene of the hanging on Friday morning, October 7.

Aside from that, the photographs were virtually identical.

Kling and Carella were studying the photographs when Meyer Meyer walked into the squadroom. They pretended they didn't know him. That was because Meyer was wearing a wig.

"Yes, sir, can I help you?" Carella asked, looking up.

"Come on," Meyer said, and started pushing his way through the gate in the railing.

Kling leaped to his feet at once, starting for the railing.

"Excuse me, sir," he said, "this is a restricted area."

"Would you please state your business, sir?" Carella said.

Meyer kept advancing into the squadroom.

Kling pulled his gun from his shoulder holster.

"Hold it right there, sir!" he shouted.

Carella's gun was already in his hand. "State your business, sir!" he shouted, moving forward.

"It's me," Meyer said. "Cut it out, will you?"

"It's *who,* sir?" Kling said. "State your goddamn business!"

"My business is kicking the asses of wise-guy flat-foots," Meyer said, and went to his desk.

"It's *Meyer!*" Carella said in mock surprise.

"I'll be a son of a gun!" Kling said.

"You've got *hair!*" Carella said.

"No kidding," Meyer said. "What's the big deal? Man buys a hairpiece, right away it's a reason for hilarity."

"Are we laughing?" Kling asked.

"You see us laughing?" Carella asked.

"Is it *real* hair?" Kling asked.

"Yes, it's real hair," Meyer said testily.

"Boy, you sure had us fooled," Carella said.

"Real hair from where?" Kling asked.

"How do I know from where? It's people who sell their hair, they make hairpieces out of it."

"Is it virgin hair?" Kling asked.

"Is it head hair or pubic hair?" Carella asked.

"The shit a man has to take up here," Meyer said, shaking his head.

"I think he looks beautiful," Kling said to Carella.

"I think he looks adorable," Carella said.

"Is this shit going to go on all morning?" Meyer said, sighing. "Nothing better to do around here? I thought you caught a homicide last week. Go arrest some shopping bag ladies, will you?"

"He's ravishing when he gets angry," Kling said.

"Those flashing blue eyes," Carella said.

"And those curly brown locks," Kling said.

"They're not curly," Meyer said.

"How much did it cost?" Kling asked.

"None of your business," Meyer said.

"Virgin pubic hair must cost a fortune," Carella said.

"Very difficult to come by," Kling said.

"How does Sarah feel about you wearing a mirkin on your head?" Carella asked, and both he and Kling burst out laughing.

"Very funny," Meyer said. "Typical crude squadroom humor. Man buys a hairpiece . . ."

"Who's that sitting in *my* chair?" a voice boomed from beyond the railing, and Arthur Brown walked into the squadroom. Brown was the color of his surname, a six-foot-four, two hundred and twenty pound detective who stood now with an amazed look on his handsome face. "Why, I do believe it's Goldilocks," he said, opening his eyes wide. "Fetch some porridge," he said to Kling. "What cute curls you have, Goldilocks."

"Another county heard from," Meyer said.

Brown approached Meyer's desk. He tiptoed around the desk, eyeing the hairpiece. Meyer didn't even look at him.

"Does it bite?" Brown asked.

"He rented it from a pet shop," Kling said.

"Ha-ha," Meyer said.

"It looks like a bird done on your head," Brown said.

"Ha-ha," Meyer said.

"Do you comb it, or just wipe it off?" Brown asked.

"Wise guys," Meyer said, shaking his head.

He'd been dreading walking in here all morning. He

knew just what would be waiting for him here when he
showed up wearing the hairpiece. He would rather have
faced a bank robber holding a sawed-off shotgun than
these smart-asses in the squadroom. He busied himself
looking over the slips on the Activity Reports spindle. He
desperately wanted a cigarette, but he'd promised his
daughter he'd quit smoking.

"What's this about the Bomb Squad being here?"
Brown asked.

Good, Meyer thought. They're getting off my goddamn rug.

"False alarm," Carella said. ' You ought to wear it in
braids," he said to Meyer.

Meyer sighed.

"So what was it?" Brown asked.

"You can sweep it up on top of your head when you go
to the Governor's ball," Kling said.

"Anti-Semites," Meyer said, and laughed when the
other men did.

"Is the Governor holding one of his balls again?"
Brown asked, and they all laughed again.

"Did you see the picture?" Carella said.

"What picture?" Brown asked.

"It was a handbag, not a bomb," Kling said. "Somebody sent us the hanging victim's handbag."

"No shit?" Brown said.

"Picture of her on her I.D. card," Carella said.

The men all looked at each other.

They were each thinking the exact same thing. They
were thinking that whoever had hanged that lady from a
lamppost *wanted* them to identify her. They had been
running all over the city for the past three days trying to
get a positive make so they'd have someplace to start.
Now somebody had made the job easy for them. He had
sent them the dead girl's handbag with identification in
it. They could only think of one person in the world who
would ever want to make things easy for the cops up

here. Or seemingly easy. None of them wanted to mention his name. But they were all thinking that's who it was.

"Maybe somebody found the handbag," Brown said.

"Read about her in the newspapers, figured he'd send the bag over to us."

"Didn't want to get involved."

"This city, nobody wants to get involved."

"Maybe," Carella said.

But they were still thinking it was the Deaf Man.

The physician conducting the autopsy for the Medical Examiner's Office had agreed with Blaney's original diagnosis at the scene, while expanding upon it somewhat: death had been caused not only by dislocation and fracturing of the upper cervical vertebrae but also by crushing of the spinal cord, typical of what occurred in legal execution by hanging. But the report went on to give an estimated time of death that was eight hours *earlier* than the moment Carella and Genero had walked out of the construction site to find the victim dangling from a lamppost.

On the telephone with Carella, the man from the Medical Examiner's Office expressed the opinion that the victim had been killed elsewhere—either by the indicated hanging or else by physical force sufficient to fracture the vertebrae and crush the spinal cord—and then transported to the scene of the discovery. The man from the Medical Examiner's Office was very careful not to say "the scene of the crime." In his opinion, the *actual* scene of the crime was not that deserted street with its abandoned buildings and its gaping construction craters. This seemed to jibe with what Carella was already thinking. Neither he nor Genero had seen anybody hanging anyplace on that street when they'd gone in to talk to the night watchman.

The address on the dead girl's I.D. card added further weight to the supposition that she had been killed somewhere else and only later transported to the lucky Eight-Seven. The girl lived in an apartment building some four miles west of the precinct territory, in a section of the city that contained its bustling garment manufacturing center. Cloak City, as the area was familiarly and historically known, had as its nucleus the workshops and showrooms that supplied ready-to-wear clothing for the rest of the nation and indeed for many countries in the non-Communist world. But in the avenues north of the factories, the tenements had been razed and luxury high-rise apartments and expensive restaurants had sprung up in their place to create a Gold Coast ambiance, attracting a show biz clientele who preferred living close to the theater district, and who joyously referred to their new neighborhood not as *Cloak* City but as *Coke* City.

Neither Carella nor Hawes—with whom he was partnered this Tuesday morning, Genero being happily away in court where he was testifying against a hot dog vendor he'd arrested for peddling without a license—knew whether estimates of the flourishing cocaine trade in this precinct were valid or not. As far as they were concerned, they had enough headaches of their own *uptown*, one of which had dragged them down here this morning. The day was one of those sparkling clear days October often lavished on the citizens of this city. Both men were glad to be out of the squadroom. On days like today, you could not help but fall in love with this city all over again.

The dead girl—whose I.D. card gave her age as almost twenty-one—had lived in one of the surviving old neighborhood buildings, a five-story, red-brick edifice covered with the soot and grime of centuries. Coatless and hatless, Carella and Hawes climbed the front stoop and rang the superintendent's bell.

"What'd you think of Meyer's wig?" Carella asked.

"What wig? You're kidding me."

"You didn't see it?"

"No. He's got a wig?"

"Yeah."

"You know why the Indian bought a hat?" Hawes asked, and the front door opened.

The girl who stood there was ten feet tall. Or at least she seemed to be ten feet tall. Both detectives had to look up at her, and neither of them were elves. She was twenty years old, Carella guessed, perhaps twenty-one, with short brown hair, luminous brown eyes, and a slender lupine face. She was wearing blue jeans and a Ramsey University sweatshirt, and she was carrying a canvas book bag printed with the words BOOK BAG.

"Police officers," Carella said, and showed her his shield. "We're looking for the super."

"We don't have a super," the girl said.

"We just rang the super's bell," Hawes said.

"Just 'cause there's a super's *bell* doesn't mean there's a *super*," the girl said, turning to Hawes. Hawes got the feeling she was thinking he was too short for her. And too old. And probably too dumb. He almost shrugged. "There hasn't been a super in this building for almost a year now," the girl said. And then, because people in this city loved nothing better than to stick it to the cops whenever they could, she added, "Maybe that's why we have so many burglaries here."

"This isn't our precinct," Hawes said defensively.

"Then what are you doing here?" the girl asked.

"Do you live here, Miss?" Carella asked.

"Of course I live here," she said. "What do you think I'm doing here? Delivering groceries?"

"Do you know a tenant named Marcia Schaffer?"

"Sure. Listen, she's in 3A, you can talk to her personally, okay? I was just on my way out, I'll be late for class."

"When's the last time you saw her?" Carella asked.

"At school Thursday."

"Ramsey U?" Hawes asked, looking at the sweatshirt.

"Brilliant deduction," the girl said.

"You went to school together?"

"Give the man another cigar."

"How long did you know her?" Carella asked.

"Since my freshman year. I'm a junior now. We're *both* juniors."

"She from here originally? The city?"

"No. Some little town in Kansas. Buffalo Dung, Kansas."

"How about you?" Hawes asked.

"Born and bred right here."

"You sound like it."

"Proud of it, too," she said.

"What was she wearing last Thursday? When you saw her?"

"A track suit. Why? We're both on the track team."

"What time was this?"

"At practice, around four in the afternoon. Why?"

"Did you see her anytime after that?"

"We took the subway home together. Listen, what . . . ?"

"Did you see her anytime after that? Anytime Thursday night?"

"No."

"See her leave the building anytime Thursday night?"

"No."

"What apartment do *you* live in?"

"3B, right across the hall from her."

"And you say she lived in 3A?"

She suddenly caught the past tense.

"She *still* lives there," she said.

"Did you see or hear anybody outside her apartment on Thursday night? Anybody knocking on the door? Anybody . . ."

"No." Her eyes narrowed. "Why are you asking these questions?"

Carella took a deep breath. "Marcia Schaffer is dead," he said.

"Don't be ridiculous," the girl said.

Both detectives looked at her.

"Marcia isn't dead," she said.

They kept looking at her.

"Don't be ridiculous," she said again.

"Can you tell me *your* name, Miss?" Carella asked.

"Jenny Compton," she said, and then at once, "but Marcia isn't dead, you've made a mistake."

"Miss Compton, we're reasonably certain the victim . . ."

"No," Jenny said, and shook her head.

"Did Miss Schaffer live here?" Hawes asked.

"She still *does,"* Jenny said. "Third floor front, apartment 3A. She isn't dead."

"We have her picture . . ."

"She isn't dead," Jenny insisted.

"Is this Marcia Schaffer?" Carella asked, and showed her a glossy blowup the P.U. had made of one of the pictures taken at the scene. It was not a very pretty picture. Jenny flinched away from it as if she'd been struck full in the face.

"Is this Marcia Schaffer?" Carella asked again.

"It looks like her, but Marcia isn't dead," Jenny said.

"Is this *also* Marcia Schaffer?" Carella asked, and showed her the I.D. card.

"Yes, that's Marcia, but . . ."

"The address on this . . ."

"Yes, Marcia *lives* here, but I know she isn't dead."

"How do you know that, Miss Compton?" Hawes asked.

"She's not dead," Jenny said.

"Miss Compton . . ."

"I saw her last Thursday *afternoon,* for Christ's sake, she can't . . ."

"She was killed sometime Thursday ni—"

"I don't *want* her to be dead," Jenny said, and suddenly burst into tears. "Shit, why'd you have to come here?"

She was ten feet tall, this girl, perhaps twenty-one years old, this woman, with city-bred smarts and a city-honed tongue, but she might have just been on her way to kindergarten class, the way she looked now, her right hand covering her face as she wept into it, the left hand clutching the book bag, standing a bit pigeon-toed, and sobbing uncontrollably while the detectives watched, saying nothing, feeling awkward and clumsy and far too overwhelmingly large for this little girl unashamedly crying in their presence.

They waited.

It was such a beautiful day.

"Aw, shit," Jenny said, "it isn't true, is it?"

"I'm sorry," Carella said.

"How . . . how . . . ?" She sniffled and then knelt to reach into her book bag, pulling out a package of tissues, ripping one free, blowing her nose, and then dabbing at her eyes. "What happened?" she said.

They never thought *murder,* unless they happened to be the ones who did the job. They always thought a car accident, or something in the subways, people were always falling under subway trains, or else an elevator shaft, there were always accidents in elevator shafts, that's the way their minds ran when you came around telling them somebody was dead, they never thought murder. And if you told them up front that the person had been *killed,* if you didn't just say the person was *dead* but actually specified *killed,* if they knew up front that a murder had been committed, they always thought gun, or knife, or poison, or bare hands, somebody beaten to death, somebody strangled to death. How did you explain that this had been a hanging? Or something made to *look* like a hanging? How did you explain to a twenty-one-year-old girl who was snuffling into a torn tissue that her girlfriend had been found hanging from a goddamn lamppost?

"Fracture of the upper cervical vertebrae," Carella said, opting for what the M.E. had told him earlier this morning. "Crushing of the spinal cord."

"Jesus!"

He still had not told Jenny that someone had *done* this to her friend. She looked at him searchingly now, realizing that a pair of detectives would not be on the doorstep asking questions if this had been a simple accident, recognizing at last that someone had *caused* Marcia Schaffer's death.

"Someone killed her, is that it?" she asked.

"Yes."

"When?"

"Thursday night sometime. The Medical Examiner's estimate puts it around seven o'clock."

"Jesus," she said again.

"You didn't see her at all on Thursday night?" Hawes asked.

"No."

"Did she mention any plans she might have had for that night?"

"No. Where . . . where did this happen?"

"We don't know."

"I mean . . . where did you *find* her?"

"Uptown."

"In the street? Somebody attacked her in the street?" Carella sighed.

"She was hanging from a lamppost," he said.

"Oh, *God!*" Jenny said, and began sobbing again.

4

DANIEL MCLAUGHLIN WAS A ROTUND LITTLE man in his late fifties, wearing dark slacks and brown shoes, a very loud sports jacket, a peach-colored shirt, a tie that looked as if it had been designed by Jackson Pollock (and further abstracted by various food stains), and a dark brown summer straw hat with a narrow brim and a feather that matched the shirt. He seemed out of breath, his face mottled and perspiring, when he came up to the detectives, who were waiting for him on the front stoop. His little brown eyes checked them out briefly, and then flicked to the overflowing garbage cans stacked near the wrought iron railing that surrounded an area below pavement level. He seemed pleased to note that the garbage cans were spilling all sorts of debris onto the sidewalk.

They had learned from Jenny that Marcia Schaffer had moved into her rent-controlled apartment at about the same time Jenny had, more than two years ago when both girls were starting at Ramsey U on athletic scholarships. Before then, Marcia had indeed lived in a small town in Kansas, not Buffalo Dung—as Jenny had earlier remarked when everything was still light and jovial and unclouded by information of violent death—but instead a place named Manhattan, which called itself The Little Apple. Carella and Hawes guessed there really *was* a place called Manhattan, Kansas.

According to Jenny, the owner of the building—the selfsame Daniel McLaughlin who now stood admiring the shit spilling from his garbage cans—had been trying

45

for the past year or more to get all of his tenants out of the
building so that he could divide his big old-fashioned
apartments into smaller units and thereby realize greater
revenues. Thus far, he'd been largely unsuccessful. Save
for a little old lady who'd moved to a nursing home, the
rest of his tenants flatly refused to budge from a neighborhood that had suddenly become chic, enjoying rents
that were impossible to find except in the worst sections
of the city, of which there were many. In an attempt to
dislodge lodgers who seemed determined to *stay* lodged,
McLaughlin had first yanked out his superintendent, and
then had begun a highly creative personal management
that last year had resulted in the water being turned off at
odd hours, garbage going uncollected, and heat not being
provided by October 15, as specified by law in this city.
Today was only the eleventh of October; it remained to
be seen whether *this* year, the heat would be turned on as
decreed, although the mild weather made the question
somewhat academic. Meanwhile, there was garbage all
over the sidewalk.

"You the detectives?" McLaughlin asked, coming up
the steps.

"Mr. McLaughlin?" Carella said.

"Yeah." He did not offer his hand. "I've got to tell
you I don't appreciate coming all the way up here to de-
liver a goddamn key."

"No other way to get in the apartment," Hawes said.

They had called him just before they'd gone to lunch in
a greasy spoon around the corner, even though the neighborhood was brimming with good French restaurants.
Each of them had eaten hamburgers and French fries,
washed down with Cokes. During lunch, Carella had
meant to ask Hawes why the Indian had bought a hat, but
he was preoccupied with the thought that a cop's normal
working-day diet was nothing the great chefs of Europe
would care to write home about. It was now one o'clock
in the afternoon, and Daniel McLaughlin was complain-

ing he'd had to come "all the way up here" from his office six blocks away.

"I don't like the idea of her being dead to *begin* with," McLaughlin said. "I don't mind having the apartment back, but suppose nobody else wants to rent it once they find out a *dead* girl was living in it?"

It seemed not to occur to him that Marcia Schaffer had been very much alive while she'd lived in his precious apartment.

"Homicide *can* be difficult," Carella said.

"Yeah," McLaughlin agreed, missing the sarcasm. "Well, I've got the key, let's go. I hope this isn't going to take forever."

"Couple of hours maybe," Hawes said. "You don't have to stay with us. If you leave the key, we'll see that it's returned to you."

"I'll bet," McLaughlin said, leaving unvoiced the suspicion that every cop in this city was a thief. "I'll take you up, come on," he said.

They followed him into the building.

The truth of what Jenny Compton had told them became immediately apparent in the small entrance lobby. A lighting fixture hung loose from the ceiling; there was no light bulb in it. The locks on several of the mailboxes were broken. The glass panel on the interior door was cracked, and the doorknob hung loose from a single screw. Further corroboration of McLaughlin's attempts to make life difficult for his intransigent tenants was manifest in the worn and soiled linoleum on the interior steps, the unwashed windows on each landing, the rickety bannisters and exposed electrical wiring. Carella wondered why someone in the building didn't simply call the Ombudsman's Office. He exchanged a glance with Hawes, who nodded bleakly.

McLaughlin stopped outside the door to 3A, fished in his pocket for a key, unlocked the door, and then looked from one detective to the other, as if trying to measure character in a few swift glances.

"Listen, I have some other things to take care of," he said. "If I leave the key, will you *really* get it back to me?"

"Scout's honor," Hawes said, deadpanned.

"I'm at McLaughlin Realty on Bower Street," McLaughlin said, handing him the key. "Well, I guess you know that, that's where you called me. I want you to understand I'm not responsible for any damage you do in here, case the girl's relatives start complaining later on."

"We'll try to be careful," Carella said.

"Make sure you get that key back to me."

"We'll see that it's returned," Hawes said.

"Yeah, I *hope,*" McLaughlin said, and went off down the hallway, shaking his head.

"Nice man," Carella said.

"Wonderful," Hawes said, and they went into the apartment.

As Jenny had suggested, the apartment was larger than those in many of the city's newer buildings, the front door opening onto a sizable entrance hall that led into a spacious living room. The apartment seemed even larger than it actually was because of the sparse furnishings, exactly what one might expect of a college girl attending school on a scholarship. A sofa was against one wall, two thrift-shop easy chairs angled into it. A bank of oversized windows was on the adjoining wall, splashing October sunlight into the room. A row of potted plants rested on the floor beneath the windows. Hawes went to them and touched the soil; they seemed not to have been watered too recently.

"You don't think McLaughlin wanted her out of the apartment *that* bad, do you?" he asked.

"Whoever pulled her up on the end of that rope had to be pretty strong," Carella said, shaking his head.

"*Fat* doesn't mean *weak,*" Hawes said.

"He look like a murderer to you?"

"No."

"There's a smell," Carella said.

"I know. But he's sure trying hard to get these people out of here."

"We ought to make some calls, put somebody on it. I hate to see him getting away with this kind of shit."

"You know anybody in the Mayor's office?"

"Maybe Rollie Chabrier does."

"Yeah, maybe."

They were referring to an assistant district attorney both men had dealt with in the past. They were roaming the living room now, not looking for anything in particular, sniffing the air, more or less, the way animals in the wild will when they enter unfamiliar territory. Technically, this was not the scene of the crime; the scene of the crime was some four miles uptown, where they had discovered the body hanging from a lamppost. But the Medical Examiner had posited the theory that Marcia Schaffer had been killed elsewhere and only later transported to where they'd discovered her. It was within the realm of possibility that she had been killed *here,* in this apartment, although at first glance there seemed to be no signs of a violent struggle of any sort. Still, the unspoken question hovered in both their minds. Hawes finally voiced it.

"Think we ought to get some technicians in here? Before we mess anything up?"

Carella considered this.

"I'd hate like hell to touch anything that may be evidence," Hawes said.

"Better call them," Carella agreed, and went to the phone. He tented a handkerchief over his hand when he picked up the receiver. He stuck the eraser end of a pencil into the receiver holes when he dialed the Mobile Crime Unit number.

The technicians arrived some twenty minutes later. They stood in the middle of the living room, looking around the place much as Carella and Hawes earlier had, just sniffing the air, getting used to the feel of it. Carella and Hawes hadn't touched a thing. They hadn't even sat on any of the chairs. They were standing almost where they'd been when Carella placed his call.

"We the first ones in here?" one of the technicians asked. Carella remembered him as somebody named Joe. Joe Something-or-other.

"Yes," Carella said. "Well, *we've* been in here a half hour or so."

"I mean, besides us. You and us."

"That's it," Carella said.

"Touch anything?" the other technician asked. Carella did not recognize him.

"Just the outside knob."

"So you want the whole works?" the first technician asked. "Dusting? Vacuuming? The twelve ninety-five job?" He smiled at his partner.

"Reduced from thirteen-fifty," his partner said, returning the smile.

"We're not sure this is the crime scene," Carella said.

"So what the hell're *we* doing here?" the first technician said.

"It *might* be," Hawes said.

"Then take the two-dollar job," the second technician suggested.

"Quick once-over," the first technician said. "Superficial, but *thorough.*" He held up a finger alongside his nose, emphasizing the point.

"Better give 'em some gloves," the second technician said.

The first technician produced a pair of white cotton gloves and handed them to Carella. "In case you decide to do any detective work," he said, and winked at his partner. He handed another pair of gloves to Hawes. Both detectives pulled on the gloves while the technicians watched.

"May I have the first dance?" the second technician said, and then they went downstairs to the van, to get all the paraphernalia they would need for tossing the apartment.

On a fireplace mantel on the wall opposite the sofa, Carella and Hawes studied the several trophies attesting to Marcia Schaffer's running ability—a silver cup, a silver plate, several medals, all earned while she was on her high school's track team. The engraved inscription on the silver plate recorded the fact that she had broken the Kansas track record three years earlier. There was a framed picture of a man and a woman, presumably her parents, reminding Carella that he had not yet called Manhattan, Kansas. That would have to come later. He did not relish having to make that call.

The technicians were back. The one Carella thought was named Joe said, "You're not fucking anything up, are you?"

The second technician put his gear down on the floor. "This a homicide or what?" he asked.

"Yes," Carella said.

"The stiff been printed already? Case we find any wild latents?"

"She's been printed," Carella said.

"Any signs of forcible entry?"

"None that we saw."

"Can we skip the window sills then?"

"Whatever you think," Carella said.

"What the hell are we *looking* for, anyway?"

"Traces of anybody else who might've been in here."

"That could be the whole fuckin' *city*," the first technician said, and shook his head. But they got to work nonetheless. The second technician was even whistling as he started dusting the mantelpiece for fingerprints.

An open doorframe, no door in it, led to the only bedroom in the apartment, large and airy, with a high ceiling and the same oversized windows overlooking the street.

There was a bed against one wall, an unpainted dresser opposite it, an unpainted desk angled into a corner. There were Ramsey University pennants on one of the walls, together with framed photographs of Marcia Schaffer in track costume, looking healthy and radiant and bursting with life. One of the pictures showed her with her blond hair blowing in the wind behind her, arms and legs pumping, mouth open and sucking in air as she broke the tape at a finish line. A gray team jacket—with the school's name lettered across the back of it in purple, and the word TRACK appliqued under the school's seal on the front—was draped over the chair near the desk. There were open books on the desk top. There was a sheet of paper in the typewriter. Carella glanced at it. Marcia Schaffer had been working on a paper for an anthropology class. *Man stands alone,* he thought, *because man alone stands.* Marcia Schaffer would never stand again, no less run. The runner had been knocked down in her twenty-first year of life.

In the bedroom closet, they found a sparse assortment of clothing—several dresses and skirts, sweaters on hangers, a ski parka, a raincoat, blue jeans, tailored slacks, a gray warmup suit with the university's name and seal on it. Together, they went through coat pockets and jacket pockets, the pockets of all the jeans and slacks. Nothing. They shook out loafers and high-heeled shoes, track shoes and sneakers. Nothing. They opened a valise on the closet shelf. It was empty. They crossed the room to the dresser, and methodically went through the clothes in the drawers there. Bras and panties, slips and more sweaters, blouses and pantyhose, knee socks and sweat socks. In a corner of the top drawer, they found a dispenser for birth control pills.

They went back into the living room where the technicians were working, and went through all the desk drawers, searching in vain for an appointment calendar. They found a small leather-bound book listing names, addresses, and telephone numbers, presumably of friends and relatives. Marcia Schaffer seemed to have known quite a few people in the city, but most of them were women, and neither Carella nor Hawes believed that a woman would have had the strength to hoist Marcia's deadweight body up onto a lamppost some twenty-five feet above the ground. In the S section of the book, Carella found a listing for *Schaffer,* no surnames following it, no address, simply a telephone number with a 913 area code preceding it. He was willing to bet this was the area code for Manhattan, Kansas. He would have to call her parents. Soon. He would have to tell them their golden girl was dead.

He sighed heavily.

"Something?" Hawes asked. He was rummaging in the wastebasket alongside the desk, studying scraps of crumpled paper.

"No, no," Carella said.

Most of the scraps in the wastebasket were handwritten notes Marcia Schaffer had made for the paper she'd been writing. There was a grocery list. There was a letter she had started and then crumpled. It began with the words, *Dear Mom and Dad, I hate to ask you for money again so soon after . . .* There was a worksheet with a list of figures she had added and then crossed out and added once again, apparently seeking a correct checkbook balance. There was a card from a place that delivered pizzas. That was all.

They went into the bathroom. Several pairs of plain white cotton panties were draped over the shower rod. An open box of super-absorbent menstrual napkins was resting on the sink below the mirror. Carella tried to remember if the Medical Examiner had mentioned anything about menstruation. He felt suddenly like an intruder. He did not want to know about anything as private and personal as Marcia Schaffer's period. But a soiled menstrual napkin was in the wastebasket under the sink. He opened the medicine cabinet. Hawes was going through the hamper near the scale, pulling out dirty pieces of laundry, examining each article of clothing.

"Blood stains here," he said.

"She was menstruating," Carella said.

"Better have the lab check them out, anyway."

"Yeah," Carella said.

Hawes began gathering the soiled clothing into a heap. He went out of the bathroom to ask the technicians about the dirty laundry. They told him to put it in a pillowcase. Carella looked into the medicine cabinet. He did not expect to find any controlled substances, and he didn't. There was the usual array of non-prescription medications, toothpaste, shampoo, conditioners, nail polish, combs, brushes, adhesive bandages, Ace bandages—presumably because she'd been a runner and prone to muscle pulls and sprains—mouth wash, barrettes, bobby pins, and the like. J.D. Salinger would have made very little of Marcia Schaffer's medicine cabinet. Carella closed the door.

A robe was hanging on a wall hook.

He took it down. The robe was a winter-weight garment, navy blue with white piping on the cuffs and around the shawl collar. The label indicated that it had been purchased at one of the city's larger department stores. The words "100% Wool" were fortified on the label with the universal symbol:

The label was further marked with the letter "L" for "Large." Carella felt in the pockets. One of them was empty. The other contained an almost-full package of Marlboro cigarettes and a gold cigarette lighter. Carella dropped these into separate evidence envelopes. Hawes was just coming back into the room with a pillowcase printed with little blue flowers.

"Were there cigarettes in her handbag?" Carella asked.

"What?"

"The girl's handbag. Do you remember cigarettes?"

"No. Why would there be cigarettes? She was on the *track* team."

"That's what I mean."

"Why? What'd you find?" Hawes asked, beginning to transfer the laundry into the pillowcase.

"A pack of Marlboros. And a Dunhill lighter."

"Is that a *man's* robe?" Hawes asked, looking up.

"Looks that way."

"How tall was she?"

"Five-eight."

Hawes looked at the robe again. "Couldn't be hers, do you think?"

"It's a large," Carella said.

Hawes nodded. "The lab'll want it for sure," he said.

The technicians were still working in the living room when Carella and Hawes came back to return the cotton gloves. Over the hum of the filtered vacuum cleaner, the one Carella thought was named Joe winked at his partner and said, "Half a day today?"

"When do you think *you'll* be finished?" Carella asked.

"A woman's work is *never* done," the other technician said.

"Think you can lock up and get the key back to us?"

"Back *where?*" the first technician said.

"The Eight-Seven. Uptown."

"All the way uptown," the second technician said, rolling his eyes. "I got a date tonight. *You* want to be responsible for the key, John?"

John, that's it, Carella thought.

"I don't want to be responsible for no fuckin' key," John said.

"Well, can you call when you think you're almost finished?" Hawes asked. "We'll send a patrolman down for it."

"They got pick-up and delivery service, the Eight-Seven," John said, and again winked at his partner.

"What's the number up there?" the other technician asked.

"377-8024," Hawes said.

John turned off the vacuum cleaner. "Let me write it down," he said. He fished in a coverall pocket for a pencil. He patted his other pockets. "Who's got a pencil?" he asked.

Hawes was already writing his last name and the precinct telephone number on a page in his notebook. He tore the page loose and handed it to John. "Ask for either one of us," he said. "Hawes or Carella."

"Horse?" the second technician said. "We got 'A Man Called Horse' here," he said to John.

"You part Indian?" John asked.

"Mohawk," Hawes lied. "Full-blooded."

"How come you ain't in construction work?" the other technician asked, and both he and John laughed. John looked at the page Hawes had torn from his notebook.

"This how you spell it in Mohawk?" he asked Hawes.

"That's the way my father always spelled it," Hawes said. "Running Deer Hawes was his name."

"What's *your* first name?" the other technician asked.

"Great Bull Farting," Hawes said, and followed Carella out of the apartment.

"That reminds me," Carella said in the hallway outside. "Why *did* the Indian buy a hat?"

"To keep his wigwam," Hawes said.

"Ouch," Carella said.

In the waning sunlight, he ran.

He had left his apartment at five-fifteen, driven up here in less than ten minutes, and then parked his car on Grover Avenue, outside the park. The park at this hour of the day was virtually empty of mothers with their baby carriages, populated now with youngsters tossing footballs, lovers strolling hand in hand, old men sitting on benches trying to read their newspapers in the fading light. Yesterday at this time, there'd been more people in the park than was usual. Yesterday had been Columbus Day—or at least the day set aside for the official *observance* of Columbus Day—and many of the shops and offices had been closed.

It annoyed him that they no longer observed a famous man's holiday when they were supposed to. Columbus Day was October 12, so why had they celebrated it two days earlier? To take advantage of a long weekend, of course. Not that *he'd* enjoyed that advantage at all. He was his own boss, and he set his own work schedule.

God, what a beautiful day it was!

Still light enough at a quarter to six to see clearly every twist and turn of the footpath along which he ran, a far cry from a cinder track, but better than nothing in this city of concrete and steel. The clocks would go back on the last Sunday in October—*Spring ahead, Fall back,* he thought—and it would start getting dark around five, five-thirty then, but in the meantime there was still the fading glow of sunshine and a cloudless blue sky overhead, he loved October, he loved this city in October.

He ran at a steady pace, nothing to win here, no one to defeat, not even a clock to race. Exercise, that's all, he thought, just exercise, running along a park path for exer-

cise, running anonymously, a tall, slender man in a gray
warmup suit without letters, running at an easy, steady
pace that soothed and comforted, as did the knowledge of
what he'd done and would continue to do.

He stopped running when he came abreast of the police
station across the street, visible beyond the low stone
wall bordering the park. Even in the late afternoon light,
he could make out the numerals 87, lettered in white on
the green globes flanking the entrance steps. Two men in
plainclothes were entering the building, both of them hatless, neither of them wearing coats—well, on a day like
today, who needed a coat? Still, he always thought of detectives as men wearing overcoats. If, in fact, they *were*
detectives. Perhaps they were only citizens coming to
make a complaint. Plenty of citizens in this city, all of
them with complaints.

He wondered if his little package had arrived yet.

He had mailed it on Saturday, took the subway all the
way out to Calm's Point to drop the package in a mailbox
there. Flat enough to squeeze into the mailbox opening,
he'd made certain of that. Weighed it at home first, made
sure the proper postage was on it. He didn't want that
package to go undelivered because of insufficient postage. There was no way it could be returned to him because he hadn't put a return address on it. That was why
he hadn't taken it to a post office. He hadn't wanted to
chance some dumb postal clerk telling him they couldn't
accept his package because there was no return address
on it. He didn't know what the exact rules were, but he
didn't want to risk a hassle. Drop it in a mailbox, the letter carrier would shrug and figure if there was enough
postage on it, somebody down the line would attempt delivery. The guys who emptied those big mailboxes probably never even *looked* at what they were picking up,
anyway. A post office was different. Clerk might see
there was no return address and even if it wasn't against
the rules, he might point it out. *No return address on this,*

you know that? Have to explain that he was sending it as a surprise, something like that, too much explaining to do. Man might remember him later on. Simpler to drop it in a mailbox. Flat enough so that it fit in a mailbox. He didn't want anyone remembering him just yet. There was plenty of time later for people to start remembering him.

All of the post offices in the city had been closed yesterday, no mail delivery anywhere; he knew for certain the package could not have been delivered yesterday. But today—unless there'd been an unusual pile-up because of the holiday—yes, it should have been delivered today.

He wondered what they'd made of it.

Getting her handbag in the mail that way.

He smiled, thinking about the looks on their faces.

Maybe next time he'd leave identification right at the scene. Make it a little easier for them. Let them know who the victim was right off. Leave the identification right in the street, under the lamppost. Didn't want to make it *too* easy for them, of course, not till the thing started building momentum. Friday's newspapers had barely mentioned the dead girl. Nothing at all in the morning papers, and no front-page headline in the sensational afternoon paper. They'd put the story on page eight, big story like that, girl found hanging from a god-damn lamppost! Next time around, they'd *know* there was a pattern. The cops would know it, too, unless they were even dumber than he thought they were. Headlines next time around, for sure.

He looked once again at the police station across the way, and then began running, smiling.

Soon, he thought.

Soon they'd know who he was.

The two women were sizing each other up.

Annie Rawles had been told that Eileen Burke was the best decoy in Special Forces. Eileen Burke had been told that Annie Rawles was a hard-nosed Rape Squad cop who d once worked out of Robbery and had shot down two hoods trying to rip off a midtown bank. Annie was looking at a woman who was five feet nine inches tall, with long legs, good breasts, flaring hips, red hair, and green eyes. Eileen was looking at a woman with eyes the color of loam behind glasses that gave her a scholarly look, wedge-cut hair the color of midnight, firm cupcake breasts, and a slender boy's body. They were both about the same age, Eileen guessed, give or take a year or so. Eileen kept wondering how somebody who looked so much like a bookkeeper could have pulled her service revolver and blown away two desperate punks facing a max of twenty years hard time.

"What do you think?" Annie asked.

"You say this isn't the only repeat?" Eileen said.

They were still sizing each other up. Eileen figured this wasn't a matter of choice. If Annie Rawles had asked for her, and if her lieutenant had assigned Eileen to the job, then that was it, they both outranked her. Still, she liked to know who she'd be working with. Annie was wondering if Eileen was really as good at the job as they'd said she was. She looked a little flashy for a decoy. Spot her strutting along in high heels with those tits bouncing, a rapist would make her in a minute and run for the hills. This was a very special rapist they were dealing with here; Annie didn't want an amateur screwing it up.

"We've got three women say they were raped more than once by this same guy. Fits the description in each case," Annie said. "There may be more, we haven't run an M.O. cross-check."

"When will you be doing that?" Eileen asked; she liked to know who she was working with, how efficient they were. It wouldn't be Annie Rawles's ass out there on the street, it would be her own.

"Working on that now," Annie said. She liked Eileen's question. She knew she was asking Eileen to put herself in a dangerous position. The man had already slashed one of the victims, left her face scarred. At the same time, that was the job. If Eileen didn't like Special Forces, she should ask for transfer to something else. Annie didn't know that Eileen was considering just that possibility, but not for any reason Annie might have understood.

"All over the city, or any special location?" Eileen asked.

"Anyplace, anytime."

"I'm only one person," Eileen said.

"There'll be other decoys. But what I have in mind for you . . ."

"How many?"

"Six, if I can get them."

"Counting me?"

"Yes."

"Who are the others?"

"I've got their names here, you want to look them over," Annie said, and handed her a typewritten sheet.

Eileen read it over carefully. She knew all of the women on the list. Most of them knew their jobs. One of them didn't. She refrained from voicing this opinion; no sense bad-mouthing anybody.

"Uh-huh," she said.

"Look okay to you?"

"Sure." She hesitated. "Connie needs a bit more experience," she said tactfully. "You might want to save her for something less complicated. Good cop, but this guy's got a knife, you said . . ."

"And he's *used* it," Annie said.

"Yeah, so save Connie for something a little less complicated." Both women understood the euphemism. "Less complicated" meant "less dangerous." Nobody wanted a lady cop slashed because she was incapable of handling something like this.

"What age groups?" Eileen asked. "The victims."

"The three we know about for sure . . . let me look at this a minute." Annie picked up another typewritten sheet. "One of them is forty-six. Another is twenty-eight. This last one—Mary Hollings, the one last Saturday night—is thirty-seven. He's raped her three times already."

"Same guy each time, huh? You're *positive* about that?"

"According to the descriptions."

"What do they say he looks like?"

"In his thirties, black hair and blue eyes . . ."

"White?"

"White. About six feet tall . . . well, it varies there. We've got him ranging from five-ten to six-two. About a hundred and eighty pounds, very muscular, very strong."

"Any identifying marks? Scars? Tattoos?"

"None of the victims mentioned any."

"Same guy each time," Eileen said, as if trying to lend credibility to it by repeating it. "That's unusual, isn't it? Guy coming back to the same victim?"

"Very," Annie said. "Which is why I thought . . ."

"With your rapists, usually . . ."

"I know."

"They don't care *who* they get, it's got nothing to do with lust."

"I know."

"So the M.O. would seem to indicate he has *favorites* or something. That doesn't jibe with the *psychology* of it."

"I know."

"So what's the plan? Cover these victims or cruise their neighborhoods?"

"We don't think they're random victims," Annie said. "That's why I'd like you to . . ."

"Then cruising's out, right?"

Annie nodded. "This last one—Mary Hollings—is a redhead."

"Oh," Eileen said. "Okay, I get it."

"About your size," Annie said. "A little shorter. What are you, five-ten, five-eleven?"

"I *wish,*" Eileen said, and smiled. "Five-nine."

"She's five-seven."

"Built like me?"

"Zoftig, I'd say."

"Bovine, *I'd* say," Eileen said, and smiled.

"Hardly," Annie said, and returned the smile.

"So you want me to be Mary Hollings, is that it?"

"If you think you can pass."

"You know the lady, I don't," Eileen said.

"It's a reasonable likeness," Annie said. "Up close, he'll tip in a minute. But by that time, it should be too late."

"Where does she live?" Eileen asked.

"1840 Laramie Crescent."

"Up in the Eight-Seven?"

"Yes."

"I have a friend up there," Eileen said.

The *friend* again, Annie thought. Her lover. The blond cop in the squadroom. King, was it? Herb King?

"Does she work, this woman?" Eileen asked. " 'Cause if she runs a computer terminal or something . . ."

"She's divorced, living on alimony payments."

"Lucky her," Eileen said. "I'll need her daily routine . . ."

"You can get that directly from her," Annie said.

"Where do we hide *her,* meanwhile?"

"She'll be leaving for California day after tomorrow. She has a sister out there."

"Better give her a wig, case he's watching the apartment when she leaves."

"We will."

"How about other tenants in the building? Won't they know I'm not . . . ?"

"We figured you could pass yourself off as the sister. I doubt he'll be talking to any of the tenants."

"Any security there?"

"No."

"Elevator operator?"

"No."

"So it's just between me and them. The tenants, I mean."

"And *him*," Annie said.

"What about boyfriends and such? What about social clubs or other places where they know her?"

"She'll be telling all her friends she's going out of town. If anyone calls while you're in the apartment, you're the sister."

"Suppose *he* calls?"

"He hasn't yet, we don't think he will. He's not a heavy breather."

"Different psychology," Eileen said, nodding.

"We figure you can go wherever she was in the habit of going, we don't think he'll follow you inside. Go in, hang around, do your nails, whatever, then come out again. If he's watching, he'll pick up the trail again outside. It should work. I *hope.*"

"I never had one like this before."

"Neither have I."

"I'll need a cross-checked breakdown," Eileen said. "On Mary Hollings and the other two victims."

"We're working that up now. We didn't think there was a pattern until now. I mean . . ."

Eileen detected a crack in the hard-nosed veneer.

"It's just . . ."

Again Annie hesitated.

"These other two . . . one's out in Riverhead, the other's in Calm's Point, it's a big city. I didn't realize till Saturday, after I talked to Mary Hollings . . . I mean, it just didn't *register* before then. That these were serial rapes. That he's hitting the same women more than once. Came to me like a bolt out of the blue. Now that we *know* there's a pattern, we're cross-checking similarities on these three victims we're *sure* were attacked by the same guy, see if we can't come up with anything in their backgrounds that might have singled them out. It's a place to start.''

"You using the computer?"

"Not only for the three," Annie said, nodding. "We're running a check on every rape reported since the beginning of the year. If there are *other* victims who were serially raped . . ."

"When do I get the printouts?" Eileen asked.

"As soon as I get them."

"And when's that?"

"I know it's your ass out there," Annie said softly.

Eileen said nothing.

"I know he has a knife," Annie said.

Eileen still said nothing.

"I'd no more risk your life than ⊥ would my own," Annie said, and Eileen thought of facing down two armed robbers in the marbled lobby of a midtown bank.

"When do I start?" she asked.

5

THE SECOND HANGING VICTIM TURNED UP IN
West Riverhead.

The 101st Precinct caught the squeal early on the
morning of October 14. This was not the rosiest precinct
in the world, but none of the cops up there had ever seen
a body hanging from a lamppost before. They had seen
all sorts of things up there, but never anything like this.
They were amazed and astonished. It took a lot to amaze
and astonish the cops of the One-Oh-One.

West Riverhead was just a short walk over the Thomas
Avenue Bridge, which separated it from Isola. Half a
million people lived on the far side of that bridge in a jag-
ged landscape as barren as the moon's. Forty-two percent
of those people were on the city's welfare rolls, and of
those who were capable of holding jobs, only twenty-
eight percent were actually employed. Six thousand abandoned buildings, heatless and without electricity, lined
the garbage-strewn streets. An estimated 17,000 drug ad-
dicts found shelter in those buildings when they were not
marauding the streets in competition with packs of wild
dogs. The statistics for West Riverhead were over-
whelming—26,347 new cases of tuberculosis reported
this past year; 3,412 cases of malnutrition; 6,502 cases of
venereal disease. For every hundred babies born in West
Riverhead, three died while still in infancy. For those
who survived, there was a life ahead of grinding poverty,
helpless anger, and hopeless frustration. It was places
like West Riverhead that caused the Russians to gloat
over how far superior for the masses was the Communist

system. Compared to West Riverhead, the 87th Precinct territory was a dairy farm in Wisconsin.

But Carella and Hawes were up here now because a smart detective on the 101st Squad remembered reading something about a girl hanging from a lamppost in the Eight-Seven, and he promptly called downtown to inform the detectives that they had another one, nobody being eager to step on the toes of somebody already investigating a case, and anyway who the hell needed a hanging victim in West Riverhead where there was enough crime up here to keep the cops busy twenty-eight hours a day? Exotic? Terrific. Who needed exotic? Better to let the Eight-Seven pick up the pieces.

Carella and Hawes got there at a little past seven in the morning.

The Homicide team had already come and gone. In this city, any crime, big or small, felony or misdemeanor, was left to the precinct that caught the initial squeal—unless *another* precinct had already caught the squeal on an obviously related crime. With a murder, the Homicide Division carefully watched over the shoulders of the investigating precinct detectives, lending their expertise where necessary, but the case technically belonged to the responding officers, with Homicide serving as a sort of clearing house. Carella and Hawes were the fortunate responding officers on another bright October day that could easily have broken the heart.

A detective named Charlie Broughan was still at the scene; Carella had worked with him before on a gang-related series of murders. There were an estimated 9,000 teenage street-gang members within the confines of the 101st. Maybe that's why Charlie Broughan looked so tired all the time. Or maybe working the Graveyard Shift up here was worse than working it anyplace else in the city. Broughan looked even wearier than he had the last time Carella saw him, a big beefy cop with a thatch of unruly brown hair and a two days' growth of beard stubble on his face. He was wearing a pale blue windbreaker, dark blue slacks, and loafers. He recognized Carella at once, came over to him, shook hands with him, and then shook hands with Hawes.

"Sorry to bother you with this shit," he said, "but I guess by the regs it's yours."

"It's ours, all right," Carella said, and looked up at the body.

"The last one was a girl, too, huh?" Broughan said.

"Yeah," Carella said.

"We didn't cut her down yet, the M.E. and everybody's still waitin'. Didn't know how you wanted to handle this."

"Mobile Crime here yet?" Hawes asked.

"Yeah," Broughan said. "Well, they *were* a minute ago. They probably went out for some coffee."

"We want to save the knot," Carella said. "Anywhere midway up the rope'll be fine."

"I'll tell the Emergency boys," Broughan said.

Carella was glad there was no one there to comment on the color of the girl's panties, which happened to be a blue as electric as the sky spreading wide and clear above the lamppost. He watched as Broughan walked over to the emergency van. The emergency cops took their time getting out their ladder, net, and bolt cutter. It was too early in the morning to work up a sweat.

"Who found her?" Carella asked Broughan.

"Got a call from an honest citizen," Broughan said, "which up here is a miracle. On his way to work—he lives about eight blocks over, in an area that ain't burned out yet—was driving by and spotted her hanging there. Actually *called* us, can you believe it?"

"What time was this?" Hawes asked.

"Clocked it in at six-oh-four. I thought the shift was about to end, I was already typing up my reports. Bang, we got somebody hanging from a lamppost." He reached into his jacket pocket, and pulled out an evidence envelope. "You'll want this," he said. "Found it under the lamppost."

"What is it?"

"The girl's wallet, I *guess*. I didn't open it, didn't want to smear anything. But I don't know any *men* who carry red wallets, do you?"

The emergency cops were cutting her down. She dropped suddenly, her skirt ballooning out over her long legs as she fell. The net sagged with her dead weight. The emergency cops lowered the net to the ground.

"Wasn't taking any chances on anybody seeing him do the job, was he?" Broughan said. "Ain't nothing in these buildings but rats, dog shit, and cockroaches."

The assistant M.E. walked over, looking bored.

Five minutes later, he expressed his opinion that the girl was dead, and that the probable cause was fracture of the cervical vertebrae.

Her name was Nancy Annunziato.

A card in her wallet identified her as a student at Calm's Point College, one of the city's five tuition-free colleges. C.P.C. was away over at the other end of the city, across the Calm's Point Bridge and the River Dix, at least an hour by car from Riverhead, an hour and a half if you took the subway. The detectives did not think anybody in his right mind would have carried a dead body on the subway, however bizarre the system had become over the years, however inured its riders had become to peculiar happenings underground. But assuming the girl had been killed elsewhere (as had supposedly been the case with Marcia Schaffer) and further assuming that the body had then been transported here to this lovely garden spot of the city, the murderer had come a hell of a long way in an attempt to cover his tracks. Why, then, had he left behind a wallet with the girl's identification in it?

The call to Manhattan, Kansas, informing Marcia Schaffer's father of her death, had been painful enough, but Carella had not had to look him in the eye when he gave him the news. This one would be more difficult. According to the I.D. card in her wallet, the girl had lived in Calm's Point, not far from the school, and presumably with her parents. This one would be face-to-face. This one would hurt both ways. He was glad Hawes would be with him, and not a jackass like Genero. Genero had once asked the wife of a murder victim if she had already arranged for a funeral plot; "It's always best to think of such things far in advance," Genero had told her. He later told Carella that his mother had already purchased funeral plots for herself and his father. "With lifetime maintenance," he'd said. Carella had wondered *whose* lifetime?

They got caught in rush-hour traffic on the way to Calm's Point, and the ride took them an hour and fifteen minutes. They did not know how bad the confrontation would be until they arrived at the house and discovered that Mr. Annunziato had suffered a heart attack only yesterday and was at the moment in the Intensive Care Unit at Saint Anthony's Hospital, some six blocks away. The neighborhood was largely Italian, a bustling ghetto that reminded Carella of the one in which he'd been born and raised. The street cries, the shouted greetings, even the clapboard two-story houses with their fig trees, all brought a rush of memory that was somehow as painful as the task that lay before him. There were no babies crying on this tree-shaded street; you never heard a baby crying in an Italian neighborhood. Whenever an Italian baby showed the slightest sign of bursting into tears, there was always a mother, an aunt, a cousin or a grandmother there to pick him up and console him. Mrs. Annunziato looked like Carella's Aunt Amelia; the resemblance only made his job more difficult.

She had thought at first that they were there to investigate the automobile accident. Her husband had been driving a car when he'd had his heart attack, and he'd smashed into another car when he lost control of the vehicle. This was how she happened to tell them, the moment they identified themselves, that he was now in intensive care, with a mild concussion in addition to the heart attack. They now had to tell her that her daughter was dead.

Hawes busied himself looking at his shoes.

Carella broke the news to Mrs. Annunziato, partially in English, partially in Italian. She listened carefully and disbelievingly. She asked for details; she was certain they were making a mistake. They showed her the dead girl's wallet. She identified it positively. They were reluctant to show her the Polaroids taken at the scene; they did not want to risk yet another heart attack. She finally burst into tears, rushing into the house to get her mother, who came out not a moment later—a short, gray-haired Italian woman dressed entirely in black, she herself crying as she pressed the detectives for yet more details. The women stood hugging each other and weeping on the sidewalk in front of the house. A crowd had gathered. An ice cream truck's bells tinkled in the bright October stillness of the tree-shaded street.

"Signore," Carella said, *"scusami, ma ci sono molti domande . . ."*

"Sì, capisco," Mrs. Annunziato said. *"Parla Inglese, per piacere."*

"Grazie," Carella said, *"il mio Italiano non è il migliore.* I have to ask these questions if we're to find who did this to your daughter, *lei capisce, signore?"*

The grandmother nodded. She was embracing Mrs. Annunziato, clinging to her, patting her, squeezing her, comforting her.

"When did you see her last?" Carella asked. *"L'ultima volta che . . ."*

"La notte scorsa," the grandmother said.

"Last night," Mrs. Annunziato said.

"A che ora?" Carella asked. "What time was that?"

"Alle sei," the grandmother said.

"Six o'clock," Mrs. Annunziato said. "She just come home from the school. She was practice."

"Scusi?" Carella said. "Practice?"

"Sì, era una corridora," the grandmother said.

"Corridora?" Carella said, not understanding the word.

"A runner," Mrs. Annunziato said. "She was on the team, *cognesce? Come si chiama? La squadra di pista, capisce? La pista* . . . how do you say? The track. She was on the track team."

There were two packets from the Police Laboratory waiting for them when they got back to the squadroom. It was still only eleven o'clock in the morning. Both men had been working the Graveyard Shift when the call had come from the 101st. They were supposed to be relieved at a quarter to eight, but it was now eleven, and the lab report was on Carella's desk, and another dead girl was awaiting autopsy in the morgue at Mercy General. In the new-penny brilliance of the squadroom, burnished October sunlight streaming through grill-covered windows opened wide to the street outside, they broke open the seal on the first packet. Meyer Meyer was sitting at his own desk, typing, his hairpiece rakishly askew on top of his head. Hawes kept looking across the room to stare at the wig. Meyer pretended he didn't know he was being observed.

The first packet contained a report on the rope section and the hangman's knot recovered at the scene, together with a report on the photographs of the knot fastening the other end of the rope to the lamppost. The rope was fashioned of a fiber called sisal, a product of the agave plant, which grew in the Indies and in some parts of Africa. Sisal rope was not quite as strong as Manila rope, which came from the abaca plant in the Philippines. A Manila rope with a one-and-a-half-inch diameter could lift a weight of 2,650 pounds. But sisal was a widely used substitute for the stronger rope, and Marcia Schaffer had weighed only a hundred and twenty-four pounds. The rope used in the hanging was the most common type: a three-strand rope which could not support as much weight as a four-strand, and nowhere near as much weight as a so-called cable-laid rope. Again, Marcia Schaffer had weighed only a hundred and twenty-four pounds.

The technician writing the report went to great lengths explaining that the fibers on the rope clearly indicated in which direction a rope had been pulled. In a legal hanging, or in a true hanging suicide, a person dropped downward when the support was pulled or kicked from under his feet. This downward motion caused the fibers of the rope to rise in a direction opposite to the fall. Conversely, if a person had been hauled *up* by rope over some sort of substructure like a tree branch, or in this case, the arm of a lamppost, the fibers rose in a direction opposite to the pulling or lifting motion. As regarded the direction of fibers in general, the technician quoted a rule to the effect that *drop down* resulted in fibers *up*, and *pull up* caused fibers *down*.

Carella and Hawes shrugged; this was all old stuff to them.

The technician went on to explain that if the fiber direction on any given rope seemed at first glance to support a finding of "true hanging" this might not necessarily be valid since the murderer might have first manually lifted an already dead body and only later manipulated the noose around its neck. This was enormously difficult to do, however, since a corpse was heavy and limp and clumsy to maneuver. Besides, the arm of the lamppost in this case was some twenty-five feet above the street. Given the height of the lamppost arm, then; given as well the downward direction of the rope fibers, the technician could only conclude that the killer had fastened the noose around the neck of the corpse, thrown the rope over the lamppost arm, and then hauled the body up, tying the loose end of the rope around the supporting post some five feet above the base.

The technician went on to report that the knot removed from behind the dead girl's neck was a true hangman's knot, the sort used in legal hanging executions. In essence, it was a variation of a slip knot, sometimes called a *running* knot—

Both detectives turned to look at each other when they came to the word "running" . . .

—fashioned for the executioner's purposes into a noose with eight or nine turns of rope above it. In this case, there were nine turns.

The technician had not expected to find any latent prints on either the rope or the knot, and he was not disappointed. He had, however, recovered fibers which when examined under the microscope were discovered not to be sisal fibers, and which he had ascertained were fibers consisting of fifty-five percent wool and forty-five percent polyester. In addition, he had found particles of human epidermis clinging to the coarse rope of the knot, and he had identified these as unpigmented skin, or, in short, skin from a white man.

The photograph of the knot tied around the lamppost— actually, the technician pointed out (intending no pun), it was *not* a *knot* but instead a *hitch*, commonly used to tie a rope to a ring, a post, or a spar. The *hitch*, then, that had fastened the end of the rope to the lamppost was called a half hitch. In the technician's opinion, the killer had chosen this particular hitch because it could be tied easily and swiftly, even—as in this case—when *two* half hitches were used in concert. It was not as strong or as safe as a timber hitch, for example, but taking into consideration the fact that the killer had a hundred and twenty-four pounds of dead weight dangling from the other end of the rope, speed and facility must have been a prime consideration. The technician concluded the report by mentioning that the half hitch was a knot familiar to virtually every sailor or fisherman on the face of the earth.

The second sealed packet contained a report on the robe (and its contents) found in the dead girl's apartment.

Upon examination of sample fibers, the robe proved to be one-hundred-percent wool, as claimed on the label. The size, as further indicated on the label, was a large— made to fit men who wore a U.S. 42. Carella wore a 42. Hawes wore a 44. A considerable quantity of hair had been vacuumed from the robe, and this had been compared with hair samples taken from the head, eyebrows, eyelashes, and genital area of Marcia Schaffer's corpse. Some of the hairs on the robe matched Marcia Schaffer's head hair. Some of them matched the pubic-area hair samples. One of them matched an eyelash. The other hairs on the robe were foreign—what the lab assistant in his report called *wild* hairs.

All of the wild hairs had dry roots, as opposed to living roots, which indicated they had fallen out and not been pulled away by force. All of the hairs had a medullary index—defined in the report as the relation between medullary diameter and whole-hair diameter—of less than 0.5, which indicated they were either human hair or monkey hair. But the air network in the medulla of these hairs was fine-grained, and the cells invisible without treatment in water; the cortex resembled a thick muff, and the pigment was fine-grained; there were thin, unprotruding scales in the cuticle, covering each other to a greater degree than would be found in the hair of an animal. The technician had determined that these hairs were indeed human, and since they measured 0.07 centimeters in diameter, that they were hairs from an *adult* human.

These same hairs, when measured under the micrometer eyepiece, were all shorter than eight centimeters, which indicated they had come either from a scalp or from a beard. The medullary index of the hairs, however, was 0.132, which seemed to indicate they were hairs from a *man's* scalp, as opposed to a woman's, whose medullary index would have been 0.148. Moreover, the ovoid shapes and the peripheral concentration of the pigment in the cortex of the hair indicated that the man was a white man.

Some of the other recovered hairs were curly and coarse, with knobby roots that indicated they had come from a man's genital area, a surmise strengthened by the fact that the medullary index was established as 0.153. Hairs from a woman's genitalia, although also curly and coarse, normally had a fine root and a medullary index of 0.114. The orange-red color of the pigment in the shaft of *all* the hairs—male or female, head, eyebrows, eyelashes or genital—together with the amount of granules present, established in support of visual findings that Marcia Schaffer and the man whose robe was found in her apartment were both blondes. Moreover, they were *natural* blondes; not a trace of any chemical dye or bleach was found on any of the hairs. A microscopic examination of the tips of the adult male head hairs revealed clean-cut surfaces that indicated the man who owned the robe had had a haircut not forty-eight hours before the hairs were deposited on the robe.

Reading all this about hair, Hawes seemed even more fascinated by Meyer's toupee. He kept looking up from the report to where Meyer sat hunched over the typewriter, and he kept wondering whether a microscopic examination of all those hairs sitting on Meyer's heretofore barren scalp would prove them to be human or animal. Meyer kept ignoring him. Meyer was thinking Hawes was trying to figure out something clever to say.

The laboratory report went on to state that the package of Marlboro cigarettes had been tested negatively for controlled substances. The cigarettes were just what they purported to be: tobacco marketed by Philip Morris Inc.

The lighter was indeed a Dunhill and not one of its many knock-offs.

There were good latent fingerprints on both the lighter and the cigarette package.

A cross-check with the Identification Section had produced no criminal record for the man who'd left his prints on both articles. But he had been fingerprinted when he enlisted in the Navy during the Vietnam War. His name was Martin J. Benson, and his last known address was 93204 Pacific Coast Highway, just outside of Santa Monica, California.

Carella and Hawes divided between them the telephone directories for all five sections of the city. Hawes hit paydirt with the Isola phone book. A Martin J. Benson was listed as living at 106 South Boulder. They were heading out of the squadroom when Hawes turned and asked Meyer, "Did you know that horse hair has a medullary index of seven point six?"—something he made up on the spot, and something Meyer did not find comical.

Boulder Street had been named at a time when the Dutch were still in possession of the city, long before construction work had reduced to rubble the huge igneous outcropping that had served as inspiration for the unimaginative appellation.

Naming the street had created a bit of a problem for the practical Dutch in that their native land was not particularly renowned for its mountainous terrain. *Rolsteen* in the Dutch language translated as "a rock that has rolled down from the top of a mountain." This particular rock, firmly rooted in the earth as it was, did not seem to have rolled down from any mountain, especially since there *were* no mountains in this part of the city—or in *any* part of the city, for that matter. On the other hand, the word *kei* in Dutch meant "a piece of rock or stone on the ground," which this rock certainly was. This rock, in fact, seemed to be growing right *out* of the ground. *Kei* also meant "paving stone" or "cobblestone," which seemed like a better word than *rolsteen* since the Dutch planned to pave the street around the rock with cobbles. So they had opted for *Keistraat* rather than *Rolsteenstraat*, which had been a good choice in that *kei* also meant, in the idiom, "being very good at something," and the Dutch had certainly been very good at paving a street around a boulder and naming it *Keistraat*. The British had simply, and again unimaginatively, translated the name from the Dutch, and Boulder Street it had become and still was, although there was no evidence of so much as a pebble on the street nowadays.

The street, perhaps because its boundaries had been defined long ago when the massive boulder actually existed, ran for two consecutive blocks east to west and then ended abruptly. Lining those two blocks was some of the choicest real estate in the city, many of the buildings dating back to Dutch times, all of them restored and in excellent condition. Neither Carella nor Hawes knew anyone who could afford to live on Boulder Street. But this was where the former sailor Martin J. Benson lived, and it did not escape their attention that it was only ten blocks from Ramsey University.

Martin J. Benson was not home when they got there at a little past noon. The superintendent, out front watering a dazzling display of chrysanthemums in huge wooden tubs near the curb, told them that he usually left for work at about eight-thirty. Mr. Benson, he informed them, worked at an advertising agency on Jefferson Avenue, uptown. Mr. Benson, he further informed them, was the Head of Creation. He made it sound as if Mr. Benson was God. The name of the advertising agency was Cole, Cooper, Loomis and Bache. The superintendent told them that the agency, under the supervision of Mr. Benson himself as Head of Creation, had invented the advertising campaign for Daffy Dots, a candy neither of the detectives had ever eaten or even heard of. They thanked him for his time, and headed uptown.

The receptionist at Cole, Cooper, Loomis and Bache was a dizzy blonde whose plastic desk plaque identified her as Dorothy Hudd—was *she* the Daffy Dot after which the candy had been named? She was wearing a pink sweater several sizes too small for her, and she seemed inordinately fond of her own breasts—if the attraction of her left hand to them was any indication of pride of ownership. Under guise of toying with a string of pearls that hung between both breasts (Hawes was becoming rather fond of them as well), her left hand nudged, explored, and covertly caressed the mounds on either side of it, causing Hawes to wonder what excesses of affection she might lavish upon them at the seashore, for example, when she was wearing nothing but a bikini. His mind boggled at the thought of what she might be like in bed, straddling him, those magnificent globes clutched in her hands. He did not mind dizzy blondes. He did not even mind dizzy brunettes.

Carella, happily married and presumably immune to such idle speculation, put away the shield he had just shown Dorothy, and asked her if Mr. Benson might have a moment to see them. Dorothy, toying with her multiple pearls, informed him that Mr. Benson was out to lunch just now and wasn't expected back till three. Carella politely asked where Mr. Benson might be lunching.

"Oh, gee, I don't know," Dorothy said.

"Would his secretary know?"

"I guess so," Dorothy said, rolling her eyes, and toying, toying, toying with the pearls, a seemingly unconscious act that was driving Hawes to distraction. "But *she's* out to lunch, too."

"Is there any way you can find out where he is?" Carella said.

"Well, gee, let me go back and ask around," Dorothy said, and swiveled her chair and her body out from behind the desk, and walked toward a door leading to the inner offices. She was wearing a tight black skirt that celebrated the return of the mini to America's shores. Hawes was appreciative. The moment she disappeared from sight, he said, "I could eat her with a spoon."

"Me, too," Carella said, destroying the myth of blind married men.

Dorothy came back some five minutes later, smiling and taking her seat behind the desk again. Her left hand went immediately to the pearls around her neck. Hawes watched, fascinated.

"Mr. Perisello told me that Mr. Benson usually eats at a place called the Coach and Four," Dorothy said, "but that's only *usually,* and maybe he isn't there today. Why don't you just come back at three?" she said, and smiled up at Hawes. "Or *anytime,*" she added.

Carella thanked her and led Hawes out of the office.

"I'm in love," Hawes said.

The Coach and Four was the kind of place neither Carella nor Hawes could afford on their Detective 2nd/Grade salaries of $33,070 a year. Designed and decorated by an American-born architect of Armenian extraction, it resembled what he *thought* an old English coaching inn must have looked like circa 1605, replete with hand-hewn timber posts and beams, leaded windows with handblown glass panes, wide-planked pegged floors (sagging here and there for authenticity), and a staff of buxom waitresses wearing dirndl skirts and scoop-necked peasant blouses that revealed rather more bosom than even Dorothy Hudd's sweater had. Hawes was beginning to think this was his lucky day.

Carella asked the hostess—a willowy brunette wearing a long black gown and high heels that seemed decidedly anachronistic in this otherwise seventeenth-century English ambiance—where Mr. Benson might be sitting, and then took out a card, scribbled a note on the back of it, and asked the hostess if she would mind delivering it to his table. He watched as she crossed the room to a corner table where two men—one of them blond, the other bald—were engaged in animated conversation, no doubt discussing their latest brilliant advertising scheme. She handed the card to the blond. He looked at the front of it, printed with a Police Department seal and Carella's name, rank, and telephone number at the Eight-Seven, and then turned the card over and read the note Carella had scrawled across the back of it. He asked the hostess something, and she pointed toward where Carella and Hawes were still standing near the reception desk, which resembled what the Armenian architect thought Dr. Johnson's writing desk and inkstand looked like over there in Gough Square in Merrie Olde England. Benson rose immediately, excused himself to the bald man sitting at the table, and then strode across the room to where they were waiting.

"Mr. Benson?" Carella asked.

"What is this?" Benson said. "I'm in the middle of lunch."

He was, Carella guessed, some six feet two inches tall, easily as tall as Hawes, with the same broad shoulders and barrel chest, eyes the color of slate, hair as golden as wheat. He was wearing a suit Carella was willing to bet was tailormade, the tie a Countess Mara, the shirt monogrammed over the left breast, the initials MJB peeping out from behind the hand-stitched lapel of the suit jacket. French cuffs showed below the jacket sleeves, where they were fastened with small, gold, diamond-studded links. A pinky ring on his left hand flashed a diamond rather larger than those on the cufflinks. Carella guessed that Heads of Creation were pulling down quite a bit of bread with their Daffy Dots campaigns.

"If you'd like to finish your lunch, we'll wait," he said.

"No, let's get it over with now," Benson said, and

looked around for a spot where they might talk privately. He settled on the bar, an oaken structure with a lead top, the length of it overhung with glasses dangling by their stems. They pulled out three stools near the end of the bar, where an old brass cash register rested on the lead top. Hawes and Carella sat on either side of Benson. Benson immediately ordered a Beefeater martini, straight up and very cold.

"So?" he said.

"So do you know anybody named Marcia Schaffer?" Carella asked, getting straight to the point.

"So that's it," Benson said, and nodded.

"That's it," Hawes said.

"What about her?" Benson asked.

"Do you know her?"

"Yes. I knew her."

"Knew her?"

The detectives were alternating their questions now, causing Benson to turn from one to the other of them.

"She's *dead,* isn't she?" Benson said. "That's why you're here, isn't it? Yes, I *knew* her. Past tense."

"How *far* in the past?" Carella asked.

"I haven't seen her in more than a month."

"Want to elaborate on that?" Hawes said flatly.

Benson turned to him. "Maybe I'd better call my lawyer," he said.

"No, maybe you'd better sit right where you are," Carella said.

Benson moved back his stool, so that he could see both detectives without having to turn from one to the other.

"Elaborate how?" he asked Hawes.

"Mr. Benson," Hawes said, "do you own a blue, hundred-percent-wool robe with white piping on the cuffs and collar?"

"Yes. Who's kidding who? You found my robe in Marcia's apartment, which is why you're here, okay? So let's cut the crap."

"Do you own a gold Dunhill lighter?"

"Yes, it was in the pocket of the robe, okay? That doesn't mean I killed her."

"Who said you killed her?" Hawes asked.

"Did anybody say you killed her?" Carella asked.

"I'm assuming you're here because . . ."

"Mr. Benson, when did you leave that robe in Miss Schaffer's apartment?" Hawes asked.

"I told you. More than a month ago."

"*When*, exactly?" Carella asked.

"Labor Day, it must have been. We spent the weekend together. In the city. The city's a perfect place to spend any holiday. Everyone's gone, you've got the whole place to . . ."

"You spent the Labor Day weekend in her apartment?"

"Yes."

"Took clothes when you went there?"

"Yes. Well, only what I needed for . . ."

"Including the robe?"

"Yes. I guess I forgot to pack it when I left."

"Forgot the robe and your lighter?"

"Yes."

"Haven't missed the lighter since Labor Day?"

"I have other lighters," Benson said.

"You smoke Marlboros, do you?"

"I smoke Marlboros, yes."

Carella took a small plastic calendar from his wallet, looked at it, and then said, "Labor Day was the fifth of September."

"If you say so. You're the one looking at the calendar."

"I say so. And you haven't seen her since, is that right?"

"That's right."

"How'd you happen to meet her, Mr. Benson?" Hawes asked.

"At Ramsey U. I was doing a guest lecture on creative advertising. I ran into her at a reception later on."

"And began dating her?"

"Yes. I'm single, there's nothing wrong with that."

"How old are you, Mr. Benson?"

"Thirty-seven. There's nothing wrong with *that*, either. Marcia was almost twenty-one. She'd have been twenty-one next month. I wasn't robbing the cradle, if that's what you're thinking."

"Did anyone say you were robbing the cradle?" Hawes asked.

"I have the feeling you both disapprove of my relationship with Marcia. Frankly, I don't give a shit *what* you think. We had some good times together."

"Then why'd you stop seeing her?"

"Who said I stopped seeing her?"

"You just told us that the last time you saw her was on Labor Day, September fifth."

"That's right."

"Have you tried to contact her since?"

"No, but . . ."

"Telephone her? Write to her?"

"Why would I write to her? We both live in the same damn *city!*"

"But you didn't phone her."

"I may have, I don't remember."

"In any case, the last time you saw her was on September fifth."

"How many times do I have to say it? Yes. Labor Day. September fifth, if that's when it was."

"That's when it was."

"So okay."

Carella looked at Hawes.

"Mr. Benson," he said, "did you have your hair cut on Saturday, September third?"

"No, I never have my hair cut on a Saturday."

"When *do* you have it cut?"

"Tuesday afternoon. We have a staff meeting at two o'clock every Tuesday, and I usually go for a haircut at four."

"You have your hair cut every Tuesday?"

"No, no. Every three weeks."

"Then you did *not* have your hair cut on Saturday, September third?"

"I did not."

"When's the *last* time you had it cut?" Hawes asked.

"Last Tuesday," Benson said.

"That would be October fourth," Carella said, looking at the calendar.

"I suppose."

"And three weeks before *that* would have been September thirteenth."

"If that's what the calendar says."

"And three weeks before *that* would have been August twenty-third."

"Where's all this going, would you mind telling me? Do I need another haircut?"

"Mr. Benson, you said you left your robe in Miss Schaffer's apartment on September fifth, the last time you saw her."

"That's right."

"And you haven't seen her since."

"I haven't."

"You didn't see her on September fifteenth, did you? Two days after you'd had a haircut?"

"I did not."

"You didn't see her on October sixth, did you? Again, two days after you'd had a haircut?"

"I didn't see her on either of those days. The last time I saw her . . ."

"Yes, you told us. Labor Day."

"Why are you lying to us?" Hawes asked gently.

"I beg your pardon."

"Mr. Benson," Carella said, "our laboratory report

indicates that you had your hair cut forty-eight hours before it was deposited on that robe. You say you left the robe there on Labor Day, but you didn't have your hair cut on September third, so either you left the robe there after an *earlier* haircut, or else you left it there after a *later* haircut, but you couldn't have left it there on September fifth, which you say is the last time you saw Marcia Schaffer.''

"So why are you lying to us?'' Hawes asked.

"Maybe I saw her *after* Labor Day,'' Benson said. "What was that date you mentioned? The haircut before this last one?''

"You tell me,'' Carella said.

"Whenever it was. The fourteenth, the fifteenth. Whenever.'' He lifted his martini glass and took a quick swallow of it.

"But not this past week, huh? Not October sixth.''

"No, I'm sure of that.''

"You did *not* see Marcia Schaffer on October sixth, two days after you had your most recent haircut? You did *not* forget your robe in her apartment on October sixth?''

"I'm positive I didn't.''

"Where *were* you on October sixth, Mr. Benson?''

"What day was that?''

"A Thursday. Thursday last week, Mr. Benson.''

"Well, I'm sure I was at work.''

"All day Thursday?''

"Yes, all day.''

"You didn't see Miss Schaffer on Thursday *night,* did you?''

"No, I'm sure I didn't.''

"How about *Wednesday* night?''

Benson sipped at his martini again.

"Did you see her on *Wednesday* night?'' Hawes asked.

"The *fifth* of October?'' Carella said.

"Mr. Benson?'' Hawes said.

"*Did* you see her that night?" Carella said.

"All right," Benson said, and put down his glass. "All right, I saw her last Wednesday night, I was with her last Wednesday night. I went there right after work, we had dinner together and spent the . . . the rest of the night . . ."

The detectives said nothing. They waited.

". . . in bed, I guess you'd say," Benson said, and sighed.

"When did you leave the apartment?" Carella asked.

"The next morning. I went directly to work from there. Marcia was on her way to school."

"This was Thursday morning, October sixth."

"Yes."

"Is that when you forgot the robe?"

"Yes."

"What time was that, Mr. Benson?"

"I left the apartment at about eight-thirty."

"And you'd had your hair cut at four o'clock on Tuesday afternoon."

"Yes."

"That's a time span of about forty hours," Carella said to Hawes.

"Close enough," Hawes said, nodding.

"Where were you Thursday night at approximately seven o'clock?" Hawes asked.

"I thought nobody was saying I killed her," Benson said.

"Nobody's said it yet."

"Then why do you want to know where I was Thursday night? That's when she was killed, isn't it? Thursday night?"

"That's when she was killed."

"So where were you Thursday night?" Carella asked.

"At seven o'clock, give or take," Hawes said.

"I was having dinner with a friend of mine."

"What friend?"

"A woman I know."

"What's her name?"

"Why do you have to drag her into this?"

"What's her name, Mr. Benson?"

"She's just a casual acquaintance, someone I met at the agency."

"She works at the agency?"

"Yes."

"What's her name?" Hawes asked.

"I'd rather not say."

Hawes and Carella looked at each other.

"How old is *this* one?" Hawes asked.

"It isn't that. She's not underage."

"Then what is it?"

Benson shook his head.

"Was it only *dinner* last Thursday night?" Carella asked.

"It was more than dinner," Benson said softly.

"You went to bed with her," Hawes said.

"I went to bed with her."

"Where?"

"My apartment."

"On Boulder Street."

"Yes, that's where I live."

"You had dinner with her at seven . . ."

"Yes."

"And got back to the apartment at what time?"

"About nine."

"And went to bed with her."

"Yes."

"What time did she leave the apartment?"

"At about one, a little later."

"What's her name, Mr. Benson?" Hawes asked.

"Look," Benson said, and sighed.

The detectives waited.

"She's married, okay?" Benson said.

"Okay," Hawes said, "she's married. What's her name?"

"She's married to a *cop*," Benson said. "Look, I don't want to get her in trouble, really. We're talking about *murder* here."

"You're telling *us?*" Carella said.

"My point . . . the point is . . . this thing is getting a lot of attention. The one last night . . ."

"Oh, you know about the one last night?" Hawes asked.

"Yes, it was on television this morning. If a cop's *wife* seems to be involved . . ."

"Involved how?" Carella asked. *"Is* she involved?"

"I'm talking about dragging her name into it. Suppose the newspapers found out? A *cop's* wife? They'd have a field day with it."

"We'll keep it a secret," Carella said. "What's her name?"

"I'd rather not say."

"Where does her husband work?" Hawes asked. "This cop?"

"I'd rather not say."

"Where were you *last* night?" Hawes asked, and suddenly leaned into Benson.

"What?" Benson said.

"Last night, *last* night," Hawes said. "When the hell was last night, Steve? You've got the calendar there."

"What?" Carella said. He'd heard Hawes, he wasn't asking what Hawes had said. He was simply surprised by the sudden anger in Hawes's voice. So okay, Benson was bedding a cop's wife. Not entirely unheard of in the annals of the department, witness Bert Kling's recent divorce premised on *exactly* such a situation. So why the sudden anger?

"What?" he said again.

"Last night's *date,*" Hawes said impatiently. "Give it to him."

"October thirteenth," Carella said.

"Where were you last night, October thirteenth?" Hawes asked.

"With . . . her," Benson said.

"The cop's wife?"

"Yes."

"In bed again?"

"Yes."

"You like to live dangerously, don't you?" Hawes said, the same anger in his voice, his blue eyes flashing, his red hair looking as if it had suddenly caught fire. "What's her name?"

"I don't want to tell you that."

"What's her fucking *name?*" Hawes said, and grabbed Benson's arm.

"Hey," Carella said, "come on."

"Her *name,*" Hawes said, tightening his grip on Benson's arm.

"I can't tell you that," Benson said.

Carella sighed heavily. "Mr. Benson," he said, "you realize . . ."

"Let go of my arm," Benson said to Hawes.

"You realize, don't you," Carella said, "that Marcia Schaffer was killed last Thursday night . . ."

"Yes, damn it, I *know* that! Let go of my *arm!*" he said to Hawes again, and tried to yank it away. Hawes's fingers remained clamped on it.

"And that your alibi for that night . . ."

"It isn't an *alibi!*"

". . . and for *last* night, when yet *another* person was . . ."

"I didn't kill either of them!"

"The only one who can verify . . ."

"Her name is Robin Steele, damn it!" Benson said, and Hawes let go of his arm.

6

THERE WERE TIMES WHEN COTTON HAWES wished he really *was* named Great Farting Bull Horse. He hated the name Hawes. It was hard to say. Hawes. It sounded like yaws, a disease of some kind, he *hated* the name. He hated the name Cotton, too. Nobody on earth was named Cotton except Cotton Mather, and he'd been dead since 1728. But Hawes's father had been a religious man who'd felt that Cotton Mather was the greatest of the Puritan priests and had named his son in honor of the colonial God-seeker who'd hunted witches with the worst of them. Conveniently, Hawes's father had chalked off the Salem trials—his father had been very good at chalking off things—as the personal petty revenges of a town feeding on its own ingrown fears. Jeremiah Hawes (why hadn't he named Hawes "Jeremiah, Jr."?) simply exonerated Cotton Mather and the role the priest had played in bringing the delusion to its fever pitch, naming his son in the man's honor. Why hadn't he named him "Lefty" instead? Hawes wasn't left-handed, but he would have preferred "Lefty" to "Cotton." Lefty Hawes. Scare the shit out of any cheap thief on the street.

There were also times when Hawes hated anyone who wasn't a cop. This went for cops' wives or girlfriends, too. If they weren't on the force, then they didn't know what the hell it was all about. You double-dated with another cop and his girlfriend, you sat there trying to tell the women that you almost got shot that afternoon, they wanted to talk about their nails instead. Some new nail polish that made your nails grow long. Guy with a .357

Magnum tries to blow you away three hours earlier, and they want to talk about their nails. If they weren't on the force, they just didn't understand. Hawes once told Meyer that *Star Wars* had it all wrong. It shouldn't have been, "May the force be with you." What it should have been, instead, was, "May *you* be with the force."

Anybody who wasn't on the force didn't really want to hear about what it was like being a cop. They all agreed that this city was a nice place to visit, but who'd want to live here? Even though they lived here, they complained about living here. But the things they complained about weren't the things that made it really difficult to live here—and impossible to work here, if you happened to be a cop. They didn't know about the underbelly. They didn't want to hear about the underbelly in this city or in *any* city. The underbelly was pale white, and it was slimy, and maggots clung to it. The underbelly was a working cop's life, day in and day out.

Cops' wives and girlfriends *understood* that their men looked at the underbelly twenty-four hours a day, but they didn't want to hear the underbelly defined. They said novenas in church, praying that their men wouldn't get hurt out there, but they didn't want to know about the underbelly, not really. Sometimes they prayed that they wouldn't have to hear about it, know about it, that pale white, maggoty-crawling underbelly. Sometimes, they tried to forget about it by going to bed with somebody who wasn't a cop. Later, they prayed forgiveness for their sins—but at least they hadn't had to touch that pale white underbelly and get its slime all over their fingers.

Robin Steele's husband worked out of the Two-Six downtown.

He was a patrolman.

He'd been on the force for three years, hardly enough time to get burned out, especially in a soft precinct like the Two-Six.

But Robin Steele had been sleeping with Martin J. Benson for the past six months now.

She confirmed that she had been with Benson on the night of October sixth, while her husband was riding shotgun in a radio motor patrol car. She confirmed that she was with him again last night, while her husband was again occupied on the city streets. She asked them please not to tell her husband any of this. She told Carella that she loved her husband very much and wouldn't want to see him hurt in any way. She knew he was in a dangerous job, and she didn't want him to have any worries on his mind when he was out there doing whatever it was he did. When Hawes asked her if she knew she wasn't the only woman in Benson's life, she said, "Oh, sure, that doesn't matter."

None of it mattered, Hawes guessed.

Except that somebody was hanging young girls from lampposts.

He guessed he called Annie Rawles because he wanted to be near a woman who was a cop. He wanted to be able to relax with somebody without having to explain what the hell a duty chart was. He wanted to be with someone who would automatically understand about the under-belly. At first he thought he might take a whack at Doro-thy Hudd of the hanging pearls and roaming fingers. He went so far as to look up her name in the Isola directory, finding a listing for a D. Hudd (why did women use only the initial of their first name in telephone directories, a sure invitation to heavy breathers?), dialed the first two numbers, and then hung up, figuring he did not want to be with a civilian on a day when a good suspect had come up with an excellent alibi.

He called the Departmental Directory instead, identi-fied himself as a working cop, told the clerk who took his rank and shield number that he was working a case with Detective Rawles of the Rape Squad, and got her home phone number in minutes. She's probably married, Hawes

thought as he dialed the number. But he hadn't seen a
wedding band on her hand. Maybe Rape Squad cops
didn't wear wedding bands. He listened to the phone
ringing on the other end.

"Hello?" a woman's voice said.

"Miss Rawles?" he said.

"Yes?"

"Cotton Hawes," he said.

"Who?" she said.

"Hawes. The Eight-Seven. You were up there last
week about a rape case, we talked briefly . . ."

"Oh, yes, hi," Annie said. "Hawes. The redheaded
one."

"Yes," Hawes said.

"You got him, is that it?" she asked.

"What?"

"The rapist."

"No, no," Hawes said. "Eileen Burke was in late this
afternoon, I gather she's been assigned . . ."

"Yes."

"But I don't think she's beginning till tomorrow."

"That's right. I just thought lightning may have
struck."

"No such luck."

There was a long silence on the line.

"So . . . uh . . . what is it?" Annie asked.

Hawes hesitated.

"Hello?" Annie said.

"Hello, I'm still here." He hesitated again. "You're
not married or anything, are you?"

"No, I'm not married," Annie said. He thought he detected a smile in her voice.

"Have you had dinner yet? I know it's past seven,
maybe you've already . . ."

"No, I haven't had dinner yet," she said. He was *sure*
she was smiling now. "I just got in a few minutes ago, in
fact."

"Would you . . . uh . . . ?"

"Sure," she said. "Want to pick me up here, or shall we meet someplace?"

"Eight o'clock sound all right?" Hawes asked.

They had dinner in a Chinese restaurant and went back to Annie's place later on. She lived in an old brick building on Langley Place, near the Three-One, which was one of the oldest precincts in the city, and which still had a coal-burning furnace in the basement. She told him that she was sure her presence in the building accounted for the fact that there hadn't been a burglary here in three years. She figured word had got around that a lady cop lived in the building. She told him this while she was pouring cognac into brandy snifters.

She was wearing a simple blue dress and blue patent-leather high-heeled pumps; he doubted she'd been dressed for work that way. She looked like any pretty civilian might look—black wedge-cut hair, brown eyes behind black-rimmed eyeglasses, the simple blue dress, a gold chain and pendant—well, no. A civilian in this city wouldn't risk wearing a gold chain. A lady cop with a .38 in her handbag might take the chance. But otherwise, she didn't *look* like a cop; some of the lady cops in this city resembled hog callers at a county fair, big guns on their hips, cartridge belts hanging, big fat asses. Annie Rawles looked like a schoolgirl. Word had it that she had blown away two hoods trying to rob a bank, but Hawes couldn't visualize it. Couldn't see her in a policeman's crouch, leveling the gun and squeezing off however many shots it had taken to deck the bastards. He tried to imagine the scene. As he accepted the brandy snifter from her, he realized he was staring.

"Something?" she said, and smiled.

"No, no," Hawes assured her. "Just remembering you're a cop."

"Sometimes I wish I could *forget* it," Annie said.

She sat beside him on the couch, tucking her legs up under her. The room was pleasantly furnished, a Franklin stove laid with cannel coal on the wall opposite the sofa, framed prints on all of the walls, a pass-through counter leading into a tidy kitchen hung with copper-bottomed pots and pans. The furniture looked like quality stuff; he remembered she earned $37,935 a year as a Detective/First. He sipped at the cognac.

"Good," he said.

"My brother brought it back from France," she said.

"What does *he* do?"

"He imports fish," she said. "Don't laugh."

"What kind of fish?"

"Salmon. Irish salmon, mostly. Very expensive stuff. Something like thirty-eight dollars a pound."

"Whoo," Hawes said. "So how come France?"

"What? Oh. A side trip. Mixing business with pleasure."

"I've never been to France," Hawes said, somewhat wistfully.

"Neither have I," Annie said.

"Popeye got to go to France, though."

"Popeye?"

"The French Connection. Did you see that movie? Not the one where he goes to France, that was lousy. The *first* one."

"Yeah, it was pretty authentic, I thought."

"Yeah, standing around in the cold, and everything. That really happened to Carella, you know."

"Who's Carella?"

"Guy I'm working these homicides with, good cop."

"What really happened to him?"

"They made him an addict. On a case he was working. They turned him on to heroin. Like with Popeye in the second *French Connection* movie. Only it happened to Carella before there even *was* that movie. I mean, *really* happened to him, never mind fiction."

"Is he okay now?"

"Oh, sure. Well, he was hooked, but not for very long, and besides they did it *to* him, you know, it wasn't a voluntary thing."

"So he kicked it."

"Oh, yeah."

"Some fun, huh? Being a cop?"

"A million laughs," Hawes said. "How'd you happen to get into it?"

"I thought it would be exciting," Annie said. "I guess it is. Don't you think it is?"

"I guess so," Hawes said.

"I was fresh out of college . . ."

"You *still* look like a college girl."

"Well, thank you."

"How old *are* you?" he asked.

"Thirty-four," Annie said immediately.

He liked that about lady cops. No bullshit. Ask a question, you got a straight answer.

"Been on the job long?"

"Eight years."

"You used to work out of Robbery, right?" Hawes said.

"Yeah. Well, I was on the Stakeout Squad before that. Right after I got the gold shield. Then Robbery, and now Rape. How about you?"

"I've been with the Eight-Seven for more years than I can count," Hawes said. "Before that, I was with the Three-Oh, a silk-stocking precinct, are you familiar with it?"

"Yes," Annie said, and nodded, and sipped at her cognac.

"I've learned a lot uptown," he said.

"I'll bet you have," Annie said.

They were silent for a moment. He wanted to ask her where she'd gone to college, what she'd majored in, whether she'd had any qualms about working with the

Stakeout Squad, whose prime purpose—before it was disbanded—was to sit in the back of stores that had been previously held up, waiting to ambush any robber who came back a second time. The Stakeout Squad had blown away forty-four armed robbers before the Commissioner decided the operation was something the Department shouldn't be too terribly proud of. Hawes wondered if she'd shot anyone while she was working with Stakeout. He had a lot of questions he still wanted to ask her. He felt he was getting to know her a little better, but there were still a lot of questions to ask. Instead, though, suddenly feeling totally relaxed and secure, he didn't ask a question at all. As if he had known her forever, he said only, "It gets to you after a while. The job."

She looked at him for what seemed like a long time before she answered.

"Yes," she said simply. "It gets to you."

They kept looking at each other.

Hawes nodded.

"Well," he said, and glanced at his watch. "If your day was anything like mine . . ."

"Rough one," she said, and nodded.

"So," he said, and rose awkwardly. "Thanks for the cognac, your brother's got good taste."

"Thanks for the dinner," she said.

She did not rise. She kept sitting right where she was, looking up at him, her legs tucked under her.

"Let's do it again sometime," he said.

"I'd love to."

"In fact . . . I've got the day off tomorrow," he said. "Maybe we could . . ."

"I don't have to be in till four," she said.

"Maybe . . . well, I don't *know*. What would *you* like to do?"

"Gee, I don't know, Marty," she said, and smiled. "What would *you* like to do?"

"I love that movie," he said.

"I do, too."

"I saw it on television again last week."

"So did I."

"You're kidding."

"No, I saw it last week."

"Late at night, right?"

"About two in the morning."

"How about that?" he said. "Both of us watching the same movie at opposite ends of the city."

"What a pity," she said.

Their eyes met.

"Well," he said, "let me call you in the morning, okay? I'll try to figure out something we can . . ."

"Let's not be dopes," Annie said.

Eileen Burke was in Kling's bed.

They had known each other intimately for the better part of eight months now, but the sex tonight had been as steamy and as improvisational as it had been the first time. When at last they expired on the separate little deaths of literary reknown, and after they exchanged the obligatory assurances that it had been as good for him as it had been for her and vice versa, and after Eileen had gone to the bathroom to pee, and after Kling had crossed the room naked to open the window to the sounds of the night traffic below, they lay back against the pillows, entwined in each other's arms, Eileen's hand resting idly on Kling's chest, his own hand gently cradling her breast.

It was a little while before Eileen told him what was troubling her.

"I've been thinking about the job," she said.

Kling had been thinking about the job, too. Kling had been thinking that the hangings up there in the Eight-Seven were the work of the Deaf Man.

"I'm not talking about this *particular* job," Eileen said. "This business of masquerading as Mary Hollings."

"The rape victim, right," Kling said.

"I mean the job *itself.*"

"Being a cop, you mean?"

"Being a particular *kind* of cop," Eileen said.

It has to be the Deaf Man, Kling was thinking. It fit with the Deaf Man's M.O. They hadn't heard from the Deaf Man in a long time, but this sure looked like the Deaf Man. Why else would anybody have bothered to make identification of the victims so easy for them?

"A decoy, I mean," Eileen said.

Kling was thinking back to the first time the Deaf Man had put in an appearance. That had been the most difficult time for the Eight-Seven because they hadn't known then what they were up against. All they'd known was that somebody was trying to force a man—what had his name been, anyway? Meyer had caught the initial squeal, a guy who'd grown up with his father, came to the squadroom to tell him—what the hell had his name been? Haskins? Baskin?

"I'm beginning to think it's demeaning," Eileen said.

"What is?" Kling asked.

"Being a decoy. I mean, aside from the fact that it smells a lot like entrapment . . ."

"Well, it's not exactly entrapment," Kling said.

"I know it isn't, but it *feels* like it is," Eileen said. "I mean, I'm out there hoping some guy will *rape* me, isn't that what it is?"

"Well, not *rape* you, actually."

"*Try* to rape me, okay?"

"So you can stop him from raping somebody else," Kling said.

"Well, yeah, that," Eileen said.

Raskin, Kling remembered. His name was David Raskin. And somebody had been trying to get him to vacate a loft on Culver Avenue, crumby little loft Raskin used for storing dresses, guy was in the dress business, right, David Raskin. First he started getting calls threatening to kill him if he didn't move out of the loft. Then the guy heckling him on the phone—they hadn't known it was the Deaf Man at the time—began sending him stationery he hadn't ordered, and then a catering service delivered folding chairs and enough food to feed the Russian army, and then an ad appeared in the two morning dailies advertising for redheads to model dresses, and that was when they tipped to what was going on: someone was referring them to Conan Doyle's *The Redheaded League,* and the someone had signed himself *L. Sordo,* which was Spanish for the Deaf Man, and he was trying to help them dope out in advance what he was planning to do.

Only he *hadn't* been trying to help them at all. He was using them the way he'd been using Raskin, misdirecting them into believing he was planning to hit the bank under Raskin's loft, when he had another bank in mind all along. Playing with them. Making them feel foolish and incompetent. Leading them a merry chase while he masterminded his break-in, probably laughing to himself all along.

Carella had got himself shot that first time the Deaf Man made himself known to the 87th Precinct.

If the Deaf Man was now responsible for the two hangings . . .

"It makes me feel like some kind of sex object," Eileen said.

"You *are* some kind of sex object," Kling said, and playfully tweaked her nipple.

"I'm serious," she said.

And while she went on to tell him that she wouldn't have been picked for this particular line of police work if she wasn't a woman, which in itself was demeaning because nobody on the force would dream of putting a *male* cop in drag to lure a rapist—had he really been listening, Kling might have protested that male cops *had* been used on such jobs—and which was entirely against the whole psychology of the rapist, anyway. A rapist wasn't interested in tits and ass, he wasn't interested in a show of leg or thigh, he was interested in satisfying his own particular *rage,* which had nothing whatever to do with sex or lust. But the sexist meatheads in the department put her on the street to parade like a hooker in the hope she would trap—yes, *trap*—some lunatic out there into dragging her in the bushes where she'd stick her gun in his mouth; it was all degrading and it made her feel slimy at night when she took off her clothes, made her feel like scrubbing herself three times over to get the filth of the job off her. What the hell was a lady like Annie Rawles doing on the *Rape* Squad when she'd already blown away two guys when she was with Robbery, what was *that* if not taking the sexist view that a woman cop was suited only for a certain *kind* of police work while a man cop had his choice of whatever the hell job he wanted?

"What job *do* you want?" Kling asked.

"I may ask for a transfer to Narcotics," she said.

"Same thing," he said. "Only then you'll be a decoy for pushers."

"It's *not* the same," Eileen said.

But Kling was still thinking about the Deaf Man.

He had blown up half the city.

That was the first time.

He had set both incendiary and explosive bombs all over the city, to divert the police, to cause panic and confusion while he went about the business of robbing a bank. Not a thought in his head of the havoc he was wreaking or of the lives lost because of his clever little escapade.

That had been the first time.

Carella tended to block out that first time because that was the time he'd been shot. He did not like to think about getting shot. He'd been shot once before then, by a pusher in Grover Park, and he hadn't enjoyed *that* particular fireworks display, either. So whenever he thought about the Deaf Man, as he was doing tonight, he tended to remember only the second and third times the Deaf Man had come around to plague them. It seemed incredible to him that there had been only three times. The Deaf Man, in his mind and in the minds of most of the detectives on the squad, was a legend, and legends were without origin, legends were omnipresent, legends were eternal. The very thought that the Deaf Man might already be back yet another time sent a small shiver of apprehension up Carella's spine. Whenever the Deaf Man arrived—and surely these hangings bore his unique stamp—the men of the Eight-Seven began behaving like Keystone Kops in a silent black-and-white film. Carella did not enjoy feeling like a dope, but the Deaf Man made *all* of them feel stupid.

He thought it a supreme irony of his life that the man who was the nemesis of the 87th Precinct advertised himself as being deaf—if, in fact, he was—while at the same time the single most important person in his life, his wife Teddy, was *truly* deaf. Nor could she speak. Not with a voice, at any rate. She spoke volumes otherwise, with her hands, with her expressive face, with her eyes. And she "heard" every word her husband uttered, her eyes fastened to his lips when he spoke or to his hands when he signed to her in the language she had taught him early on in their marriage.

Teddy was talking to him now.

They had just made love.

The first words she said to him were, "I love you."

She used the informal sign, a blend of the letters "i," "l," and "y," her right hand held close to her breast, the little finger, index finger and thumb extended, the remaining two fingers folded down toward her palm. He answered with the more formal sign for "I love you": first touching the tip of his index finger to the center of his chest; then clenching both fists in the "a" handsign, crossing his arms below the wrists, and placing his hands on his chest; and finally pointing at her with his index finger—a simple "I" plus "love" plus "you."

They kissed again.

She sighed.

And then she began telling him about her day.

He had known for quite some time now that she was interested in finding a job. Fanny had been with them since the twins were born, and she ran the house efficiently. The twins—Mark and April—were now eleven years old, and in school much of the day. Teddy was bored with playing tennis or lunching with the "girls." She signed "girl" by making the "a" handsign with her right fist, and dragging the tip of her thumb down her cheek along the jawline; to make the word plural, she rapidly indicated several different locations, pointing with her extended forefinger. More than *one* girl. Girls. But her eyes and the expression on her face made it clear that she was using the word derogatively; she did not consider herself a "girl," and she certainly didn't consider herself one of the "girls."

Carella, listening to this—he was in fact *listening,* even though he was *watching*—thought about the second time the Deaf Man had come into the precinct's busy life. Again, it had been Meyer who'd initially been contacted, purely by chance since he was the one who'd answered the ringing telephone. The Deaf Man himself was on the other end of the line, promising to kill the Parks Commissioner if he did not receive five thousand dollars before noon. The Parks Commissioner was shot dead the following night.

Well, I went to this real estate agency on Cumberland Avenue this morning, Teddy was saying with her hands and her eyes and her face. I'd written them a letter answering an ad in the newspaper, telling them what my experience had been before we got married and before I became a mother—

(Carella remembered. He had met Theodora Franklin

while investigating a burglary at a small firm on the fringe of the precinct territory. She had been working there addressing envelopes. He had taken one look at the brown-eyed, black-haired beauty sitting behind the typewriter, and had known instantly that this was the woman with whom he wished to share the rest of his life.)

—and they wrote back setting up an appointment for an interview. So I got all dolled up this morning, and went over there.

To express the slang expression "dolled up," she first signed "x," stroking the curled index finger of the handsign on the tip of her nose, twice. To indicate "doll" was in the past tense, she immediately made the sign for "finished." For "up" she made the same sign anyone who was not a deaf-mute might have made: She simply moved her extended index finger upward. Dolled up. Carella got the message, and visualized her in a smart suit and heels, taking the bus to Cumberland Avenue, some two miles from the house.

And now her hands and her eyes and her mobile face spewed forth a torrent of language. Surprise of all surprises, she told him, the lady is a deaf-mute. The lady cannot *hear,* the lady cannot *speak,* the lady—however intelligent her letter may have sounded, however bright and perky she may appear in person—possesses neither tongue nor ear, the lady simply will not *do!* This despite the fact that the ad called only for someone to type and file. This despite the fact that I was reading that fat bastard's lips and understanding every single word he said— which wasn't easy since he was chewing on a cigar—this despite the fact that I can *still* type sixty words a minute after all these years, ah, the hell with it. Steve, he thought I was *dumb* (she tapped the knuckles of the "a" handsign against her forehead, indicating someone stupid), the obvious mate to *deaf,* right? (she touched first her mouth and then her ear with her extended index finger), like ham and eggs, right? Deaf and *dumb,* right? Shit, she

said signing the word alphabetically for emphasis,
S-H-I-T!

He took her in his arms.

He was about to comfort her, about to tell her that
there were ignorant people in this world who were incapable of judging a person's worth by anything but the
most obvious external evidence, when suddenly she was
signing again. He read her hands and the anger in her
eyes.

I'm not quitting, she said. *I'll get a goddamn job.*

She rolled into him, and he felt her small determined
nod against his shoulder. Reaching behind him toward
the nighttable, he snapped off the bedside light. He
could hear her breathing in the darkness beside him. He
knew she would lie awake for a long time, planning her
next move. He thought suddenly of the Deaf Man again.
Was *he* lying awake out there someplace, planning *his*
next move? Another girl hanging from a lamppost? Another young runner knocked down in her prime? But
why?

That second time around, he had senselessly killed the
Parks Commissioner, and then the Deputy Mayor (and a
handful of unselected targets who happened to be in the
immediate vicinity when the Deputy Mayor's car exploded) and then had threatened to kill the Mayor himself, all as part of his grander scheme. The scheme? To
extort five thousand dollars from each of a hundred selected wealthy citizens. The dubious reasoning for
believing they would pay? Well, the Deaf Man had
warned his previous targets in advance, hadn't he? And
then had carried out his threats. And now he was promising to strike *without* warning if his new targets didn't
pay. So what would five thousand dollars mean to men
who were worth millions? Even figuring on a mere one-
percent return, the Deaf Man's expenses would be more
than covered. Never mind that he had already killed two
selected victims and a handful of innocent bystanders.

Never mind that he planned to kill yet a third, the Mayor himself. All part of the game. Fun and games. Everytime the Deaf Man put in an appearance, a laugh riot was all but guaranteed. For everyone but the cops of the 87th Precinct.

If those young girls hanging from lampposts were harbingers of something bigger the Deaf Man planned, the Eight-Seven was in for more trouble than it already had or needed. Carella shuddered with the thought, and suddenly pulled his wife close.

Sarah Meyer was wondering how to tell her husband that she thought their daughter should go on the pill. Meyer was wondering whether she liked his hairpiece. He was also wondering if the Deaf Man was once again in their midst. Not in their *immediate* midst, since he knew that he and Sarah were alone in bed together, but in the midst of hanging young women from lampposts.

Meyer did not like the Deaf Man. It had been Meyer's misfortune, on three separate occasions now, to be the first detective contacted by the Deaf Man. Well, that wasn't quite true. The first time around, it had been Dave Raskin who'd contacted him *about* the Deaf Man, who they didn't even know was deaf at the time, if he really *was* deaf, which maybe he wasn't. There were a lot of things they didn't know about the Deaf Man. Like who he was, for example. Or where he'd been all these years. Or why he was back now, if indeed he *was* back, which Meyer hoped he wasn't, but feared he was.

All Meyer wanted to do was ask Sarah if she liked him better *with* his hairpiece or *without* his hairpiece. He was not wearing his hairpiece to bed. If she told him she liked him better *with* it, he would get out of bed and put it on, and then he would make wild passionate love to her. Either way, with or without the hairpiece, he planned to make wild passionate love to her. He did not want to be thinking about the Deaf Man. He wanted to be thinking instead about Sarah's splendid legs, thighs, and breasts.

Sarah was worrying about their only daughter, Susan, who was sixteen years old. More specifically, Sarah was worried about genetics. Her husband had told her on more occasions than she could count that she was blessed with splendid legs, thighs, and breasts. She wasn't so sure now how she felt about her legs or thighs, but she agreed that she had very good breasts, and there was nothing she liked better (well, *almost* nothing) than having her breasts fondled. That was where genetics came in. She did not have to worry about her older boy, Alan, so far as genetics were concerned. Nor did she have to worry about her youngest son, Jeff. Alan was seventeen and Jeff was thirteen and the only thing she had to worry about where *they* were concerned was the possibility that they might begin smoking dope or something, in which case Meyer would break their respective heads. But genetics, ah, genetics.

Susan, from all external evidence, had inherited the splendid legs, thighs, and breasts Meyer was always telling Sarah she possessed. She had also inherited Sarah's bee-stung lips, her own and Meyer's blue eyes, plus blond hair that came from God knew where, and all of this put together made for a very attractive young lady who Sarah hoped was not as fond of being fondled as she herself was.

That was why Sarah wanted to suggest to Meyer that they both suggest to Susan that Susan suggest to their family doctor that perhaps he ought to put her on the pill. Sarah did not know whether or not her daughter was still a virgin. Susan had become awfully close-mouthed about personal matters in the past several months, a possible sign that she had already been initiated by some hot-blooded high school cowboy (I'll *kill* him, Sarah thought), or, on the other hand, a possible sign that she was seriously *considering* initiation. Either way, Sarah did not want her daughter to become pregnant at the age of sixteen.

The problem, however, was explaining all of this to Meyer.

It was Sarah's firm belief that Meyer thought their daughter had never been kissed.

Simultaneously, they both began speaking.

"I've been thinking . . ."

"Sarah, do you . . . ?"

They both fell silent.

"Go ahead," Meyer said. "You first."

"No, you first."

Meyer took a deep breath.

"They're kidding me about the hairpiece," he said.

"Who?"

"The guys."

"So?"

"*All* the guys," Meyer said.

"So?"

"So . . . Sarah . . . do *you* like the hairpiece?"

"It's not me who has to like it," Sarah said. "It's on *your* head."

"Well . . . do you think I look better with it or without it?"

Sarah considered this for what seemed a long time.

"Meyer," she said, "I love you with hair or without hair. To me, you're *you,* with hair or without hair. You can go around bald, if you like, or you can wear the wig you've already got, or you can buy a blond wig or a red-headed wig, you can grow a mustache or a beard, or you can paint your toenails purple, whatever you do I'll love you. Because I love you," she said.

"I love you, too," he said, and hesitated. "But do you like the wig?"

"You want an honest answer?"

"Yes."

"I love to kiss your shiny bald head," she said.

"Then I'll burn the wig," he said.

"Yes, burn it."

"Tomorrow," he said.

"Whenever," she said.

"Okay," he said, but he wasn't sure he would burn it. He sort of liked the way he looked in it. The wig made him look like a *detective*. He liked looking like a detective. He liked *being* a detective. Except when the Deaf Man was around. Why did the Deaf Man have to be around again? If it *was* the Deaf Man. But who else would be hanging girls from lampposts and then leaving identification around to make the job easy? It had to be the Deaf Man. He wondered suddenly if the Deaf Man wore a wig? The Deaf Man was blond, Carella had positively identified him that time he'd got shot. A tall blond man wearing a hearing aid in his right ear. But suppose the blond hair was a wig. Suppose the Deaf Man was really bald? Would they have to start calling him the *Bald* Man? Did people call Meyer himself the *Bald* Man behind his back? Was he known throughout the 87th Precinct as the *Bald* Detective? Throughout the entire *city* perhaps? The world? He did not want to be known as the *bald* anything. He wanted to be known as Meyer Meyer. Himself.

Sarah was talking.

He had missed the first several words of what she was saying, but it had something to do with people growing up to be beautiful and naturally attracting the attention of other people. He remembered the last time the Deaf Man had come to plague them. Why didn't he pick on some other precinct, what the hell was it with him? Why the Eight-Seven? Sent photographs to them. Sent each photograph *twice*. Made it easy for them—well, not *so* easy, a philanthropist he wasn't. But threw the challenge in their laps: Dope out what these pictures mean, and you'll know what I'm up to this time. The pictures, once they doped them out, indicated that he was going to rob another bank. And rob a bank he did. *Twice*. Sent in a team he knew would be caught if the detectives had properly figured out the pictures he'd sent them, and then sent in a *second* team an hour and a half later. Almost got away with it, too. Called himself "Taubman" that time around. "Taubman" was German for the Deaf Man. *Der taube mann*. God, Meyer hoped he wasn't back again.

"So what do you think?" Sarah said.

"I hope he isn't back again," Meyer said aloud.

"Who?"

"The Deaf Man."

"Did you hear anything I said?"

"Well, sure, I . . ."

"Or are *you* deaf, too?" Sarah asked.

"What is it?" Meyer said.

"I asked you about Susan."

"What about Susan?"

"She's sixteen."

"I know she's sixteen."

"She's beautiful."

"Like her mother."

"Thank you. She's beginning to attract boys."

"She's been attracting them since she was twelve," Meyer said.

"You *know* that?"

"Of *course* I know it, am I blind? In fact, I've been meaning to ask you. Don't you think it's time she saw a doctor?"

"A doctor?" Sarah said.

"Yeah. To prescribe the pill for her."

"Oh," Sarah said.

"I know the idea may be upsetting to you . . ."

"No, no," Sarah said.

"But I think it's best to take the necessary precautions. Really. This isn't the Middle Ages, you know."

"I know," Sarah said.

"So will you talk to her?"

"I'll talk to her," Sarah said. She was silent for a moment. Then she whispered, "I love you, you know that?" and kissed his shiny bald head.

Hawes loved to undress women.

He especially loved undressing women who wore eyeglasses. Taking off their eyeglasses was tantamount to stripping them naked. A woman looked particularly soft and desirable once her eyeglasses were removed. He loved to kiss the closed eyelids of a woman whose eyeglasses he had just removed. When he started to take off Annie's eyeglasses, she said, "No, don't."

They were in her bedroom. They had carried their brandy snifters into her bedroom, and they were sitting on the edge of Annie's king-sized bed. They had kissed once, gently and exploratively, and then he started to take off her eyeglasses, and he was thinking now that it was starting wrong. If a woman refused to let you take off her eyeglasses, how would she react when you asked her to swing from the chandelier?

When Hawes was seventeen years old, he had dated a girl who wore eyeglasses, and he had done something he thought was very clever. He had gently taken her eyeglasses from the bridge of her nose, and had breathed on both lenses, and when she asked him why he was doing that, he replied, "So you won't be able to see what my hands are doing." The girl had asked him to drive her home at once. He had since learned not to breathe on girls' eyeglasses; you could fog up a potential situation that way. The situation with Annie Rawles seemed fraught with potential, but she had just told him not to take off her eyeglasses, and he was thinking he had pulled a gaffe equal to the one when he was but a mere callow youth. He looked at her, puzzled.

"I want to see you," she whispered.

He kissed her again. She kissed very nicely, her lips parting slightly to receive his, soft and pliable, a slight inhalation of breath causing an airtight seal between their mouths, he wondered how Sam Grossman at the lab would have explained the phenomenon of such a vacuum, lips pressing to lips, inhalation causing suction suddenly disrupted by the intrusion of probing tongues—he knew suddenly that everything was going to be all right, eyeglasses or no.

The first time was the most important time; he always listened skeptically when any of the squadroom pundits declared that sex got better as it went along, you learned with practice. In his experience, if the first time wasn't any good, the next time would be worse, and the time after that would be impossible. In police work, that was an adage: A bad situation can only get worse. It applied to sex as well. He got a little dizzy kissing Annie Rawles, a sure indication that everything was going to be very good indeed. He could not recall ever having grown dizzy just kissing someone. *There's magic in your lips, Kate,* he thought, and wondered which Shakespearean play that was from, or had Spencer Tracy said it to Katharine Hepburn in some movie? *There's magic in your lips,* he thought, and said aloud, "There's magic in your lips."

"Kate," Annie whispered. *"Henry the Fifth,"* and kissed him again.

It was funny how dizzy he got kissing her. His head was actually buzzing. Not too many people knew how to kiss nowadays. People rushed through kissing as if it were the curtain-raiser to the play itself, an introduction to be hurried through before the real performance started—*Henry the Fifth?* Was that where the line came from? He'd known once, he was sure, but he'd forgotten. Had Annie been an English major in college? Had she been a *kissing* major? Jesus, he really did like kissing her. He was reluctant to stop kissing her. He had never in his life felt that he'd be content to spend a night just kissing somebody, but he was close to feeling that now. He remembered that there were things besides kissing, but feeling the way he did—feeling! *That* was one of the other things besides kissing.

Once, when he was nineteen, he had dated a girl who *didn't* wear eyeglasses, and he had done something else he thought was very clever, with almost the identical result. He had touched the lapel of the jacket the girl was wearing, and he had asked, "Can this be wool?" And then he had touched the collar of the blouse she was wearing, and he had asked, "Can this be silk?" And then he had put his hand on her breast and asked, "Can this be felt?" The girl hadn't asked him to drive her home, the way the girl with the eyeglasses had. Instead, she just got out of the car and *walked* home.

Hawes wondered now if he should touch Annie's breast. He was having a very good time kissing her, but he was beginning to think he should `touch` something, too, and her breast seemed a good place to start. His hand was cupped under her chin, he was drinking kisses from her mouth. He allowed his hand to slide tentatively over her throat, and past her collar bone, and onto the silky-feeling fabric of the blue dress she was wearing, and then onto her left breast—

"No, don't," Annie said.

He thought at once that there were some things grown men never learn, even if they'd been burned often as teenagers. He also thought that he'd been wrong about things going right. Maybe Annie was one of those ladies who thought it was perfectly okay to kiss the night away, something he himself had thought was okay just a moment earlier, but which was not *really* okay for consenting adults in the privacy of their own home, although the home was hers and not his. He was very confused all at once, in addition to being very dizzy.

"I want you to undress me first," Annie whispered.

He was suddenly more excited than he'd ever been in his life. More excited than that first time on the roof with Elizabeth Parker (everytime he saw Andy Parker in the squadroom, he thought of Elizabeth Parker, although the two were not related) when he was sixteen years old and she'd had to teach him where to find it. More excited than that time with a black whore in Panama, when he was twenty years old and serving in the U.S. Navy, a joyously beautiful woman who had taught him more about sex in two hours than he'd learned the rest of his life. (He had never mentioned this to Brown; one day he thought he might.) More excited than that time at a dinner party when the married woman sitting next to him and wearing a slinky green gown cut to her navel slid her hand under the table and onto his thigh, close to his groin, and said while forking shrimp cocktail into her deliciously wicked mouth, "Do you find you have to use your gun often, Detective Hawes?"

She looked like a schoolteacher in her simple blue dress, Annie Rawles did. Eyeglasses perched on her nose, a faint smile on her mouth. She turned her back to him as if she were about to write something on the blackboard. "The zipper," she said, and lowered her head, even though she wore her black hair in a wedge cut that exposed the back of her slender neck and the place at the top of her dress where the zipper tab nestled. He kissed the back of her neck. He felt her shudder. He reached for the zipper tab and lowered the zipper on her back, exposing the line of her brassiere strap, a blue paler than the dress, crossing her pale white skin. He was reaching for the brassiere clasp, when again she said, "No, don't," and turned to face him, and shivered out of the dress, allowing it to cascade over her hips to her ankles. She stepped out of the dress.

She was wearing lingerie out of the pages of *Penthouse,* the schoolteacher vanishing in the crumpled pile of simple blue dress on the carpet, the hard-nosed cop transformed in the wink of an instant into a hard-porn sex goddess. A flimsy, lace-edged, pale blue bra lifted her cupcake breasts, revealing the sloping tops of both, and—in the instance of her left breast—carelessly exposing the roseate and a stubby pink nipple already erect to bursting. The gold chain and pendant dangled between them, as if seeking sanctuary. She wore a garter belt under sheer panties of the same pale blue hue, the darker outline of her black pubic triangle forming a swelling mound at the joining of her legs, the garters taut against firm white thighs. She suddenly seemed full-blown without her protective blue dress, not half so thin as he'd imagined her to be, hips rounded and womanly, shapely legs molded by blue nylons tapering to narrow ankles and high-heeled, patent leather shoes.

A wisp of black hair curled recklessly from under the lace-edged leg of the sheer panties.

He was suddenly and outrageously erect. Her eyes moved to the bulge inside his trousers, and the smile she flashed him was as knowing as the one the black whore in Panama had given him when she'd opened the backstreet door of her narrow crib to his timorous knocking. Fiona, her name had been. Fiona of the two short hours and thousand lingering nights.

He moved toward her, suffocating on a musk he imagined or actually breathed.

"No, don't," she said.

He stopped.

He had the terrible feeling that this was going to be like that time in Los Angeles when he'd gone out there to extradite an armed robber, and a twenty-three-year-old television starlet had performed an elaborate striptease for him before packing him off with a peck on the cheek. "But that white streak in your hair is really *very* cute, honey," she'd told him as she closed the door behind him. Back at his sleazy hotel in downtown L.A. that night, he had actually considered tinting the streak red, like the rest of his hair. He'd had a good time with the robber on the plane back, though; the guy had a wonderful sense of humor, even in handcuffs.

"Now you," Annie whispered.

She helped him out of his jacket. She undid the knot on his tie, and then she snapped the tie out from under his collar as though she were cracking a whip. She unbuttoned the top button of his shirt. She unbuttoned all the buttons on his shirt. She kissed his chest, and then eased the shirt from his trousers. She unbuttoned the cuffs. She helped him out of the shirt, and then she tossed it across the room, where it landed on her blue dress. She took his belt out of his trouser loops. She undid the button on his pants. She lowered his zipper. She reached into his trousers and said, "Oh, my."

Five minutes later, they were in bed together.

Hawes was naked. Annie was wearing nothing but the gold chain and pendant. He would have to ask her, sometime, why she refused to take off the pendant and chain. For now, he was content to know that he was making contact with another human being, and for the rest of the night he would not have to think about anything but loving her. The fact that she was a screamer unsettled him a bit. The last screamer he'd had was a court stenographer who also happened to wear eyeglasses. She'd worn her glasses to bed. But she'd screamed loud enough to wake the dead everytime she achieved orgasm. Annie screamed almost as loud and equally as often. She told him not to worry about it; everybody in the building knew she was a cop. He had completely forgotten she was a cop.

And he had also completely forgotten that the person hanging young girls from lampposts up there in the Eight-Seven might just possibly be the Deaf Man.

Arthur Brown had already forgotten the passing thought that their lamppost murderer might be the Deaf Man. Brown had as much respect for the Deaf Man as anybody on the squad, but the way Brown figured it, a killer was a killer, and they were all the same to him; they were all *bad* guys, and he was the *good* guy, and besides he wanted to get his wife in bed.

Brown's daughter Connie was asleep already. Brown's wife Caroline was in the den, watching television, Brown was in the bathroom, toweling himself after a long hot shower. He looked at himself in the bathroom mirror and saw the same handsome Arthur Brown staring back at him. He smiled at his mirror reflection. He was feeling good tonight. Tonight, he would take Caroline to the stars and the moon and back again. Still smiling, he walked naked into the bedroom. He draped the damp towel over the back of the chair, spotted the morning newspaper on the floor where Caroline had left it, and immediately reached down to pick it up. He folded two pages of the newspaper open, tore out a hole in the center of the now-single large page, and grinned from ear to ear.

When Brown walked into the den, he was wearing only the morning newspaper. His penis stuck out through the hole he had torn in the page. Caroline looked up.

"Well, well," she said.

In an exaggerated watermelon dialect, Brown said, "You s'pose it true what de white folk say 'bout de size o' de black man's organ?"

"Not on the evidence," Caroline said.

"Will you settle anyhow?" Brown asked.

Caroline went to him and tore the newspaper to shreds.

7

FROM WHERE HE SAT IN THE STANDS WATCHing Darcy Welles, he knew at once that she had the right stuff. Even more so than the other two. He could tell just by the way she moved during the warmup.

It was another clear bright October day, and the sky over the university track was virtually cloudless and as piercingly blue as heat lightning. Beyond the track, he could see the huge bulk of the football stadium, and still beyond that the stone tower that dominated the school quadrangle. It was not a bad campus for a city as large as this one, where you couldn't really expect wide areas of lawn or tree-shaded quadrangles. He had walked through it on Saturday, getting the feel of the place, making himself at home here, wanting to feel entirely at ease when he approached the girl later on. He always felt comfortable with women, anyway. Women took to him. They thought he was very offbeat, perhaps a little eccentric, but they were fond of him. Men gave him trouble. Men wouldn't put up with his little idiosyncrasies. Abruptly walking out of a restaurant when he'd had enough to eat and was feeling tired. Frequently breaking appointments. Refusing to share in ridiculous innuendoes about their sexual exploits. Men gave him a pain in the ass. He liked women.

He watched the girl.

The season was still several months away—January if she'd be competing in any indoor events, March for the beginning of the major outdoor races—but of course a runner trained all year round, had to if he or she hoped to stay in condition. Just as important for a woman as for a man, maybe more so. She had already taken three laps around the track—wearing the school's track suit, maroon with a dark blue "C" over the left breast and the university name across the back of the jacket—taking the first lap very slowly (he'd timed her at three minutes), gradually increasing her speed until she'd done the third lap in two minutes. She was on the fourth lap now, jogging the first fifty yards, running the next fifty, coming all the way around and doing the last fifty at top speed. She rested for several moments, sucking in great gulps of air, and then she began doing arm swings, thirty seconds for each arm, rotating the arm from her shoulder in a full circle, her fist clenched. Trunk bends now—she knew the warmup routine, this girl—and now hand bounces and hula hoops, a minute of wood choppers, another minute of side winders. She lay on the grass beside the track, on her back, put her hands under her hips and did thirty seconds or so of air-bicycling, and then leg overs and leg lifts and leg spreads, making the simple exercises seem somehow graceful. She was going to be one hell of a sprinter, this girl.

Another girl was coming over to her now. Possibly a member of the team, possibly just a friend who had come to watch her work out. The other girl wasn't wearing a track suit. Plaid skirt and knee socks, blue cardigan sweater. He hoped she would not hang around when he approached Darcy. Today was a Wednesday, the third day of a normal workout week. On Monday, she'd undoubtedly practiced short sprints from the blocks, sixty yards, a hundred and twenty yards, something like that, it varied in different training programs. Yesterday, she'd probably done nine runs halfway around the track, walking back for recovery after each of the first two 220-yard sprints, walking the full length of the track after the third, sixth, and ninth runs. In most programs, the training got more exacting as you moved deeper into the week, peaking on Friday, tapering off on Saturday with weight lifting, and then allowing a day of rest on Sunday (even God rested on Sunday) before the cycle resumed again on Monday. None of the pre-season training was as severe or as concentrated as when the competitive season began, of course. Darcy Welles was just getting back into running trim again after a summer and early fall of off-season training. He visualized her running along country roads back in Ohio, where she made her home. The newspaper accounts of her ability had been very encouraging. Her best high school time for the hundred-yard dash had been twelve-three, which wasn't at all bad when you considered that Evelyn Ashford's recent record was ten seventy-nine. "I wasn't thinking about anything, I just ran," Ashford said at Colorado Springs. "I didn't seem to wake up until the last twenty meters. When I crossed the line, I thought 'That was nothing special. Maybe eleven-one.' " Ten seventy-nine! When they told her the time, she said, "I'm stunned. Just stunned. Stunned." Well, your Evelyn Ashfords were few and far between. Even someone like Jeanette Bolden, when she was in high school her personal best was eleven sixty-eight, whittled that down to eleven-eighteen when she ran second to Ashford at Pepsi. That eleven-second barrier, that was the thing. You could thank Wilma Rudolph for that. But Darcy Welles was still young, a freshman here at Converse, and she had the right stuff. Olympics caliber, Darcy Welles was. It was a shame he had to kill her.

She was obviously impatient talking to the other girl, eager to get back to the workout. The other girl went on for what seemed like forever, and then smiled and waved and walked off. A visible look of relief crossed Darcy's face. She took off the warmup suit and folded it neatly on the bench bordering the track. She was wearing track jersey and pants, no number on the jersey, the shorts slit partially up the side to allow easier movement of her muscular legs and thighs. She stood at the starting line for a moment, surveying the track, and then she placed her left foot just behind the line, stooped over it, right foot and left arm back, right arm up, took a deep breath, and was off from a standing start.

He clicked his stopwatch again, timing her as she went through her longer third-day sprints, adding to yesterday's distance by half now, running 330 yards in forty-five seconds, walking for five minutes after each of the three runs. She was beginning to sweat through her jersey and pants. He watched her carefully as she zippered open her carry bag, took out her blocks and placed the lead block some fifteen inches behind the starting line. She measured the distance for the rear block, adjusting both blocks carefully. She stood up, sniffed the brisk autumn air, put her hands on her hips, hesitated a moment and then knelt into the blocks. She was such a pretty girl, black-haired and blue-eyed, nineteen years old—it was a pity she had to die.

Her form was excellent.

Some coach back there in Ohio had taught her well.

He could almost hear the silent command in her head: *On your marks!*

Left leg reaching back for the rear block. Right leg moving back to touch the front block with her toes. Hands behind the line now, not quite touching it, thumbs pointing inward. Weight on the left knee, the right foot, and both hands. Head level. Eyes looking out some three feet ahead of the line.

Set!

Hips rising. Body rocking forward to move the shoulders ahead of the line. Soles of both feet pressed hard against the blocks. Eyes still fixed on that imaginary spot three feet ahead. A spring tensed for sudden release.

Bang!

The sound of an imaginary gun in her head and in his, and her arms were suddenly pumping, the right arm pistoning forward, the left arm thrusting back, the legs pushing simultaneously at both blocks, left leg reaching out to take that first long important step, right leg thrusting hard against the block, and she was off!

God, what a glorious runner!

He timed her at nine seconds, give or take, for each of the half-dozen 60-yard sprints, watching as she walked back for recovery after each one. She was drenched with sweat when finally she came back to the bench to take a towel from her carry bag and to wipe her face and arms with it. She put on the jacket of her warmup suit. There was a chill in the late afternoon air.

He smiled, and put the stopwatch back into his pocket.

She was walking away from the track, head bent in seeming thought, even her jacket soaked through with perspiration, a high sheen of sweat on her long legs, when he approached her.

"Miss Welles?" he said.

She stopped, looked up in surprise. Her blue eyes searched his face.

"Corey McIntyre," he said. *"Sports USA."*

She kept studying him.

"You're putting me on," she said.

"No, no," he said, and smiled, and reached into his pocket for his wallet. From the wallet, he took a small lucite-enclosed card. He handed it to her. She looked at it.

SPORTS USA

PRESS

Writer-Reporter _Corey McIntyre_

"Gee," she said, and handed the card back to him.

"You *are* Darcy Welles, aren't you?" he asked.

"Uh-huh," she said, and nodded.

She was, he guessed, five-feet-eight or -nine inches tall. Her eyes were almost level with his. She was studying him, waiting.

"We're preparing an article for our February issue," he said.

"I'll bet," she said. She was still skeptical. He was still holding the card in his hands. He was tempted to show it to her again. Instead, he put it back in his wallet.

"On young female athletes," he said. "We won't be concentrating exclusively on *track* stars, of course . . ."

"Oh, sure, *stars,*" she said, and rolled her eyes.

"Well, you *have* attracted some attention, Miss Welles."

"That's news to me," she said.

"I have your complete file. Your record in Ohio was an impressive one."

"It was okay, I guess," Darcy said.

She was glowing from the workout. Her skin looked fresh, her eyes sparkling. There was that about athletes. All of them, men or women, all looked so goddamn healthy. He envied her youth. He envied her daily regimen.

"Much more than just okay," he said.

"Right now, if I can break twelve, I'll go dancing in the streets."

"You looked good out there today."

"You were watching, huh?"

"Timed those last sprints at about nine seconds each."

"Sixty yards at nine isn't worth much."

"For practice, it's not bad."

"If I'm going to do the hundred in twelve, I've got to shave that down to seven."

"Is that what you're aiming for? Twelve?"

"Eleven would be better, huh?" she said, and grinned. "But this isn't the Olympics."

"Not yet," he said, and returned the smile.

"Oh, sure. Maybe not *ever,*" she said.

"Your personal best in Ohio was twelve-three, am I right?"

"Yeah," she said, and pulled a face. "Pretty shitty, huh?"

"No, pretty good. You should *see* some of the high school records."

"I've seen them. Last year, a girl in California ran it in eleven-eight."

"Eloise Blair."

"That's right."

"We'll be interviewing her as well. She's at U.C.L.A. now."

"What do you mean, interviewing?" Darcy said.

"I thought I mentioned . . ."

"Yeah, but what do you mean?"

"Well, we'd like to do an interview with you."

"What do you mean? For *Sports USA?*"

"For *Sports USA,* yes."

"Come on," she said, and pulled a face that made her look twelve years old. "Me? In *Sports USA?* Come on."

"Well, not you *alone.* But we'll be concentrating on female athletes . . ."

"College athletes?"

"Not all of them. And not all of them track stars."

"Here we go with the *stars* again," she said, and again rolled her eyes.

"We'll be covering swimming, basketball, gymnastics . . . well, we're trying to make it as comprehensive as we can. And forgive me if I use the word again, but we're trying to zero in on the young American women of today who may very well *become* the stars of tomorrow."

"Twelve-three for the hundred yard dash is a star of tomorrow, huh?" Darcy said.

"At *Sports USA*," he said solemnly, "we're not entirely unaware of what's happening in the sports world."

She studied his face again, nodding, digesting all that he'd told her. "I wish you hadn't seen me today," she said at last. "I was really rotten today."

"I thought you had great style."

"Yeah, some style. Sixty yards in nine seconds, that's really terrific style."

"Did you do much running this summer?"

"Every day. Well, not Sundays."

"What sort of a routine did you follow?"

"You really interested in this?" she asked.

"I am. In fact . . . if I could have a little of your time later this evening, perhaps we can go into it at greater length. I'm primarily interested in your goals and aspirations, but anything you can tell me about your early interest in running, or your training habits . . ."

"Listen, are you for real?" she said.

"I beg your pardon."

"I mean, is this Candid Camera or something?"

She looked around suddenly, as though searching for a hidden camera. They were standing quite alone on the edge of the track. She studied an oak in the near distance as a possible place for Allen Funt to be hiding. She shrugged, shook her head, and turned back to him again.

"This isn't Candid Camera," he said, and smiled. "This is Corey McIntyre of *Sports USA,* and I'm interviewing young female athletes for an article we plan to run in our February issue. We'll be concentrating somewhat heavily on track in order to take advantage of the season's start, but we'll also be covering . . ."

"Okay, okay, I believe you," she said, and shook her head again, and grinned. "Sheeesh," she said, "I can't believe it."

"Believe it."

"Okay," she said. "So you want to interview me, okay, I believe it."

"Do you think you can spare some time tonight?"

"I've got a heavy test coming up in Psych tomorrow."

"Oh, that's too bad," he said. "How about . . . ?"

"But I think I know the stuff already," she said. "Tonight'll be fine, provided I get to bed early."

"Why don't we have dinner together?" he suggested. "I'm pretty sure I can do the interview in one meeting, and then—if you don't mind, that is—I'd like to set up a convenient time for a photographer to . . ."

"A photographer, sheesh," she said, grinning.

"If that's all right with you."

"Yeah, sure," she said. "I can't believe this, I've got to tell you."

"Would eight o'clock be all right?" he asked.

"Yeah, fine. Boy."

"If you can start thinking about some of the things I mentioned . . ."

"Yeah, aspirations and goals, right."

"Early interest in . . ."

"Right."

"Training habits . . ."

"Okay, sure, that's easy."

"Any anecdotes about running . . . well, we'll cover all that tonight. Where shall I pick you up? Or would you rather meet me?"

"Well, can you stop by the dorm?"

"I had in mind a midtown restaurant. It might be easier if you took a taxi."

"Sure, whatever you say."

"Get a receipt. *Sports USA*'ll pick up the tab."

"Okay. Where?" she said.

"Marino's on Ulster and South Haley. Eight o'clock sharp."

"Corey McIntyre," she said. "*Sports USA*. Wow."

* * *

In the stillness of Nancy Annunziato's bedroom, her mother and grandmother silently moving around the house outside the closed door, Carella and Hawes went through the dead girl's belongings. There had been no need to call in the lab technicians; this room could not possibly have been the scene of the crime. And yet, they went through her personal effects as delicately as if they were preserving evidence for later admission at a trial. Neither of the men mentioned the Deaf Man. If the Deaf Man had been responsible for Nancy Annunziato's death, if he had slain both her and Marcia Schaffer, then they were dealing with a wild card in a stacked deck. They preferred, for now, to believe that there was a reasonably human motive for the murders, that the crimes had not been concocted in the Deaf Man's computerized brain.

Hawes was now reading the girl's training diary.

Carella was looking through her appointment calendar.

Nancy had been killed on October 13. The medical examiner's report on the postmortem interval—premised on body temperature, lividity, degree of decomposition, and rigor mortis—had estimated the time of death as approximately 11:00 P.M. The lab had come up negative for any fingerprints on the wallet found at the scene; the killer, though conveniently providing identification of the girl, had nonetheless wiped the wallet clean before dropping it at her feet. They now had only her personal record of events to help them reconstruct where she'd been and what she'd been doing on the day of her murder.

Her training diary revealed that on Thursday, October 13, Nancy Annunziato had awakened at 7:30 A.M. She had recorded her early morning pulse rate as 58. She had gone to bed the night before at 11:00 P.M. (A flip back through the pages revealed that this was her usual bedtime; yet on the night of her murder, she had been abroad in the city someplace at that hour.) Her body weight at awakening had been one hundred and twenty pounds. She had recorded the place of her daily workout as "Outdoor track, C.P.C.," and had described the running surface as "Synthetic." She had recorded the day's temperature (at the time of her workout) as sixty-four degrees, and had described the day as fair, with low humidity and no wind. She had begun her workout at 3:30 P.M.

She had detailed the workout that day as "usual warmup," followed by four 80-yard sprints from blocks, with walkbacks for recovery and a full-track walk after the last sprint; four 150-yard sprints around the turn from running starts, with walkbacks for recovery; and six 60-yard sprints from blocks, again with walkbacks after each sprint. She had listed the total distance run as 1,280 yards, her weight before the workout as a hundred and twenty-one pounds and after it as a hundred and nineteen pounds. Under the words "Fatigue Index," she had scribbled the number "5," which Hawes assumed was midway on a scale of 1 to 10. She had ended her workout at 4:15 P.M.

Her mother had already told them that she'd arrived home after practice that day at 6:00 P.M. Calm's Point College was only fifteen minutes by subway from the Annunziato house. That left an hour and a half of unaccountable time. There was nothing in the dead girl's appointment calendar that gave any clue as to how she had spent that hour and a half. Presumably, she had showered at school and changed back into street clothes. That narrowed the gap to an hour. Had she gone to the school library? Had she stopped to chat with friends? Or had she encountered the man who'd later killed her?

Her appointment calendar for Thursday, October 13, read:

French Notes - Holly

Bio Exam

Sports USA !!!

"What's this?" Carella asked. "A magazine?"

Hawes looked at the page.

"Yeah," he said. "She's got a stack of them there on the dresser."

"Probably went on the stands that day," Carella said.

"Reminder to pick it up, huh?"

"Maybe. See if she's got the issue that came out last week, will you?"

Hawes walked to where a pile of some dozen magazines were scattered over the dresser top.

"Sports Illustrated," he said. *"Runners World.* Yeah, here it is. *Sports USA.* The October seventeenth issue. Would that be it?"

"I guess so. They usually date them a week ahead, don't they?"

"I think so."

"Anything special in it?"

"Like what?"

"Who knows? Tips on how to run a mile in thirty-eight seconds."

Hawes began leafing through the magazine.

"They really work hard, don't they?" he said idly.

"Can you imagine *doing* that kind of exercise?" Carella said, shaking his head.

"Give me a heart attack," Hawes said.

'Anything?" Carella asked.

"Mostly football."

He was still leafing through the magazine.

"Nice looking lady here," he said, and showed Carella a picture of a young woman in a wet tank suit. "Little broad in the beam, but nice."

He started flipping backward through the magazine.

"Hey," he said.

"What?"

He showed Carella the page he had turned to, and indicated the masthead.

SPORTS USA

Editor-in-Chief: John Wilson Spiers
President: L. Carter Knowles
Chairman of the Board: Andrew Nelson
Executive Vice President: Lloyd Pierce
Editorial Director: Martin Goldblum

Managing Editor: Louis Caputo
Assistant Managing Editors: Roger Paxton,
James Harris, Richard Canaday

Art Director: David Greenspan

Senior Editors: George Franklin, Joseph Haley,
Rebecca Bonnie, Elliot Bradley, Harold Newton.

Associate Editors: Stephen Amstedt, Mary Jane
Allister, Guy De Santis, David Husson.

Staff Writers: Peter Wittke, Andrew Wright,
Jill Germain, Paul Mellon, Arthur Sachs, John Goche.

Writer-Reporters: Edward Pankowski, Daniel
Bernard, Werner Schneider, Corey McIntyre, Frank
Brosset, John William Ashworth, L.J. Armstrong,
Arnold Bernal, Paula Booth, Emilio Cagliotti.

Photographers: STAFF: Jim Bye, Audrey Eshelby,
C.F. Fleming, Joseph Raynor, Albert Ticknor,
Jeremy Gaines, Peter Houston, Herbert Rollet.
CONTRIBUTING: Derek Pike, Michael Quested,
Thomas Addison, Lois Coles, Joseph Peskett.

"Why'd she circle that particular name?" Carella said.

"Maybe her mother knows," Hawes said.

Mrs. Annunziato did not know.

"Corey McIntyre?" she said. "No, I don't know the name."

"Your daughter never mentioned him to you?"

"Mai. Never."

"Or this magazine? *Sports USA?"*

"She gets this magazine all the time. The others too. Anything about sports or runners, she gets."

"But none of the other copies of this magazine have this name circled," Carella said. "It's only in this issue. The October seventeenth issue."

"I don't know," Mrs. Annunziato said.

She seemed pained not to be able to supply the detectives with the information they needed. She had still not told her husband that their daughter was dead. The funeral had taken place three days ago, but he did not yet know that she was dead. And now she could not help the detectives with what they wanted to know about this name that was circled in one of her daughter's magazines.

"This man wouldn't have called the house or anything, would he?" Carella asked.

"No, I don't remember. No, not that name."

"Mrs. Annunziato, you told us your daughter got home at six o'clock on the day she was killed."

"Yes. Six o'clock." She did not want to talk about the day her daughter had been killed. She had still not told her husband that she was dead.

"Can you tell us again what she was wearing?"

"School clothes. A skirt, a blouse. A jacket, I think."

"But that's not what she was wearing when she was found."

"No?"

"She was wearing a green dress and green shoes."

"Yes."

"Because she changed after she got home, isn't that what you told us?"

"Yes."

"Into more dressy clothes."

"Yes."

"Because she was going out, you said."

"Yes, she told me she was going out."

"But she didn't say where she was going."

"She *never* told me," Mrs. Annunziato said. "Young girls today . . ." She shook her head.

"Didn't mention where she was going or whether she was meeting someone."

"No."

"You told us she left the house around seven. A little after seven."

"Yes."

"Does she have a car?"

"No. A taxi came for her."

"She called a taxi?"

"Yes."

"Do you know what taxi company she called?"

"No. It was a yellow taxicab that came."

"But she didn't tell you where she was going."

"No."

"Mrs. Annunziato, your daughter usually went to bed at eleven o'clock, didn't she?"

"Yes. She had to be at school early."

"Were you here at home on the night she was killed?"

"No, I was at the hospital. That was the day my husband had his heart attack. I was at the hospital with him. He was in Intensive Care. It was nine o'clock he had the accident. On his way home."

"From work?"

"No, no, his club. He belongs to this club. It's old friends of his, bricklayers like him. They have a club, they meet once a month."

"Your husband is a bricklayer?" Hawes said.

"Yes. A bricklayer. A *union* bricklayer," she said, as though wishing to give the job more stature.

"And he suffered his heart attack at nine o'clock that night."

"That's when the hospital called me. I went right over."

"This was after your daughter had left the house."

"Yes."

"Then she didn't know your husband was in the hospital."

"No, how could she know?"

"You went directly to the hospital after they called you . . ."

"Yes."

"What time did you get home again? From the hospital?"

"I was there all night."

"You stayed there all night?"

"He was in Intensive Care," she said again, in explanation.

"What time did you get home the next morning?"

"A little after nine."

"Then you didn't know your daughter hadn't been home at all that night, is that right?"

"I didn't know."

"Was your *mother* home on the night your daughter was killed?"

"Yes."

"Did *she* mention anything to you—when you got home the next morning—about your daughter being out all night?"

"She sometimes did that."

"Your daughter? Stayed out all night sometimes?"

"Young girls today," Mrs. Annunziato said, and shook her head. "When I was a girl . . . my father would have *killed* me," she said. "But today . . ." She shook her head again.

"So it wasn't unusual for your daughter to sometimes stay away from home for the entire night."

"Not a lot. But sometimes. She says . . . she told us it was with a girlfriend, she would be staying at a girlfriend's house. So who knows, a girlfriend or a boyfriend, who knows? It's better not to ask. Today, it's better not to ask, not to know. She was a good girl, it's better not to know.''

"And you don't know who this man Corey McIntyre might be? Your daughter never mentioned him to you."

"Never."

A call to *Sports USA* at their offices on the Avenue of the Americas in New York City advised Carella that there was indeed a man named Corey McIntyre who worked for them as a writer-reporter. But Mr. McIntyre lived in Los Angeles, and he was usually assigned to cover events in southern California, working as their special correspondent there. Carella told the man on the other end of the line that he was investigating a murder, and would appreciate having Mr. McIntyre's address and phone number. The man told him to wait. He came back a few minutes later and said he guessed it would be all right, and then gave Carella what he wanted.

Los Angeles, Carella thought. Terrific. What do we do now? Let's say McIntyre *is* our man. Let's say he was here in the city on October sixth when somebody killed Marcia Schaffer, and again on October thirteenth when somebody, presumably the same person, killed Nancy Annunziato. Let's say I call him and ask him where he was on those nights, and he hangs up, and runs for Mexico or wherever. Great. He leafed through his personal telephone directory, found a listing for the L.A.P.D., dialed the number, and asked for the Detective Division. A man came on the line.

"Branigan," he said.

"Detective Carella in Isola," Carella said. "I've got a problem."

"Let's hear it," Branigan said.

Carella told him about the murders. He told him about the name circled in Nancy Annunziato's copy of *Sports USA.* He told him that the man lived in L.A. He told him that he was afraid a phone call might spook him, if indeed he was the killer. Branigan listened.

"So what is it?" he said at last. "You want somebody to drop in on him, is that it?"

"I was thinking . . ."

"First of all," Branigan said, "suppose we go there, okay, first of all? And suppose the guy says he was out bowling those nights, and we say 'Thank you very much, sir, can you tell us who you were bowling with?' and he gives us the names of three other guys, okay, that's first of all. Then suppose we leave the house to go check on those three other guys who maybe don't exist, so what does our man do meanwhile? If our man's the killer, he runs to China. He does just what you're afraid he'll do, anyway, so what's the use of wasting time out here? If he's the killer, he ain't about to tell us he was Back East there doing the number on those girls, is he? Especially when he's probably smart enough to know we ain't got jurisdiction to arrest him without specific charges pending on your end."

"I thought if you *really* questioned him . . ."

"You got Miranda-Escobedo back there, or are you working in Russia? You're saying we go to his house, right, this is in the second place. And he doesn't have anything that looks good for where he was those two nights, or maybe he even tells us he was *there* on those nights, Back East there, which I don't think he'd be stupid enough to do if he's the killer and there are two cops standing on his doorstep. But let's say he sounds maybe not like *real* meat but at least a hamburger medium rare and we say, 'Sir, would you mind accompanying us downtown because there are a few more questions we'd like to ask you?' So he puts on his hat, and we take him here and we sit him down and read him Miranda because this ain't a field investigation anymore, Carella, this is now a situation where an investigation is *focusing* on a man, and he is technically in police custody, and we cannot ask him any questions until he knows his rights. So suppose he says he doesn't *want* to answer any questions, which is his privilege? Then what? You expect us to charge him with two counts of Murder One on the say-so of a call from the East?''

"No, I certainly wouldn't . . ."

"Of course not, because if you were on *our* end of the deal, and if *we* called *you* to go talk to some guy, you'd recognize what kind of trouble you were buying, wouldn't you? The Supreme Court doesn't like lengthy interrogations or incommunicado detention, Carella. If this guy clams up, what do we do then? Hold him here till you can hop a plane out? L.A.P.D. would get its ass in a sling so tight we wouldn't be able to shit for a month.''

"I hear you," Carella said.

"Look, Carella, I recognize your problem. You call this guy on the phone, you start asking him questions, he thinks right away 'Uh-oh,' and he reaches for his hat. But it seems to me you've got to take that chance. Anyway, how do you know it's not somebody Back East just picked the man's name out of the magazine and used it? This guy out here may be clean as a whistle.''

"I realize that."

"Carella," Branigan said, "it's been nice talking to you, but I got headaches, too.''

There was a click on the line.

Nothing ventured, nothing gained, Carella thought, and looked up at the squadroom clock. Seven-thirty. It was still only four-thirty on the Coast. The night watch had relieved at a quarter to four here. Hawes was busy at his desk, typing up the report on what they'd learned at the Annunziato house. Both detectives had been working the day watch since a quarter to eight this morning. Carella was tired; there was nothing he wanted more than a drink and a hot shower. He looked again at the slip of paper on which he'd written Corey McIntyre's address and phone number. Okay, here goes nothing, he thought, and dialed the 213 area code and then the number. A woman picked up after the fourth ring.

"Hello?" she said.

"Corey McIntyre, please," Carella said.

"This is his wife," the woman said. "May I know who's calling?"

"Detective Carella of the Eighty-seventh Squad," he said. "In Isola."

"Just a moment," the woman said.

He could hear voices mumbling in the background. He heard a man say, quite distinctly, *"Who?"* Carella waited.

"Hello?" the voice on the other end said.

"Mr. McIntyre?"

"Yes?" Puzzlement in the voice. Or was it wariness?

"Corey McIntyre?"

"Yes?"

"Is this the Corey McIntyre who works for *Sports USA?*"

"Yes?"

"Mr. McIntyre, I'm sorry to bother you this way, but would the name Nancy Annunziato mean anything to you?"

Silence on the other end of the line.

"Mr. McIntyre?"

"I'm thinking," he said. "Annunziato?"

"Yes. Nancy Annunziato."

"No, I don't know her. Who is she?"

"How about Marcia Schaffer?"

"I don't know her, either. Sir, can you tell me . . . ?"

"Mr. McIntyre, were you in the East on October the thirteenth? That was a Thursday night. Last Thursday night."

"No, I was right here in L.A. last Thursday night."

"Can you remember what you were doing?"

"What is this?" McIntyre said. "Diane, what were we doing last Thursday night?"

In the background, Carella heard the woman say, "What?"

"Last Thursday night," McIntyre called to her. "This guy wants to know what we were . . . listen," he said into the phone again, "what's this in reference to, would you mind telling me?"

"We're investigating a series of murders . . ."

"So what's that got to do with me?"

"I'd appreciate it if . . ."

"Listen, I'm going to hang up," McIntyre said.

"No, I wish you wouldn't," Carella said.

"Give me a good reason *why* I shouldn't."

Carella took a deep breath.

"Because a copy of *Sports USA* in the most recent victim's possession had your name circled in it."

"*My* name?"

"Yes, sir. On the page with the masthead. Page four. Your name, sir. Corey McIntyre. Under Writer-Reporters."

"Who's this? Is this you, Frank?"

"Is it Frank again?" his wife said in the background.

"This is Detective Stephen Louis Carella of the Eighty-seventh . . ."

"Frank, if this is another one of your harebrained . . ."

"Mr. McIntyre, I assure you . . ."

"What's your number there?" McIntyre said.

"377-8034," Carella said.

"In Isola, did you say?"

"Yes."

"I'll call you back," McIntyre said. "Collect," he added, and hung up.

He called back ten minutes later. The collect person-to-person call went through the switchboard downstairs, and was transferred to the squadroom, where Carella accepted charges.

"Okay," McIntyre said, "you're a genuine cop. Now what's this about my name circled in the magazine?"

"In the dead girl's room," Carella said.

"So what's that supposed to mean?"

"That's what I'm trying to find out."

"Was she killed last Thursday, is that it?"

"Yes, sir."

"Okay. You want to know where I was last Thursday? Here's where I . . ."

"Tell him where we were," his wife said in the background, loudly and angrily.

"My wife and I were at a dinner party in Brentwood," McIntyre said. "The party took place at the home of Dr. and Mrs. Joseph Foderman. We got there at a little before eight . . ."

"Give him the address," his wife said.

". . . and we left at a little after twelve. There were . . ."

"And the telephone number," she said.

"There were eight of us there in addition to the host and hostess," McIntyre said. "I can give you the names of the other guests, if you'd like them."

"I don't think that will be necessary," Carella said.

"Do you want the Fodermans' address?"

"Just the telephone number, please."

"You plan to call them?"

"Yes, sir."

"To tell them I'm a suspect in a *murder?*"

"No, sir. Just to ascertain that you were in fact there last Thursday night."

"Do me a favor, will you? Tell them some guy Back East is using my name, will you, please?"

"I'll do that, sir."

"And I'd sure like to know who he *is,*" McIntyre said.

"So would we," Carella said. "May I have that number, please?"

McIntyre gave him the number, and then said, "I'm sorry I yelled at you."

"Don't apologize," his wife said in the background.

There was a sharp click on the line.

Carella sighed and dialed the number McIntyre had just given him. He spoke to a woman named Phyllis Foderman who told him that her husband was at the hospital just then, but asked if she could be of any assistance. Carella told her who he was and from where he was calling, and then he said they had reason to believe someone here in the city was using Corey McIntyre's name, and they were trying to ascertain the whereabouts of the *real* Mr. McIntyre for last Thursday night, October 13. Mrs. Foderman told him at once that Corey McIntyre and his wife Diane had been with them at a small dinner party here in Brentwood, and that six other people besides her and her husband could vouch for that fact. Carella thanked her and hung up.

In this city, any licensed taxicab was required to turn in to the Hack Bureau a record of all calls made that day, listing origin and time of pickup, destination, and time deposited at destination. This because very few taxi passengers ever looked at the name or number of the driver on the card prominently displayed on the dashboard, and often would have to call the bureau to inquire about a parcel or a personal belonging carelessly left behind in a cab. By cross-checking, the bureau could come up with the name and number of the driver, and follow up on the loss. This was almost always an academic exercise; nearly everything left in a taxicab vanished from sight in ten seconds flat. But a side-effect of such scrupulously kept and computerized records was that the police department had access to a minute-by-minute record of pickup locations and destinations.

Carella's call to the Hack Bureau, on a special twenty-four-hour hot line, was routinely made and routinely answered. He identified himself and told the woman on the other end of the line that he wanted the final destination of a pickup at 207 Laurel Street in Calm's Point at approximately seven o'clock on the night of October 13.

"The computer's down," the woman told him.

"When will it be *up* again?" Carella asked.

"Who knows with computers?" the woman said.

"Can you check the records manually?"

"Everything goes into the computer," she said.

"I'm investigating a homicide," Carella said.

"Who isn't?" the woman said.

"Can you call me at home later tonight? When the computer's working again?"

"Be happy to," she said.

Darcy Welles had taken a taxi to Marino's restaurant on Ulster and South Haley, and had asked the driver for a receipt which she handed across the table the moment she sat down opposite the man she thought was Corey McIntyre of *Sports USA*. He was, she supposed, somewhere in his late thirties, not bad-looking for someone that old, and really in pretty good condition no matter *what* age he was. Somehow, he looked familiar. She'd been thinking about that ever since she first met him this afternoon, but she still couldn't place where she'd seen him before.

"I checked the magazine, you know," she said, as he signaled the waiter to their table.

"I'm sorry?" he said, tilting his head as if he hadn't quite heard her.

"To see if you were legit," Darcy said, and smiled. "I looked for your name in the front, where they list all the editors and everything."

"Oh, I see," he said, and returned the smile. "And am I legit?"

"Yeah," she said, and shook her head, embarrassed. "I'm sorry, but . . . well . . . it isn't every day of the week *Sports USA* comes knocking on my door."

"Yes, sir, can I help you?" the waiter said. "Something to drink before dinner?"

"Darcy?"

"I'm in training," she said.

"A glass of wine?"

"Well . . . I'm really not supposed to."

"Some white wine for the lady," he said. "And I'll have a Dewar's on the rocks."

"Yes, sir, a white wine and a Dewar's on the rocks. Would you like to see menus now? Or would you like to wait a bit?"

"We'll wait."

"No hurry, sir," the waiter said. "Thank you."

"This is really nice," Darcy said, looking around the restaurant.

"I hope you like Italian food," he said.

"Who doesn't?" she said. "I just have to watch the calories, that's all."

"We ran an article once that said an athlete needs something like twice the number of calories a non-athlete requires."

"Well, I sure like to *eat,* I'll tell you that," Darcy said.

"A daily caloric intake of four thousand calories isn't unusual for a runner," he said.

"But who's counting?" she said, and laughed.

"So," he said. "Tell me about yourself."

"You know, it's funny, but . . ."

"Would you mind if I used a tape recorder?"

"What? Oh. Gee, I don't know. I mean, I've never . . ."

He had already placed the pocket-sized recorder on the table between them. "If it makes you uncomfortable," he said, "I can simply take notes."

"No, I guess it'll be all right," she said, and looked at the recorder. She watched as he pressed several buttons.

"The red light means it's on, the green light means it's taping," he said. "So. You were about to say."

"Only that it was funny how your questions this afternoon started me thinking. I mean, who can *remember* how I first got interested in running? You know what my mother said?''

"Your mother?"

"Yeah, when I called her. She said I . . .''

"You called her in Ohio?"

"Oh, sure. I mean how often does little Darcy Welles get interviewed by *Sports USA?*''

"Was she pleased?"

"Oh, my God, she almost wet her pants. Oops, that thing's going, isn't it?'' she said, and looked at the recorder. "Anyway, she said I probably first started running because my brother *chased* me a lot.''

"That's a wonderful anecdote.''

"But I think . . . I started *really* thinking about it, you know . . . and I think the reason I went into running is because of how *good* it makes me feel, do you know what I mean?''

"Yes,'' he said.

"White wine for the lady,'' the waiter said, and placed her glass on the table. "And a Dewar's on the rocks for you, sir.''

"Thank you,'' he said.

"Shall I bring the menus now, sir?''

"In a bit,'' he said.

"Thank you, sir,'' the waiter said, and padded off.

"I don't mean only *physically* good . . . there's that, you know, your body feels so well-tuned . . .''

"Yes.''

"But how it makes me feel *mentally,* too. When I'm running that's all I can think of, just *running,* you know?''

"Yes.''

"Nothing else is in there cluttering up my head, do you know what I mean?''

"Yes.''

"I feel . . . I feel as if everything's clean and white in

my head. I can hear my own breathing, and that's the only sound in the world . . ."

"Yes."

"And all the little problems, all the junky stuff just disappears, you know? It's as if . . . as if it's snowing inside my head, and the snow is covering up all the garbage and all the petty little junk, and it's leaving everything clean and white and pure. That's how I feel when I'm running. As if it's Christmas all year round. With everything white and soft and beautiful."

"Yes," he said, "I know."

Carella called the Hack Bureau again from home that night.

It was nine-thirty. The twins were asleep, and Teddy was sitting across from him in the living room, looking through the Want Ad sections of both the morning and the afternoon papers, circling ads that seemed of interest. A man answered the phone this time. Carella asked for the woman he'd spoken to earlier.

"She's gone," the man said. "She went home at eight. I relieved her at eight."

"How's the computer doing?"

"What do you mean, how's it doing? It's doing fine. How should it be doing?"

"It was down when I called at seven-thirty."

"Well, it's up now."

"Didn't she leave a message that I was to be called?" Carella asked. "This is Detective Carella, I'm working a homicide."

"I don't see nothing here on the message board," the man said.

"Okay, I'm trying to trace a call originating at 207 Laurel Street in Calm's Point . . ."

"When?" the man asked. Carella visualized him sitting before a computer keyboard, typing.

"October thirteenth," he said.

"Time?"

"Seven P.M., more or less."

"207 Laurel Street," the man repeated. "Calm's Point."

"Right."

"Yeah, here it is."

"Where'd he take her?" Carella asked.

"1118 South Haley."

"In Isola?"

"Isola."

"What time did he drop her off?"

"Quarter to eight."

"Any indication what that might be? Apartment house? Office building?"

"Just the address."

"Thank you," Carella said.

"Anytime," the man said, and hung up.

Carella thought for a moment, and then looked through his notebook to see if he had a number for the Fire Investigation Bureau. There was no listing on his page of frequently called numbers. He dialed the 87th Precinct. Dave Murchison was the desk sergeant on duty. He told Carella they were having a reasonably quiet night, and then asked to what he owed the pleasure of the call. Carella told him he needed the night number for the Fire Investigation Bureau.

It was twenty minutes to ten when he placed the call.

"F.I.B.," the man on the other end said.

"This is Detective Carella, Eighty-seventh Squad," he said. "I'm investigating a homicide."

"Yep," the man said.

"I've got an address on South Haley, I want to know whether it's business or residence."

"South Haley," the man said. "That's the Four-One Engine, I think. I'll give you the number there, they'll be able to tell you. Just a second."

Carella waited.

"That's 914-3700," the man said. "If Captain Healey's there, give him my regards."

"I will, thanks," Carella said.

It was a quarter to ten when he placed the call to Engine Company Forty-One. The fireman who answered the phone said, "Forty-first Engine, Lehman."

"This is Detective Carella, Eighty-seventh Squad," Carella said.

"How do you do, Carella?" Lehman said.

"I'm working a homicide . . ."

"Phew," Lehman said.

". . . and I'm trying to zero in on 1118 South Haley. What do you have for it? Is it an apartment building? An office building?"

"I can hardly hear you," Lehman said. "Will you guys pipe down?" he shouted. Into the phone again, he said, "They're playing poker. What was that address again?"

"1118 South Haley."

"Let me check the map. Hold on, okay?"

Carella waited. In the background, someone shouted "Holy shit!" and he wondered who had just turned over his hole card to reveal a royal flush.

"You still with me?" Lehman said.

"Still here."

"Okay. 1118 South Haley is a six-story building, offices on the upper floors, restaurant at ground level."

"What's the name of the restaurant?"

"Marino's," Lehman said. "I never ate there, but it's supposed to be pretty good."

"Okay, thanks a lot."

"Guy just had four aces," Lehman said, and hung up.

Carella looked through the Isola directory for a listing for Marino's. He dialed the number, identified himself to the man who answered the phone, and then said, "I was wondering if you could check back through your reservations book for the night of October thirteenth, that would have been Thursday last week.''

"Sure, what time?" the man said.

"Eight o'clock, around then.''

"What's the name?"

"McIntyre. Corey McIntyre.''

He could hear pages being turned on the other end of the line.

"Yes, here it is," the man said. "McIntyre at eight o'clock.''

"For how many?" Carella asked.

"Two.''

"Would you remember who he was with?''

"No, I'm sorry, we get a lot of customers, I couldn't possibly . . . wait a minute. McIntyre, you said?''

"McIntyre, yes.''

"Just a second.''

He could hear the pages turning again.

"Yeah, that's what I thought,'' the man said.

"What's that?''

"He's here tonight.''

"What?''

"Yeah, came in at eight o'clock, reservation for two. Table number four. Just a second, okay?''

Carella waited.

The man came back onto the phone.

"Sorry,'' he said. "He left about five minutes ago.''

"Who was he with?''

"The waiter says a young girl.''

"Jesus!'' Carella said. "How late are you open?''

"Eleven-thirty, twelve, it depends. Why?''

"Keep the waiter there,'' Carella said, and hung up.

The parking garage was two blocks from the restaurant. A sign on the wall advised any interested motorist of the exorbitant fees charged for parking a car here in the heart of the city, and promised that if the car was not delivered within five minutes from the time the claim check was stamped, there would be no charge at all. His claim check had been stamped seven minutes ago. He could hear the shriek of rubber as an attendant better suited for competition in the Grand Prix drove an automobile down around the hairpin turns of the garage ramp, hoping to beat the time limit, and possibly to save his job. He wondered if they'd really let him get away without paying. He was not about to argue over two or three minutes. He did not want anything to delay him tonight.

"You really don't have to drive me back to the dorm, you know," Darcy said. "I could take a cab, really."

"My pleasure," he said.

"Or the subway," she said.

"The subways are dangerous," he said.

"I ride them all the time."

"You shouldn't."

His car came into sight around the last curve in the ramp. The driver, a Puerto Rican in his fifties, got out of the car and said, "Ri' on d'button. Fi'minutes."

He did not contradict the driver. He gave him a fifty-cent tip, held the door open for Darcy, closed it behind her, and then went around to the driver's side. The car was a fifteen-year-old Mercedes-Benz 280 SL. He had bought it when the money was still pouring in. The media ads, the television commercials. That was then. This was now.

"Fasten your seat belt," he told her.

Hawes was in bed with Annie Rawles when the telephone rang. He looked at the bedside clock. It was ten minutes to ten.

"Let it ring," Annie said.

He looked into her eyes. His eyes said he had to answer it; her eyes acknowledged this sad fact of police work. He rolled off her and lifted the receiver.

"Hawes," he said.

"Cotton, it's Steve."

"Yeah, Steve."

"I hope I'm not interrupting anything."

"No, no," he said, and rolled his eyes at Annie. Annie was naked except for the gold chain and pendant. She toyed with the chain and pendant. He had still not asked her why she never took off the chain and pendant. He had meant to ask her that first night, last week, but he hadn't. He had meant to ask her tonight, when she'd worn the chain and pendant even in his shower. He had not. "What is it, Steve?" he said.

"Our man just left Marino's restaurant at 1118 South Haley. Can you get over there and talk to the waiter who served him?"

"What's the rush?" Hawes asked.

"He had a young girl with him."

"Shit, I'm on my way," Hawes said.

"I'll meet you there," Carella said. "As soon as I can."

Both men hung up.

"I have to go," Hawes said, getting out of bed.

"Shall I wait here for you?" Annie asked.

"I don't know how long it'll be. We may have a lead."

"I'll wait," Annie said. She paused. "If I'm asleep, wake me." She paused again. "You know how," she said.

"This is really very nice of you," Darcy said. "Going out of your way like this."

"Simply my way of thanking you for a wonderful interview," he said.

They were on the River Highway now, heading eastward toward the university farther uptown. They had just passed under the Hamilton Bridge, the lights on its suspension cables and piers illuminating the dark waters of the River Harb below. Somewhere on the river, a tugboat sounded its horn. On the opposite bank, the adjoining state's highrise towers tried boldly and pointlessly to compete with the magnificent skyline they faced. The dashboard clock read 10:07. The traffic was heavier than he thought it would be; usually, you caught your commuters leaving the city between five and six o'clock, your theatergoers heading home at eleven, eleven-thirty. He kept his eyes on the road. He did not want to risk an accident. He did not want to become embroiled in anything that might cause him to lose her. Not when he was so close.

"You think you got everything you need?" she asked.

"It was a *very* good interview," he said. "You're very articulate."

"Oh, sure," she said.

"I'm entirely sincere. You have a knack for probing your deepest feelings. That's very important."

"You think so?"

"I wouldn't say so otherwise."

"Well . . . you're very easy to talk to. You make it all . . . I don't know. It just sort of flows, talking to you."

"Thank you."

"Would you do me a favor?"

"Certainly."

"This'll sound stupid."

"Well, we won't know until you ask, will we?"

"Could you . . . could I hear what my voice sounds like?"

"On tape, do you mean?"

"Yeah. That's stupid, right?"

"No, that's entirely normal."

He reached into his jacket pocket and handed the recorder to her.

"See the button marked Rewind?" he said. "Just press it."

"This one?"

He took his eyes from the road for a moment.

"That's the one. Well, wait, first flip the On-Off button . . ."

"Got it."

"Now rewind it."

"Okay."

"And now press the Play button."

She pressed the button. Her voice came into the car mid-sentence.

" . . . even *think* of the Olympics right now, you know what I mean? It seems like a dream to me, the idea of Olympics competition somewhere down the line . . ."

"God, I sound *awful!*" she said.

". . . I never even consciously think about it. All I'm concerned with right now is becoming the best runner I can possibly be. If I can break twelve, well *then,* maybe *then* I can start thinking about . . ."

"Like a six-year-old," she said, and pressed the Stop button. "How could you bear *listening* to all that junk?"

"I found it very informative," he said.

"You want this back in your pocket, or can I leave it here on the seat?"

"Could you run it forward for me, please?"

"What do I press?"

"Fast Forward. Just until you get to blank tape again."

She experimented as he drove, running the tape forward, stopping it, and finally getting it past the last of their conversation in the restaurant. "That should do it," she said. She turned the recorder off completely. "In your pocket? Yes? No?"

"Please," he said.

"Hey, you're missing the exit," she said.

"There's something I want to show you," he said. "Do you have a minute?"

The blue sign indicating Hollis Avenue and Converse University flashed by overhead.

"Well, sure," she said, "I guess so." She hesitated. "What do you want to show me?"

"A statue," he said.

"A statue?" She pulled a face. 'What kind of statue?"

"Did you know there's a statue of a runner in this city?"

"No. You're kidding me. Who'd want to put up a statue of a runner?"

"Ah-ha," he said. "I *thought* you'd be surprised."

"Where is it? A *runner?*"

"Not far from here. If you have a minute."

"I wouldn't miss it for the world," she said. She hesitated again, and then said, "You're fun, you know that? You're really a fun guy to be with."

There was no siren on Carella's private car. Driving as fast as he could, running as many red lights as he possibly could without smashing into any pedestrians or cars, it nonetheless took him half an hour to get to the restaurant. By that time, Hawes had already talked to the waiter, and was talking to the maitre d' who'd taken McIntyre's reservation on the phone. The moment Carella came in, Hawes said, "Excuse me," and walked over to him. Carella seemed out of breath, as if he'd *trotted* all the way from Riverhead.

"What've we got?" he asked.

"A little," Hawes said. "Guy who made the phone reservation said he was Corey McIntyre . . ."

"Who's in Los Angeles," Carella said.

"Right, but who was here *last* week, too, the guy who's *calling* himself Corey McIntyre. The maitre d' confirmed that, but he checked back through his book, and there's nothing for a McIntyre before then, the guy who's *calling* himself McIntyre."

"What's he look like?"

"Just this side of forty, the waiter said. About five ten

or eleven, hundred and seventy pounds, brown hair and brown eyes, mustache, no visible scars or tattoos. Wearing a dark brown suit, tan tie, brown shoes. No overcoat, according to the lady in the checkroom.''

''How'd he pay for dinner?''

''No luck there, Steve. Cash.''

''What about the girl?''

''The waiter says she looked about eighteen, nineteen. Slender . . . well, wiry was the word he used. I thought only men were wiry,'' Hawes said and shrugged. ''Anyway, wiry. About five-eight or five-nine, tall girl, the waiter said. Black hair, blue eyes.''

''Did the waiter catch her name?''

''Darcy. When he asked them if they wanted drinks before dinner, the guy said, 'Darcy?' The girl said she wasn't supposed to. She told him she was in training.''

''Another athlete?'' Carella said. ''Jesus!''

''Another *runner*, Steve.''

''How do you know?''

''The waiter heard them talking about running. About how good running made her feel. This was when he was bringing their drinks to the table. The girl had white wine, the guy had Dewar's on the rocks.''

''Reliable witness?'' Carella asked.

''Sharp as a tack. Memory like an elephant.''

''What else?''

''The guy was taping her,'' Hawes said. ''Put a recorder on the table, taped every word she said. Well, he turned it off while they were eating, but he started taping again when they were on coffee. The waiter said he kept asking her questions, as if it was an interview or something.''

''He didn't happen to catch her *last* name, did he?''

''You expect miracles?''

''What was she wearing?''

''Red dress and red high-heeled shoes. Red barrette in

her hair. The hair was pulled back. Not a pony tail, but pulled back and fastened with the barrette.''

"We ought to *hire* the waiter,'' Carella said. "How'd they leave?''

"Doorman outside asked if they needed a taxi, our guy told him no.''

"So did they walk away, or what? Did he see them get into a car?''

"They walked.''

"Which way?''

"North. Toward Jefferson.''

"They may *still* be walking,'' Carella said. "What precinct is this? Midtown South, isn't it?''

"To Hall Avenue. Then it's North.''

"Let's get it on the radio to *both* precincts. If they're walking, one of the cars may spot them.''

"You know how many garages there are in the side streets around here? Suppose the guy was driving?''

"That's *our* job,'' Carella said.

He had turned off the parkway just before the toll booth that separated Isola from Riverhead, and was driving southward now toward the Diamondback River and the park bordering its northern bank. The statue, he had told her, was in the park. He doubted that anyone else in the city knew the statue even existed; that's what he had told her. She seemed keen on seeing the statue, but he could tell that the streets through which they now drove were making her a little nervous. The old Maurice Avenue fishmarket was on their right, its windows shattered by vandals, its once-white walls adorned with spray-painted graffiti. Just beyond that was the century-old building that housed the 84th Precinct, green globes flanking the front steps. He had taken this street deliberately, hoping the sight of a police station would reassure her. He drove past the several police cars angled into the curb out front. A uniformed cop was just coming down the front steps.

"Good to know they're around, isn't it?" he said.

"You said it. This is *some* neighborhood."

It had, at one time, been a fine neighborhood indeed, but the Bridge Street Section, as it was called, had deteriorated over the years until it resembled all too many other rundown areas of the city, its streets potholed, its buildings crumbling, many of them in fact abandoned. Years ago, when the police department chose Bridge Street as the location for one of its precincts, the street had been a lively thoroughfare brimming with merchant shops, the nucleus of which was the huge fish market close to the River Harb, where—back then—the clear waters had made possible a daily harvest of fresh fish. Now the river was polluted and the neighborhood scarcely habitable. He could not understand why it was called Bridge Street. The nearest bridges were to the east and west—the Hamilton Bridge that spanned the River Harb and connected two states; and the shorter bridge running over Devil's Bight to join Riverhead with Isola. Nor was there any bridge at either end of the park bordering the Diamondback River, at which point Bridge Street ended in a perpendicular fusing with Turret Road. There were no turrets in evidence, either, though perhaps there had been when the Dutch or the British were here. Turret Road certainly *sounded* British. In any case, Bridge Street ran directly into it, and ended, and the Bridge Street Park began on the other side of Turret Road.

"Here we are," he said.

The dashboard clock read 10:37.

"Spooky around here," Darcy said.

"It's well-patroled," he said.

He was lying. He had scouted the park on three separate nighttime occasions, and he hadn't seen a single policeman on its paths, despite the park's proximity to the police station. Moreover, the park was known to be dangerous at night, and a pedestrian abroad in it after nine o'clock was a rare sight. He had seen only two people in the park on his previous nocturnal outings: a sailor and a girl who looked like a hooker on her knees before him in the bushes.

He parked the car some distance from the nearest streetlamp, came around to the passenger side at the curb, and opened the door for her. As she stepped out of the car, he reached into his pocket and snapped on the recorder.

"Will we be able to *see* this statue?" she asked. "It looks dark in there."

"Oh, there are lights," he said.

There were, in fact, lampposts inside the park. The old-fashioned vertical sort, a single post supporting a globe-enclosed light bulb at the top of the pole. No arms arcing out over the path. He considered this a drawback. This time, he would have preferred hanging her right where he killed her, in a deserted park in another precinct.

The park was bordered by a low stone wall on the Turret Road side and a cyclone fence on the far side near the Diamondback River. He had no intention of taking her that deep into the park. He planned to do this at once, as soon as they had cleared the entrance. The entrance was an opening in the wall defined by two higher stone pillars flanking it. A globe-enclosed light bulb topped each of the pillars, but the lamps were out just now; he had shattered both of them two nights ago. The sidewalk and the park path beyond were in almost complete darkness.

"Should have brought a flashlight," Darcy said.

"Vandals," he said. "But there's a lamppost just a little ways in."

They entered the park.

"Who's this a statue *of*, anyway?" she asked.

"Jesse Owens," he said.

He was lying again. The only statue in the park was an equestrian statue of an obscure colonel who, according to the bronze plaque at its base, had fought bravely in the Battle of Gettysburg.

"Really? Here? I thought he was from Cleveland."

"You know the name, do you?"

"Well, sure. He ran the socks off everybody in the world . . . when was it?"

"1936. The Berlin Olympics."

"Made a fool of Hitler and all his Aryan theories."

"Ten-six for the hundred meter," he said, nodding. "Broke the world record at twenty-point-seven for the two-hundred, and *also* won the four-hundred meter relay."

"Not to mention the broad jump," Darcy said.

"You *do* know him then," he said, smiling, pleased.

"Of *course* I know him, I'm a *runner,*" she said, and that was when he made his move.

He intended to do this as swiftly and as easily as he had with the other two. A modified arm drag, designed neither to take her down nor to bend her over at the waist but instead to force her body weight over to her left foot, exposing her side. With her left arm extended, he would move up under her armpit, and before she could turn her head, would clamp his hand at the back of her neck in a half nelson. Swinging around behind her, he would move his other hand up under her right armpit and clasp it at the back of her neck to complete a full nelson. Then he would press her head straight downward, forcing her chin onto her chest and, by exerting pressure, cracking her spine.

The full nelson, because it was so dangerous, could be used by wrestlers only in international competition, and then provided that it was applied at a ninety-degree angle to the spinal column. Once the hands were locked behind an opponent's head, a body shift to the right or left was mandatory to create the legal angle before applying pressure. He was not concerned with legal angles. He was concerned only with dispatching her effectively, soundlessly, and as quickly as possible. His experience with the other two had taught him that he could apply the hold and the necessary pressure to break her neck in twenty seconds. But this time, the girl wasn't having any of it.

The instant he locked his hand around her wrist, she shouted, ''Hey!'' and immediately took a step away from him, trying to free herself. Pulling her into him again, he tried to maneuver his arm up under hers to apply the first half of the nelson, but she jabbed her free elbow into his ribs and then, her back still partially to him, stamped on the insole of his foot with her high-heeled shoe.

The pain in his foot was excruciating, but he would not release his hold on her wrist. They struggled fiercely and soundlessly, their dancing feet rasping over the light cover of fallen leaves underfoot, their bodies intercepting light from the lamppost ahead and casting fitful shadows on the path. She would not allow him to get under her arm. She kept trying to free her wrist, pulling away, attacking whenever he tried to get under that arm to apply his hold. As she came at him again, her right hand clawing at his face, he punched her. His closed left fist caught her in the center of her chest, between her compact athlete's breasts, knocking the wind out of her. He hit her again, in the face this time, and he kept punching her in anger at the difficulty she was causing, her refusal to cooperate in her own demise. A short sharp jab broke her nose. Blood spilled onto his fist and stained the front of her red dress a darker crimson. She was gasping for breath now, her blue eyes wide in fright. He punched her in the mouth, shattering her front teeth, and as she started to fall toward him, he quickly maneuvered his arm up under hers, applied the hold at the back of her neck, and then moved completely behind her, his groin tight against her buttocks. Supporting her, looping his free arm under her armpit, and over the back of her head, he locked the fingers of both hands behind her neck, spread his legs wide to distribute his weight, and swiftly applied pressure.

He heard the cracking snap of her spine.

It sounded like a rifle shot on the still October air.

The girl collapsed against him.

He looked swiftly ahead on the path, and then picked her up in his arms and turned toward the park entrance.

A man was standing in the opening flanked by the shattered light globes. Illumination from the lamppost up the street cast his angled shadow between the two stone pillars.

The man took one look and ran like hell.

8

DETECTIVE FIRST/GRADE OLIVER WEEKS SAID, "Well, well."

It was very rare that you saw a white person up here. The white people up here in Diamondback were either cops or mailmen or garbage collectors or somebody come uptown to get his ashes hauled by a hooker. It was also rare to see a white person up here who was also a white *woman*. The neighborhood had a lot of what Ollie called "high yeller girls," but they weren't white, of course. If you had the teensiest drop of black blood in you, you weren't white, not the way Ollie Weeks figured it, anyway. So it was rare to see a white girl up here at eight o'clock on a Thursday morning, and it was even more rare to see her hanging from a lamppost. The Homicide dicks thought it was rare, too. They were all commenting how rare it was when the man from the Medical Examiner's Office arrived.

The M.E. told them it wasn't so rare at all, the girl hanging from the lamppost. He asked them didn't they read the newspapers or watch television? Didn't they know two *other* girls had been found in similarly compromising situations within the past two weeks, hanging up there on lampposts where everybody could look up under their dresses? The assembled crowd of policemen all looked up under the dead girl's dress. She was wearing red panties under her red dress.

"Still," Ollie said, "it's rare up here in the Eight-Three you find anybody dead but a nigger."

One of the patrolmen setting up the barricades and the

Crime Scene signs was black. He made no comment about Ollie's derogatory remark because Ollie outranked him in spades (the patrolman actually thought this, without recognizing the Freudian association) and besides Fat Ollie Weeks didn't know that the word "nigger" was derogatory. If Fat Ollie Weeks had been Secretary of the Interior, the now-famous line would have read, "I got a nigger, a broad, two kikes, and a crip." That was simply the way Fat Ollie Weeks talked. He meant no harm. He was always telling people he meant no harm, that was just the way he talked. "Some of my best friends are niggers," Fat Ollie Weeks was fond of proclaiming. In fact, Ollie thought the best detective on the Eighty-third—other than himself, of course—was a nigger. He was always telling anyone who'd listen that Parsons was one of the best fuckin' nigger cops in this city.

When they cut the girl down some ten minutes later, the detectives and the M.E. gathered around her as if they were in a floating crap game.

"Did a nice number on her beforehand, didn't he?" one of the Homicide dicks said. His name was Matson.

"Knocked half her teeth out," the other one said. His name was Manson. This was a bad name for a cop, and he was always getting ribbed about it.

"Broke her nose, looks like."

"Not to mention her neck," the M.E. said. "Whose case is this?"

"Mine," Ollie said. "Lucky me."

"Your cause of death is fracture of the cervical vertebrae."

"That blood on her dress?" Matson asked.

"No, it's gravy," Ollie said. "What the fuck you think it is?"

"Where?" Manson asked.

"Across the tits," Matson said.

"Nice little Jennifers," Manson said.

"I never heard that expression before," Matson said.

"Jennifers? It's a common expression."

"I never heard it in my life. Jennifers? That's supposed to be tits, Jennifers?"

"Where I grew up, everybody called them Jennifers," Manson said, offended.

"Where the fuck was *that?*" Ollie said.

"Calm's Point," Manson said.

"Figures," Matson said, and shook his head.

"You might want to cross-check on the other two," the M.E. suggested.

"She's got two *more?*" Manson said, attempting a bit of humor after the put-down following his use of the word "Jennifers" which when he was growing up *was* a common word used to define tits, even *big* tits—well, no, those were Jemimas.

"The other two *victims,*" the M.E. said.

"You guys want this?" the black patrolman said, walking over.

Meyer was sitting at his desk, wearing his wig and typing. The wig kept slipping a little, which made him look devil-may-care. He saw a huge bulk standing outside the slatted railing that separated the squadroom from the corridor outside. For a moment, he thought it was Fat Ollie Weeks. He blinked. It *was* Fat Ollie Weeks. Meyer immediately felt like taking a shower. Weeks usually smelled like a cesspool, and anyone standing close to him wondered why he did not draw flies. Weeks also was a bigot. Meyer didn't need him in the squadroom today. He didn't need him in the squadroom *ever.* But here he was, as big as Buddha, at ten in the morning.

"Anybody home?" he said from the railing, and then opened the gate and walked in. Meyer was alone in the squadroom. He said nothing. He watched Ollie as he approached the desk. Little pig eyes in a round pig face. Fat belly bulging over the belt of his trousers. Wrinkled sports jacket that looked as if it had been slept in for a week. Big Fat Ollie Weeks floating toward the desk like a barrage balloon.

"Detective Weeks," he said, flashing his buzzer. "The Eight-Three."

"No kidding?" Meyer said. What the hell *was* this? Ollie knew him, they had worked together before.

"I been up here before," Ollie said.

"Oh, really?" Meyer said.

"Yeah, I know all the guys up here," Ollie said. "Used to be a little bald Jewish person working up here."

Meyer did not mind being called "bald" (not *much*, he didn't) which was what he was when he wasn't wearing his wig, nor did he mind being called a "Jewish person," which was also what he was, but at a bit more than six feet tall he did not think he was "little," and anyway when Ollie put all the words together as "a little bald Jewish person," they sounded like a slur.

"I am that little bald Jewish person," he said, "and cut the crap, Ollie."

Ollie's little pig eyes opened wide. "Meyer?" he said. "Is that you? I'll be damned!" He began circling the desk, studying Meyer's hairpiece. "It's very becoming," he said. "You don't look Jewish no more."

Meyer said nothing. I need him, he thought. I really *need* him.

"I've been meaning to call you," Ollie said.

I'm glad you didn't, Meyer thought.

"Didn't some guy write a book using your name in it one time?"

"Some *lady*," Meyer said.

"Used the name Meyer Meyer for a person in her book, right?" Ollie said.

"A *character* in the book," Meyer said.

"That's even worse," Ollie said. "Reason I mention

it—you familiar with 'Hill Street Blues'? It's a television show.''

"I'm familiar with it," Meyer said.

"I caught a rerun last week musta been. They had a guy on it I think they stole from me."

"What do you mean, stole from you?"

"This cop. A narc cop . . ."

"You're not a narc cop, Ollie."

"Don't I know what I am? But I *been* on narcotics cases, same as you. First time I *met* you guys was on a narcotics case, in fact. Some guys smuggling shit inside little wooden animals, remember? That was the first time I worked with you guys up here."

"I remember," Meyer said.

"That was before 'Hill Street Blues' was even a dream in anybody's head."

"So what's the point, Ollie?"

"The point is this guy's name was Charlie Weeks. On the show. Charlie, not Ollie. But that's pretty close, don't you think? Charlie and Ollie. With the same last name? Weeks? I think that's very close, Meyer."

"I still don't see . . ."

"This other guy—they got a Jewish person on the show, too, his name is Goldblume, one of your paisans, huh? This guy Goldblume, he's telling the boss up there, this Furillo, that Weeks is trigger-happy . . . especially when the target is *black*. What Weeks says at one point is, 'Freeze, niggers, or I'll blow your heads off.' Also, he manhandles suspects. I mean, he's a regular shithead, this Charlie Weeks."

"So?"

"So am *I* a shithead?" Ollie asked. "Is *Ollie* Weeks a shithead? Is *Ollie* Weeks the kind of cop who goes around mistreating suspects?"

Meyer said nothing.

"Is *Ollie* Weeks the kind of cop who has anything but *respect* for niggers?"

Meyer still said nothing.

"What I'm thinking of doing," Ollie said, "is suing the company makes 'Hill Street Blues.' For putting a cop on television has a name sounds exactly like mine and who's a prejudiced person goes around shooting niggers and roughing up guys he's interrogating. That kind of shit can give a *real* cop a bad name, never mind they call him *Charlie* Weeks on their fuckin' T.V. show."

"I think you have a case," Meyer said flatly.

"Did *you* sue that time?"

"Rollie advised me against it. Rollie Chabrier. In the D.A.'s Office."

"Yeah, I know him," Ollie said. "He told you not to, huh?"

"He said I should be flattered."

"Yeah, well, I ain't so fuckin' *flattered*," Ollie said. "There's such a thing as goin' too far, am I right or am I right? Matter of fact, I been meanin' to talk to Carella up here, 'cause I think *he's* got a case, too."

"How do you figure that?"

"Well, don't Furillo sound a lot like Carella to you? I mean, how many wop names are there in this world that got three vowels and four condiments in them, and *two* of those condiments happen to be the same in both names? Two *l*'s, Meyer! Carella and Furillo, those names sound a whole lot alike to me, like Charlie Weeks and Ollie Weeks. Does Carella wear a vest all the time?"

"Only when he's expecting a shootout," Meyer said.

"No, I mean a regular vest, like from a suit, a *suit* vest. 'Cause this guy Carillo . . . Furillo, I mean . . . he's always wearing a vest. I think Carella oughta look into it."

"Wearing a vest, you mean?"

"No, the similarity of the names, I mean. You think those guys out there ever heard of us?"

"What guys?"

"The ones out in California who are putting together

that T.V. show and winning all the Emmys. You think they ever heard of Steve Carella and Ollie Weeks?''

"Probably not," Meyer said.

"I mean, we ain't exactly *famous*, either one of us," Ollie said, "but we been around a long time, man. A long fuckin' time. To me, it ain't a coincidence."

"So sue them," Meyer said.

"Prolly cost me a fortune," Ollie said. "Anyway, Steve and me'll still be here long after that fuckin' show turns to cornflakes."

"Cornflakes?"

"Yeah, in the can. The celluloid, the film. Long after it crumbles into cornflakes."

"So is that why you came up here?" Meyer said. "To ask me . . ."

"No, that's just somethin' been botherin' me a long time. The way 'Hill Street Blues' looks like *us*, Meyer. Even their fuckin' *imaginary* city looks like this one, don't it? I mean, shit, Meyer, we're real cops, ain't we?''

"I would say we're real cops, yes," Meyer said.

"So those guys are only make-believe, am I right or am I right? Using names that sound like *real* fuckin' cops in a *real* fuckin' city. It ain't fair, Meyer."

"Where is it written that it has to be fair?" Meyer said.

"Sometimes you sound like a fuckin' rabbi, you know that?" Ollie said.

Meyer sighed heavily.

"Why *did* you come up here?" he asked. "If you don't plan to sue . . ."

"I got a stiff hanging on a lamppost this morning. Found this at the scene," Ollie said, and tossed a tape cassette onto Meyer's desk.

From where Annie Rawles sat at her desk, she could see most of the lower part of the island that was Isola. The sky outside was blue and clear, causing the buildings towering into it to appear knife-edged. She wondered how much longer the good weather would last. This was already the twentieth of the month, usually a time when November's imminent presence was at least suggested.

The Rape Squad's offices were on the sixth floor of the new Headquarters Building downtown, a glass and steel structure that dominated the skyline and dwarfed the lower buildings that housed the city's municipal, judicial, and financial institutions. Before the new building went up—God, she couldn't remember how many years ago, and she wondered why everyone still referred to it as "new"—the Rape Squad had been based in one of the city's oldest precincts, a ramshackle structure midtown, near the overhead ramp of the River Highway. Rape victims were reluctant to report the crime of rape to the police, anyway; they suspected, correctly in many cases, that the police would give them as difficult a time as the rapist had. One look at the decrepit old building on Decatur Street had dissuaded many a victim from entering to discuss the crime further with specialists trained to deal with it. The new Headquarters Building did much to calm such fears. It had the orderly, sterile look of a hospital, and it made victims feel they were telling their stories to medical people rather than to cops, who they felt—again correctly—belonged to a paramilitary organization. Annie was grateful for the new offices in the new building; they made her job easier.

So did the computer.

She had told Eileen Burke that she was running a computer cross-check in an attempt to discover whether the same man had serially raped more women than the three victims about whom they were already positive. She had also told her that they were working up a cross-check on the victims themselves, trying to zero in on any similarities that may have attracted the rapist to them.

For the first cross-check, she had asked the computer operator—a man improbably name Binky Bowles—to go back to the beginning of the year, even though the first of the already positive victims had reported the offense only last April, six months back. The files on every reported rape, anywhere in the city, were already in the computer. Binky had only to press the appropriate keys to retrieve the name of any woman reporting a second, third, fourth, or even fifth occurrence after the original one. Much to Annie's surprise, there had been thirteen serial rape victims this year.

The first of these was a woman named Lois Carmody, who'd reported the initial assault to the 112th Precinct in Majesta on March 7. Her name came up three more times, each time for the same precinct in Majesta. The most recent serial victim—a woman name Janet Reilly—had been raped for the second time only last week, four days after Mary Hollings had reported *her* rape to the 87th Precinct. Both of the Reilly rapes had been committed in Riverhead. Their man—if indeed the same man was responsible for the serial rapes of thirteen women—had been very busy. He had also chosen his victims seemingly at random in each of the five sections that made up the greater city; Annie ruled out location as a unifying factor.

Binky's job got a bit more difficult after that.

Retrieving the files on each of the thirteen women, he isolated the descriptions they'd given of the man who'd assaulted them, and further broke down those descriptions as to race, age, height, weight, color of hair, color of eyes, visible scars or tattoos, and weapon used (if any) during the commission of the crime. Annie debated asking him to feed in descriptions of the clothing each assailant had been wearing, but decided this would be irrelevant. Clothing could easily change with the seasons; the earliest of the reported serial rapes went back to March. Binky asked the computer to spew out the victims' names in the order of the dates on which each had

reported the first rape. The breakdown that came from
the dot-matrix printer looked liked this:

Victims	Description of Assailants by Occurrence
Lois Carmody	1) White . . . 30 . . . 5'10" . . . 180 lbs . . . hr brwn . . . eys blu . . . no vis s/t . . . swtchbld knf.
	2) Same as occurrence one.
	3) Same as occurrence one.
	4) Same as occurrence one.
Mary Jane Moffit	1) Black . . . 19 . . . 6'0" . . . 200 lbs . . . hr blck . . . eys brwn . . . scar over lft eye . . . no tatt . . . no wpn.
	2) White . . . 27-30 . . . 5'9" . . . 170 lbs . . . hr blnd . . . eys brwn . . . no vis s/t . . . handgun.
Blanca Diaz	1) White . . . 25-30 . . . 6'0" . . . 200 lbs . . . hr brwn . . . eys blu . . . no vis s/t . . . swtchbld knf.
	2) Same as occurrence one.
	3) Same as occurrence one.
Patricia Ryan	1) White . . . 30-35 . . . 5'10" . . . 180 lbs . . . hr brwn . . . eys blu . . . no vis s/t . . . swtchbld knf.
	2) Same as occurrence one.
	3) Same as occurrence one.
Vanessa Hughes	1) White . . . 21 . . . 6'0" . . . 200 lbs . . . hr brwn . . . eys blu . . . no vis s . . . tatt rt hnd word love in hrt . . . icepick.

	2)	Black . . . 25-30 . . . 6'4" . . . 220 lbs . . . hr blck . . . eys brwn . . . no vis s/t . . . handgun.
Vivienne Chabrun	1)	White . . . 30-35 . . . 6'0" . . . 180 lbs . . . hr brwn . . . eys blu . . . no vis s/t . . . swtchbld knf.
	2)	Same as occurrence one.
	3)	Same as occurrence one.
Elaine Reynolds	1)	Black . . . 42 . . . 5'8" . . . 150 lbs . . . hr blck . . . eys hzl . . . no vis s/t . . . ktchn knf.
	2)	Hispanic . . . 17 . . . 6'0" . . . 170 lbs . . . hr blck . . . eys brwn . . . no vis s . . . tatt penis flower design . . . handgun.
Angela Ferrari	1)	White . . . 32 . . . 6'0" . . . 190 lbs . . . hr brwn . . . eys blu . . . no vis s/t . . . swtchbld knf.
	2)	Same as occurrence one.
	3)	Same as occurrence one.
	4)	White . . . 21 . . . 5'7" . . . 160 lbs . . . hr blnd . . . eys grn . . . no vis s/t . . . no wpn.
Terry Cooper	1)	White . . . 32 . . . 6'2" . . . 190 lbs . . . hr brwn . . . eys blu . . . no vis s/t . . . swtchbld knf.
	2)	Same as occurrence one.
Cecily Bainbridge	1)	White . . . 30 . . . 6'0" . . . 180 lbs . . . hr brwn . . . eys blu . . . no vis s/t . . . swtchbld knf.
	2)	Same as occurrence one.

Clara Preston	1)	White . . . 50-55 . . . 5'6" . . . 140 lbs . . . hr blck . . . eys brwn . . . scar rt thumb . . . pinky mssng lft hnd . . . no tatt . . . handgun.
	2)	White . . . 16 . . . 5'6" . . . 240 lbs . . . hr brwn . . . eys brwn . . . no vis s/t . . . no wpn.
Mary Hollings	1)	White . . . 30 . . . 5'10" . . . 180 lbs . . . hr brwn . . . eys blu . . . no vis s/t . . . swtchbld knf.
	2)	Same as occurrence one.
	3)	Same as occurrence one.
Janet Reilly	1)	White . . . 28 . . . 6'2" . . . 200 lbs . . . hr brwn . . . eys blu . . . no vis s/t . . . swtchbld knf.
	2)	Same as occurrence one.

Annie automatically eliminated any victim who had been serially raped by obviously different men—a black man and a white man, for example, or any two men of widely divergent descriptions—chalking these off as coincidental occurrences in a city populated with mad dogs. She was able to cull out four of the possible thirteen victims in this way, and held in abeyance a decision on Angela Ferrari, who'd been raped four times, but who'd described her *last* assailant as someone different from the others, whom she'd described identically. This left eight strong candidates and a relatively strong ninth.

Each of the nine women had described the multiple rapist as white. Each had reported that he had brown hair and blue eyes, no visible scars or tattoos, and had used a switchblade knife as a weapon.

Three of the women had said the rapist was five-feet ten-inches tall.

Four of them had said he was an even six feet tall.

Two had said he was six-feet two-inches tall.

The descriptions from the various women indicated that the rapist weighed somewhere between a hundred and eighty and two hundred pounds, with the majority—five women—saying he weighed a hundred and eighty.

As for his age, he had been variously described as 28 by one of the women, somewhere between 25 and 30 by another, 30 by three of the women, 32 by two of them, and somewhere between 30 and 35 by the remaining two.

It seemed to Annie that she was reasonably safe in assuming their man was white, thirty years old, six feet tall, and weighing a hundred and eighty pounds. There seemed no doubt that he had brown hair, blue eyes, and no visible scars or tattoos. There was also no doubt that he was carrying a switchblade knife—or that he had used it on at least one occasion, the third time he'd raped Blanca Diaz. She left Binky to the onerous task of checking through the computerized Known Rapist files, hoping he'd come up with a man or men who answered the composite description and whose M.O. included threats with a switchblade knife.

At her desk now, she went through the initial D.D. reports and subsequent profiles on the victims themselves, searching for any similarity or similarities that may have singled them out as victims. She prepared her notes on a scratch sheet, and then worked them up in the form of a chart, again listing the women's names in order of first reported rape.

* * *

Name	Age	Race	EthnicBG	Religion	Marital Status	Children	Rape?	Sodomy?
Lois Carmody	32	White	Irish	Catholic	Married	2	Yes	No
Blanca Diaz	46	Hispanic	Puerto Rican	Catholic	Married	4	Yes	No
Patricia Ryan	22	White	Irish	Catholic	Single	None	Yes	No
Vivienne Chabrun	28	White	French	Catholic	Single	None	Yes	No
Angela Ferrari	34	White	Italian	Catholic	Married	2	Yes	No
Terry Cooper	26	Black	African	Catholic	Single	None	Yes	No
Cecily Bainbridge	34	Black	Jamaican	Catholic	Divorced	3	Yes	No
Mary Hollings	37	White	English	Catholic	Divorced	None	Yes	No
Janet Reilly	19	White	Irish	Catholic	Single	None	Yes	No

Studying the chart, Annie made some notes she planned to have Binky put into the computer later. According to her calculations, most of the victims were white: six as against two black and one Hispanic. All of them were Catholic. Three were married, four were single, and two were divorced. Five of the victims were childless. One of them had four children. Another had three. The remaining two had two children each. The women's ethnic backgrounds were varied, with the largest number of them—three—being Irish. Their ages ranged from a low of 19 in the case of Janet Reilly to a high of 46 as concerned Blanca Diaz, the only Hispanic victim. Discounting these two extremes, Annie came up with an average age of about thirty—the same age as the rapist.

She looked at the chart again.

It seemed odd to her that all of the victims were Catholic. It seemed further odd that none of them had been sodomized. That simply didn't jibe with the M.O. of most rapists. Would Binky Bowles—she smiled everytime she thought of his name—come up with a knifewielder who matched the description the women had given and who further specialized in rape alone? Was he afraid one of them might bite it off? Put the son of a bitch out of business forever. Serve him right.

She didn't have enough data.

She looked through the D.D. reports and profiles again, taking notes, and then prepared another rough chart she would later ask Binky to feed into the computer for a more sophisticated evaluation than her own.

Name	City of Origin	Profession	Education	Clubs and Organizations	Hobbies and Sports
Lois Carmody	Washington, D.C.	Housewife	2 yrs. coll.	Catholic Daughters, YWCA	Needlepoint, tennis
Blanca Diaz	Mayaguez, P.R.	Housewife	2 yrs. high school	None	Embroidery, dancing, guitar
Patricia Ryan	Native	Student	B.A., 1st yr. M.A. in Comp Lit	Harvard Club, Calm's Point Symphony	Violin, travel, swimming
Vivienne Chabrun	Reims, France	Translator	Equivalent French B.A.	Alliance des Femmes Francaises	Skiing
Angela Ferrari	Native	Housewife	B.A., M.A.	YWCA, League Women Voters, Girl Scouts, PTA	Aerobics, tennis, ice skating, photography, crafts
Terry Cooper	Columbia, S.C.	Postal Clerk	High school grad	None	Bowling
Cecily Bainbridge	Kingston, Jamaica	Domestic	Elementary School	None	None
Mary Hollings	Long Beach, Ca.	Unemployed (Formerly travel agent)	B.A.	Intrepids Club	Travel, photography
Janet Reilly	Native	Student	1st yr. coll.	Zeta Chi, Newman Club, History Club Cheerleaders Squad, Chorus	Videogames, jogging, tennis

A mixed bag if ever there was one. Housewives, students, a blue collar worker (literally, since she was a postal clerk), a domestic, a translator and a former travel agent now living on the proceeds of alimony. Three natives of the city, the rest from all over creation. Education ranging from elementary school to a masters degree. Clubs and organizations, sports and hobbies ranging from—God, what a woman this Angela Ferrari seemed to be! Only thirty-four years old, married and with two children, she'd still found the time to get her masters degree, and was presently engaged in more activities than a colony of ants. And how about Janet Reilly? Nineteen years old, in her first year of college, and already involved in enough extra-curricular pursuits to keep the entire freshman class busy. So the son of a bitch rapes them. Caught Janet twice and Angela four—no, wait a minute. Angela was the one who'd described one rapist differently: twenty-one years old, five-foot-seven, a hundred and sixty pounds, blond hair and green eyes, no weapon. Had she been hysterical on that occasion? Or had *another* son of a bitch decided to take advantage of someone he knew had already been raped repeatedly? The way so many lunatics will jump on a bandwagon once it starts rolling, to cash in on the notoriety of the originator.

She looked at the computer printout again.

Lois Carmody: raped four times by the same man. Blanca Diaz, a forty-six-year-old housewife with four kids: three times. Patricia Ryan: three times. Vivienne Chabrun: three times. Angela Ferrari: three times for sure by the same man, yet another time by someone else. Cecily Bainbridge: twice. Mary Hollings: three times. Janet Reilly: twice.

Why the same women again and again?

Why?

She went back over the original D.D. reports, trying to find a pattern, trying to zero in on the link. Each of the women had been raped at night. Even in the case of Mary Hollings, the last time the rapist had struck—coming into her apartment this time—it was still dark, even though it was technically Friday *morning,* October 7. She traced back through the D.D. reports on Mary. The first reported rape was on June 10, a Friday. The next was on September 16, another Friday.

Well, coincidence maybe.

She looked at the D.D. reports on Janet Reilly.

She had been raped for the first time on September 13, a Tuesday night. And she had been raped again little more than a week ago, on October 11—*another* Tuesday night.

Okay. Okay, Annie thought. Take it easy now. Do them in order, check off the dates on all the D.D. reports against the computer printout of names. I need a calendar, where the hell's a calendar?

She opened the top drawer of her desk, rummaged around for a calendar, found one already marked with appointments, and then opened her notebook to the first several pages, where there were blank calendars for both this year and next. She carried the notebook to the copying machine in the corner of her office, and then made a dozen copies of this year's calendar—one for each of the victims, three spares for errors. Back at her desk again, she headed nine of the calendars with different names, and then—referring to the D.D. reports on each woman—began circling dates:

* * *

Lois Carmody

JANUARY						
SUN	MON	TUE	WED	THU	FRI	SAT
						1
2	3	4	5	6	7	8
9	10	11	12	13	14	15
16	17	18	19	20	21	22
23	24	25	26	27	28	29
30	31					

FEBRUARY						
SUN	MON	TUE	WED	THU	FRI	SAT
		1	2	3	4	5
6	7	8	9	10	11	12
13	14	15	16	17	18	19
20	21	22	23	24	25	26
27	28					

MARCH						
SUN	MON	TUE	WED	THU	FRI	SAT
		1	2	3	4	5
6	(7)	8	9	10	11	12
13	14	15	16	17	18	19
20	21	22	23	24	25	26
27	28	29	30	31		

APRIL						
SUN	MON	TUE	WED	THU	FRI	SAT
					1	2
3	(4)	5	6	7	8	9
10	11	12	13	14	15	16
17	18	19	20	21	22	23
24	(25)	26	27	28	29	30

MAY						
SUN	MON	TUE	WED	THU	FRI	SAT
1	2	3	4	5	6	7
8	(9)	10	11	12	13	14
15	16	17	18	19	20	21
22	23	24	25	26	27	28
29	30	31				

JUNE						
SUN	MON	TUE	WED	THU	FRI	SAT
			1	2	3	4
5	6	7	8	9	10	11
12	13	14	15	16	17	18
19	20	21	22	23	24	25
26	27	28	29	30		

JULY						
SUN	MON	TUE	WED	THU	FRI	SAT
					1	2
3	4	5	6	7	8	9
10	11	12	13	14	15	16
17	18	19	20	21	22	23
24	25	26	27	28	29	30
31						

AUGUST						
SUN	MON	TUE	WED	THU	FRI	SAT
	1	2	3	4	5	6
7	8	9	10	11	12	13
14	15	16	17	18	19	20
21	22	23	24	25	26	27
28	29	30	31			

SEPTEMBER						
SUN	MON	TUE	WED	THU	FRI	SAT
				1	2	3
4	5	6	7	8	9	10
11	12	13	14	15	16	17
18	19	20	21	22	23	24
25	26	27	28	29	30	

OCTOBER						
SUN	MON	TUE	WED	THU	FRI	SAT
						1
2	3	4	5	6	7	8
9	10	11	12	13	14	15
16	17	18	19	20	21	22
23	24	25	26	27	28	29
30	31					

NOVEMBER						
SUN	MON	TUE	WED	THU	FRI	SAT
		1	2	3	4	5
6	7	8	9	10	11	12
13	14	15	16	17	18	19
20	21	22	23	24	25	26
27	28	29	30			

DECEMBER						
SUN	MON	TUE	WED	THU	FRI	SAT
				1	2	3
4	5	6	7	8	9	10
11	12	13	14	15	16	17
18	19	20	21	22	23	24
25	26	27	28			

Blanca Diaz

JANUARY						
SUN	MON	TUE	WED	THU	FRI	SAT
						1
2	3	4	5	6	7	8
9	10	11	12	13	14	15
16	17	18	19	20	21	22
23	24	25	26	27	28	29
30	31					

JULY						
SUN	MON	TUE	WED	THU	FRI	SAT
					1	2
3	4	5	6	7	8	9
10	11	12	13	14	15	16
17	18	19	20	21	22	23
24	25	26	27	28	29	30
31						

FEBRUARY						
SUN	MON	TUE	WED	THU	FRI	SAT
		1	2	3	4	5
6	7	8	9	10	11	12
13	14	15	16	17	18	19
20	21	22	23	24	25	26
27	28					

AUGUST						
SUN	MON	TUE	WED	THU	FRI	SAT
	1	2	3	4	5	6
7	8	9	10	11	12	13
14	15	16	17	18	19	20
21	22	23	24	25	26	27
28	29	30	31			

MARCH						
SUN	MON	TUE	WED	THU	FRI	SAT
		1	2	3	4	5
6	7	8	9	10	11	12
13	14	(15)	16	17	18	19
20	21	22	23	24	25	26
27	28	29	30	31		

SEPTEMBER						
SUN	MON	TUE	WED	THU	FRI	SAT
				1	2	3
4	5	6	7	8	9	10
11	12	13	14	15	16	17
18	19	20	21	22	23	24
25	26	27	28	29	30	

APRIL						
SUN	MON	TUE	WED	THU	FRI	SAT
					1	2
3	4	(5)	6	7	8	9
10	11	(12)	13	14	15	16
17	18	19	20	21	22	23
24	25	26	27	28	29	30

OCTOBER						
SUN	MON	TUE	WED	THU	FRI	SAT
						1
2	3	4	5	6	7	8
9	10	11	12	13	14	15
16	17	18	19	20	21	22
23	24	25	26	27	28	29
30	31					

MAY						
SUN	MON	TUE	WED	THU	FRI	SAT
1	2	(3)	4	5	6	7
8	9	10	11	12	13	14
15	16	17	18	19	20	21
22	23	24	25	26	27	28
29	30	31				

NOVEMBER						
SUN	MON	TUE	WED	THU	FRI	SAT
		1	2	3	4	5
6	7	8	9	10	11	12
13	14	15	16	17	18	19
20	21	22	23	24	25	26
27	28	29	30			

JUNE						
SUN	MON	TUE	WED	THU	FRI	SAT
			1	2	3	4
5	6	7	8	9	10	11
12	13	14	15	16	17	18
19	20	21	22	23	24	25
26	27	28	29	30		

DECEMBER						
SUN	MON	TUE	WED	THU	FRI	SAT
				1	2	3
4	5	6	7	8	9	10
11	12	13	14	15	16	17
18	19	20	21	22	23	24
25	26	27	28			

Patricia Ryan

JANUARY						
SUN	MON	TUE	WED	THU	FRI	SAT
						1
2	3	4	5	6	7	8
9	10	11	12	13	14	15
16	17	18	19	20	21	22
23	24	25	26	27	28	29
30	31					

JULY						
SUN	MON	TUE	WED	THU	FRI	SAT
					1	2
3	4	5	6	7	8	9
10	11	12	13	14	15	16
17	18	19	20	21	22	23
24	25	26	27	28	29	30
31						

FEBRUARY						
SUN	MON	TUE	WED	THU	FRI	SAT
		1	2	3	4	5
6	7	8	9	10	11	12
13	14	15	16	17	18	19
20	21	22	23	24	25	26
27	28					

AUGUST						
SUN	MON	TUE	WED	THU	FRI	SAT
	1	2	3	4	5	6
7	8	9	10	11	12	13
14	15	16	17	18	19	20
21	22	23	24	25	26	27
28	29	30	31			

MARCH						
SUN	MON	TUE	WED	THU	FRI	SAT
		1	2	3	4	5
6	7	8	9	10	11	12
13	14	15	16	17	18	19
20	21	22	(23)	24	25	26
27	28	29	30	31		

SEPTEMBER						
SUN	MON	TUE	WED	THU	FRI	SAT
				1	2	3
4	5	6	7	8	9	10
11	12	13	14	15	16	17
18	19	20	21	22	23	24
25	26	27	28	29	30	

APRIL						
SUN	MON	TUE	WED	THU	FRI	SAT
					1	2
3	4	5	6	7	8	9
10	11	12	13	14	15	16
17	18	19	(20)	21	22	23
24	25	26	27	28	29	30

OCTOBER						
SUN	MON	TUE	WED	THU	FRI	SAT
						1
2	3	4	5	6	7	8
9	10	11	12	13	14	15
16	17	18	19	20	21	22
23	24	25	26	27	28	29
30	31					

MAY						
SUN	MON	TUE	WED	THU	FRI	SAT
1	2	3	4	5	6	7
8	9	10	11	12	13	14
15	16	17	18	19	20	21
22	23	24	(25)	26	27	28
29	30	31				

NOVEMBER						
SUN	MON	TUE	WED	THU	FRI	SAT
		1	2	3	4	5
6	7	8	9	10	11	12
13	14	15	16	17	18	19
20	21	22	23	24	25	26
27	28	29	30			

JUNE						
SUN	MON	TUE	WED	THU	FRI	SAT
			1	2	3	4
5	6	7	8	9	10	11
12	13	14	15	16	17	18
19	20	21	22	23	24	25
26	27	28	29	30		

DECEMBER						
SUN	MON	TUE	WED	THU	FRI	SAT
				1	2	3
4	5	6	7	8	9	10
11	12	13	14	15	16	17
18	19	20	21	22	23	24
25	26	27	28			

Vivienne Chabrun

JANUARY						
SUN	MON	TUE	WED	THU	FRI	SAT
						1
2	3	4	5	6	7	8
9	10	11	12	13	14	15
16	17	18	19	20	21	22
23	24	25	26	27	28	29
30	31					

JULY						
SUN	MON	TUE	WED	THU	FRI	SAT
					1	2
3	4	5	6	7	8	9
10	11	12	13	14	15	16
17	18	19	20	21	22	23
24	25	26	27	28	29	30
31						

FEBRUARY						
SUN	MON	TUE	WED	THU	FRI	SAT
		1	2	3	4	5
6	7	8	9	10	11	12
13	14	15	16	17	18	19
20	21	22	23	24	25	26
27	28					

AUGUST						
SUN	MON	TUE	WED	THU	FRI	SAT
	1	2	3	4	5	6
7	8	9	10	11	12	13
14	15	16	17	18	19	20
21	22	23	24	25	26	27
28	29	30	31			

MARCH						
SUN	MON	TUE	WED	THU	FRI	SAT
		1	2	3	4	5
6	7	8	9	10	11	12
13	14	15	16	17	18	19
20	21	22	23	24	25	26
27	28	29	30	(31)		

SEPTEMBER						
SUN	MON	TUE	WED	THU	FRI	SAT
				1	2	3
4	5	6	7	8	9	10
11	12	13	14	15	16	17
18	19	20	21	22	23	24
25	26	27	28	29	30	

APRIL						
SUN	MON	TUE	WED	THU	FRI	SAT
					1	2
3	4	5	6	7	8	9
10	11	12	13	14	15	16
17	18	19	20	21	22	23
24	25	26	27	28	29	30

OCTOBER						
SUN	MON	TUE	WED	THU	FRI	SAT
						1
2	3	4	5	6	7	8
9	10	11	12	13	14	15
16	17	18	19	20	21	22
23	24	25	26	27	28	29
30	31					

MAY						
SUN	MON	TUE	WED	THU	FRI	SAT
1	2	3	4	5	6	7
8	9	10	11	12	13	14
15	16	17	18	(19)	20	21
22	23	24	25	26	27	28
29	30	31				

NOVEMBER						
SUN	MON	TUE	WED	THU	FRI	SAT
		1	2	3	4	5
6	7	8	9	10	11	12
13	14	15	16	17	18	19
20	21	22	23	24	25	26
27	28	29	30			

JUNE						
SUN	MON	TUE	WED	THU	FRI	SAT
			1	(2)	3	4
5	6	7	8	9	10	11
12	13	14	15	16	17	18
19	20	21	22	23	24	25
26	27	28	29	30		

DECEMBER						
SUN	MON	TUE	WED	THU	FRI	SAT
				1	2	3
4	5	6	7	8	9	10
11	12	13	14	15	16	17
18	19	20	21	22	23	24
25	26	27	28			

Angela Ferrari

JANUARY						
SUN	MON	TUE	WED	THU	FRI	SAT
						1
2	3	4	5	6	7	8
9	10	11	12	13	14	15
16	17	18	19	20	21	22
23	24	25	26	27	28	29
30	31					

JULY						
SUN	MON	TUE	WED	THU	FRI	SAT
					1	2
3	4	5	6	7	8	9
10	11	12	13	14	15	16
17	18	19	20	21	22	23
24	25	26	27	28	29	30
31						

FEBRUARY						
SUN	MON	TUE	WED	THU	FRI	SAT
		1	2	3	4	5
6	7	8	9	10	11	12
13	14	15	16	17	18	19
20	21	22	23	24	25	26
27	28					

AUGUST						
SUN	MON	TUE	WED	THU	FRI	SAT
	1	2	3	4	5	6
7	8	9	10	11	12	13
14	15	16	17	18	19	20
21	22	23	24	25	26	27
28	29	30	31			

MARCH						
SUN	MON	TUE	WED	THU	FRI	SAT
		1	2	3	4	5
6	7	8	9	10	11	12
13	14	15	16	17	18	19
20	21	22	23	24	25	26
27	28	29	30	31		

SEPTEMBER						
SUN	MON	TUE	WED	THU	FRI	SAT
				1	2	3
4	5	6	7	8	9	10
11	12	13	14	15	16	17
18	19	20	21	22	23	24
25	26	27	28	29	30	

APRIL						
SUN	MON	TUE	WED	THU	FRI	SAT
					1	2
3	4	5	6	7	8	9
10	(11)	12	13	14	15	16
17	18	19	20	21	22	23
24	25	26	27	28	29	30

OCTOBER						
SUN	MON	TUE	WED	THU	FRI	SAT
						1
2	3	4	5	6	7	8
9	10	11	12	13	14	15
16	17	18	19	20	21	22
23	24	25	26	27	28	29
30	31					

MAY						
SUN	MON	TUE	WED	THU	FRI	SAT
1	2	3	4	5	6	7
8	9	10	11	12	13	14
15	16	17	18	19	20	21
22	23	24	25	26	27	28
29	(30)	31				

NOVEMBER						
SUN	MON	TUE	WED	THU	FRI	SAT
		1	2	3	4	5
6	7	8	9	10	11	12
13	14	15	16	17	18	19
20	21	22	23	24	25	26
27	28	29	30			

JUNE						
SUN	MON	TUE	WED	THU	FRI	SAT
			1	2	3	4
5	(6)	7	8	9	10	11
12	(13)	14	15	16	17	18
19	20	21	22	23	24	25
26	27	28	29	30		

DECEMBER						
SUN	MON	TUE	WED	THU	FRI	SAT
				1	2	3
4	5	6	7	8	9	10
11	12	13	14	15	16	17
18	19	20	21	22	23	24
25	26	27	28			

She hesitated. The three dates she had just circled were the dates for identifications of the same man. The man Angela had described *differently*—the wild card, so to speak—had raped her on June 28. On the calendar, Annie marked that date with an X.

Angela Ferrari

JANUARY								JULY						
SUN	MON	TUE	WED	THU	FRI	SAT		SUN	MON	TUE	WED	THU	FRI	SAT
						1							1	2
2	3	4	5	6	7	8		3	4	5	6	7	8	9
9	10	11	12	13	14	15		10	11	12	13	14	15	16
16	17	18	19	20	21	22		17	18	19	20	21	22	23
23	24	25	26	27	28	29		24	25	26	27	28	29	30
30	31							31						

FEBRUARY								AUGUST						
SUN	MON	TUE	WED	THU	FRI	SAT		SUN	MON	TUE	WED	THU	FRI	SAT
		1	2	3	4	5			1	2	3	4	5	6
6	7	8	9	10	11	12		7	8	9	10	11	12	13
13	14	15	16	17	18	19		14	15	16	17	18	19	20
20	21	22	23	24	25	26		21	22	23	24	25	26	27
27	28							28	29	30	31			

MARCH								SEPTEMBER						
SUN	MON	TUE	WED	THU	FRI	SAT		SUN	MON	TUE	WED	THU	FRI	SAT
		1	2	3	4	5						1	2	3
6	7	8	9	10	11	12		4	5	6	7	8	9	10
13	14	15	16	17	18	19		11	12	13	14	15	16	17
20	21	22	23	24	25	26		18	19	20	21	22	23	24
27	28	29	30	31				25	26	27	28	29	30	

APRIL								OCTOBER						
SUN	MON	TUE	WED	THU	FRI	SAT		SUN	MON	TUE	WED	THU	FRI	SAT
					1	2								1
3	4	5	6	7	8	9		2	3	4	5	6	7	8
10	(11)	12	13	14	15	16		9	10	11	12	13	14	15
17	18	19	20	21	22	23		16	17	18	19	20	21	22
24	25	26	27	28	29	30		23	24	25	26	27	28	29
								30	31					

MAY								NOVEMBER						
SUN	MON	TUE	WED	THU	FRI	SAT		SUN	MON	TUE	WED	THU	FRI	SAT
1	2	3	4	5	6	7				1	2	3	4	5
8	9	10	11	12	13	14		6	7	8	9	10	11	12
15	16	17	18	19	20	21		13	14	15	16	17	18	19
22	23	24	25	26	27	28		20	21	22	23	24	25	26
29	(30)	31						27	28	29	30			

JUNE								DECEMBER						
SUN	MON	TUE	WED	THU	FRI	SAT		SUN	MON	TUE	WED	THU	FRI	SAT
			1	2	3	4						1	2	3
5	6	7	8	9	10	11		4	5	6	7	8	9	10
12	(13)	14	15	16	17	18		11	12	13	14	15	16	17
19	20	21	22	23	24	25		18	19	20	21	22	23	24
26	27	28⊗	29	30				25	26	27	28			

Terry Cooper

JANUARY						
SUN	MON	TUE	WED	THU	FRI	SAT
						1
2	3	4	5	6	7	8
9	10	11	12	13	14	15
16	17	18	19	20	21	22
23	24	25	26	27	28	29
30	31					

FEBRUARY						
SUN	MON	TUE	WED	THU	FRI	SAT
		1	2	3	4	5
6	7	8	9	10	11	12
13	14	15	16	17	18	19
20	21	22	23	24	25	26
27	28					

MARCH						
SUN	MON	TUE	WED	THU	FRI	SAT
		1	2	3	4	5
6	7	8	9	10	11	12
13	14	15	16	17	18	19
20	21	22	23	24	25	26
27	28	29	30	31		

APRIL						
SUN	MON	TUE	WED	THU	FRI	SAT
					1	2
3	4	5	6	7	8	9
10	11	12	13	14	15	16
17	18	19	20	21	22	23
24	25	26	27	28	29	30

MAY						
SUN	MON	TUE	WED	THU	FRI	SAT
(1)	2	3	4	5	6	7
8	9	10	11	12	13	14
15	16	17	18	19	20	21
22	23	24	25	26	27	28
29	30	31				

JUNE						
SUN	MON	TUE	WED	THU	FRI	SAT
			1	2	3	4
5	6	7	8	9	10	11
12	13	14	15	16	17	18
(19)	20	21	22	23	24	25
26	27	28	29	30		

JULY						
SUN	MON	TUE	WED	THU	FRI	SAT
					1	2
3	4	5	6	7	8	9
10	11	12	13	14	15	16
17	18	19	20	21	22	23
24	25	26	27	28	29	30
31						

AUGUST						
SUN	MON	TUE	WED	THU	FRI	SAT
	1	2	3	4	5	6
7	8	9	10	11	12	13
14	15	16	17	18	19	20
21	22	23	24	25	26	27
28	29	30	31			

SEPTEMBER						
SUN	MON	TUE	WED	THU	FRI	SAT
				1	2	3
4	5	6	7	8	9	10
11	12	13	14	15	16	17
18	19	20	21	22	23	24
25	26	27	28	29	30	

OCTOBER						
SUN	MON	TUE	WED	THU	FRI	SAT
						1
2	3	4	5	6	7	8
9	10	11	12	13	14	15
16	17	18	19	20	21	22
23	24	25	26	27	28	29
30	31					

NOVEMBER						
SUN	MON	TUE	WED	THU	FRI	SAT
		1	2	3	4	5
6	7	8	9	10	11	12
13	14	15	16	17	18	19
20	21	22	23	24	25	26
27	28	29	30			

DECEMBER						
SUN	MON	TUE	WED	THU	FRI	SAT
				1	2	3
4	5	6	7	8	9	10
11	12	13	14	15	16	17
18	19	20	21	22	23	24
25	26	27	28			

Cecily Bainbridge

JANUARY						
SUN	MON	TUE	WED	THU	FRI	SAT
						1
2	3	4	5	6	7	8
9	10	11	12	13	14	15
16	17	18	19	20	21	22
23	24	25	26	27	28	29
30	31					

JULY						
SUN	MON	TUE	WED	THU	FRI	SAT
					1	2
3	4	5	6	7	8	9
10	11	12	13	14	15	16
17	18	19	20	21	22	23
24	25	26	27	28	29	30
31						

FEBRUARY						
SUN	MON	TUE	WED	THU	FRI	SAT
		1	2	3	4	5
6	7	8	9	10	11	12
13	14	15	16	17	18	19
20	21	22	23	24	25	26
27	28					

AUGUST						
SUN	MON	TUE	WED	THU	FRI	SAT
	1	2	3	4	5	6
7	8	9	10	11	12	13
14	15	16	17	18	19	20
21	22	23	24	25	26	27
28	29	30	31			

MARCH						
SUN	MON	TUE	WED	THU	FRI	SAT
		1	2	3	4	5
6	7	8	9	10	11	12
13	14	15	16	17	18	19
20	21	22	23	24	25	26
27	28	29	30	31		

SEPTEMBER						
SUN	MON	TUE	WED	THU	FRI	SAT
				1	2	3
4	5	6	7	8	9	10
11	12	13	14	15	16	17
18	19	20	21	22	23	24
25	26	27	28	29	30	

APRIL						
SUN	MON	TUE	WED	THU	FRI	SAT
					1	2
3	4	5	6	7	8	9
10	11	12	13	14	15	16
17	18	19	20	21	22	23
24	25	26	27	28	29	30

OCTOBER						
SUN	MON	TUE	WED	THU	FRI	SAT
						1
2	3	4	5	6	7	8
9	10	11	12	13	14	15
16	17	18	19	20	21	22
23	24	25	26	27	28	29
30	31					

MAY						
SUN	MON	TUE	WED	THU	FRI	SAT
1	2	3	4	5	6	(7)
8	9	10	11	12	13	14
15	16	17	18	19	20	21
22	23	24	25	26	27	28
29	30	31				

NOVEMBER						
SUN	MON	TUE	WED	THU	FRI	SAT
		1	2	3	4	5
6	7	8	9	10	11	12
13	14	15	16	17	18	19
20	21	22	23	24	25	26
27	28	29	30			

JUNE						
SUN	MON	TUE	WED	THU	FRI	SAT
			1	2	3	(4)
5	6	7	8	9	10	11
12	13	14	15	16	17	18
19	20	21	22	23	24	25
26	27	28	29	30		

DECEMBER						
SUN	MON	TUE	WED	THU	FRI	SAT
				1	2	3
4	5	6	7	8	9	10
11	12	13	14	15	16	17
18	19	20	21	22	23	24
25	26	27	28			

Mary Hollings

JANUARY							JULY						
SUN	MON	TUE	WED	THU	FRI	SAT	SUN	MON	TUE	WED	THU	FRI	SAT
						1						1	2
2	3	4	5	6	7	8	3	4	5	6	7	8	9
9	10	11	12	13	14	15	10	11	12	13	14	15	16
16	17	18	19	20	21	22	17	18	19	20	21	22	23
23	24	25	26	27	28	29	24	25	26	27	28	29	30
30	31						31						

FEBRUARY							AUGUST						
SUN	MON	TUE	WED	THU	FRI	SAT	SUN	MON	TUE	WED	THU	FRI	SAT
		1	2	3	4	5		1	2	3	4	5	6
6	7	8	9	10	11	12	7	8	9	10	11	12	13
13	14	15	16	17	18	19	14	15	16	17	18	19	20
20	21	22	23	24	25	26	21	22	23	24	25	26	27
27	28						28	29	30	31			

MARCH							SEPTEMBER						
SUN	MON	TUE	WED	THU	FRI	SAT	SUN	MON	TUE	WED	THU	FRI	SAT
		1	2	3	4	5					1	2	3
6	7	8	9	10	11	12	4	5	6	7	8	9	10
13	14	15	16	17	18	19	11	12	13	14	15	(16)	17
20	21	22	23	24	25	26	18	19	20	21	22	23	24
27	28	29	30	31			25	26	27	28	29	30	

APRIL							OCTOBER						
SUN	MON	TUE	WED	THU	FRI	SAT	SUN	MON	TUE	WED	THU	FRI	SAT
					1	2							1
3	4	5	6	7	8	9	2	3	4	5	6	7	8
10	11	12	13	14	15	16	9	10	11	12	13	14	15
17	18	19	20	21	22	23	16	17	18	19	20	21	22
24	25	26	27	28	29	30	23	24	25	26	27	28	29
							30	31					

MAY							NOVEMBER						
SUN	MON	TUE	WED	THU	FRI	SAT	SUN	MON	TUE	WED	THU	FRI	SAT
1	2	3	4	5	6	7			1	2	3	4	5
8	9	10	11	12	13	14	6	7	8	9	10	11	12
15	16	17	18	19	20	21	13	14	15	16	17	18	19
22	23	24	25	26	27	28	20	21	22	23	24	25	26
29	30	31					27	28	29	30			

JUNE							DECEMBER						
SUN	MON	TUE	WED	THU	FRI	SAT	SUN	MON	TUE	WED	THU	FRI	SAT
			1	2	3	4					1	2	3
5	6	7	8	9	(10)	11	4	5	6	7	8	9	10
12	13	14	15	16	17	18	11	12	13	14	15	16	17
19	20	21	22	23	24	25	18	19	20	21	22	23	24
26	27	28	29	30			25	26	27	28			

Janet Reilly

JANUARY						
SUN	MON	TUE	WED	THU	FRI	SAT
						1
2	3	4	5	6	7	8
9	10	11	12	13	14	15
16	17	18	19	20	21	22
23	24	25	26	27	28	29
30	31					

FEBRUARY						
SUN	MON	TUE	WED	THU	FRI	SAT
		1	2	3	4	5
6	7	8	9	10	11	12
13	14	15	16	17	18	19
20	21	22	23	24	25	26
27	28					

MARCH						
SUN	MON	TUE	WED	THU	FRI	SAT
		1	2	3	4	5
6	7	8	9	10	11	12
13	14	15	16	17	18	19
20	21	22	23	24	25	26
27	28	29	30	31		

APRIL						
SUN	MON	TUE	WED	THU	FRI	SAT
					1	2
3	4	5	6	7	8	9
10	11	12	13	14	15	16
17	18	19	20	21	22	23
24	25	26	27	28	29	30

MAY						
SUN	MON	TUE	WED	THU	FRI	SAT
1	2	3	4	5	6	7
8	9	10	11	12	13	14
15	16	17	18	19	20	21
22	23	24	25	26	27	28
29	30	31				

JUNE						
SUN	MON	TUE	WED	THU	FRI	SAT
			1	2	3	4
5	6	7	8	9	10	11
12	13	14	15	16	17	18
19	20	21	22	23	24	25
26	27	28	29	30		

JULY						
SUN	MON	TUE	WED	THU	FRI	SAT
					1	2
3	4	5	6	7	8	9
10	11	12	13	14	15	16
17	18	19	20	21	22	23
24	25	26	27	28	29	30
31						

AUGUST						
SUN	MON	TUE	WED	THU	FRI	SAT
	1	2	3	4	5	6
7	8	9	10	11	12	13
14	15	16	17	18	19	20
21	22	23	24	25	26	27
28	29	30	31			

SEPTEMBER						
SUN	MON	TUE	WED	THU	FRI	SAT
				1	2	3
4	5	6	7	8	9	10
11	12	(13)	14	15	16	17
18	19	20	21	22	23	24
25	26	27	28	29	30	

OCTOBER						
SUN	MON	TUE	WED	THU	FRI	SAT
						1
2	3	(4)	5	6	7	8
9	10	(11)	12	13	14	15
16	17	18	19	20	21	22
23	24	25	26	27	28	29
30	31					

NOVEMBER						
SUN	MON	TUE	WED	THU	FRI	SAT
		1	2	3	4	5
6	7	8	9	10	11	12
13	14	15	16	17	18	19
20	21	22	23	24	25	26
27	28	29	30			

DECEMBER						
SUN	MON	TUE	WED	THU	FRI	SAT
				1	2	3
4	5	6	7	8	9	10
11	12	13	14	15	16	17
18	19	20	21	22	23	24
25	26	27	28			

On a separate sheet of paper, she listed all nine names again, and then—referring to the calendar entries for each name—made yet another list.

Lois Carmody: March 7, April 4, April 25, May 9. All Monday nights.

Blanca Diaz: March 15, April 12, May 3. Tuesday nights.

Patricia Ryan: March 23, April 20, May 25. Wednesday nights.

Vivienne Chabrun: March 31, May 19, June 2. Thursdays.

Angela Ferrari: April 11, May 30 and June 13 for description of same man. All Monday nights. June 28 for the wild card. A Tuesday night.

Terry Cooper: May 1, June 19. Both Sunday nights.

Cecily Bainbridge: May 7, June 4. Saturday nights.

Mary Hollings: June 10, September 16, October 7. Fridays.

Janet Reilly: September 13, October 11. Tuesdays.

She studied the list.

Okay. Same woman on the same night of the week. But what the hell did it *mean?* His choice of a night for any given woman may have been premised on a study of her habits. Maybe Vivienne Chabrun went to a meeting of L'Alliance des Femmes Françaises on Thursday nights. Maybe Lois Carmody played tennis on Monday nights. Maybe Janet Reilly sang with the chorus on Tuesday nights. Who the hell knew?

She leafed through the calendars.

Vivienne Chabrun had been raped for the first time on the last day of March, the second time seven weeks later on May 19, and then again two weeks after that on the second of June. All Thursday nights. Terry Cooper had been raped on the first of May, and then seven weeks later, on June 19. Sunday nights. Patricia Ryan had been raped on March 23, again four weeks later on April 20, and then not again till May 25, five weeks after the April date. Wednesday nights. There seemed to be no discernible pattern until Annie went back through the calendars again, and studied the one for Lois Carmody, the first of the serial victims.

Lois Carmody

JANUARY						
SUN	MON	TUE	WED	THU	FRI	SAT
						1
2	3	4	5	6	7	8
9	10	11	12	13	14	15
16	17	18	19	20	21	22
23	24	25	26	27	28	29
30	31					

JULY						
SUN	MON	TUE	WED	THU	FRI	SAT
					1	2
3	4	5	6	7	8	9
10	11	12	13	14	15	16
17	18	19	20	21	22	23
24	25	26	27	28	29	30
31						

FEBRUARY						
SUN	MON	TUE	WED	THU	FRI	SAT
		1	2	3	4	5
6	7	8	9	10	11	12
13	14	15	16	17	18	19
20	21	22	23	24	25	26
27	28					

AUGUST						
SUN	MON	TUE	WED	THU	FRI	SAT
	1	2	3	4	5	6
7	8	9	10	11	12	13
14	15	16	17	18	19	20
21	22	23	24	25	26	27
28	29	30	31			

MARCH						
SUN	MON	TUE	WED	THU	FRI	SAT
		1	2	3	4	5
6	(7)	8	9	10	11	12
13	14	15	16	17	18	19
20	21	22	23	24	25	26
27	28	29	30	31		

SEPTEMBER						
SUN	MON	TUE	WED	THU	FRI	SAT
				1	2	3
4	5	6	7	8	9	10
11	12	13	14	15	16	17
18	19	20	21	22	23	24
25	26	27	28	29	30	

APRIL						
SUN	MON	TUE	WED	THU	FRI	SAT
					1	2
3	(4)	5	6	7	8	9
10	11	12	13	14	15	16
17	(18)	19	20	21	22	23
24	(25)	26	27	28	29	30

OCTOBER						
SUN	MON	TUE	WED	THU	FRI	SAT
						1
2	3	4	5	6	7	8
9	10	11	12	13	14	15
16	17	18	19	20	21	22
23	24	25	26	27	28	29
30	31					

MAY						
SUN	MON	TUE	WED	THU	FRI	SAT
1	(2)	3	4	5	6	7
8	(9)	10	11	12	13	14
15	16	17	18	19	20	21
22	23	24	25	26	27	28
29	30	31				

NOVEMBER						
SUN	MON	TUE	WED	THU	FRI	SAT
		1	2	3	4	5
6	7	8	9	10	11	12
13	14	15	16	17	18	19
20	21	22	23	24	25	26
27	28	29	30			

JUNE						
SUN	MON	TUE	WED	THU	FRI	SAT
			1	2	3	4
5	6	7	8	9	10	11
12	13	14	15	16	17	18
19	20	21	22	23	24	25
26	27	28	29	30		

DECEMBER						
SUN	MON	TUE	WED	THU	FRI	SAT
				1	2	3
4	5	6	7	8	9	10
11	12	13	14	15	16	17
18	19	20	21	22	23	24
25	26	27	28			

First rape: Monday, March 7.

Second rape: Four weeks later. Monday, April 4.

Third rape: Three weeks later. Monday, April 25.

Fourth rape: Two weeks later. Monday, May 9.

Annie looked at the calendar again. Four weeks, three weeks, two weeks. If he'd raped her again after that, would there have been an interval of only *one* week?

She looked at the calendar for Angela Ferrari.

Hit for the first time on April 11. Four weeks after that would have been May 9. Nothing on that date. Three weeks after May 9 was May 30. Yep, he'd hit her again on the thirtieth. And two weeks after that was—right on the nose! He'd raped her again on June 13.

Okay, hold it, Annie thought, take it easy.

Cecily Bainbridge: First rape on Saturday, May 7. Next rape four weeks later on Saturday, June 4. Blanca Diaz, right on schedule: First rape on March 15, next one four weeks later on April 12, the one after that—when he'd cut her—three weeks later on May 3. Mary Hollings . . . well, this was a tough one.

Raped for the first time on Friday, June 10, and then not again till Friday, September 16. Annie started counting off weeks on the calendar. Four weeks after June 10 was July 8. Three weeks after that was July 29. Two weeks after that was August 12. A week after that was August 19. Starting the cycle all over again, four weeks after August 19 was September 16, the exact date Mary Hollings had been raped for the second time. And three weeks after that was the seventh of October, the date of the most recent attack on her.

Janet Reilly: Raped on the thirteenth of September and then again exactly four weeks later, on October 11.

But if this *was* a pattern—four weeks, three weeks, two weeks—then how did it tie in with the seemingly patternless calendars for Vivienne Chabrun, Terry Cooper and Patricia Ryan?

Vivienne Chabrun: First rape, March 31. Four weeks

after that was April 28. No circle on her calendar for that date. But three weeks after the twenty-eighth was May 19, and he'd hit her on that date, and again *two* weeks after that, on June 2!

Okay. Okay now.

Terry Cooper: Hit for the first time on May 1, nothing four weeks later on May 29, but hit again three weeks after that on June 19!

Come on, Patricia, Annie thought, and looked at the last calendar.

Patricia Ryan: Raped on March 23. Four weeks after that was April 20, marked with another circle on the calendar. Three weeks after that was May 11 . . . nothing. But hold it. She'd been raped again on May 25, only *two* weeks after the May 11 date.

Maybe it didn't *matter* whether the intervals were exactly spaced so long as . . .

Was it possible?

Was he trying to make sure he got each of them at spaced intervals of a *week*, never mind how the intervals fell provided that he didn't *duplicate* any week? If not, why rape each of them on different nights, the same night for each woman? Had the son of a bitch worked out a calendar for each of his victims? Hit them at specified intervals, so long as he didn't duplicate the weeks one, two, three, four as indicated for any given woman? Skip a week, skip two weeks, six weeks, it didn't matter. All he had to do was count off the weeks to make sure he picked up the cycle again.

But why?

What the hell kind of freak were they dealing with here?

Annie made up one last calendar, listing *all* the dates of the multiple rapes, and labeling it "Cumulative."

Cumulative

JANUARY								JULY						
SUN	MON	TUE	WED	THU	FRI	SAT		SUN	MON	TUE	WED	THU	FRI	SAT
						1							1	2
2	3	4	5	6	7	8		3	4	5	6	7	8	9
9	10	11	12	13	14	15		10	11	12	13	14	15	16
16	17	18	19	20	21	22		17	18	19	20	21	22	23
23	24	25	26	27	28	29		24	25	26	27	28	29	30
30	31							31						

FEBRUARY								AUGUST						
SUN	MON	TUE	WED	THU	FRI	SAT		SUN	MON	TUE	WED	THU	FRI	SAT
		1	2	3	4	5			1	2	3	4	5	6
6	7	8	9	10	11	12		7	8	9	10	11	12	13
13	14	15	16	17	18	19		14	15	16	17	18	19	20
20	21	22	23	24	25	26		21	22	23	24	25	26	27
27	28							28	29	30	31			

MARCH								SEPTEMBER						
SUN	MON	TUE	WED	THU	FRI	SAT		SUN	MON	TUE	WED	THU	FRI	SAT
		1	2	3	4	5						1	2	3
6	7	8	9	10	11	12		4	5	6	7	8	9	10
13	14	15	16	17	18	19		11	12	13	14	15	16	17
20	21	22	23	24	25	26		18	19	20	21	22	23	24
27	28	29	30	31				25	26	27	28	29	30	

APRIL								OCTOBER						
SUN	MON	TUE	WED	THU	FRI	SAT		SUN	MON	TUE	WED	THU	FRI	SAT
					1	2								1
3	4	5	6	7	8	9		2	3	4	5	6	7	8
10	11	12	13	14	15	16		9	10	11	12	13	14	15
17	18	19	20	21	22	23		16	17	18	19	20	21	22
24	25	26	27	28	29	30		23	24	25	26	27	28	29
								30	31					

MAY								NOVEMBER						
SUN	MON	TUE	WED	THU	FRI	SAT		SUN	MON	TUE	WED	THU	FRI	SAT
1	2	3	4	5	6	7				1	2	3	4	5
8	9	10	11	12	13	14		6	7	8	9	10	11	12
15	16	17	18	19	20	21		13	14	15	16	17	18	19
22	23	24	25	26	27	28		20	21	22	23	24	25	26
29	30	31						27	28	29	30			

JUNE								DECEMBER						
SUN	MON	TUE	WED	THU	FRI	SAT		SUN	MON	TUE	WED	THU	FRI	SAT
			1	2	3	4						1	2	3
5	6	7	8	9	10	11		4	5	6	7	8	9	10
12	13	14	15	16	17	18		11	12	13	14	15	16	17
19	20	21	22	23	24	25		18	19	20	21	22	23	24
26	27	28	29	30				25	26	27	28			

The attacks had started in March, four that month, spaced eight days apart on successive nights of the week. Lois Carmody on March 7. Blanca Diaz on March 15. Patricia Ryan on March 23. Vivienne Chabrun on March 31.

In April, he'd hit Lois Carmody again on the fourth, added Angela Ferrari as a new victim on the eleventh, hit Blanca Diaz again on the twelfth, Patricia Ryan on the twentieth, and Lois Carmody yet another time on the twenty-fifth.

Two new victims in May, Terry Cooper and Cecily Bainbridge, for a total of seven hits that month.

Another frenzy of activity in June—five hits that month with Mary Hollings added as a new victim and Lois Carmody dropped from his calendar after a total of four consecutive hits spaced four weeks, three weeks, and two weeks apart.

Nothing in July or August.

Or at least nothing reported.

In September he'd hit Mary Hollings again, and had added Janet Reilly to his list.

In October—so far—just Mary and Janet.

Why nothing for July and August?

And would he soon pick up again on the victims he'd only raped two or three times? Was four his goal? Why four? Or had they not yet heard the last of Lois Carmody?

Too many questions, Annie thought.

Plus the *big* unanswered one.

Why these *particular* women?

Why?

In the October stillness of the squadroom, the windows open to a golden wash of late morning sunlight that seemed more fitting for August, the four detectives stood around Meyer's desk, listening to the tape cassette. Ollie Weeks had heard it before, but he was listening intently nonetheless, as if trying to memorize the words. Meyer,

Carella, and Hawes were hearing it for the first time, and separately trying to recall what the Deaf Man's voice sounded like.

There were two people on the cassette.

Darcy Welles and the man they knew only as Corey McIntyre.

> McINTYRE: The red light means it's on, the green light means it's taping. So. You were about to say.
>
> DARCY: Only that it was funny how your questions this afternoon started me thinking. I mean, who can *remember* how I first got interested in running? You know what my mother said?
>
> McINTYRE: Your mother?
>
> DARCY: Yeah, when I called her. She said I . . .
>
> McINTYRE: You called her in Ohio?

"Sounds a little nervous there, don't he?" Ollie said.

"Shhh," Carella said.

> DARCY: . . . get interviewed by *Sports USA?*
>
> McINTYRE: Was she pleased?

"Nervous as hell, you ask *me,*" Ollie said. "Kid called her mother to tell her who she's having dinner with . . ."

"You want us to listen to this, or you want to talk?" Hawes said.

"This is all bullshit, anyway," Ollie said, "this part of it. She talks about her brother, she talks about how terrific running makes her feel . . . here, right here."

> DARCY: . . . how *good* it makes me feel, do you know what I mean?
>
> McINTYRE: Yes.

* * *

"Guy *knows* how good it makes her feel," Ollie said. "Knows all about running."

"Will you please shut the hell up?" Meyer said.

"This is just shit where the waiter comes in with the drinks and asks them if they want to see menus . . . here's what I mean, listen to this. The guy keeps agreeing how *good* running makes you feel, listen. It's yes, yes, yes, all the way down the line."

DARCY: . . . snow is covering up all the garbage and all the petty little junk, and it's leaving everything clean and white and pure. That's how I feel when I'm running. As if it's Christmas all year round. With everything white and soft and beautiful.

McINTYRE: Yes, I know. Shall we look at the menus now? I'll just turn this off for a minute.

"He turns it off here," Ollie said, "and he don't turn it on again till later. But most of the stuff is just Q and A about running, and once she calls him 'Mr. McIntyre,' who you say was in L.A. at the time, huh, Steve?"

"Yes," Carella said.

"I marked a place we ought to listen to, unless you really want to hear what kind of training a runner does, which to me is all bullshit," Ollie said. "Can I run it ahead a bit?"

Without waiting for an answer, Ollie put the recorder on Fast Forward. He stopped the tape a bit past the mark and then fiddled with the controls, jockeying the tape back and forth until he found what he wanted.

"Yeah, here it is," he said. "Listen."

McINTYRE: Well, I can't thank you enough, Darcy. That was just the kind of material I was looking for.

DARCY: I hope so, anyway.

McINTYRE: It was, believe me. Would you like more coffee?

DARCY: No, I'd better get moving. What time is it, anyway?

MCINTYRE: A quarter to ten.

"Gives us a time," Ollie said. "Very nice of him."

DARCY: . . . realize it was so late. I have to look over that Psych material again.

MCINTYRE: I can give you a lift back to school, if you like.

"Here it comes," Ollie said.

DARCY: No, that's okay . . .

MCINTYRE: My car's parked right around the corner, near Jefferson. We can walk over to the garage, if you like . . .

DARCY: Well, gee, that's very nice of you.

MCINTYRE: Let me get the check.

"He turns off the machine here," Ollie said.

"Is that it?"

"There's more. But the guy just located the garage for us, so it should be pretty easy to find it, don't you think? Right around the corner, near Jefferson. How many garages . . . ?"

"We've already hit a dozen of them," Hawes said.

"Well, this should make it easier. You checked the phone books for Corey McIntyres?"

"None in the city," Carella said.

"So he was just usin' that guy's name out West, huh?"

"Looks that way."

"He won't be usin' it no more," Ollie said.

"What do you mean?"

"Listen," he said, and pointed to the recorder. "He

musta turned it on again just before he killed her. Wanted a permanent record, huh? The guy must be nuts.''

The detectives listened.

"There's the click," Ollie said. "Here it comes."

DARCY: Will we be able to *see* this statue? It looks dark in there.

McINTYRE: Oh, there are lights.

DARCY: Should have brought a flashlight.

McINTYRE: Vandals. But there's a lamppost just a little ways in.

"Where you suppose they are?" Ollie asked.

"Shhh," Meyer said.

DARCY: Who's this a statue *of,* anyway?

McINTYRE: Jesse Owens.

DARCY: Really? Here? I thought he was from Cleveland.

McINTYRE: You know the name, do you?

DARCY: Well, sure. He ran the socks off everybody in the world . . . when was it?

McINTYRE: 1936. The Berlin Olympics.

DARCY: Made a fool of Hitler and all his Aryan theories.

McINTYRE: Ten-six for the hundred meter. Broke the world record at twenty point seven for the two-hundred, and *also* won the four-hundred meter relay.

DARCY: Not to mention the broad jump.

McINTYRE: You *do* know him then.

DARCY: Of *course* I know him, I'm a *runner.*

"Here it comes," Ollie said.

The sounds of scuffling, heavy breathing, rasping, a thud, a gasp for breath, and another thud, and yet another, and now more gasping, fitful, frenzied.

"He's beating the shit out of her," Ollie said. "You should see how she looked when we found her . . ."

And then, suddenly, a sharp click.

"What's that?" Meyer asked. "Did he turn off the recorder?"

"No, sir," Ollie said.

"I thought I heard . . ."

"You did. That's the girl's neck breaking."

Silence on the tape now. Ten seconds, twenty seconds. Then the sound of footsteps moving quickly. Other footsteps, fading. A car door slamming. Another car door. The sound of an automobile engine starting. Then, over the purr of the engine, McIntyre's voice.

McIntyre: Hello, boys, it's me again. This won't be the last one. But it's the last you'll hear of Corey McIntyre. 'Bye now.

Silence.

The detectives looked at each other.

"That's it?" Hawes asked.

"That's all she wrote," Ollie said.

"Wants to get caught, doesn't he?" Meyer said.

"Looks that way to me," Ollie said. "Otherwise why leave us a tape zeroing in on the garage and giving us a voice print we can later match up we get a good suspect? First thing we got to do . . ."

"We?" Carella said.

"Why, sure," Ollie said. "I don't like young girls getting their necks broke by no fuckin' idiot. I'm gonna be workin' this one with you."

The detectives looked at him.

"We'll have a good time," Ollie said.

Which they found less than reassuring.

9

THE FIRST EDITION OF THE CITY'S AFTERNOON tabloid hit the stands at eleven-thirty that morning. The headline blared:

THIRD YOUNG CO-ED
MURDERED

Below the headline was a photograph of Darcy Welles hanging from a lamppost in the Eighty-third Precinct. The brief text under the photograph read:

Nineteen-year-old Darcy Welles, freshman track star at Converse University, became the third victim early this morning of the Road Runner Killer. Story page 4.

It was not unusual for this particular newspaper to label killers in a manner that would appeal to the popular imagination; its parentage was in London, where such sensationalism was commonplace. The police would have wished otherwise. Handy labels never helped in the apprehension of a murderer; if anything they made matters more difficult because they encouraged either phone calls or letters from cranks claiming to be "the Nursemaid Murderer," or "the Mad Slasher," or "the .32-Caliber Killer," or whoever else the newspapers had dreamed up. Their killer had now been named: the Road Runner Killer. Terrific. Except that it made their job harder. The story on page 4 read like a paperback mystery written by a hack:

In the cold early light of this morning's dawn, detectives of the 83rd Precinct in Isola's Diamondback area came upon the third victim in a now indisputably linked series of murders. In each instance, the victim has been a young woman. In each instance, the young woman was a college track star. In each instance, the victim's neck was broken, and she was found hanging from a lamppost in different deserted areas of the city. The Road Runner Killer is loose in the city, and not even the police can guess when and where he will strike next.

The story went on to relate in detail the circumstances surrounding the previous deaths of Marcia Schaffer and Nancy Annunziato, and then advised the reader to turn to page 6 for a profile on Darcy Welles and an interview with her parents in Columbus, Ohio. The profile on Darcy seemed to have been pilfered from the files at Converse University. It sketched in her educational background, tracing her years through elementary, junior high, and high school, and then went on to list all the track competitions she had entered, giving the results of each. The profile was accompanied by a photograph of Darcy in high school graduation cap and gown. A line of text under the photograph identified Darcy simply as *Victim Number Three: Darcy Welles*.

The interview with her parents had been conducted via the telephone at nine o'clock that morning, presumably immediately after a stringer sitting police calls in Diamondback had phoned in with news of the girl hanging from the lamppost. The reporter who spoke to both Robert Welles and his wife Jessica wrote in his interview that he had been the one to break the news of their daughter's murder, and that for the first five minutes of his conversation with them, they had been "sobbing uncontrollably" and "scarcely coherent." He had plunged ahead regardless, and had elicited from them a description of

Darcy that showed her to be a good, hard-working girl, dedicated to running but nonetheless maintaining a solid B-average in high school and "now in college." When their just-spoken words "now in college" registered on them, both parents had broken into tears again "with the realization that their daughter was no longer in fact a college student, their daughter was now a third grisly victim of the Road Runner Killer."

Darcy's older brother was a man named Bosley "Buzz" Welles, who worked as a computer programmer for the IBM branch office in Columbus. She'd had no steady boyfriends when she was living at home, but she was an attractive popular girl who had many friends of both sexes. So far as Mr. and Mrs. Welles knew, she had not been dating anyone since she'd started her freshman year at Converse in September. Her parents told the reporter that she had recently been contacted by the magazine *Sports USA* regarding an article they were preparing on promising young women athletes, and was in fact scheduled to be interviewed on the night she was murdered. Mr. and Mrs. Welles did not remember the name of the man who was to conduct the interview. On his own initiative, the reporter had called the editorial offices of *Sports USA* in New York, and had been told that they knew of no such article in preparation.

"Is it possible, then," the reporter editorialized in the distinctive style of his paper, "that the Road Runner Killer is representing himself as someone who works for *Sports USA*, thereby gaining the confidence of his young victims before leading them to slaughter?"

You bet your ass, Ollie thought, reading the article.

He was sitting beside Carella in a car they'd checked out not ten minutes earlier, heading downtown. Hawes was sitting in back. He did not like having his usual seat usurped by Ollie, but at the same time he did not envy Carella having to sit so close to him. He noticed that Carella had opened the window on the driver's side of the car. Wide.

"Listen to this," Ollie said, and began reading aloud. " 'If this is indeed the case . . .' "

"If *what* is indeed the case?" Hawes asked.

"Somebody palming himself off as a reporter from *Sports USA*," Ollie said, and began reading aloud again. " 'If this is indeed the case, the baffled policemen of this city might make note of it. And they might do well to warn any young female athletes at universities or colleges against accepting at face value anyone who represents himself to them as a reporter or journalist.' "

Alf Miscolo, in the Clerical Office of the Eight-Seven, had already typed up and photocopied a letter dictated by Lieutenant Byrnes for hand-delivery to every college and university in the city. The detectives had, in fact, debated whether the letter should go out to high schools as well.

"There's more," Ollie said. "This guy here, he all of a sudden remembers this is supposed to be an interview with Mom and Dad, and not a story giving advice to the police department. You ready? 'Mr. and Mrs. Welles were sobbing again as we ended our telephone conversation. The wires between here and Columbus hummed with their grief, a grief shared by parents all over this city, a grief that seemed to echo the words: "Find the Road Runner Killer." ' "

"Beautiful," Hawes said.

"Page opposite has pictures of the other two girls," Ollie said, "hanging from lampposts like Christmas ornaments. Whole fuckin' *paper* is full of the murders. They even got comments from the cops in New York who were handling the 'Son of Sam' killings, and a story by the reporter who covered it there, trying to find comparisons in M.O.s. It's headlined 'Psycho Similarities.' I'm surprised they didn't dig up Jack the Ripper. If this doesn't drive our man underground, nothing will. I'm glad the parents didn't remember his name, the name he gave the girl. Otherwise Corey McIntyre out in L.A.'d find himself splashed all *over* this rag.''

Ollie folded the newspaper and threw it into the back seat. It hit Hawes's knee and fell to the floor of the car.

"Give 'em time," Hawes said. "They'll get to it."

"They wanna be cops," Ollie said, "why don't they join the force? They wanna be reporters, they should shut the fuck up and not stick their noses in police work. You're coming to Haley, you know that?" he said to Carella.

"I know it."

"Which garages did you hit already?" Ollie asked.

"I've got the list," Hawes said.

" 'Cause this one is supposed to be right around the corner from the restaurant, near Jefferson."

"I thought we hit everything in a five-block radius," Hawes said.

"Yeah, well maybe you missed one, huh, Red?" Ollie said.

Hawes didn't like anyone to call him "Red." He preferred Lefty to Red. He preferred Great Bull Moose Farting to Red.

"My name's Cotton," he said mildly.

"That's a dumb name," Ollie said.

Hawes silently agreed with him.

"I think I'll call you 'Red,' " Ollie said.

"Okay," Hawes said. "And I'll call you 'Phyllis.' "

"Phyllis?" Ollie said. "Where'd you get Phyllis from? *Phyllis?* There's a space," he said to Carella.

"I see it," Carella said.

"In case you didn't," Ollie said. "Way you guys missed a garage right around the corner from the restaurant, who knows if you can see parking spaces or not?"

Carella pulled into the space. He threw down the visor with its attached notice that this was a police officer on a duty call, just in case some overzealous patrolman hadn't met his quota of parking tickets today. The three detectives got out of the car. Carella locked all the doors. He knew some cops from the Six-One who'd had their car stolen from the curb while they were inside a liquor store investigating an armed robbery.

"So where are we?" Ollie said. "Restaurant's on Ulster and South Haley, this is what?"

"Ulster and Bowes."

"So what we should do," Ollie said, "is go back to the restaurant, use that as our starting point. Then we go up to the corner closest to Jefferson and fan out left and right from there. He said right around the corner, didn't he? Near Jefferson?"

"That's what he said," Carella said. "But right around the corner could mean anything."

"What could right around the corner mean but right around the corner?" Ollie said. "Am I right, Red? Or am I right?"

Hawes winced.

"Ollie," he said, "I really don't like being called 'Red.'"

"So I'll call you 'Cotton,' will you like that better?"

"I would."

"Okay, okay. But if I had a dumb name like 'Cotton,' I'd prefer being called almost anything else, I got to tell you. Am I right, Steve-a-rino? Or am I right?"

Carella said nothing.

The detectives walked back to the restaurant.

"Fancy joint," Ollie commented. "Guy must have plenty of bread, he takes his victims here before he zonks them. Okay, now to the corner. You guys with me? I want to show you how to find a garage."

The garage was not right around the corner.

It was a block up from the corner, and then a half-block to the north, toward Jefferson Avenue. It was one of the garages Carella and Hawes had hit on the night of the Welles murder. They had spoken then to a little Puerto Rican parking attendant named Ricardo Albareda who could not remember seeing a young girl in a red dress with a man wearing a dark brown suit, a tan tie, and brown shoes. They had gone on to give Albareda the same description the waiter at Marino's had given Hawes: five feet ten or eleven, a hundred and seventy pounds, brown hair and brown eyes, a mustache. Albareda still couldn't remember the couple.

Albareda was on duty now. He explained that he usually worked the day shift, but that last night he'd been filling in for his friend who was home sick. He told the detectives that he didn't get home till two o'clock last night, and he had to be at work again at eight this morning. He told the detectives that he was very tired. He told them all this with a marked Spanish accent.

"Look, shithead," Ollie said reasonably, *"this* is the fuckin' garage, you unnerstan' English? *This* is where they were, and I want you to start rememberin' right away, or I'm gonna kick your little spic ass all around the block, you think you got that?"

"If I cann remember them, I cann remember them," Albareda said. He shrugged and looked at Carella.

"We questioned him fully last night," Carella said. "If the man can't remember them, then he can't re . . ."

"That was last night," Ollie said, "and this is today. And this is Detective Ollie Weeks," he said, turning to Albareda, "who don't take no for an answer unless somebody wants to be in serious trouble like for spitting on the sidewalk."

"I dinn spit on no si'walk," Albareda said.

"When I hit you in the mouth, shithead, you're gonna be spittin' blood and teeth on the sidewalk, and that's a misdemeanor."

"Look, Ollie . . ." Hawes said.

"Keep out of this, Red," Ollie said. "We're talkin' a quarter to ten, somewhere in there," he said to Albareda. "Young girl in a red dress, her picture's all over the newspaper today, she got *killed* last night, you unnerstan' that, shithead? With a guy twice her age, has a mustache like yours, okay, Pancho? Start rememberin'."

"I don' r'member nobody with a mustash like mine," Albareda said.

"How about a young girl in a red dress?"

"I don' r'member her."

"How many fuckin' girls in red dresses you get here at a quarter to ten? What were you doin', Albareda? Jerkin' off in the toilet with *Playboy,* you didn't notice a girl in a red dress?"

"We get lotsa girls they wearin' red," Albareda said defensively.

"At a quarter to ten last night? You had lots of girls wearing red?"

"No, not lass night. I'm juss sayin'."

"Who else was working here last night? Were you all alone, you dumb spic shithead?"

"There wass ony two of us. There wass s'pose to be t'ree, but . . ."

"Yeah, your amigo was home in bed suckin' his own dong. So who else was here?"

"Thass not why there wass two of us."

"Then why?"

" 'Cause *another* man s'pose to be here, an' *he* wass sick, too."

"A regular epidemic, huh? What're you all comin' down with, herpes? So who was the other guy with you?"

"Anìbal."

"Annabelle?"

"Anìbal. Anìbal Perez. He works all the time d'night shiff."

"The night *shiff,* huh, Pancho? You got his number?"

"*Sì,* I haff his number."

"Call him up. Tell him to get his ass down here in ten minutes flat or I'll go find him and hang *him* from a lamp-post."

"He lives all the way Majesta."

"Tell him to take a taxi. Or would he like a squad car pulling up in front of his house?"

"I'll call him," Albareda said.

Perez arrived some forty minutes later. He looked very bewildered. He glanced at Albareda for some clue as to what was going on, and then he looked at the one he figured to be the most sympathetic of the cops, a fat man like himself.

"Whass goin' on?" he asked.

"You here last night at a quarter to ten?"

"*Sí.*"

"Talk English," Ollie said, "this is America. You see my two friends here last night askin' questions?"

"No."

"He wass upstairs when they come aroun'," Albareda said.

"Very sloppy," Ollie said to Carella, "you didn't check to see there was more than one guy here. Okay, Pancho," he said to Perez, forgetting he'd been calling Albareda the same name, "*now* you're downstairs, and *now* we want to know did you see a young girl in a red dress last night about a quarter to ten with a guy about forty years old, brown hair and brown eyes, a mustache like your amigo here got."

"*Sí,*" Perez said.

"I tole you to talk English," Ollie said. "You saw them?"

"I saw them."

"Young girl nineteen years old? Red dress?"

"Yes."

"Guy about forty wearing a brown suit . . ."

"Yes."

"Okay, now we're getting someplace," Ollie said. "What kind of car was he driving?"

"I don' r'member," Perez said.

"You the one who got the car for them?"

"I'm the one, yes."

"So what kind of car was it?"

"I don' r'member. We get lots of cars here. I drive them up, I drive them down, how you 'speck me to r'member what kind of car this car or that car wass?"

"When you talk to me, you get that tone out of your voice, you hear me, Pancho?"

"Yes, sir," Perez said.

"That's better," Ollie said. "So you don't remember the car, huh?"

"No."

"Was it a big car, a little car, what kind of car was it?"

"I don' r'member."

"You're a great pair, you two fuckin' spics," Ollie said. "Where do you keep your receipts?"

"What?"

"Your receipts, your receipts, you want me to speak Spanish, or is this the United States?"

"Puerto Rico is also the United States," Perez said with dignity.

"That's what *you* think," Ollie said. "When a guy comes in to park his car, there's a ticket, right? You fill in the license plate number on both halves of the ticket, right? And you tear off the bottom part and you give that to the customer for when he comes back to claim his car, right? You followin' me so far? That's called a claim check, what you give the guy who parks his car. Okay, you throw the *top* part of the ticket in a box, and when the guy comes back with *his* half of the ticket, you match them up, and that's how you know what floor you parked his car on. So where do you keep them tickets, the receipts?"

"Oh," Perez said.

"Comes the dawn," Ollie said. "You got them receipts someplace?"

"In d'cashier's office. Lass night's tickets, you mean?"

"That's what we're talking about here, last night. You also stamp those tickets, don't you? With the time the guy came in, and the time the guy comes back to claim his car. Okay, I want to see every ticket for anybody came in around eight o'clock and left around a quarter to ten. Now that's easy, ain't it? In fact, that's what my friends here shoulda done last night, but better late than never, right? Show me the tickets.''

"The cashier hass them,'' Perez said. "In the office.''

The cashier was a black girl in her late twenties. She looked up when the detectives came into the small office. Ollie winked at Carella and then said, "Hello, sweetie.''

"I ain't *your* sweetie nor nobody else's,'' the girl said.

"You mean you ain't my little chocolate Tootsie Roll?''

"What *is* this?'' she said.

"Police officers, Miss,'' Hawes said, and showed her his shield. "We have reason to believe . . .''

"We want to see your ticket stubs for last night,'' Ollie said. "Anything that came in at eight, a little before eight, and left around a quarter to ten.''

"We don't file them that way,'' the girl said. "By time.''

"How *do* you file them?''

"By the numbers on the tickets.''

"Okay,'' Ollie said, "drag out all the tickets, we'll look through them ourselves.''

"Here?'' the girl said. "I got work to do here.''

"So do we,'' Ollie said.

The work took them close to two hours. They divided the tickets between them, isolated all those that had been stamped with an "in'' time of seven-thirty or later, and then went through these for any with an "out'' time between nine-forty-five and ten o'clock. They came up with three tickets and three license plate numbers.

One of the tickets was marked: Chev-38L4721.

The second was marked: Benz-604J29.

The third was marked: CadSav-WU3200.

"The rest is duck soup,'' Ollie said.

* * *

Eileen Burke did not like this job. First of all, she did not like being a woman other than herself. Next, she did not like living in another woman's apartment. And lastly, she did not like a masquerade that made it impossible for her to see Bert Kling. Annie had told her that she could not see Bert while she was posing as Mary Hollings. If the rapist spotted her in the company of a man he had not previously seen, he might just possibly smell a trap. This would not do. Eileen was the bait. If the rat sniffed anything rancid about the offered piece of cheese, he just might run for the hills.

Mary's apartment was done in what Eileen would have called Victorian cum Peter Lorre. That was to say it somewhat resembled Count Dracula's castle, lacking only its warmth. The walls throughout were painted a green that was the exact color to be found in any squadroom in the city. The rugs on the floors in the living room and bedroom were tattered Orientals that had known better snake charmers tootling their flutes upon them. The living room draperies resembled the ones Miss Haversham refused to open in *Great Expectations* although Eileen had to admit they were somewhat less dust-laden. And the clutter was unimaginable—even if it was Eileen's own.

The clutter was deliberate.

In the several days Eileen had spent in orientation with Mary before her departure for Long Beach, she had come to learn that the woman was a slob. Perhaps it had to do with having been divorced. Or perhaps it had to do with having been raped. Either way, it was unimaginable. On her first visit to the apartment, Eileen saw panties, slips, blouses, sweaters, and slacks piled in heaps on the floors, sofas, backs of chairs, shower curtain rods, and dresser tops. Socks and pantyhose and nylons like a horde of snakes whose backs had been broken. "I usually tidy up on Saturday or Sunday," Mary explained. "There's no sense trying to keep up with it during the week.'' Eileen had simply nodded. She'd been there to *learn* about the woman, not to criticize her. That first meeting had taken place on Wednesday morning, October 12. They had met again the next day, Eileen familiarizing herself with the apartment and with Mary's everyday routine. On the fourteenth, Mary left for California, leaving behind her what appeared to be the debris of a vast army of very unsanitary women. On Saturday, Eileen had cleaned up the mess.

That was five days ago.

The clothes that littered the apartment now were her own; she had carried them in over a period of days, usually in shopping bags lest anyone watching might become suspicious of suitcases. The dirty dishes in the sink were dishes she herself had used. But this was only Thursday, and Mary did not normally clean up the apartment until Saturday or Sunday. If someone was watching, Eileen wanted everything to look the same as it always did. *If* someone was watching. She could not be sure. She hoped he was. That's why she was here.

On the living room side—the one featuring Miss Haversham's fine musty drapes—the windows faced the street twelve stories below. Eileen had opened the drapes the moment she'd moved in, the better to be seen—*if* anyone was watching. It was easier to watch on the bedroom side of the apartment. The window there, covered with venetian blinds that hadn't been cleaned since Venice was but a mere trickle from a leaky water faucet, opened onto a wide areaway and a building some twenty feet opposite this one. Anyone behind any of the windows or on the roof could easily see into the apartment. Eileen hoped he had binoculars. Eileen hoped he was getting a good look, and she further hoped that he would make his move soon. On Saturday, she would pick up the clothing she had deliberately scattered all over the apartment and take it down to the washing machines in the basement. On

Sunday, she would start all over again with a clean slate, so to speak. But she didn't know how long she could go on living in the midst of all this disorder. Her own apartment, by comparison, was as spartan as a monk's cell.

She had complained to Kling about the mess not half an hour ago—on the telephone, of course. He had listened patiently. He had told her he hoped this job would be over soon. He had told her he missed her. He had asked how long Annie expected to keep her in that apartment, wearing another woman's nightgown to bed . . .

"I wear my own nightgown," Eileen had said.

"So suppose he's watching you?" Kling asked. "He sees a different nightgown, he figures 'Uh-oh, this is an imposter in there.' "

"Mary could have bought some *new* nightgowns," Eileen said. "All she does all morning long is shop, anyway. Until noon. Mary gets up at nine every morning and Mary takes two hours to shower and dress, is what Mary does. Don't ask me what takes Mary two hours to shower and dress. I've had the lieutenant call me at home on emergencies, and I was out of the place in ten minutes flat, fresh as a daisy and looking neat as a pin."

"To coin a couple of phrases," Kling said.

"Nobody likes a smart ass," Eileen said. "Anyway, Mary leaves her apartment at eleven o'clock every morning, and she shops until one. I was in four department stores this morning, Bert. I almost bought you a very sexy pair of undershorts."

"Why *almost?* An almost gift isn't a gift at all."

"I figured if he was watching me, he'd wonder why I was buying a pair of men's undershorts."

"Have you caught any glimpse of him yet?"

"No. But I have a feeling he's around."

"What kind of feeling?"

"Just a feeling, you know? While I was having lunch—Mary has lunch at one o'clock sharp every day—

every *weekday,* that is. On Saturdays, she doesn't set the alarm, she just sleeps as late as she likes. Sundays, too."

"Maybe I'll sneak over there on Sunday morning, pretend I'm the guy come to fix the plumbing or something."

"Good idea," Eileen said. "My plumbing can *use* some fixing, believe me. Anyway, while I was having lunch today . . ."

"Yeah, what happened?"

"I had a feeling he was there."

"In the restaurant?"

"Mary doesn't eat in restaurants. Mary eats in health food joints. I have had more damn bean sprouts in the past week . . ."

"But he was there, huh?"

"I don't *know.* I'm just saying it was a *feeling.* The place was full of mostly women, but there were maybe six guys in there and at least three of them could've been him. I mean, according to the description we got from the victims. White, thirty-ish, six feet tall, a hundred and eighty pounds, brown hair, blue eyes, no visible scars or tattoos."

"Could be anybody in the city."

"Don't I know it?"

There was a long silence on the line.

"I have a great idea," Kling said.

"About the rapist?"

"No, about us."

"Oh-*ho,*" she said.

"Want to hear it?"

"Sure."

"Why don't you go take a shower . . ."

"Uh-huh."

"And then put on your nightgown . . ."

"Uh-huh."

"And then get into your nice, warm bed . . ."

"*Mary's* bed, you mean."

"Mary's bed, right. And then I'll call you back. How does that sound?"

"I don't want to go to bed yet," Eileen said. "It's only ten o'clock."

"So? Mary gets up at nine o'clock every weekday morning, doesn't she? Besides, I didn't say you should go to *sleep*, I just said you should go to *bed*."

"Oh, I get it," Eileen said. "You want to make an obscene phone call, right?"

"Well, I wouldn't call it exactly *that*," Kling said.

"What *would* you call it exactly, you dirty old man?"

"Dirty, yes. Old, no. What do you say?"

"Sure, give me half an hour or so."

"Half an *hour*? Didn't you tell me you sometimes get calls from your lieutenant on emergencies or something and you're showered and dressed in ten minutes flat? What's gonna take you half an hour now?"

"If I'm gonna get an obscene phone call, I want to put on some perfume," Eileen said, and hung up.

She was in the shower when the phone rang again. She was surprised; it wasn't like Bert to call back five minutes after she'd asked him to give her a half-hour. She decided to let the phone ring. It kept ringing. And ringing. And ringing. She got out of the shower, wrapped a bath towel around herself, and went back into the bedroom—sidestepping the piles of debris she had littered all over the floor in an attempt at simulating Mary's lifestyle—and then went into the living room, where the phone was still ringing. She picked up the receiver.

"Hello?" she said.

"Eileen?"

A woman's voice.

"Yes?"

"This is Mary Hollings."

"Oh, hi," she said. "I'm sorry, I didn't recognize your voice."

"I'm not interrupting anything, am I?"

"I was just in the shower," Eileen said. "That's what took me so long to get to the phone. Are you calling from California?"

"Yes. This is an imposition, I know, but . . ."

"Not at all," Eileen said. "What is it?"

"Well . . . I'm supposed to pay my rent on the fifteenth of the month. And the thing is . . . I took my small checkbook out here to pay any bills that were forwarded . . ."

"You asked the post office to forward your mail?" Eileen asked at once.

"Well . . . yes."

There was a silence on the line.

"Did I do something wrong?" Mary asked.

"No, no, that's fine," Eileen said.

She didn't think it was so fine. Every morning, as part of the routine Mary had described to her, she'd gone down to the mailbox, surprised to find only third class mail—magazines, solicitations, and so on. No first class mail. This had seemed odd to her; even if no friends or relatives ever sent Mary a letter, there surely should have been bills. Now she had the answer. Mary had asked the post office to forward her mail to Long Beach, undoubtedly specifying that the order applied to first class mail only. But if the rapist had been watching Mary before she'd gone to California, would he have seen her when she went to the post office? And if he'd followed her inside, would he have seen her filling out a CHANGE OF ADDRESS card? And if so, did he now know that the woman living in Mary Hollings's apartment wasn't Mary Hollings at all? Eileen didn't like it one damn bit. The silence on the phone lengthened.

At last, Mary said, "I thought I'd paid the rent before I left. I usually try to pay it two or three days before it's due. I send it to this company that manages the building, they're called Reynolds Realty, Inc."

"Uh-huh," Eileen said.

"But I took only my *small* checkbook out here, the one I usually carry in my handbag . . ."

"Uh-huh."

"And what I normally do is I pay the rent from the *big* checkbook. The one with three checks on a page, do you know the kind I mean?"

"Uh-huh," Eileen said.

"So I have no way of checking," Mary said, "on whether I paid the rent or not. I wouldn't want to come home and discover I've been dispossessed or something."

"So . . . uh . . . what is it?" Eileen said.

"I wonder if you'd do me a favor."

"Sure."

"You're in the living room, aren't you? That's where the phone is, so that's where I guess you are."

"That's where I am," Eileen said.

Dripping all over your Oriental rug, she thought, but did not say.

"Well, in the desk where the phone is . . ."

"Uh-huh."

"The bottom drawer on the righthand side . . ."

"Uh-huh."

"There's my *big* checkbook. The one I didn't take out here. Because I figured I could pay any forwarded bills from my *small* checkbook."

"Okay," Eileen said.

"Would you mind terribly looking at the checkbook, the *big* one, and seeing if I paid the rent? If I paid it, it would be around October twelfth or thirteenth, sometime around then. Could you please look?"

"Sure, just a sec," Eileen said.

She opened the bottom drawer on the righthand side of the desk, rummaged around under some folders and loose sheets of paper and found the checkbook.

"I've got it," she said, "let me take a look."

She pulled the chair out from the kneehole, sat, turned on the desklamp, and opened the checkbook.

"October twelfth or thirteenth," she said.

"Around then," Mary said.

"October seventh," she said aloud, turning the pages of stubs in the binder, "October ninth . . . what was the name of the place again?"

"Reynolds Realty, Inc."

"October eleventh," Eileen said, "October . . . here it is. October twelfth, Reynolds Realty, Inc., six hundred and fourteen dollars. The stub is marked 'Rent due 10/15.' I guess you paid it, Mary."

"What a relief," Mary said. "I really was worried that they'd change the lock on the door or something. I'd get home and find . . ." She hesitated. "When do you think that'll be?" she asked. "My coming home, I mean. Have you had any luck yet?"

"Not a nibble," Eileen said.

"Because . . . my sister's a lovely person, and she's very happy to see me and all . . . but I've been here almost a week now . . ."

"Yes, I know."

"And I have the feeling I'm overstaying my welcome a bit."

"Uh-huh."

"Not that she's *said* anything to me . . ."

"I understand."

"But you begin to sense things, you know?"

"Yes."

"So . . . when do you think you'll be finished there? I mean, how long will you keep doing this? If he doesn't show up, I mean."

"I'll have to discuss that with Detective Rawles," Eileen said. "I don't know how long she plans to keep the job running. Can I get back to you sometime tomorrow?"

"Oh sure, there's no rush. I mean, my sister isn't

throwing me out into the street or anything. I was just wondering, that's all.''

"I'll try to find out. And I'll get back to you.''

"You have the number here in Long Beach, don't you?''

"Yes, you gave it to me.''

"Well,'' Mary said. "Good luck.''

"Thank you.''

"Goodbye now.''

"Goodbye, Mary.''

There was a click on the line. Eileen replaced the receiver on its cradle, and looked at her watch. If she didn't hurry, she'd miss the first obscene phone call she'd ever had in her life. She was heading back for the bedroom when the phone rang again. She looked at her watch again. Bert? Fifteen minutes early? Mary again, asking her to look up something *else* in the checkbook? She went back to the desk and lifted the receiver.

"Hello?''

"Eileen?''

She recognized the voice at once.

"Hello, Annie,'' she said, "how are you?''

"The question is how're *you?*''

"Surviving,'' Eileen said. "What's up?''

"Have you got a minute?''

"Barely,'' she said, and looked at her watch again.

"Oh?'' Annie said. "Plans for tonight?''

"Sort of,'' Eileen said.

She did not think it wise to explain to Detective First/Grade Anne Rawles exactly what those plans were. The plans, in fact, were somewhat vague in her own mind. But she had read books, ah yes, she had read books. All sorts of fantasies were dancing through her head.

"You going out or something?'' Annie asked.

"No, not tonight. I was out *last* night. I went to a movie.''

"Any sign of him?"

"No."

"Were you alone?"

"As alone as anyone can be," Eileen said.

"I'm sorry about that, but . . ."

"Sure, don't sweat it. I just got a call from Mary Hollings, she . . ."

"From California?"

"Yeah. She wants to know when I'll be getting out of here."

"Maybe sooner than you think," Annie said.

"You calling off the job?"

"No."

"Then what?"

"I've got some stuff that might interest you," Annie said and began telling her about the pattern she'd detected while working on the computer printouts. Eileen looked at her watch. Automatically, she moved a pad into place before her on the desk and began taking notes as Annie told her about the four-week, three-week, two-week cycle. As she continued listening, she jotted down the dates on which Mary Hollings had been raped: June 10, September 16, and October 7.

"That doesn't jibe," she said. "There's a long gap between June and September."

"Yeah, but if you count off the weeks—have you got a calendar there?"

"Just a sec," Eileen said, and turned to the front page of Mary's checkbook. "Yeah, go ahead."

"Just count out the weeks with me," Annie said. "First rape, June tenth. Four weeks after that, July eighth. Three weeks after that, July twenty-ninth . . . are you following me?"

"Yeah?" Eileen said, puzzled.

"Okay. Two weeks after that, August twelfth. A week after that, August nineteenth. End of cycle. You beginning to see it?"

"Not yet."

"Then stay with me. Four weeks after August nineteenth was September sixteenth . . . have you got those dates I gave you for the Hollings rapes?"

"Yes. September sixteenth, right, here it is."

"Right. And when's the next one?"

"October seventh."

"Exactly three weeks later," Annie said. "And what's two weeks after that?"

"October twenty-first."

"Tomorrow," Annie said.

"So you think . . ."

"I think . . . look, who knows *how* this creep's mind is working? There may not be a pattern at all, this may all be coincidence. But if there *is* a pattern, then Mary Hollings is the only victim he's hit on Fridays and tomorrow's Friday, and it happens to be two weeks from the *last* time she was raped."

"Yeah," Eileen said.

"What I'm saying . . ."

"I got it."

"I'm saying be careful tomorrow."

"Thanks."

"You think you might need a backup on this?"

"We might spook him. I'll chance it alone."

"Eileen . . . really. Be *very* careful."

"Okay."

"He has a knife."

"I know."

"He's used it before . . ."

"I know."

"So watch your step. He pulls that knife, don't ask questions, just blow him away."

"Okay." She hesitated. "When do you think he'll make his move?" she asked.

"It's always been at night," Annie said.

"So I got all day tomorrow to shop, and eat lunch in

health food joints, and go to the museum or whatever, right?''

Annie laughed, and then sobered immediately.

''While you're doing all that,'' she said, ''keep an eye out for him. If he's going to hit tomorrow night, he may be tracking you.''

''Okay.''

''You sure you don't want a backup?''

Eileen wasn't sure. But she said, ''I don't want to lose him.''

''I'm not talking about *men*. We can throw a couple of lady cops in there.''

''He might smell them. We're too close now, Annie.''

''Okay. But remember what I said. If he pulls that . . .''

''I've got it all.'' She looked at her watch again. ''That it?''

''Good luck,'' Annie said, and hung up.

Two good lucks in the same night, Eileen thought as she put the receiver back on the cradle. I'm going to need it, that's for damn sure. It was almost ten-thirty. If Bert was nothing else, he was punctual. She went back into the bedroom, debating putting on a nightgown, and decided on a pair of panties instead. She was about to draw the blinds when the telephone rang again. She went back into the living room, and picked up the receiver.

''Hello?'' she said.

''Honey, it's me,'' Kling said.

''Yes, Bert. I was just about to . . .''

''Listen, I'm sorry, but we got some names and addresses from Motor Vehicles on these hangings. The loot just phoned me, he wants us to hit them in three teams.''

''Oh,'' Eileen said.

''So . . . uh . . . it'll have to wait, I guess.''

''Yeah, I guess so,'' Eileen said.

''Maybe tomorrow night,'' Kling said.

''Maybe.''

''I gotta run, Meyer's picking me up in five minutes.''

"Okay, darling. Be careful."

"You, too."

There was a click on the line. Eileen hung up and walked back into the bedroom. As she was reaching for the hanging cords on the venetian blinds, it suddenly occurred to her that Bert's idea wouldn't have worked, anyway, there wasn't a phone in the bedroom.

Sighing, she pulled the blinds shut.

From where he crouched behind the parapet of the roof opposite, binoculars to his eyes, he saw the blinds closing, his view into the bedroom suddenly replaced by a rectangle of light as impenetrable as a brick wall.

He'd been watching her ever since nightfall. Would have preferred following her all day long, but that was impossible. He wasn't free until four, sometimes five, each afternoon. Even getting away at night was difficult, the excuses he had to make. Didn't want to be away on *too* many nights because the nights dictated by the calendar had to be absolutely certain ones. Whatever else happened to fall on these nights, he'd say no, sorry I have to be someplace else. Here, there, anywhere. His excuses were bought. Not always without question, but always bought in the long run. He was a determined person. People had learned a long time ago that there was no sense trying to argue him out of any position he'd taken.

Mary Hollings should have learned that by now. Three times already. Tomorrow night would be the fourth time. Four should be enough, but five was better. If you could catch them five times, you were reasonably certain you had them right where you wanted them. He debated whether he should try going into her apartment again tomorrow night. Probably not. Too risky. Almost fell off the damn fire escape last time, lost his footing as he was climbing up, too risky. Left by the front door afterward, a lot safer, ran down the stairs, came out onto the street, hung around until he saw the police car arriving, knew she would call the police, she had each and every time.

Tomorrow night, he'd try to catch her on the street. Unless she didn't go out. She'd gone to a movie last night, walked home afterward, perfect time to have caught her again, but he preferred doing it by the calendar. Too careless the other way. If you had a plan, you should follow it. Anyway, there were too many of them now. If you didn't follow the calendar, you could lose track of which one was due, and then the whole plan would be screwed up. Even if opportunity seemed to present itself, as it had last night, it was better to show restraint and follow the dictates of the calendar.

Very busy tonight, Ms. Mary Hollings.

Strutting around the apartment as if she was *looking* for it to happen. Maybe she was. Damn hypocrites, all of them. All wanted the same thing, but pretended they were doing it for other reasons. Tried to sanitize the act by giving it loftier meaning. Tried to impose that meaning upon others. Denied the sex act itself as a means to an end. Never mind what they *really* felt about sex, never mind the little acts they did in private when he was watching them, forget all that. Pure in their minds, oh yes, but in their hearts—

The heart was quite another matter. The heart and the slit between the legs. Never mind what cause was being propounded in the head. The heart and the slit were what *really* governed them. Mary Hollings tonight. Stripping naked with the blinds open. Building here how many feet across the areaway? Anyone could have been watching. Wouldn't even *need* binoculars to see what she was advertising, red hair and red bush, tits like melons. Ms. Mary Hollings who advocated a policy that denied sexuality in favor of *femaleness*, the same *femaleness* shared by any beast of the field. Dashed past the open blinds wearing nothing but a towel later on. Came back into the bedroom and put on a pair of panties. Stood admiring herself at the mirror, the blinds still open. Left the bedroom again to go into the living room—he knew the layout of the apartment, he'd been in there.

In *her,* too.

Three times.

Tomorrow night would be number four for Ms. Mary Hollings.

Tomorrow night.

would've hijacked tomorrow without knowing there was a
```
...
```
tickets at the garage, without which nobody from MVB

10

ON THE NIGHT OF DARCY WELLES'S MURDER, three men had parked automobiles between the hours of eight and ten in the garage around the corner from Marino's restaurant. Lieutenant Byrnes decided it would be best to hit all three tonight. If one of them was a murderer, tomorrow couldn't come soon enough. But even if all three were clean, the chances of catching them at home tonight seemed better than waiting till morning. Tomorrow was Friday, a work day. If these men held jobs, a visit to their homes in the morning would net three zeros. Questions would have to be asked of whoever opened the door, and further visits would have to be made to their places of work. Better to do it tonight; the early bird catches the worm, and besides he who hesitates is lost. So went the lieutenant's reasoning.

Five of the detectives working the three teams would have preferred staying home in bed rather than chasing all over the city after a man who only *maybe* was the actual perpetrator. "Perpetrator" was the word Ollie Weeks used. He was the sixth detective making up the three teams of two men each, and he much preferred being out in the city on a hunt than staying home in an apartment even *he* admitted was seedy. Lieutenant Byrnes wasn't too sure about the protocol of allowing Ollie to participate in a potential bust. Ollie argued that the third stiff had been found up in the Eighty-third, hadn't she, and so he had every right to go along. "Besides," he pointed out subtly, "I was the one got them fuckin' tickets at the garage, without which nobody from MVB would've been able to come up with these names and addresses, so let's cut the shit, okay, Loot?''

The men set off for different parts of the city at approximately ten-thirty. Carella got lucky; he was teamed with Ollie Weeks. He rolled his eyes heavenward as they went downstairs to check out an unmarked sedan. Ollie was dressed rather nattily for Ollie. He was wearing a plaid mackinaw and a deerstalker hat; the weather, so mild until now, had turned raw when the sun sank below the horizon; the October honeymoon seemed to be over. Carella, still wearing what he'd put on this morning, felt a little chilly, and he hoped the sedan was one with a working heater. It wasn't.

The owner of the Mercedes-Benz with the 604J29 license plate number lived not ten minutes away from the station house. His name was Henry Lytell.

"That name sounds familiar," Ollie said. He was driving. Carella was leaning over beside him, banging on the heater with the heel of his hand, trying to get it to work. "Don't that sound familiar to you? Henry Lytell?"

"No, it doesn't," Carella said. "Okay, I give up, the hell with it!"

"You guys oughta get some new cars," Ollie said.

Carella grunted, pulled up the collar on his sports jacket, and tried to hunch down into it.

"What I do," Ollie said, "I always keep extra gear in the trunk of my car, case it turns cold, or starts rainin' or somethin', this city."

"Um," Carella said.

"What we shoulda done, we shoulda taken *my* car 'steada this beat-up shebang. Up in the Eight-Three, we got brand new cars—Mercurys and Fords. The lieutenant comes out back everytime we bring one in, makes sure we didn't put a scratch on it. We know how to live up in the Eight-Three. That name sounds very familiar, Henry Lytell. Ain't he an actor or something?''

"It doesn't ring a bell," Carella said.

"Lytell, Lytell, I'm sure that's somebody's name," Ollie said.

Carella did not mention that since Lytell *was* somebody's name, then it *had* to be somebody's name. Carella was thinking he should have worn his long johns to work this morning.

"It's the Henry throws me," Ollie said. "What's the address again?"

"843 Holmes."

"Like Sherlock."

"The same."

"We hit paydirt, we share the collar, that clear?" Ollie said. "Credit goes to *both* precincts."

"You bucking for Commissioner?" Carella said.

"I'm happy with what I am," Ollie said. "But fair is fair."

"Aren't you cold in here?" Carella said.

"Me? No. You cold?"

"Yes."

"It's supposed to rain," Ollie said.

"Will that make it warmer?"

"I'm only saying."

They were silent for several moments.

"Did Meyer mention what I said about 'Hill Street Blues'?" Ollie asked.

"No," Carella said.

"About suing 'Hill Street Blues'?"

"No, he didn't. Who's suing 'Hill Street Blues'?"

"I think you and me should sue them."

"Why?"

"Don't you think Furillo sounds like Carella?"

"No," Carella said.

"Don't you think *Charlie* Weeks sounds like *Ollie* Weeks?"

"No."

"You don't?"

"No. Charlie Weeks sounds like Charlie Weeks."

"To me, they sound almost like the same name."

"The way *Howard* Hunter sounds like *Evan* Hunter."

"That ain't the same at all."

"Or the way *Arthur* Hitler sounds like *Adolph* Hitler."

"Now you're making a joke of it," Ollie said. "Anyway, I'll bet there ain't a single person in the whole world named Hitler nowadays. Not even in Germany is there a kraut named Hitler. Everybody named Hitler already changed his name to something else."

"So why don't you change your name to something else? If Charlie Weeks is bothering you, change your name to Ollie *Jones* or something."

"Why don't Charlie Weeks change *his* name to something else?" Ollie said. "Why don't *Furillo* change his name to something else?"

"I don't see any connection between Furillo and Carella," Carella said.

"Why you so irritated tonight?"

"I'm not irritated, I'm cold."

"We're about to make a collar, and the man is irritated."

"You don't *know* we're about to make a collar," Carella said.

"I feel it in my bones," Ollie said. "Here we are."

He double-parked alongside a station wagon parked at the curb in front of Henry Lytell's building. The building was a six-story brick, no doorman. They went into the small entrance alcove and checked out the mailboxes.

"Lytell, H.," Ollie said. "Apartment 6B. Top floor. I hope there's an elevator. Don't that name sound familiar to you? Lytell?"

"No," Carella said. It was as cold in the entrance alcove as it had been in the car, the kind of damp, penetrating cold that surely promised rain.

Ollie rang the bell button in the panel set alongside the

mailboxes. He kept leaning on the button. There was no answering buzz on the inner door.

"You suppose there's a super in this dump?" he asked, checking the bell-button panel. "No such luck," he said, and pressed the button opposite the name Nakura, for apartment 5A. An answering buzz sounded at the inner door. Ollie grabbed for the knob and pushed the door open.

"Thank God for small favors," he said, walking toward the small elevator at the back of the hall. He pressed the call button. The detectives waited. "These old buildings," Ollie said, "the elevators're as slow as a nigger in August."

"I have some advice for you," Carella said.

"Yeah, what's that?"

"Don't ever get yourself partnered with Arthur Brown."

"Why? Oh, you mean what I just said? That was a figure of speech."

"Brown might not think so."

"Sure, he would," Ollie said, "he's got a good sense of humor, Brown. What's wrong with what I just said, anyway? It's a figure of speech."

"I don't like your figures of speech," Carella said.

"Come on, come on," Ollie said, and patted him on the back. "Don't be so irritated tonight, Steve-a-rino. We're about to make a collar."

"And please don't call me Steve-a-rino."

"What should I call you? Furillo? You want me to call you Furillo?"

"My name is Steve."

"Furillo's name is *Frank*. The sergeant there, he calls him 'Francis' all the time. Maybe I'll call you Stephen. Would you like me to call you 'Stephen,' Stephen?"

"I would like you to call me Steve."

"Okay, Steve. You like 'Hill Street Blues,' Steve?"

"I don't like cop shows," Carella said.

"Where the fuck's the elevator?" Ollie said.

"You want to walk up?"

"Six flights? No way."

The elevator finally got there. The men entered. Ollie pressed the button for the sixth floor. The doors closed.

"Speed this thing makes, we'll be up there next Tuesday," Ollie said.

On the sixth floor, they found apartment 6B on the wall opposite the elevator, two doors down.

"Better flank it," Ollie said. "Lytell may be the one likes to break necks."

His pistol was already in his right hand.

They flanked the door, Carella on the left, Ollie on the right. Ollie pressed the doorbell button. They heard chimes sounding inside. Nothing else. Ollie pressed the button again. More chimes. He put his ear to the wood, listening. Nothing.

"Quiet as a graveyard," he said. "Back away, Steve."

"What for?"

"I'm gonna kick it in."

"You can't do that, Ollie."

"Who says?" Ollie said, and raised his right knee.

"Ollie . . ."

Ollie's leg pistoned out in a flat-footed kick at the lock. The lock sprang, the door flew inward. The apartment beyond was dark.

"Anybody home?" Ollie said, and moved into the apartment in a policeman's crouch, fanning the air ahead of him with his pistol. "Get the light," he said to Carella.

Carella felt for a light switch on the wall inside the door. He found it, and snapped it upward.

"Police!" Ollie shouted, apparently to no one. "Cover me," he said to Carella and moved deeper in the apartment. Carella kept his pistol leveled on the area in front of Ollie. What the hell am I *doing?* he thought. This is *illegal*. Ollie snapped on the living room light. The room was empty. On one wall there was an oversized oil painting of a male runner in jersey and shorts, the number ten on the front of the jersey, the man taking long strides, legs reaching, arms pumping. It looked like a knockoff of the paintings that guy did for *Playboy* magazine, Carella couldn't remember his name. There were doors on either side of the living room, both of them closed. Without a word, the detectives fanned out, Ollie taking the door on the right, Carella the one on the left. Both rooms were bedrooms and nobody was in either of them.

"Let's toss the joint," Ollie said.

"No," Carella said.

"Why not?"

"We shouldn't even be *in* here," he said, and thought at once of the patient who asked his psychiatrist to give him a farewell kiss on his final visit to the office. The psychiatrist said, *"Kiss* you? I shouldn't even be lying here on the *couch* with you."

"But we *are* in here," Ollie said. "You can *see* we're in here, can't you?"

"Illegally," Carella said.

"Steve, Steve," Ollie said paternally, shaking his head. "Let me tell you a little fairytale, do you like fairytales, Steve?"

"Ollie, do you know you're fooling around with the Poi . . ."

"Listen to my fairytale, okay?" Ollie said. "Two honest, hardworking cops go out one night to check on a possible suspect. They get to the suspect's apartment—which happens to be this very apartment we are now standing in—and guess what they find? They find that some burglar has already broken into the place and made a fuckin' shambles of it. Like the good, honest, hardworking cops they are, they report the burglary to the local precinct—what*ever* the fuck precinct this is—and then they go on their merry way. How does that sound to you, Steve? Or don't you like fairytales?''

"I love fairytales," Carella said. "Here's one for you, okay? It's called the Poison Tree, and it . . .''

"Ah, yes, m'boy, the Poison Tree," Ollie said, falling into his world-famous W.C. Fields imitation. "The Poison Tree, yes, yes, sounds vaguely familiar.''

"The Poison Tree is about a cop who failed to follow legal guidelines before searching for an icepick in a sewer. The cop searched around in the sewer muck, and he found this bloody icepick, and a good suspect's fingerprints were all over it, but the cop's information about that icepick had been obtained illegally, Ollie, and the D.A. told him it was the fruit of the poison tree, and the case got kicked out of court, and the murderer is probably using that same icepick on a hundred other people right this minute. The Poison Tree Doctrine, Ollie. How long have you been a cop, Ollie?''

"Ah, yes, the Poison Tree Doctrine," Ollie said, still being W.C. Fields.

"We are in here without a warrant," Carella said, "we have broken down a citizen's door, and we are in here illegally. Which means that any evidence we find in here . . .''

"I see your point, m'boy," Ollie said. "Would it disturb you overly, however, if I snooped around a bit? Without touching anything?''

"Ollie . . .''

"Because that's what I'm *gonna* do," Ollie said in his own voice, "even if it disturbs the shit out of you. We're here to see if this guy has any connection with the murders. If he *does* . . .''

"We're here to find out if this guy *parked* his car . . .''

"We already *know* that! That ain't why we're here, Steve.''

"We're here to *talk* to the man!''

"Well, the man ain't here, is he? Do you see the man here? So who do we talk to? The four walls?"

"We talk to a magistrate about getting a search warrant. That's the proper . . ."

"No, we talk to the man's *appointment* calendar to see where he is tonight, and then we go *find* the man, and we talk to him *personally*."

"And when a judge . . ."

"A judge ain't gonna know we talked to the man's appointment calendar, is he? I already told you, Steve, when we got here we walked in on a 10–21, and that's what I'm gonna call in before we walk out of here. In the meantime, I'm gonna look through the man's desk and see if he kept an appointment calendar."

Carella watched as Ollie walked to the desk across the room and opened the top drawer.

"See?" Ollie said. "Easy. The man is making it easy for us."

He turned from the desk, and showed Carella an appointment calendar.

"Now what we do," Ollie said, "is open the calendar to October . . . like this."

He opened the calendar.

"And we look for October twentieth, which is today's date . . . well, well, take a look at this, Steve. This is a very talkative calendar, the man has here."

Carella looked.

For October sixth, the night Marcia Schaffer was killed, Lytell had written her name into his calendar, and beneath that the name of her school, Ramsey University. For October thirteenth, he had written in "Nancy Annunziato" and then "Marino's." For last night, he had put down Darcy Welles's name and "Marino's" again.

"You seeing all this?" Ollie asked.

"I'm seeing it."

"You see what he's got written down for tonight?"

For tonight, Lytell had written the name "Luella Scott" and—

"Six to five, she's a nigger," Ollie said.

—and the word "Folger" which could only stand for Folger University, up in Riverhead.

Ollie closed the appointment calendar.

"Should take us half an hour to get there, twenty minutes if we hit the hammer," he said. "Let me call in this burglary we discovered, and then let's get the fuck out of here—before he breaks *her* neck, too."

It was always Arthur Brown's luck to catch Diamondback.

Anytime he had to go anyplace outside the precinct, he seemed to catch Diamondback. He figured it was departmental policy. Send all your black cops up to black Diamondback whenever they had to leave the confines of the Eight-Seven.

It was difficult for a black cop up here in Diamondback. A lot of the black people up here, they weren't exactly on the side of law and order, and when they saw a black cop coming around they figured he was a traitor to the cause. Brown didn't know *what* cause. He guessed that all the honest cab drivers, clergymen, salesclerks, letter carriers, stenographers, secretaries, and other hard-working people up here also wondered what cause the pimps, pushers, prostitutes, numbers runners, burglars, armed robbers, and petty thieves felt a cop like Arthur Brown was betraying. The only cause *he* respected was the one that told you to be the best possible person you *could* be in a world gone rotten. Diamondback was the world as rotten as it could ever get. He wouldn't live up here in Diamondback even if he was some guy cleaning out toilets for a living—which was what he sometimes felt he actually *did* for a living.

He had noticed over the years that not too many black lawyers, doctors, engineers, or architects lived up here in

Diamondback—not in *this* part of Diamondback, anyway. If any black who'd made it decided to live in Diamondback at *all*, it was in the fringe area known as Sweetloaf. If Arthur Brown had to live in Diamondback, he guessed he would want to live in Sweetloaf. The only trouble with Sweetloaf was that the population there was entirely black. Brown felt there was something very wrong about the population of *anyplace* being entirely *anything*. Except maybe the population of China. But even that troubled him a little. How did those people over there in China manage to get through a day without seeing anybody who had blond hair and blue eyes? Didn't it get boring just seeing everybody walking around with black hair and brown eyes? Brown was glad he didn't live in China. He was also glad he didn't live in Diamondback. But here he was again, ten minutes to eleven and smack in the heart of Diamondback, talking to a man who owned a Cadillac Seville with the license plate WU3200.

Both he and Hawes had known the minute the MVB came back with an address in Diamondback that this probably wasn't their man. The waiter at Marino's had described the guy with Darcy Welles as white. There were some white people living up here, Brown guessed, but they were few and far between. So the odds were at least a hundred to one that the guy who answered the door for them would be black (which he was) and the odds on a black man up here driving a brand new Cadillac Seville were at least a thousand to one that he was either dealing dope or hustling broads.

Willy Bartlett was hustling broads.

They spent exactly five minutes with him while he told them he was downtown last night dropping off a "girlfriend" of his, and they knew they were wasting even those five minutes because he was the wrong color to begin with.

Then again, Brown thought, maybe every black man in this *city* is the wrong color to begin with.

* * *

Eileen Burke couldn't sleep.

It was eleven o'clock, and she had already set Mary's alarm for 9:00 A.M., which meant that if she could manage to get to sleep without thinking of all sorts of things, she would get ten hours sleep before the alarm went off. That was a lot of sleep. Whenever she was in Bert's bed, or vice versa, she averaged six hours a night—if she was lucky. Tonight, she was in Mary's bed, and she couldn't sleep, and she guessed it was because she had so many things to think about. One of those things was Bert out there knocking on a door that maybe had a killer behind it. Another thing was the possibility that the rapist would come knocking on *her* door—*Mary's* door—tomorrow night sometime. Neither of the thoughts were conducive to sleep.

It was too bad Bert had to go out tonight. Whatever he'd planned for them to do on the telephone, Eileen was positive it would have put her in a good mood for sleeping afterward. If tomorrow night *really* came down the way Annie expected it would, then Eileen would need a good night's sleep tonight. The trouble was, thinking about tomorrow night made it very difficult to fall asleep tonight. Eileen kept wondering if Annie had got those dates right. Or if any of that four-week, three-week, and so-on jazz made any sense at all. What I *should* do, she thought, is get up and look at the calendar again. Instead of lying here worrying about whether tomorrow night's really going to be the night at all.

She snapped on the light beside the bed, threw the covers back, and swung her legs down to the floor. It was very cold in the apartment—that was October for you. Nice one day, freeze your ass off the next. She put on her robe and then worked her way around the piles of dirty laundry on the floor (I'll wash all these on Saturday morning, she thought), went to the bedroom door and reached beyond it for the living room light switch.

At the desk, she turned on the small lamp, and opened the top drawer, hoping to find a calendar that was larger and easier to read than the one at the front of Mary's checkbook—the *big* one, as Mary had called it. She found nothing but a little plastic calendar with a dry cleaner's name and phone number on it, the kind you tuck into a wallet. Besides, it was *last* year's calendar. She opened the bottom drawer on the right-hand side of the desk, fished out the checkbook again, and turned to the front of it.

The notes she had made while talking to Annie were still on the desk. She began ticking off the dates on the calendar, counting off the weeks. Well, Annie seemed to be right. Even allowing for the summer hiatus (how come no rapes in July and August, she wondered?) the pattern seemed clear. Tomorrow was Friday the twenty-first, and if their man acted as they expected he would, Mary Hollings was due for another visit. Out of curiosity, Eileen began leafing through the checkbook, locating the stubs for the checks Mary had written on the days she'd been raped.

June 10. Heavy activity, lots of bills to pay, all those shopping excursions Mary makes every day. Department stores all over the city, telephone company, electric company—Eileen counted ten checks written on that day alone. She flipped forward to September 16.

Equally heavy there, this lady sure ran up bills, those alimony checks had to be pretty hefty. A check made out to Reynolds Realty, Inc. (little late last month, huh, Mary? Your rent's due on the fifteenth), another to a play subscription series at a theater down in the Quarter, another to an organization called A.I.M. (marked CONTRIBUTION), a stub for a check written to Albert Cleaners (the people who'd provided her with last year's pocket size calendar), another stub for a check made out to Citizens Savings Bank (marked RENEWAL—SAFETY DEPOSIT

BOX), a check to American Express, another to Visa, and that was it.

What the hell is A.I.M.? Eileen wondered. Sounds like an organization supporting a citizen's right to bear arms. Ready, aim, fire. Was Mary a gun nut? Terrific. Support your local gun group and make life easier for all the cheap thieves in the world. A.I.M. Association of International Murderers? Allied Independent Maniacs? Am I Macho?

Eileen shrugged.

On October 7, Mary had written only six checks, two of them to department stores in the city (naturally), one to the Bowler Art Museum (again marked CONTRIBUTION), another to Raucher TV-Radio Repair, one for $5.75 made payable to Lombino's Best Pizza (had she sent out for a pizza that night? And paid the delivery boy with a check?), and the last for a whopping $1,650 made payable to someone named Howard Moscowitz. The stub was marked LEGAL FEES.

So what's A.I.M.? Eileen thought.

She hated mysteries.

She flipped back to the beginning of the checkbook. Maybe Mary had made a previous donation to A.I.M. And maybe she had written on the stub its full and doubtlessly honorable name. Amalgamated Indolent Masochists perhaps? Or Academy of Islamic Mosques? Or how about Avoid Intolerant Males? Or Are Iguanas Mammals?

Mary had made three contributions to A.I.M. during the past year. A hundred dollars in January. Fifty dollars in March. And a final fifty dollars on September 16, the second time she'd been raped. Undoubtedly in response to quarterly solicitations. There was no clue on the stubs as to what the acronym (if indeed it was one) stood for. Each was marked simply A.I.M.—CONTRIBUTION.

Eileen yawned.

This was better than counting sheep.

The Isola telephone directory was resting on the desk
alongside the phone. She pulled it to her, flipped it open
to the A listings, and began running her finger down the
page:

> A-I Bookshops, Inc. . . .
> A-I Systems . . .
> AIC Investigations . . .
> AID Photo . . .
> AIG, Ltd. . . . .
> AIHL Dental Labs . . .
> A.I.M. . . .

There it is, she thought, and copied the information on
a sheet of paper:

> A.I.M.
> 832 Hall Avenue
> 388-7400

Right here in the city, she thought. Maybe I ought to
ask Annie to check on it. Three contributions to the same
outfit. Might be important.

She yawned again.

She turned off the desk lamp, turned off the living
room light, and went back into the bedroom. She put her
robe at the foot of the bed, got under the covers, and lay
thinking for a moment. A.I.M. Sleep, she thought? Go to
sleep. Come on, Morpheus, where are you? A.I.M. Anyone Inviting Morpheus? The ayes have it. She reached up
to turn off the bedside lamp.

The clock read ten minutes past eleven.

The owner of the Chevy Citation with the license plate
number 38L4721 lived in Majesta. It took Meyer and
Kling forty minutes to get there from the squadroom.
Kling looked at his watch as they were parking the car

outside the housing development in which Frederick
Sagel lived. Twelve minutes past eleven. It was seventeen minutes past eleven by the time they knocked on his
third-floor apartment. A woman's voice yelled, "Who's
there?" She sounded alarmed. In this city, a knock on the
door at anytime past ten—when you were supposed to
know where your children were—could be considered
ominous.

"Police," Meyer said. He was weary; it had been a
long day. He did not want to be out here knocking on
anybody's door, especially if a murderer happened to be
behind it.

"Who?" the woman asked incredulously.

"Police," Meyer repeated.

"Well . . . just a minute, okay?" she said. Kling put
his ear to the door. He heard the woman say, in a sort of
stage whisper, "Freddie, it's the cops," and then a
man—presumably Freddie, who was also presumably
Frederick Sagel—said, *"What?"*

"The cops, the cops," the woman said impatiently.

"Well, Jesus, let me put something on," Sagel said.

"He's getting dressed," Kling said to Meyer.

"Um," Meyer said.

Sagel—if this *was* Sagel—was wearing a robe over pajamas when he opened the door. He was about twenty-
five years old, Meyer guessed, a plump little man
standing some five-feet-seven-or-eight inches tall, with a
bald head and dark brown eyes. Meyer pitied him the
bald head; he himself was wearing his toupee. But one
look at him—Sagel or not—told both detectives that he
was not the man who'd been described by the waiter at
Marino's. The man who'd been with Darcy Welles on
the night of her murder was—according to the waiter—in
his forties, about five-feet-ten-inches tall, with brown
hair and brown eyes. Nonetheless, on the off chance that
the waiter had been mistaken, they went through the routine.

"Frederick Sagel?" Meyer asked.

"Yes?"

"All right to come in a minute?" Kling said.

"What for?" Sagel asked.

In the apartment behind him, they could see a woman—presumably the one who'd answered their knock at the door, and presumably Sagel's wife—wearing a robe and turning the dial on a television set that had the volume down very low. She had curlers in her hair. That's why Meyer figured she was Sagel's wife and not his girlfriend.

"We'd like to ask you a few questions," Kling said, "if that's all right with you."

"What about?" Sagel said. He was standing in the doorway, looking either like a fire hydrant or an outraged Englishman defending the entrance to his sacrosanct castle.

"About where you were last night," Meyer said.

"What?" Sagel said.

"We'd all be a lot more comfortable if we could come in," Kling said.

"Well . . . I guess so," Sagel said, and stepped aside.

The moment the detectives were in the apartment, Sagel's wife turned on her heel, went through a door opening off the living room, and closed the door behind her. Modesty, Meyer thought.

"Well . . . uh . . . why don't you sit down?" Sagel said.

The detectives sat side by side on a sofa facing the television screen. On the screen, two people were negotiating a drug deal. Kling guessed one of them was an undercover narc. On television, if you saw any two people exchanging money for cocaine, one of them had to be an undercover narc. He wondered suddenly if Eileen had been serious about asking for transfer to the Narcotics Squad. He also wondered what she was doing right this minute. What he'd planned for tonight, what he'd planned to ask her to do when he phoned her—

". . . you park it at a garage on South Columbia?" Meyer was saying. "Between Garden and Jefferson—closer to Jefferson, actually?"

"Yeah, sure," Sagel said, looking puzzled.

"That's where you parked your car last night?" Meyer said. "A Chevy Citation with the license plate—what's the number, Bert?"

Kling looked at his notebook.

"38L4721," he said.

"That's the number . . . I guess," Sagel said. "I mean, who the hell can remember his license plate number? That sounds like it, though. I guess."

"And you parked your car at this garage at eight o'clock, is that right?" Meyer said.

"Around eight, yes."

"Where'd you go after you parked the car, Mr. Sagel?"

"To my office."

"You went to your office at eight o'clock at *night?*" Kling asked.

"Yes, sir."

"Why'd you do that?" Meyer asked.

" 'Cause I forgot my work."

"Your work?"

"I'm an accountant. I left my work at the office—by accident. The stuff I was supposed to work on last night. I do a lot of work at home. We have a computer at the office, but I'll tell you the truth, I don't trust it. So what I usually do is I take the printouts home and I check them against my *own* figures, the figures I made by *hand,* you know what I mean? That way, I'm sure."

"So . . . as I understand this," Meyer said, "you parked the car at eight o'clock . . ."

"That's right."

"And went up to your office to get the work you'd left behind . . ."

"That's right."

"Mr. Sagel, did you go back to the garage at ten o'clock? To reclaim your car?"

"Yes, sir."

"Mr. Sagel, why did it take you two hours to pick up your work?"

"It didn't. I stopped for a drink. There's a restaurant near my building, the building where my office is, and it's got a nice bar. So I stopped in there for a drink before I went to get the car."

"What restaurant was that?" Kling asked.

"A place called Marino's," Sagel said.

"You were in *Marino*'s last night?" Meyer asked.

"Yes, sir."

"How long were you there?"

"I musta got there around eight-fifteen, and I guess I stayed an hour or so. Had a few drinks, you know? Sitting at the bar. Bullshitting with the bartender. You know how it is when you're sitting at a bar."

"What time did you leave Marino's, Mr. Sagel?"

"I told you. Nine-fifteen, nine-thirty, in there."

"And you got to the garage at ten."

"Yeah, about ten o'clock, it must've been."

"What took you so long to get to the garage?"

"Oh, I don't know. I was walking around, looking in the store windows. I walked up to Jefferson and looked in the store windows. It was such a nice night, you know."

"When you were at the garage picking up your car . . ."

"Yeah?"

"Did you happen to notice a girl wearing a red dress?"

"No, I didn't see any girl in a red dress."

"Tall girl in a red dress. Five-eight or -nine . . ."

"Five-eight ain't tall," Sagel said. *"I'm* five-eight, and that ain't tall."

"Black hair and blue eyes?"

"No, I didn't see nobody like that at the garage."

"Or in the restaurant. Did you happen to see her in the restaurant?"

"I didn't look in the restaurant. I told you, I was sitting at the bar."

"Mr. Sagel," Meyer said, "do you know anyone named Darcy Welles?"

"Oh, I get it," Sagel said.

"What do you get, Mr. Sagel?"

"That's what this is about. Okay, I get it. The girl somebody hung from a lamppost last night, okay, I get it."

"How do you know about that?" Meyer said.

"Are you kidding? It's in all the papers. Also, it was on television tonight, just *now* as a matter of fact, the Eleven O'Clock News. I was in my pajamas watching the news when you guys knocked on the door. It was all about this Darcy Welles girl hanging from a lamppost like the other two. You got to be deaf, dumb, and blind not to know about those girls hanging from lampposts. Helen!" he shouted suddenly. "Come in here a minute, will you? This is rich, you guys thinking I had something to do with it."

They did not, in fact, think he had anything to do with it.

There is a ring to the truth, and it shatters the night like a hammer striking a gong.

But they listened nonetheless while Helen Sagel told them that her husband had left the apartment at about twenty after seven last night, just after they'd finished dinner, because he'd forgotten his work at the office and he wanted to do some checking of the figures on the computer printouts, and he'd got back at about ten-thirty, a quarter to eleven, something like that, and he smelled as if he'd had a few drinks. He had worked on his figures until midnight and then he'd come to bed where she was already asleep, but he woke her up when he turned on the light.

"Okay?" Helen said. "Is that it? Can I go back to bed now?"

"Yes, ma'am, thank you," Meyer said.

"Knocking on people's doors in the middle of the night," Helen muttered and left the living room again.

"Sorry about this," Meyer said to Sagel. "But we have to check these things out, you know."

"Oh, sure," Sagel said. "I hope you catch him."

"We're trying, sir, thank you," Meyer said.

"May I ask you a question?" Sagel said.

"Certainly."

"Is that a wig you're wearing?"

"Well . . . yes, it is," Meyer said.

"I've been thinking of getting one," Sagel said. "Not like *that* one, I mean a *good* one. A wig nobody can tell you're wearing, you know what I mean?"

"Uh . . . yes," Meyer said.

"Well, good night," Kling said. "Thanks for your time, Mr. Sagel."

"Good night," Meyer mumbled.

He was silent all the way down to the street. It was windier outside than it had been when they entered the building. It looked as if it might begin raining anytime now.

"I look pretty shitty in this thing, huh?" Meyer asked.

Kling didn't answer for a moment.

"Bert?" Meyer said.

"Well . . . yeah, Meyer, I guess you do," Kling said.

"Yeah," Meyer said.

He took the wig off his head, walked to the row of garbage cans outside the building, lifted the lid off one of them, and tossed the wig inside.

"Easy come, easy go," he said, and sighed.

But his head felt colder without all that hair on it.

He sure hoped it wouldn't start raining.

* * *

Folger Road had taken its name from Folger University, which sat at the bottom end of a wide boulevard that climbed upward to skewer one of the city's larger business areas. Carella once tried explaining to an out-of-towner who only *thought* he lived in a real city that you could take someplace like downtown San Diego, for example, and easily lose it in any one of the separate areas that conglomerately formed *this* city—which was, of course, the *only* city in the world. Well, Carella had to take that back. He'd never been to London or Paris or Rome or Tokyo or any of those other bustling places that he supposed were real cities, too. But trying to explain to this guy from Muddy Boots, Iowa, that his entire *city* could disappear overnight in an area like the Quarter, or the Lower Platform, or even Ashley Heights —well, that had been impossible. You had to understand cities. You had to understand that a section like Folger Road, with its bright lights and its stores and its blaring traffic and its teeming humanity was the equivalent of *eighteen* cities like Mildew, Florida, or Broken Back, Arizona.

The university *itself* was probably the size of a city like Lost Souls, Montana. Founded by the Catholic Church back in 1892—a bad year for Lizzie Borden—it then consisted of several massive stone buildings in an area still surrounded by open farmland. The name "Riverhead" was a bastardization of "Ryerhert," in itself an abbreviation of "Ryerhert's Farms." Once upon a time, when the world was young and the Dutch were snugly settled in the city, the land adjacent to Isola was owned by a patroon named Pieter Ryerhert. Ryerhert was a farmer who at the age of sixty-eight grew tired of rising with the chickens and going to bed with the cows. As the metropolis grew, and the need for housing beyond Isola's limited boundaries increased, Ryerhert sold or donated most of his land to the expanding city, and then moved

down to Isola, where he lived the gay life of a fat, rich
burgher. Ryerhert's Farms became simply Ryerhert, but
this was not a particularly easy name to pronounce. By
the time World War I rolled around, and despite the fact
that Ryerhert was Dutch and not German, the name really
began to rankle, and petitions were circulated to change it
because it sounded too Teutonic, and therefore probably
had Huns running around up there cutting off the hands
of Belgian babies. It became Riverhead in 1919. It was
still Riverhead—but not the Riverhead it had been back
then in 1892 when the Catholic Church decided it would
be a good idea to start educating the people up here in the
hinterlands.

The university now occupied some twelve square acres
of valuable land which, if sold at going real estate prices,
would have caused the Pope to perform a ceremonial
mass and a little dance through the streets of Warsaw.
The entire campus was surrounded by a high stone wall
that had undoubtedly kept the largely Italian-American
masons in Riverhead busy for the better part of a century.
Fifteen years ago, the university had begun admitting
women—something the Pope had not yet seen fit to do
with his clergy. At the administration building, Carella
and Ollie spoke to a bleary-eyed clerk manning the Student Directory phone and learned that Luella Scott was
indeed one of the women students here, and that she lived
on campus in a freshman dorm named Hunnicut.

In the car, driving toward the dorm on the campus's
wide, tree-lined roads, Ollie said, "That sounds dirty,
don't it? For a Catholic school, I mean? Hunnicut? That
sounds dirty to me."

The dorms at Folger University were not co-
educational. A freshman with her nose buried in a text-
book looked up from a desk in the lobby when the
detectives knocked on the locked, glass-paneled entrance
door. A sign on the desk read RECEPTION. Ollie indicated that she should unlock the door. The girl shook her

head. Ollie took out his wallet and opened it to his blue-and-gold detective's shield. He held the shield up to one of the glass panels. The girl shook her head again.

"They got better security here than we got at Police Headquarters," he said to Carella. Then, at the top of his voice, he bellowed. "Police! Open the door!"

The girl got up from behind the desk, and walked to the door.

"What?" she said.

"Police, police!" Ollie shouted. "You see the badge? Open the goddamn *door!*"

"I'm not allowed to open the door," the girl said. "And don't curse."

They could barely hear her through the glass panels that separated them from the inside.

"You see this?" Ollie shouted, and rapped the shield against the glass. "We're cops! Open the door! *Cops!*" he shouted. *"Police!"*

The girl leaned in close to the glass and studied the shield.

"I'm gonna shoot that little bitch," Ollie said to Carella. "Open the door!" he yelled.

The girl unlocked the door.

"Only students are allowed in," she said primly. "We lock the doors at ten o'clock, you have to have your own key to get in after ten."

"Then why're you sitting behind a desk says Reception, you're not letting anybody in?" Ollie asked.

"Reception ends at ten o'clock," the girl said.

"What *is* this?" Ollie said. "Saturday Night Live?"

"Saturday nights, we lock the doors at midnight," the girl said.

"So what're you doing *sitting* down here if you ain't recepting anybody?" Ollie said.

"I *was* on Reception," the girl said, "but I went off at ten. I was doing my homework. My roommate keeps the radio on all the time."

"Pretend for a minute you're *still* on Reception," Ollie said. "You know a girl named Luella Scott?"

"Yes?" the girl said.

"Where is she?"

"Third floor, room sixty-two," the girl said. "But she isn't here just now."

"Where is she?" Carella asked.

"She went to the library."

"When?"

"She left here at about nine."

"Where's the library? On campus here?"

"Yes, of *course* on campus," the girl said.

"Where?"

"Two dorms down, past Baxter, cross the quadrangle, two more dorms till you come to a small sort of cloister and the library's just past that."

"Was she alone?" Ollie asked.

"What?"

"When she *left* here. Was she alone?"

"Yes."

"Come on," Ollie said.

"Me?" the girl said, but the detectives were already outside and running up the path.

She'd been easy to identify. One of the three black girls on the team. The other two were seniors, he knew what they looked like from newspaper stories he'd researched in the public library. Luella Scott was the new one. Skinny little kid, looked as if she'd be gasping for breath after only a few steps, but oh she was fast, ran like the wind, fast, fast. Smart, too. Entered college this fall when she was only seventeen. He liked that, her being seventeen. The newspapers would really go to town on a seventeen-year-old girl.

All that coverage today.

He was almost home free.

This one should do it.

Luella Scott should do it.

From where he stood beneath the old maple tree, its yellowing leaves rattling in the fresh wind, he could see the lighted windows of the library building, but he could not spot Luella anyplace inside. There was only one entrance to the library, and she'd gone in there at a little after nine o'clock, he'd followed her over from her dorm, not much security on this campus except for the high stone walls, you'd think they'd be more careful with such a large female student body and rapists running loose all over the city. Went in at a little past nine, couldn't have come out anyplace else because there wasn't anyplace else to come out *of.* Had to come out right here, where he was waiting.

He looked at his watch.

Almost eleven-thirty.

What was taking her so long?

Well, she probably studied a lot. You don't get into college at seventeen unless you're a hard worker. You could be smart as hell, but if you didn't crack those books, it didn't matter. Smart girl, Luella Scott, but he wished she'd hurry it up in there. He also wished she would be the last one. He hoped this time would do the trick. He didn't want to walk in and give himself up, they'd think he was crazy or something. *Sure, mister, you killed four girls, terrific, mister, go watch some more television, okay?*

Break this one in half, he wasn't careful. Skinny little thing.

Hoist her up over the lamppost arm, should be easy. Couldn't weigh more than a hundred pounds, this one. Where'd she find the stamina to *run* the way she did? God, she was fast!

He looked up at the sky.

He hoped it wouldn't start raining.

Still, rain had its benefits. Not too many people out on the street when it was raining, get the job done without any interference. That guy last night when he was carrying Darcy out of the park. He'd thought that would do it, the old fart seeing him. Hoped he'd go to the police when he read about it in this morning's paper—*Hey, guess what, I saw this guy carrying a dead girl out of Bridge Street Park last night, I'll bet he was the guy who hung that girl from a lamppost!* Cops probably wouldn't have believed him even if he did go in to report what he'd seen. *Sure, mister, go back to the park and sleep it off, okay?* Or maybe he *had* gone in, told them what he'd seen, and the cops were playing it cool, telling the newspapers they had no leads when all the while they were closing in on him. He hoped so. He hoped they'd finally get off their asses and *catch* him. He couldn't wait to read the newspapers when they finally caught him. Oh, wow!

The Road Runner Killer.

Change *that* name soon enough, you could bet on that.

Lightning.

Lightning all over the newspapers again.

A fierce gust of wind shook the branches overhead, sent leaves tumbling down in a golden shower. The leaves, driven by the wind, rasped over the path winding past the library steps. Where the hell *are* you? he thought. He planned to follow her only a little way back to the dorm, get her on that dark stretch of path before it opened into the quadrangle again. Dark there, perfect there. Couldn't risk Corey McIntyre again, make it *too* easy for them, they'd think he was crazy. Couldn't have the papers saying he was crazy. That was the one thing—

One of the library doors was opening.

Luella came out onto the wide, flat top step, her arms full of books. She looked too skinny to be carrying all those books. He felt like going up to her, asking her if she'd like some help with the books. She was adjusting a long woolen muffler around her neck now, pulling up the collar of her pea coat, skinny little girl in a big pea coat probably belonged to her brother or somebody, somebody in the family who was a sailor, you got a lot of black kids enlisting in the service these days. He tried to remember whether his research had turned up anything about her brother being a sailor? Nothing in the stories he'd read, nothing he could remember. Easy to forget things, though. Look at how easily they'd forgotten him.

She was coming down the steps now.

She coughed. Probably had a cold. Bad for a runner, she should be taking better care of herself, skinny little thing like that.

She walked past the tree.

The wind came up again.

She hadn't seen him.

He waited until she was a good fifty yards ahead of him, and then he fell into step behind her. He was grateful for the rasping of the wind-driven leaves on the path; they covered any sound his track shoes made.

"What'd she say the name of that dorm was?" Ollie asked.

"Baxter," Carella said.

"So where are the names? How you supposed to know one dorm from another?"

"She said the second dorm down."

"So how can you tell the difference between a dorm and any of these other buildings?"

"I think this one is Baxter," Carella said.

"So where's the quadrangle? Everything looks the same here. Fuckin' college looks like a monastery."

"There it is," Carella said. "Up ahead."

She was through the cloister now, unaware of his presence behind her, the leaves swirling on the path, rising on the air again in tainted tatters. Ahead of her was a section of path lighted at its eastern end by a single lamppost, dark until it opened onto the quadrangle where another lamppost stood. He knew she was fast, he would have to get to her before she bolted, he didn't want her to get away. She was fast, yes—but he was faster. He waited until she passed beneath the lamppost, and then he broke from a standing start, his shoes pounding on the pavement, the leaves scattering as if in sudden panic. She heard him, but she was too late. As she started to turn, he pounced on her.

The surprise was total, her eyes opening wide in shock, her jaw dropping, a scream starting somewhere in her throat—he clamped his hand over her mouth.

She bit him.

He pulled his hand back.

The scream erupted, shattering the night.

They had come through the quadrangle and were entering the path at its western end, dark beyond the lamppost, when they heard the scream. Ollie's gun was in his hand an instant before Carella reached for his holster. Both men began running.

Up ahead, they saw the figures struggling in the dark, the man towering over the girl, the girl kicking and punching at him as he tried to turn her back to him. The wind was stronger now, rattling the branches of the trees lining the path, blasting leaves onto the air like demons trailing fire.

"Police!" Ollie shouted and fired over his head.

The man turned.

They could not see his face in the dark, they could see only the motion of his turning. Carella thought for a moment he would use the girl as a shield, holding her from behind—one of his arms was looped under hers now, his right hand clamped over the back of her neck—but instead he released her suddenly and began running.

"The girl!" Carella said urgently, and began running after him.

He had wanted to say, "See if the girl's all right," or "Take care of the girl," but the man was off like the wind unleashing leaves everywhere on the night, and as Carella ran past the girl lying on the path now, he did not even turn to see if Ollie had understood him.

He had not run this hard since he was a kid in high school. Track wasn't his sport; he'd played right field on the school's baseball team, and his serious running had been confined to chasing high flies or rounding third base on a locomotive dash for home. That had been a long time ago; only on television and in movies did cops chase all over the city trying to nail a runaway suspect.

The man ahead of him was too fast.

Carella fired his pistol into the darkness, and the muzzle flash and ensuing explosion—like lightning and thunder on the night—coincided with a rain as sudden as it was fierce, almost as if his squeezing the trigger had served as a release mechanism, the lever action opening a hopper somewhere above. The rain was all-consuming. It pelted the path and the trees arching overhead, combining with the wind to create a multi-colored shower of water and withering leaves. He pounded through the rain and the falling leaves, gasping for breath, his heart lurching in his chest, certain he would lose Lytell—if this *was* Lytell—knowing the man was simply too fast for him.

And then suddenly, up ahead, he saw Lytell lose purchase on the wet leaves underfoot, his arms flailing out for balance as his feet went out from under him. He fell to the sodden path sideways, his left shoulder hitting the asphalt, the blow of the impact softened somewhat by the covering of leaves. He was getting to his feet again when Carella ran up to him.

"Police," Carella said breathlessly. "Don't move."

Lytell smiled.

"What took you so long?" he said.

11

IT WAS STILL RAINING WHEN THE MAN FROM
the D.A.'s office arrived at the 87th Precinct. He did not
get there till six the next morning, by which time Ollie
and Carella had already searched—armed with a magistrate's warrant this time—Henry Lytell's premises at 843
Holmes Street. Several articles they had found in the
apartment were on the desk in Lieutenant Byrnes's office
when the assistant D.A. arrived. A stenographer recorded the presence of Lieutenant Byrnes, Detectives
Carella and Weeks, and Assistant District Attorney
Ralph Jenkins. The stenographer also recorded the date,
Friday, October 21, and the time the interrogation took
place, 6:05 A.M. Jenkins read Lytell his rights. Lytell
said he understood them, and further stated that he did
not wish his own attorney present during the questioning.
Jenkins began the Q and A.

Q: May I have your full name, please?
A: Henry Lewis Lytell.
Q: And your address, Mr. Ly—
A: You probably know me as Lightning Lytell. That's
   what the reporters used to call me. Back then.
Q: Yes. Mr. Lytell, may I have your address, please?
A: 843 Holmes Street.
Q: Here in Isola?
A: Yes, sir.
Q: Are you employed, Mr. Lytell?
A: Yes, sir, I am.
Q: In what line of work?

255

A: You understand, don't you, that I'm a *runner*. I mean, that's what I *am*. How I earn my living has nothing to do with what I really *am*.

Q: How *do* you earn your living, Mr. Lytell?

A: I'm a researcher.

Q: For whom? What sort of research?

A: A free-lance researcher. For advertising agencies, writers, anybody needing information about any particular subject or subjects.

Q: And your place of business is where?

A: At home. I work out of my apartment.

Q: Do you set your own hours, Mr. Lytell?

A: Yes. That's the only good thing about the job, the freedom it gives me. To do other things. I try to run every day for at least—

Q: Mr. Lytell, can you tell me where you were and what you were doing on the night of October sixth? That would have been a Thursday night, two weeks ago.

A: Yes, sir. I was with a runner from Ramsey University. A girl on the track team.

Q: Her name, please.

A: Marcia Schaffer.

Q: When you say you were *with* her . . .

A: I was with her first in her apartment where I represented myself as a man named Corey McIntyre of *Sports USA* magazine. Then—

Q: You told Miss Schaffer you were someone named Corey McIntyre?

A: Yes, sir.

Q: How did you come upon this name?

A: I got it from the masthead of the magazine.

Q: And Miss Schaffer accepted you as a person from the magazine?

A: I had an I.D. card.

Q: Where did you get an I.D. card?

A: I made it. I used to work for an advertising agency. This was, oh, eight, nine years ago, after all the hullaballoo was dying down. I learned a lot in the art department, I know how to do these things.

Q: What things?

A: Making up a card that looks legitimate. Getting it laminated.

Q: You were working in the art department of an advertising agency?

A: No, no. But I knew art directors, I was always hanging around with them. I was working directly with one of the creative assistants, you see. Trying to dream up campaigns involving sports, you see. That's why I was hired in the first place. Because of my athletic expertise.

Q: As I understand this, then, you were working at an advertising agency some eight or nine years ago . . .

A: Yes.

Q: When did you begin doing independent research, Mr. Lytell?

A: Three years ago.

Q: And you've been so employed since?

A: Running is what I *really* do.

Q: Yes, but to earn a living . . .

A: Yes, I do research work.

Q: Getting back to the night of October sixth. You went to Miss Schaffer's apartment and represented yourself as an employee of *Sports USA*—

A: A *writer-reporter* for *Sports USA*.

Q: A writer-reporter, yes. And then what?

A: I told her we were preparing an article on promising young runners.

Q: She accepted this?

A: Well, I know all *about* running, that's what I *am*, a runner. So naturally, I knew what I was talking about. Yes, she accepted me.

Q: And then what?

A: I asked her if she'd like to have dinner with me. To do the interview.

Q: Did you, in fact, have dinner with Miss Schaffer that night?

A: Yes. At a seafood place near her apartment. There're lots of good restaurants in that neighborhood, we just picked one at random.

Q: What time was this, Mr. Lytell?

A: Early. Six o'clock, I think. Early.

Q: You took her to dinner at six o'clock?

A: Yes. So I could do the interview. She was very excited about the interview.

Q: What happened then?

A: What do you want me to say?

Q: Whatever you wish to say. Tell me what happened after dinner.

A: I killed her. I already told that to the detectives here.

Q: Where did you kill her?

A: In my apartment. I told her I wanted to continue the interview, and I suggested that we finish it over a cognac in my apartment. She said she didn't want a cognac—she was in training, you know, runners have a very strict training regimen—but she said if I had a Coke or something, that would be fine.

Q: What time did you get to your apartment?

A: Seven-thirty?

Q: And then what happened?

A: She was—I think she was looking at a painting I have hanging in the living room, it's a painting of a male runner—and I came up behind her and applied a full nelson. I used to do some wrestling before I got interested in track. There's no comparison, you know. Wrestling is a sweaty form of one-on-one combat, whereas running . . .

Q: You killed her by applying a full nelson?

A: Yes. To break her neck.

Q: At what time was this, Mr. Lytell?

A: A little before eight, I guess.

Q: Lieutenant Byrnes, the medical examiner's estimate of the post mortem interval puts the time of death at approximately 7:00 P.M., doesn't it?

A: (Byrnes) Yes, sir.

Q: Mr. Lytell, what did you do then?

A: I watched some television.

Q: You . . .

A: I wanted to wait till the streets got deserted. So I could carry her down to the car. The rope was already in the trunk, I'd put it in the trunk earlier that day.

Q: How long did you watch television?

A: Until about two in the morning.

Q: Then what?

A: I carried her down to the car. I checked the street from the window first, my living room faces the street. I didn't see anybody around, so I carried her down, and put her in the front seat. She looked like she was sleeping. I mean, sitting there in the car.

Q: What did you do next?

A: I drove her up here.

Q: By up here . . .

A: The neighborhood up here.

Q: Why up here?

A: I didn't pick it specifically. I was looking for a deserted place. I found this construction site with a row of abandoned buildings on the other side of the street, and I thought it would be a good place.

Q: A good place for what?

A: To hang her.

Q: Why did you hang her, Mr. Lytell?

A: It seemed a good way.

Q: A good way?

A: Yes.

Q: To do what?

A: Just a good way.

Q: Mr. Lytell . . . did you also kill a young woman named Nancy Annunziato?

A: Yes, sir.

Q: Can you give me the details of that?

A: It was the same as the first one. I told her I was with *Sports USA,* I took her to dinner, I . . .

Q: When was this, Mr. Lytell?

A: On the night of October thirteenth. I met her for dinner at Marino's, that's a midtown restaurant, very nice. She lived all the way out in Calm's Point, you see, she agreed to meet me at the restaurant. Eight o'clock. I made the reservation for eight o'clock. We did most of the interview during dinner, and then we went back to my apartment, same as the last one, same as the Schaffer girl. We talked some more—she was a big talker, Nancy—and then I . . . well . . . you know.

Q: You killed her.

A: Yes. I used a full nelson again.

Q: What time was this?

A: Ten-thirty, eleven.

Q: Lieutenant Byrnes, does that jibe with the medical examiner's estimate?

A: (Byrnes) Yes, sir.

Q: What did you do then, Mr. Lytell?

A: Same as the other one. Took her down to the car, drove around looking for a deserted place to hang her. I didn't want to do it up here again. I'd already tried to help the detectives up here . . .

Q: Help them?

A: Yes. By sending them Marcia's handbag. I took the keys out first, though. I threw away the keys to her apartment.

Q: Why did you do that?

A: To help them.

Q: Help them with what?

A: Well, just to help them.

Q: You thought throwing away her keys would help . . .

A: No, no, I did *that* so it wouldn't be *too* easy for them. What I mean was I sent them the handbag. So they could identify her, you see?

Q: Why did you want to help them?

A: Well, I just did. But they seemed . . . excuse me, gentlemen . . . they seemed to be moving very slowly on it, you know? So I didn't want to hang Nancy's body up here again, I figured I'd try my luck with another precinct.

Q: Lieutenant Byrnes, where was the second victim found?

A: (Byrnes) In west Riverhead, sir. The Hundred and First Precinct.

Q: Is that where you took Nancy Annunziato, Mr. Lytell?

A: I guess so. I mean, I didn't know the number of the precinct or anything. It was in Riverhead, though, where all the burned-out buildings are. *That* part of Riverhead.

Q: West Riverhead.

A: I guess that's what it's called.

Q: Mr. Lytell, did you hang Nancy Annunziato's body from a lamppost in West Riverhead?

A: Yes, I did.

Q: At what time was that?

A: Sometime in the middle of the night.

Q: Can you give me an approximate time?

A: Three in the morning? I guess it was around then.

Q: Lieutenant Byrnes, would you know at what time the Hundred and First Precinct received notification of discovery?

A: (Byrnes) Steve?

A: (Carella) Detective Broughan clocked the call in at 6:04 A.M.

A: (Lytell) I left her wallet under the lamppost.

Q: Why did you do that?

A: Help them out, you know. I was hoping maybe the cops there were a little smarter than the ones in this precinct—excuse me.

Q: Why did you want the cops to be smart?

A: Well, you know.

Q: No, I don't. Can you explain that to me?

A: Help them out a little, you know?

Q: Why are you smiling, Mr. Lytell?

A: I don't know.

Q: Do you realize you're smiling?

A: I guess I'm smiling.

Q: Tell me about Darcy Welles. Did you kill her, too?

A: Yes, I did.

Q: When?

A: Wednesday night.

Q: October nineteenth?

A: I guess that was the date.

Q: Well, here's a calendar, and here's Wednesday night. Was it October nineteenth?

A: Yes, October nineteenth.

Q: Can you tell me about that?

A: Look, I can go on all night here, but the important thing . . .

Q: Yes, what's the important thing, Mr. Lytell?

A: I killed her the same as the others, okay? Exactly the same. The restaurant, the interview . . . well, not exactly. I didn't take Darcy to my apartment. I was getting scared of doing that, afraid someone might see me and . . .

Q: But you told us earlier that you wanted to help the cops, you wanted the cops to . . .

A: Well, yes. But I didn't want my neighbors thinking I was molesting young girls or anything. So I took her to this park further uptown, the Bridge Street Park.

Q: And killed her there?

A: Yes.

Q: Again applying a full nelson?

A: Yes.

Q: And where did you take *her* afterward, Mr. Lytell?

A: To Diamondback. I was *really* scared up there, I've got to tell you. Everybody's *black* up there, you know. But it worked out okay. I got her up on the lamppost all right.

Q: What time was this, Mr. Lytell?

A: Oh, I don't know. Twenty to eleven, a quarter to eleven?

Q: Mr. Lytell, did you attempt to kill a girl named Luella Scott last night?

A: Yes, sir, I did. I attempted to kill her.

Q: If you had succeeded in your attempt, would you later have *hanged* Miss Scott as well?

A: Yes, sir, that was my plan.

Q: Why?

A: I don't understand your question.

Q: Why did you *hang* these young girls, Mr. Lytell? What was the purpose of that?

A: To make them visible.

Q: Visible?

A: To attract attention to them.

Q: Why did you want attention attracted to them?

A: Well, you know.

Q: I don't know.

A: So everybody would realize.

Q: Realize what?

A: About them.

Q: *What* about them?

A: That they were murdered by the same person.

Q: You.

A: Yes.

Q: You wanted everyone to know that *you* had murdered them?

A: No, no.

Q: Then what *did* you want everyone to know?

A: I don't know *what* I wanted them to know, damn it!

Q: Mr. Lytell, I'm trying to understand . . .

A: What the hell is it you don't understand? I've already told you . . .

Q: Yes, but hanging these girls . . .

A: That was the idea.

Q: What was the idea?

A: Jesus, I don't know how to make it any plainer.

Q: You say you hanged them to attract attention to them . . .

A: Yes.

Q: . . . to make everyone realize they'd been murdered by the same person.

A: Yes.

Q: Why, Mr. Lytell?

A: Are we finished here? Because if we are . . .

Q: We told you earlier that you can end this whenever you want to. All you have to do is tell us you don't want to answer any further questions.

A: I don't mind answering questions. It's just that you're asking all the *wrong* questions.

Q: What questions would you like me to ask, Mr. Lytell?

A: How about the *gold* sitting there? Doesn't *that* interest you at all?

Q: By the gold, are you referring to these medals Detectives Weeks and Carella found in your apartment?

A: I don't know who found them there.

Q: But they're yours, are they not?

A: Well, whose do you *think* they are?

Q: These are Olympic medals, are they not?

A: Olympic *gold* medals. You're not looking at bronze there, mister.

Q: Did you win these medals, Mr. Lytell?

A: Come on, don't be ridiculous. Were you living on Mars?

Q: Sir?

A: How old are you, anyway?

Q: I'm thirty-seven, sir.

A: So where were you fifteen years ago? You were twenty-two years old, am I right? Didn't you watch television? Didn't you know what the hell was going *on* in the world?

Q: You won these medals fifteen years ago, is that what you're saying?

A: Listen to the guy, will you? Three gold medals, he's acting as if it never happened!

Q: I'm not a sports fan, Mr. Lytell. Perhaps you can tell me a little more about it.

A: Sure, that's the whole damn trouble. People forget, that's the trouble. Three gold medals—I was on the Johnny Carson show, for Christ's sake. Lightning Lytell, that's how he introduced me, Lightning Lytell. That's what they all called me. That's what the reporters covering the games started calling me. I was on the cover of every important sports magazine in this country, I couldn't go anyplace without people stopping me on the street, "Hey, Lightning!" "How ya doin', Lightning?" I was *famous!*

We did a thing, Johnny and me, where we pretended to have a race, you know, just a short sprint across the stage, and he did that famous take of his, Johnny, his take, you know his take? 'Cause I was halfway across the stage before he even heard the starting gun. Reaction time is very important, you know. Jesse Owens used to favor a bunch start, used to set his front block eight inches from the line, the rear block twelve inches behind that. You have to set your blocks for what feels right for you, it's a personal thing. Bobby Morrow—he was triple gold winner in the 1956 games—he used to set his front block twenty-one inches from the line, and his rear block back fourteen inches from that. It varies. The first guy who ran the metric short sprint in ten seconds flat—this was Armin Hary—he used to set his blocks at twenty-three and thirty-three. You have to explode out of the blocks—that's a common expression you hear all the time in running, you *explode* out of the blocks. Just moving out of them fast isn't the way you win races. You have to *explode* out of those blocks like a rocket coming out of a silo.

When I won the triple gold—this was fifteen years back, I was only twenty-four years old, man, I was off like *lightning* . . . well, that's where I got the nickname. Lightning. Talk about exploding! It was lightning and thunder, *boom,* out of the blocks and no stopping me! Well, hell, *three* gold medals! The one-hundred, the two-hundred, and the relay! I was anchor in the relay. At the handoff, we were five yards behind Italy, running third in the race! Jimmy was coming in really fast, man, he was stepping, but I was ready to explode the second I got that baton! *Boom!* I ran that last hundred meters in eight-six! Incredible! I made up all that lost distance and won going away! Hell, I won them *all* in my day. You name them, I won them. High school, college, AAU, NCAA, invitationals, Olympic trials—all of them, you name them.

You know what it means to be a winner? You know what it means to be the *best* at what you do? Do you have any concept of what that means? Do you know anything at *all* about the sheer exuberance of running to *win?* When you get out there, you not only want to *beat* the other guy, you want to *murder* him, do you know what I mean? You want to run him right into the ground, you want him to collapse behind you and start vomiting up his guts, you want him to know he has met his match, man, and he has succumbed, he has *lost!* You get out there, you're behind that starting line there, and the world funnels down to just the track, the whole world becomes that turf or cinder and you're already streaking down it like lightning in your mind, you're already hitting the string even though the race hasn't started yet. And you do your little dance in your shoes, your shoes tickle the cinder or the turf, tap-tap-tap, and you hear the starter's whistle, and you keep doing your little jig, sucking in great big gulps of oxygen, and everything inside you is boiling up, ready to boil over, ready to explode when you hear that call to the marks, crouching into the blocks, waiting for the gun—and the gold.

But they forget, don't they? They forget what you did, what you were. All those commercials I made— God, the money was pouring in—*everybody* wanted Lightning Lytell to endorse his product. Shit, I was signed by William Morris, have you ever heard of William Morris? They're a talent agency in New York and L.A., they've got offices all over the world, they were going to make me a *movie* star! Damn well on the way to doing it, too, all those commercials, you couldn't turn on your television set without seeing me on the screen holding up a product, Lightning Lytell—"You think *I'm* fast? Wait'll you see how fast this razor shaves you"—all of it, everything from orange juice to vitamin capsules, I was all over the screen. I was a household word, Lightning Lytell. But then it . . . you know . . . it falls apart somehow. You stop getting offers, they told me it was overexposure, they told me people were getting too used to seeing my face on the screen. And suddenly you're not a movie star, you're not even a television pitchman, you're just Henry Lewis Lytell again, and nobody knows who the hell you are.

They forget.

You . . . want to remind them, you know what I mean?

You want to remind them.

Q: Is that why you committed these murders, Mr. Ly-
    tell? To remind them?

A: No, no.

Q: Is that why you hanged these young women? To cre-
    ate a sensation that would—

A: No, no. Hey, no.

Q: —*remind* people you were still around?

A: I'm the fastest human being on *earth!*

Q: Is that why?

A: The fastest human being.

The detectives were all staring at him now. Lytell was
looking at the three gold medals on Lieutenant Byrnes's
desk. Assistant District Attorney Jenkins picked up one
of the medals, held it in the palm of his hand and stared at
it thoughtfully. When he looked up at Lytell again, Lytell
seemed lost in reverie, listening perhaps to the distant
sound of a starting gun, the roar of a stadium crowd as he
thundered down the track.

"Is there anything you'd like to add to this?" Jenkins
asked.

Lytell shook his head.

"Anything you'd like to change or delete?"

Lytell shook his head again.

Jenkins looked at the stenographer.

"That's it then," he said.

At eleven o'clock that morning, Eileen called Annie
Rawles to ask her how she thought she should proceed
that night. Should she stay home, or should she go out? It
was still raining; the rain might dissuade their man. It
was Annie's opinion that he wouldn't try coming into the
apartment again. He undoubtedly knew the last rape had
been reported to the police, and he couldn't risk the possibility that the apartment was staked out. Annie thought
he would try to hit Eileen on the street if he could, and
only try the apartment as a last resort.

"So you want me to go out, huh?" Eileen asked. "In the rain."

"Supposed to get worse tonight," Annie said. "So far, it's trickled off to a nice steady drizzle."

"What's so nice about a steady drizzle?" Eileen asked.

"Better than lightning and thunder, no?"

"Is *that* what we're supposed to get?"

"According to the forecast."

"I'm afraid of lightning," Eileen said.

"Wear rubber-soled shoes."

"Sure. Where do you think I should go? Another movie? I went to a movie Wednesday night."

"How about a disco?"

"Not Mary's style."

"He may think that's odd, two movies in the same week. Why don't you go out for an early dinner? If he's as eager to get to you as we think he is, he may make his move as soon as it's dark."

"Ever try getting raped on a full stomach?" Eileen said.

Annie laughed.

"Get back to me later, okay?" she said. "Let me know what you plan."

"I will," Eileen said.

"That it?"

"One other thing. What's A.I.M.?"

"This is a riddle, right?"

"No, this is something Mary contributed to three times this year. Total of two hundred bucks, all of them marked in her checkbook as contributions. I was thinking . . . if it's some kind of nutty handgun organization . . ."

"Yeah, I follow. Let me run it through the computer, okay?"

"They've got an office right here in the city," Eileen said. "Get back to me, will you? I'm curious."

Annie got back to her at a little before one o'clock.

"Well," she said, "you want to hear this list?"

"Shoot."

"It's a long one."

"I don't have anyplace to go till six-thirty "

"Oh? What'd you decide?"

"Dinner at a place called Ocho Rıos, three blocks from here. Mexican joint."

"You like Mexican food?"

"I like the idea that it's only three blocks from here. That means I can *walk* it. A taxi might scare him off. I'll tell you, Annie, I hope he makes his play on the street, I don't want him coming here to the apartment. More room to swing outside, you follow me?"

"However you want it."

"I'll pace out the terrain this afternoon, get the feel of it. I don't want him jumping out of some alley I don't know exists."

"Good," Annie said. "Here's this A.I.M. stuff, the list is as long as my arm, don't bother to write it down. What we have . . . are you listening? We have an organization called Accuracy In Media, and another one called Advance in Medicine. We've got the American Institute for Microminiaturization, and the Asian Institute of Management. We've got the American Indian Movement, the American Institute of Musicology, the Association for the Integration of Management, the Australian Institute of Management . . ."

"These are all *real?*"

"Honest to God. *Plus* the Australian Institute of Metals, the American Institute of Man, and an organization called Adventure In Movement for the Handicapped."

"Which of them is on Hall Avenue?" Eileen asked.

"I was saving that for last. 832 Hall, is that the address you have?"

"Yes."

"Okay, it's something called Against Infant Murder."

"Against Infant Murder, huh?"

"Yep. 832 Hall Avenue."

"What is it? Some kind of anti-abortion group?"

"They didn't define it as such when I called them. They said they were simply pro-life."

"Uh-huh. Any connection with Right to Life?"

"None that I can see. They're strictly local."

There was a long silence on the line.

"You think any of the *other* victims made contributions to this group?" Eileen asked.

"I'll be talking to all of them this afternoon, either on the phone or in person. If it turns out they *did* . . ."

"Yeah, it may be a thread."

"It may be more than that. All the victims were Catholics, you know."

"I *didn't* know."

"Yeah. And Catholics aren't supposed to use artificial means of birth control."

"Only the rhythm method, right. *Some* Catholics."

"Most, I thought. Are you Catholic?"

"You have to ask? With a name like *Burke?*"

"What do *you* use?"

"I'm on the pill."

"So am I."

"What is it you're thinking, Annie?"

"I don't know yet, I want to see how this checks out with the victims. But if all of them *did* contribute to A.I.M.. . ."

"Uh-huh," Eileen said.

There was another long silence on the line.

"I almost hope . . ."

"Yeah?"

"I hope they didn't," Annie said. "I hope Mary Hollings was the only one, a wild card."

"Why?"

"Because otherwise it's too damn ghoulish," Annie said.

* * *

Teddy's appointment at the law offices was for three o'clock that afternoon. She arrived at twenty minutes to, and waited downstairs until two-fifty, not wanting to seem too eager by arriving early. She really wanted the job; the job sounded perfect to her. She was dressed in what she considered a sedate but not drab manner, wearing a smart suit over a blouse with a stock tie, pantyhose color-coordinated with the nubby brown fabric of the suit, brown shoes with French heels. The lobby of the building was suffocatingly hot after the dank drizzle outdoors, and so she took off her raincoat before she got on the elevator. At precisely 3:00 P.M. sharp, she presented herself to the receptionist at Franklin, Logan, Gibson and Knowles and showed her the letter she had received from Phillip Logan. The receptionist told her Mr. Logan would see her in a few moments. At ten minutes past three, the receptionist picked up the phone receiver—it must have buzzed, but Teddy had not heard it—and then said Mr. Logan would see her now. Reading the girl's lips, Teddy nodded.

"First doorway down the hall on your right," the girl said.

Teddy went down the hallway and knocked on the door.

She waited a few seconds, allowing time for Logan inside to have said, "Come in," and then turned the doorknob and went into the office. The office was spacious, furnished with a large desk, several easy chairs, a coffee table and banks of bookcases on three walls. The fourth wall was fashioned almost entirely of glass that offered a splendid view of the city's towering buildings. Rain slithered down the glass panels. A shaded lamp cast a glow of yellow illumination on the desk top.

Logan rose from behind the desk the moment she entered the room. He was a tall man wearing a dark blue suit, a white shirt, and a striped tie. His eyes were a shade lighter than the suit. His hair was graying. Teddy guessed he was somewhere in his early fifties.

"Ah, Miss Carella," he said, "how kind of you to come. Please sit down."

She sat in one of the easy chairs facing his desk. He sat behind the desk again and smiled at her. His eyes looked warm and friendly.

"I assume you can . . . uh . . . read my lips," he said. "Your letter . . ."

She nodded.

"It was very straightforward of you to describe your disability in advance," Logan said. "In your letter, I mean. Very frank and honest."

Teddy nodded again, although the word *disability* rankled.

"You are . . . uh . . . you *do* understand what I'm saying, don't you?"

She nodded, and then motioned to the pad and pencil on his desk.

"What?" he said. "Oh. Yes, of *course*, how silly of me."

He handed the pad and pencil across to her.

On the pad, she wrote: *I can understand you completely.*

He took the pad again, read what she'd written, and said, "Wonderful, good." He hesitated. "Uh . . . perhaps we should move that chair around here," he said, "don't you think? So we won't have to be passing this thing back and forth."

He rose quickly and came to where she was sitting. Teddy got up, and he shoved the easy chair closer to the desk and to the side of it. She sat again, folding her raincoat over her lap.

"There, that's better," he said. "Now we can talk a bit more easily. Oh, excuse me, was my back to you? Did you get all of that?"

Teddy nodded, and smiled.

"This is all very new to me, you see," he said. "So. Where shall we begin? You understand, don't you, that the job calls for an expert typist . . . I see in your letter that you can do sixty words a minute . . ."

I may be a little rusty just now, Teddy wrote on the pad.

"Well, that all comes back to you, doesn't it? It's like roller skating, I would guess."

Teddy nodded, although she did not think typing was like roller skating.

"And you *do* take steno . . ."

She nodded again.

"And, of course, the filing is a routine matter, so I'm sure you can handle that."

She looked at him expectantly.

"We like attractive people in our offices, Miss Carella," Logan said, and smiled. "You're a very beautiful woman."

She nodded her thanks—modestly, she hoped—and then wrote: *It's* Mrs. *Carella.*

"Of course, forgive me," he said. "Theodora, is it?"

She wrote: *Most people call me Teddy.*

"Teddy? That's charming. Teddy. It suits you. You're extraordinarily beautiful, Teddy. I suppose you've heard that a thousand times . . ."

She shook her head.

". . . but I find that most compliments bear repeating, don't you? Extraordinarily beautiful," he said, and his eyes met hers. He held contact for longer than was comfortable. She lowered her eyes to the pad. When she looked up again, he was still staring at her. She shifted her weight in the chair. He was still watching her.

"So," he said. "Hours are nine to five, the job pays two and a quarter to start, can you begin Monday morning? Or will you need a little time to get your affairs in order?"

Her eyes opened wide. She had not for a moment believed it would be this simple. She was speechless, literally so, but speechless beyond that—as if her mind had suddenly gone blank, her ability to communicate frozen somewhere inside her head.

"You *do* want the job, don't you?" he said, and smiled again.

Oh, yes, she thought, oh God, *yes!* She nodded, her eyes flashing happiness, her hands unconsciously starting to convey her appreciation, and then falling empty of words into her lap when she realized he could not possibly read them.

"*Will* Monday morning be all right?" he asked.

She nodded yes.

"Good then," he said, "I'll look forward to seeing you then."

He leaned toward her.

"I'm sure we'll get along fine," he said, and suddenly, without warning, he slid his hand under her skirt. She sat bolt upright, her eyes opening wide, too shocked to move for an instant. His fingers tightened on her thigh.

"Don't you think so, Miss Car . . . ?"

She slapped him hard, as hard as she could, and then rose at once from her chair, and moved toward him, her teeth bared, her hand drawn back to hit him again. He was nursing his jaw, his blue eyes looking hurt and a trifle bewildered. Words welled up inside her, words she could not speak. She stood there trembling with fury, her hand still poised to strike.

"That's it, you know," he said, and smiled.

She was turning away from him, tears welling into her eyes, when she saw more words forming on his lips.

"You just blew it, dummy."

And the last word pained her more than he possibly could have known, the last word went through her like a knife.

She was still crying when she came out of the building into the falling rain.

* * *

Annie had been unable to reach three of the victims by telephone, but the five she *did* manage to contact told her they had been contributors to A.I.M. She spent the rest of the afternoon trying the addresses she had for the remaining three victims. Two of them were still out when she got there, but Angela Ferrari informed her that she was a pro-life supporter and had contributed not only to A.I.M. but to Right to Life as well. It was almost six o'clock when she rang Janet Reilly's doorbell. Janet was the most recent of the serial rape victims, and—at only nineteen—the youngest of them. A college student, she lived at home with her parents, and had just got there from a meeting of the Newman Club when Annie arrived.

Her parents were not happy to see Annie. They were both working people, and they'd got home just before their daughter, only to answer the door a few minutes later on the Rape Squad again. Their daughter had been raped for the first time on September 13. They thought she'd gone through enough horror then to have lasted her a lifetime, but it had happened to her again on October 11, the horror escalating, the terror a constant thing now. They did not want her to answer any further questions from the police. All they wanted was to be left alone. They all but closed the door in Annie's face until she promised this would be the very last question.

Janet Reilly answered the question positively.

She had indeed made a small contribution to a pro-life organization called A.I.M.

Annie left the apartment at ten minutes past six. From a pay phone on the corner, she tried to reach Vivienne Chabrun, the only victim she had not yet spoken to. Again, there was no answer at her apartment. She now knew for certain, however, that eight of the nine victims had made contributions in varying amounts to A.I.M., and it seemed to her that this information would be valuable to Eileen. She deposited the coin again, and dialed the number at Mary Hollings's apartment. She let the phone ring ten times. There was no answer.

Eileen was already on her way to dinner.

A musician roamed from table to table, strumming his guitar and singing Mexican songs. When he got to Eileen's table, he played "Cielito Lindo" for her, optimistically, she thought; the sky outside had been bloated with threatening black clouds when she'd entered the restaurant. The rain had stopped entirely at about four in the afternoon, but the clouds had begun building again at dusk, piling up massively and ominously overhead. By six-fifteen, when she'd left the apartment to walk here, she could already hear the sound of distant thunder in the next state, beyond the river.

She was having her coffee—the wall clock read twenty minutes past seven—when the first lightning flash came, illuminating the curtained window facing the street. The following boom of thunder was ear-shattering; she hunched her shoulders in anticipation, and even so its volume shocked her. The rain came then, unleashed in fury, enforced by a keening wind, battering the window and pelting the sidewalk outside. She lighted a cigarette and smoked it while she finished her coffee. It was almost seven-thirty when she paid her bill and went to the checkroom for the raincoat and umbrella she'd left there.

The raincoat was Mary's. It fit her a bit too snugly, but she thought it might be recognizable to him, and if the rain came—as it most certainly had—visibility might be poor; she did not want to lose him because he couldn't *see* her. The umbrella was Mary's, too, a delicate little red plaid thing that was more stylish than protective, especially against what was raging outside just now. The rainboots were Eileen's. Rubber with floppy tops. She had chosen them exactly because the tops *were* floppy. Strapped to her ankle inside the right boot was a holster containing a lightweight Browning .380 automatic pistol,

her spare. Her regulation pistol was a .38 Detective's
Special, and she was carrying that in a shoulder bag slung
over her left shoulder for an easy cross-body draw.

She tipped the checkroom girl a dollar (wondering if
this was too much), put on the raincoat, reslung the
shoulder bag, and then walked out into the small entry alcove. A pair of glass doors, with the word *Ocho* engraved on one and *Rios* on the other, faced the street
outside, lashed with rain now. Lightning flashed as she
pushed open one of the doors. She backed inside again,
waited for the boom of thunder to fade, and then stepped
out into the rain, opening the umbrella.

A gust of wind almost tore the umbrella from her
grasp. She turned into the wind, fighting it, refusing to
allow it to turn the umbrella inside out. Angling it over
her face and shoulders, using it as a shield to bully her
way through the driving rain, she started for the corner.
The route she had traced out this afternoon would take
her one block west on a brightly lighted avenue—
deserted now because of the storm—and then two blocks
north on less well-lighted streets to Mary's apartment.
She did not expect him to make his move while she was
on the avenue. But on that two-block walk to the
apartment—

She suddenly wished she'd asked for a backup.

Stupid, playing it this way.

And yet, if she'd planted her backups, say, on the
other side of the street, one walking fifty feet ahead of
her, the other fifty feet behind, he'd be sure to spot them,
wouldn't he? Three women walking out here in the rain
in the classic triangle pattern? Sure to spot them. Or suppose she'd planted them in any one of the darkened doorways or alleyways along the route she'd walked this
afternoon, and suppose he checked out that same route,
saw two ladies lurking in doorways—not many hookers
up here, and certainly none on the side streets where
there wasn't any business—no, he'd tip, he'd run, they'd

lose him. Better without any backups. And still, she wished she had one.

She took a deep breath as she turned the corner off the avenue.

The blocks would be longer now.

Your side streets were always longer than your streets on the avenue. Maybe twice as long. Plenty of opportunity for him in there. Two long blocks.

It was raining inside the floppy tops of the boots. She could feel the backup pistol inside the right boot, the butt cold against the nylon of her pantyhose. She was wearing panties *under* the pantyhose, great protection against a knife, oh, sure, great big chastity belt he could slash open in a minute. She was holding the umbrella with both hands now, trying to keep it from being carried away by the wind. She wondered suddenly if she shouldn't just throw the damn thing away, put her right hand onto the butt of the .38 in her bag—*He pulls that knife, don't ask questions, just blow him away.* Annie's advice. Not that she needed it.

Alley coming up on her right. Narrow space between two of the buildings, stacked with garbage cans when she'd passed it this afternoon. *Too* narrow for action? The guy wasn't looking to *dance,* he was looking to *rape,* and the width of the alley seemed to preclude the space for that. Ever get raped on top of a garbage can? she asked herself. *Don't ask questions, just blow him away.* Dark doorway in the building beyond the alley. Lights in the next building and the one after that. Lamppost on the corner. The sky suddenly split by a streak of lightning. Thunder booming on the night. A gust of wind turned the umbrella inside out. She threw it into the garbage can on the corner and felt the immediate onslaught of the rain on her naked head. Should have worn a hat, she thought. Or one of those plastic things you tie under your chin. Her hand found the butt of the .38 in her shoulder bag.

She crossed the street.

Another lamppost on the corner opposite.

Darkness beyond that.

An alley coming up, she knew. Wider than the first had been, a car's width across, at least. Nice place to tango. Plenty of room. Her hand tightened on the gun butt. Nothing. Nobody in the alley that she could see, no footsteps behind her after she passed it. Lighted buildings ahead now, looking potbelly warm in the rain. Another alley way up ahead, two buildings down from Mary's. What if they'd been wrong? What if he *didn't* plan to hit tonight? She kept walking, her hand on the gun butt. She skirted a puddle on the sidewalk. More lightning, she winced; more thunder, she winced again. Passing the only other alley now, dark and wide, but not as wide as the last one had been. Garbage cans. A scraggly wet cat sitting on one of the cans, peering out at the falling rain. Cat would've bolted if somebody was in there, no? She was passing the alley when he grabbed her.

He grabbed her from behind, his left arm looping around her neck and yanking her off her feet. She fell back against him, her right hand already yanking the pistol out of her bag. The cat shrieked and leaped off the garbage can, skittering underfoot as it streaked out into the rain.

"Hello, Mary," he whispered, and she pulled the gun free.

"This is a knife, Mary," he said, and his right hand came up suddenly, and she felt the sharp tip of the blade against her ribs, just below her heart.

"Just drop the gun, Mary," he said. "You still have the gun, huh, Mary? Same as last time. Well, just drop it, nice and easy, drop it on the ground, Mary."

He prodded her with the knife. The tip poked at the lightweight raincoat, poked at the thin fabric of her blouse beneath it, poked at her ribs. His left arm was still looped around her neck, holding her tight in the crook of his elbow. The pistol was in her hand, but he was behind her, and powerless in his grip, and the pressure of the knife blade was more insistent now.

"Do it!" he said urgently, and she dropped the pistol.

It clattered to the alleyway floor. Lightning shattered the night. There was an enormous boom of thunder. He dragged her deeper into the alley, into the darkness, past the garbage cans to where a loading platform was set in the wall some three feet above the floor. A pair of rusted iron doors were behind the platform. He threw her onto the platform, and her hand went immediately into the top of her floppy rubber boot, groping for the butt of the Browning.

"Don't force me to cut you," he said.

She yanked the pistol out of its holster.

She was bringing it up into firing position, when he slashed her.

She dropped the gun at once, her hand going up to her face where sudden fire blazed a trail across her cheek. Her hand came away wet, she thought it was the rain at first, but the wet was sticky and thick, and she knew it was blood—he had cut her cheek, she was bleeding from the cheek! And suddenly she was overcome by a fear she had never before known in her life.

"Good girl," he said.

There was another flash of lightning, more thunder. The knife was under her dress now, she dared not move, he was picking at the nylon of the pantyhose with the knife, catching at it, plucking at it; she winced below, tightened there in horrified reaction, afraid of the knife, fearful he would use it again where she was infinitely more vulnerable. The tip of the blade caught the fabric, held. There was the sound of the nylon ripping, the whisper of the knife as it opened the pantyhose over her crotch and the panties underneath. He laughed when he realized she was also wearing panties.

"Expecting a rape?" he asked, still laughing, and then slashed the panties, too, and now she was open to the cold of the night, her legs spread and trembling, the rain beating down on her face and mingling there with the blood, washing the blood from her cheek burning hot where the gash crossed it, her eyes widening in terror when he placed the cold flat of the knife against her vagina and said, "Want me to cut you here, too, Mary?"

She shook her head, *No, please.* Mumbled the words incoherently. Said them aloud at last, "No, please," trembling beneath him as he moved between her legs and put the knife to her throat again. "Please," she said. "Don't . . . cut me again. Please."

"Want me to fuck you instead?" he asked.

She shook her head again. *No!* she thought. But she said instead, "Don't cut me again."

"You want to get fucked instead, isn't that right, Mary?"

No! she thought. "Yes," she said. *Don't cut me,* she thought. Please.

"Say it, Mary."

"Don't cut me," she said.

"Say it, Mary!"

"Fuck me in . . . instead," she said.

"You want my baby, don't you, Mary?"

Oh, God, no, she thought, *oh, God,* that's *it!* "Yes," she said, "I want your baby."

"The hell you do," he said, and laughed.

Lightning tore the night close by. Thunder boomed into the alleyway, immediately overhead, echoing.

She knew all the things to do, knew all about going for the eyes, clawing at the jelly of the eyes, blinding the bastard, she knew all about that. She knew what to do if he forced you to blow him, knew all about fondling his balls and taking him in your mouth, and then biting down hard on his cock and squeezing his balls tight at the same time, knew all about how to send a rapist shrieking into the night in pain. But a knife was at her throat.

The tip of the sharp blade was in the hollow of her

throat where a tiny pulse beat wildly. He had slashed her face, she could still feel the slow steady ooze of blood from the cut, fire blazing along the length of the cut from one end to the other. The rain pelted her face and her legs, her skirt up around her thighs, the cold, wet concrete of the platform beneath her, the rusted iron doors behind her. And then—suddenly—she felt the rigid thrust of him below, against her unreceptive lips, and thought he would tear her with the force of his penetration, rip her as if with the knife itself, still at her throat, poised to cut.

She trembled in fear, and in shame, and in helpless desperation, suffering his pounding below, sobbing now, repeatedly begging him to stop, afraid of screaming lest the knife pierce the flesh of her throat as surely as he himself was piercing her flesh below. And when he shuddered convulsively—the knife tip trembling against her throat—and then lay motionless upon her for several moments, she could only think *It's over, he's done,* and the shame washed over her again, the utter sense of degradation caused by his invasion, and she sobbed more scathingly. And realized in that instant that this was not a working cop here in a dark alley, her underwear torn, her legs spread, a stranger's sperm inside her. No. This was a frightened *victim,* a helpless violated *woman.* And she closed her eyes against the rain and the tears and the pain.

"*Now* go get your abortion," he said.

He rolled off her.

She wondered where her gun was. Her guns.

She heard him running out of the alley on the patter of the rain.

She lay there in pain, above and below, her eyes closed tight.

She lay there for a very long while.

Then she stumbled out of the alley, and found the nearest patrol box, and called in the crime.

And fainted as lightning flashed again, and did not hear the following boom of thunder.

12

ANNIE WENT OUT WITH A VENGEANCE.

Knowing what had happened to Eileen the night before, visualizing her torn and bleeding in that rain-swept alley, she knew only that the son of a bitch had to be stopped, and she prayed to God that when she caught up with him she simply didn't shoot him dead before asking his name. She did not know what had happened to Teddy Carella yesterday afternoon in Philip Logan's office; she did not, in fact, even know Steve Carella except as the Chinese-looking detective who'd been sitting at one of the desks the first time she'd walked into the 87th Precinct squadroom. But had she known either of them, had she known that Teddy had been submitted to her own baptism of fire yesterday, she would have considered it only a less severe manifestation of what had happened to Eileen.

The call from Sergeant Murchison had come at exactly ten minutes to eight, five minutes after a radio motor patrol car from the Eight-Seven responded and found Eileen lying unconscious on the sidewalk under the call box. Annie had listened silently while Murchison gave her the news. She thanked him, put on her raincoat, and went out into the street where the lightning and thunder were gone but the rain persisted. By the time she arrived at the hospital, twelve stitches had already been taken in Eileen's cheek. The emergency room doctor reported that Eileen had been sedated and was now asleep; they planned to keep her overnight for observation because she'd been in a state of shock when they admitted her. He

would not allow Annie to see her, even though she tried
to pull rank. Annie went home, called A.I.M. on the off
chance someone might be there—it was almost ten
o'clock by then—got no answer, and then looked up the
home number of Polly Floyd, the A.I.M. supervisor
she'd spoken to on the phone yesterday. She got no answer. She kept trying until midnight. Still no answer. She
tossed and turned all night long, waiting for morning.

Again there was no answer when she called the A.I.M.
offices at 9:00 A.M. She tried again at nine-fifteen and
once more at nine-thirty, and then she dialed Polly
Floyd's home number. The phone rang repeatedly. Annie counted a dozen rings and was about to hang up when
Polly at last answered the phone. Annie told her that she
wanted to come to the office. Polly said the office was
closed on Saturdays. Annie told her to open it. Polly said
that was impossible. Annie told her to open it and to have
the entire staff assembled there by eleven o'clock. Polly
said she had no intention of doing anything of the sort.
Annie took a deep breath.

"Miss Floyd," she said, "I have a police officer in the
hospital who was brought in last night with a knife
wound that required twelve stitches. I can go all the way
downtown to ask a judge for a search warrant, but I've
got to tell you, Miss Floyd, I'll be mean as hell if I have
to go through all that trouble. What I'm suggest-
ing . . ."

"Is this some sort of coercion?" Polly said.

"Yes," Annie answered.

"I'll see if I can round up the staff for you."

"Thank you," Annie said, and hung up.

The A.I.M. offices were at 832 Hall Avenue, above a
bookstore that was going out of business. The building
was six stories high, and the A.I.M. offices were on the
third floor. Annie arrived there at a little before eleven.
The small reception area beyond the frosted glass door
looked like something a down-at-the-heels private eye

might have inhabited were it not for the posters on all four walls. The posters were blown-up photographs showing fetuses in various stages of development. Across the top of each photo were the words "Against Infant Murder," lettered in red and designed to look like dripping blood. Polly Floyd herself resembled a fetus in an advanced stage of development, a tiny, pink-faced, pink-fisted lady with short blond hair and a mouth that looked as if it had never been kissed and never *wanted* to be kissed. Well, maybe Annie was wrong on that score; the woman hadn't answered her phone at midnight last night, and it had taken her forever to get to it at nine-thirty this morning.

Polly Floyd was in high dudgeon when Annie walked in. She immediately began complaining about police states and honest citizens being subjected to—

"I'm sorry," Annie said, not sounding sorry at all. "But, as I told you on the phone, this is a matter of some urgency."

"What does your *cop* have to do with *us?*" Polly asked. "If someone got himself stabbed . . ."

"Herself," Annie said.

"Even so, what . . . ?"

"Where's your staff?" Annie asked abruptly. They were standing alone in the small reception room with its pictures of fetuses. Polly still hadn't taken off her coat. Undoubtedly, she expected a brief meeting.

"They're waiting in my office," she said.

"How many on the staff?"

"Four."

"Including you?"

"In addition to me."

"Any of them men?"

"One."

"I want to see him," Annie said.

Seeing him was the first thing she wanted to do.

She had called the hospital again a half-hour ago, before leaving her apartment, to check on Eileen's condition, and to talk to her if possible. When Eileen answered the phone in her room, she sounded drowsy, but she told Annie she was feeling okay—considering. Her description of the man who'd attacked her jibed exactly with the description the previous victims had given: White, thirtyish, six feet tall, a hundred and eighty pounds. Brown hair, blue eyes, no visible scars or tattoos.

The man waiting in Polly Floyd's office was a scrawny black man in his sixties, about five feet eight inches tall, with brown eyes behind tortoise shell eyeglasses, and a fringe of white hair circling his otherwise bald head.

There were three other people waiting in the room, all of them women.

Annie asked them to sit down.

Polly stood just inside the door, annoyed by this invasion of A.I.M.'s offices, further annoyed by the easy takeover of her own *private* office.

Annie asked the gathered staff if any of them were familiar with any of the following names, and then read them off: Lois Carmody, Terry Cooper, Patricia Ryan, Vivienne Chabrun, Angela Ferrari, Cecily Bainbridge, Blanca Diaz, Mary Hollings and Janet Reilly.

Everyone in the room agreed that the names sounded familiar.

"They've all been contributors to A.I.M. at one time or another," Annie said. "Isn't that right?"

None of the staff knew if that was why the names sounded familiar to them.

"How many contributors do you *have?*" Annie asked.

Everyone on the staff looked at Polly Floyd.

"I'm sorry, but that's *our* business," Polly said. She was still standing just inside the doorway. She had not yet taken off her raincoat. Her arms were folded across her chest.

"Do you keep a list of your contributors?" Annie asked her.

"Yes, but the list is confidential."

"Who has access to that list?" Annie asked.

"All of us. Everyone on the staff."

"But you say the list is confidential."

"Limited to staff access," Polly said.

"Well," the black man with the fringe of white hair said, "that isn't quite . . ."

"In any event," Polly interrupted, "the list is not available for police scrutiny."

Annie turned to the man.

"I don't believe I caught your name, sir," she said.

"Eleazar Fitch," he said.

"I like biblical names," Annie said, and smiled.

"My father's name was Elijah," Fitch said, and returned the smile.

"You were saying, Mr. Fitch, about this list . . . ?"

"Whatever it is you're investigating," Polly cut in, "we're not interested in involvement."

"Involvement?" Annie said.

"Involvement, yes. We don't want A.I.M. linked in any way to the stabbing of a policewoman."

"Which happens to be a Class-C felony," Annie said, "punishable by three to fifteen years in prison. Rape, on the other hand . . ."

"Rape?" Polly said, and her pink face went white.

"Rape, Miss Floyd, is a Class-B felony, and you can get twenty-five years for that. This police officer was raped last night. Cut and raped, Miss Floyd. We have good reason to believe that her assailant is also responsible for the rapes of nine other women, eight of whom were contributors to A.I.M. What I want to know . . ."

"I'm sure their donations to A.I.M. had nothing whatever . . ."

"How can you know that for sure, Polly?" Fitch asked.

Polly Floyd turned pink again. Fitch stared at her for a moment, and then looked at Annie again.

"We sell our mailing list," he said.

"To whom?" Annie said at once.

"To any responsible organization that—"

"Polly, you *know* that isn't true," Fitch interrupted, and turned to Annie again. "We'll let anyone who makes a sizable donation have the list."

"What do you consider sizable?" Annie asked.

"Anything over a hundred dollars."

"So if I sent you a hundred dollars and requested your mailing list . . ."

"You'd get it in a minute."

"Provided," Polly said, "you *also* told us how you planned to *use* the list."

"Is that true, Mr. Fitch?"

"We'll send it to anyone interested in the pro-life movement," Fitch said. "Express a sincere interest in the movement, request the mailing list, and send us a check for a hundred bucks. That's it."

"I see," Annie said.

"We're not Right To Life, you know," Polly said defensively. "We don't have giant corporations and trust funds making contributions to us. We're new, we only started two years ago, we have to support our efforts by whatever means possible and ethical. There's nothing wrong with supplying mailing lists to interested contributors, you know. You can buy or rent a mailing list for *anything!*"

"How many mailing lists have you distributed since the beginning of the year?" Annie asked.

"I have no idea," Polly said.

"No more than ten," Fitch said.

"All here in the city?"

"Most of them. Some of them were out of town."

"How many in the city?"

"I don't know, I'd have to look at the files."

"You have the names and addresses on file?"

"Oh, yes."

"I'd like to see them, please."

"Giving you those names would be tantamount to invading the privacy of people who may not *wish* their privacy invaded," Polly said.

Annie looked at her. She did not mention that telling a woman what she could or could not do about her own pregnancy might *also* be invading the privacy of someone who might not wish to have her privacy invaded.

She said only, "I guess I'll have to get that court order, after all."

"Give her the names," Polly said.

Eileen was sitting up in bed, her hands flat on the sheet, when Kling entered the room. Her head was turned away from him. The window oozed raindrops, framed a gray view of buildings beyond.

"Hi," he said.

When she turned toward the door, he saw the bandage on her left cheek. A thick wad of cotton layers covered with adhesive plaster tape. She'd been crying; the flesh around her eyes was red and puffy. She smiled and lifted one hand from the sheet in greeting. The hand dropped again, limply, white against the white sheet.

"Hi," she said.

He came to the bed. He kissed her on the cheek that wasn't bandaged.

"You okay?" he asked.

"Yeah, fine," she said.

"I was just talking to the doctor, he says they'll be releasing you later today."

"Good," she said.

He did not know what else to say. He knew what had happened to her. He did not know what to say.

"Some cop, huh?" she said. "Let him scare me out of both my guns, let him . . ." She turned her face away again. Rain slithered down the window panes.

"He raped me, Bert."

"I know."

"How . . . ?" Her voice caught. "How do you feel about that?"

"I want to kill him," Kling said.

"Sure, but . . . how do . . . how do you feel about me getting raped?"

He looked at her, puzzled. Her head was still turned away from him, as though she were trying to hide the patch on her cheek and by extension the wound that testified to her surrender.

"About letting him rape me," she said.

"You didn't *let* him do *anything.*"

"I'm a cop," she said.

"Honey . . ."

"I should have . . ." She shook her head. "I was too scared, Bert," she said. Her voice was very low.

"I've been scared," he said.

"I was afraid he'd kill me."

She turned to look at him.

Their eyes met. Tears were forming in her eyes. She blinked them back.

"A cop isn't *supposed* to get that scared, Bert. A cop is supposed to . . . to . . . I threw away my *gun!* The minute he stuck that knife in my ribs, I panicked, Bert, I threw away my *gun!* I had it in my hand but I threw it away!"

"I'd have done the same . . ."

"I had a spare in my boot, a little Browning. I reached into the boot, I had the gun in my hand, ready to fire, when he . . . he . . . cut me."

Kling was silent.

"I didn't think it would hurt that much, Bert. Getting cut. You cut yourself shaving your legs or your armpits, it stings for a minute but this was my *face*, Bert, he cut my *face*, and oh, *Jesus*, how it *hurt!* I'm no beauty, I know that, but it's the only face I have, and when he . . ."

"You're gorgeous," he said.

"Not anymore," she said, and turned away from him again. "That was when I—when he cut me and I lost the second gun—that was when I knew I . . . I'd do . . . I'd do anything he wanted me to do. I *let* him rape me, Bert. I *let* him do it."

"You'd be dead otherwise," Kling said.

"So damn helpless," she said, and shook her head again.

He said nothing.

"So now . . ." Her voice caught again. "I guess you'll always wonder whether I was asking for it, huh?"

"Cut it out," he said.

"Isn't that what men are supposed to wonder when their wives or their girlfriends get . . . ?"

"You *were* asking for it," Kling said. "That's why you were out there, that was your job. You were doing your job, Eileen, and you got hurt. And that's . . ."

"I also got *raped!*" she said, and turned to him, her eyes flashing.

"That was part of getting hurt," he said.

"No!" she said. *"You've* been hurt on the job, but nobody ever *raped* you afterward! There's a difference, Bert."

"I understand the difference," he said.

"I'm not sure you do," she said. "Because if you did, you wouldn't be giving me this 'line of duty' bullshit!"

"Eileen . . ."

"He didn't rape a *cop,* he raped a *woman!* He raped *me,* Bert! *Because* I'm a woman!"

"I know."

"No, you *don't* know," she said. "How *can* you know? You're a man, and men don't get raped."

"Men get raped," he said softly.

"Where?" she said. "In prison? Only because there aren't any women handy."

"Men get raped," he said again, but did not elaborate.

She looked at him. The pain in his eyes was as deep as the pain she had felt last night when the knife ripped across her face. She kept studying his eyes, searching his face. Her anger dissipated. This was Bert sitting here with her, this was not some vague enemy named Man, this was Bert Kling—and *he*, after all, was not the man who'd raped her.

"I'm sorry," she said.

"That's okay."

"I shouldn't be taking it out on you."

"Who else?" he said, and smiled.

"I'm sorry," she said. "Really."

She searched for his hand. He took her hand in both his own.

"I never thought this could happen to me," she said, and sighed. "Never in a million years. I've been scared out there, you're always a little scared . . ."

"Yes," he said.

"But I never thought *this* could happen. Remember how I used to kid around about my rape fantasies?"

"Yes."

"It's only a fantasy when it isn't *real*," she said. "I used to think . . . I guess I thought . . . I mean, I was *scared*, Bert, even with backups I was scared. But not of being *raped*. Hurt, maybe, but not *raped*. I was a *cop*, how could a cop possibly . . . ?"

"You're still a cop," he said.

"You better believe it," she said. "Remember what I was telling you? About feeling degraded by decoy work? About maybe asking for a transfer?"

"I remember."

"Well, now they'll have to blast me out of this job with dynamite."

"Good," he said, and kissed her hand.

" 'Cause I mean . . . doesn't *somebody* have to be out there? To make sure this doesn't happen to *other* women? I mean, there has to be *somebody* out there, doesn't there?''

"Sure," he said. "You."

"Yeah, me," she said, and sighed deeply.

He held her hand to his cheek.

They were silent for several moments.

She almost turned her face away again.

Instead, she held his eyes with her own and said, "Will you . . . ?"

Her voice caught again.

"Will you love me as much with a scar?"

Sometimes you got lucky first crack out of the box.

There had not been ten requests for mailing lists, as Eleazar Fitch had surmised, but only eight. Three of them were from out-of-towners who wished to start local pro-life groups of their own, and who were looking for organization support from previous contributors. Five of them were in the city: A group to support the strict surveillance of books on library shelves had requested the mailing list; a group opposed to young girls seeking birth control advice without the consent of their parents had also requested the list of contributors to A.I.M.; a group opposed to euthanasia had contributed a hundred dollars and asked for the list; an organization opposing the passage of the Equal Rights Amendment had similarly requested the list. Only one of the requests had been made by a single individual. His letter to A.I.M. stated that he was preparing an article for a magazine named *Our Right*, and that he was interested in contacting supporters of A.I.M. with a view toward soliciting their opinions on pro-life.

His name was Arthur Haines.

Today was Saturday. Annie was hopeful that Arthur Haines would be home when she visited him. The address to which the mailing list had been sent was in a complex of garden apartments in a residential section of

Majesta. It was still raining lightly when she got there. The walks outside were covered with wet leaves. Lights were showing inside many of the apartments, even though it was not yet 1:00 P.M. She found the address—a first-floor apartment in a red-brick three-story building—and rang the doorbell. The living room drapes were open. From where she stood outside the front door, she could see obliquely into the room. Two little girls—she guessed they were eight and six respectively—were sitting on the floor, watching an animated cartoon on the television screen. The eldest of the two nudged her younger sister the moment she heard the doorbell, obviously prodding her to answer it. The younger girl pulled a face, got to her feet and came toward the front of the apartment, passing from Annie's line of sight. From somewhere inside, a woman's voice yelled, "Will one of you kids get the *door,* please?"

"I'm *here,* Mom!" the younger girl answered, just inside the door now. "Who is it?" she said.

"Police officer," Annie said.

"Just a minute, please," the girl said.

Annie waited. She could hear voices inside, the little girl telling her mother the *police* were at the door, the mother telling her daughter to go back and watch television.

Just inside the door now, the woman said, "Yes, who is it, please?"

"Police officer," Annie said. "Could you open the door, please?"

The woman who opened the door was eminently pregnant, and possibly imminently so. It was almost one in the afternoon, but she was still wearing a bathrobe over a nightgown and she looked as bloated as anyone could possibly look, her huge belly starting somewhere just below her breasts and billowing outward, a giant dirigible of a woman with a doll's face and a cupid's bow mouth, no lipstick on it, no makeup on her eyes or face.

"Yes?" she said.

"I'm looking for Arthur Haines," Annie said. "Is he here?"

"I'm Lois Haines, his wife. What is it, please?"

"I'd like to talk to him," Annie said.

"What about?" Lois said.

She stood in the doorway like a belligerent elephant, frowning, obviously annoyed by this intrusion on a rainy Saturday.

"I'd like to ask him some questions," Annie said.

"What about?" Lois insisted.

"Ma'am, may I come in, please?"

"Let me see your badge."

Annie opened her handbag and took out the leather fob to which her shield was pinned. Lois studied it, and then said, "Well, I wish you'd tell me what . . ."

"Who is it, honey?" a man's voice called.

Beyond Lois, who still stood in the doorway refusing entrance, her shoulders squared now and her belly aggressively jutting, Annie could see a tall, dark-haired man coming from the rear of the apartment. Lois stepped aside only slightly, turning to him, and Annie got a good look as he approached: Thirty-ish, she guessed. Easily six feet tall. A hundred and eighty pounds if he weighed an ounce. Brown hair and blue eyes.

"This woman wants to see you," Lois said. "She says she's a policeman."

The word "policeman" amused Annie, but she did not smile. She was busy watching Haines as he came into the small entrance foyer now, a pleasant smile on his face.

"Well, come in," he said. "What's the matter with you, Lo? Don't you know it's raining out there? Come in, come in," he said, and extended his hand as his wife stepped aside. "What's this about, officer?" he said, shaking hands with Annie. "Am I illegally parked? I thought alternate side of the street regulations didn't apply on weekends."

"I don't know where you're parked," Annie said. "I'm not here about your car, Mr. Haines."

The three of them were standing now in an uneasy knot in the entrance foyer, the door closed against the rain, the two little girls turning their attention from the animated cartoon to the visitor who said she was a cop. They had never seen a real-life lady cop before. She didn't even *look* like a cop. She was wearing a raincoat and eyeglasses spattered from the rain outside. She was carrying a leather bag slung from her left shoulder. She was wearing low-heeled walking shoes. The little girls thought she looked like their Aunt Josie in Maine. Their Aunt Josie was a social worker.

"Well, what is it then?" Haines said, "How can we help you?"

"Is there someplace we can talk privately?" Annie asked, glancing at the children.

"Sure, let's go in the kitchen," Haines said. "Honey, is there any coffee left on the stove? Would you care for a cup of coffee, Miss . . . I'm sorry, I didn't get your name."

"Detective Anne Rawles," Annie said.

"Well, come on in," Haines said.

They went into the kitchen. Annie and Haines sat at the kitchen table. As Lois started for the stove, Annie said, "Thank you, Mrs. Haines, I don't care for any coffee."

"Fresh brewed this morning," Lois said.

"Thank you, no. Mr. Haines," Annie said, "did you write to an organization called A.I.M., requesting a list of their contributors?"

"Why, yes, I did," Haines said, looking surprised. His wife was standing near the stove, watching him.

"How'd you plan to use that list?" Annie asked.

"I was preparing a paper on the attitudes and opinions of pro-life supporters."

"For a magazine, is that right?"

"Yes."

"Are you a writer, Mr. Haines?"

"No, I'm a teacher."

"Where do you teach, Mr. Haines?"

"At the Oak Ridge Middle School."

"Here in Majesta?"

"Yes, just a mile from here."

"Do you frequently write articles for magazines, Mr. Haines?"

"Well . . ." he said, and glanced at his wife, as if deciding whether he should lie or not. She was still watching him intently. "No," he said, "not as a usual practice."

"But you thought you might like to write this *particular* article . . ."

"Yes. I enjoy the magazine, I don't know if you've ever seen it. It's called *Our Right,* and it's published by a non-profit organization in . . ."

"So you contributed a hundred dollars to A.I.M. and asked for their mailing list, is that right?"

"Yes."

"You gave somebody a hundred *dollars?*" Lois said.

"Yes, darling, I told you about it."

"No, you didn't," she said. "A hundred *dollars?*" She shook her head in amazement.

"How much did you expect to get for this article you were writing?" Annie asked.

"Oh, I don't know what they pay," Haines said.

"Did the magazine *know* you were writing this article?"

"Well, no. I planned to write it and then simply submit it."

"Send it to them."

"Yes."

"Hoping they would take it."

"Yes."

"Did you ever actually write this article, Mr. Haines?"

"Uh . . . no . . . I never got around to it. I'm very involved in extra-curricular activities at the school, you see. I teach English, and I'm faculty advisor for the school newspaper, and I'm also advisor for the drama club and the debating club, so it sometimes gets a bit hectic. I'll get around to it, though."

"Have you yet contacted any of the people on the mailing list A.I.M. supplied?"

"No, not yet," Haines said. "I will, though. As I say, when I find some free time . . ."

"What did you say this article was going to be about?" Lois asked.

"Uh . . . pro-life," Haines said. "The movement. The aims and attitudes of . . . uh . . . women who . . . uh . . ."

"When did you get to be such a big pro-lifer?" Lois asked.

"Well, it's a matter of some interest to me," Haines said.

His wife looked at him.

"Has been for a long time," he said, and cleared his throat.

"That's news to me, the fuss you made about *this* one," Lois said, and clutched her belly as if it were an overripe watermelon.

"Lois . . ."

"Totally news to me," she said, and rolled her eyes. "You should have heard him when I told him I was pregnant again," she said to Annie.

Annie was watching him.

"I'm sure that's of absolutely no interest to Miss Rawles," Haines said. "As a matter of fact, Miss Rawles—should I call you Detective Rawles?"

"Either way is fine," Annie said.

"Well, Miss Rawles, I wonder if you can tell me why

you're here. Has my letter to A.I.M. caused some sort of problem? Surely, an innocuous request for a mailing list . . ."

"I still can't get over your paying a hundred *dollars* for a mailing list," Lois said.

"It was a tax deductible contribution," Haines said.

"To a *pro*-life organization?" Lois said, shaking her head. "I can't believe it." She turned to Annie and said, "You live with a man for ten years, you *still* don't really know him, do you?"

"I guess not," Annie said. "Mr. Haines, do you know whether the following names were on the mailing list you received from A.I.M.?" She opened her notebook and began reading. "Lois Carmody, Blanca Diaz, Patricia Ryan . . ."

"No, I don't know any of those names."

"I didn't ask you if you *knew* them, Mr. Haines. I asked if they're on that list you got from A.I.M."

"I would have to check the list," Haines said. "If I can even *find* it."

"Vivienne Chabrun?" Annie said. "Angela Ferrari? Terry Cooper . . ."

"No, I don't know any of those people."

"Cecily Bainbridge, Mary Hollings, Janet Reilly?"

"No," Haines said.

"Eileen Burke?"

He looked puzzled for an instant.

"No," he said. "None of them."

"Mr. Haines," Annie said, slowly and deliberately, "can you tell me where you were last night between seven-thirty and eight o'clock?"

"At the school," Haines said. "The kids put the newspaper to bed on Friday night. That's where I was. In the newspaper office at the Oak Ridge Middle . . ."

"What time did you leave here last night, Mr. Haines?"

"Well, actually, I didn't come home. I had some papers to correct, and I guess I went directly from the faculty lounge to the newspaper office. To meet with the kids.''

"What time was that, Mr. Haines? When you met with the kids.''

"Oh, four o'clock. Four-thirty. They're very hard-working kids, I'm really proud of the newspaper. It's called the Oak Ridge . . .''

"What time did you get home last night, Mr. Haines?''

"Well, it only takes ten minutes to get here. It's only a mile down the road. Actually, a mile and three-tenths.''

"So what time did you get home?''

"Eight o'clock? Wasn't it somewhere around eight, Lo?''

"It was closer to ten," Lois said. "I was already in bed.''

"Yes, somewhere in there," Haines said. "Sometime between eight and ten.''

"It was ten minutes to ten exactly," Lois said. "I looked at the clock when I heard you come in.''

"So you were in the school's newspaper office . . .''

"Yes, I was.''

"From four o'clock yesterday afternoon . . .''

"Well, more like four-thirty. I'd say it was four-thirty.''

"From four-thirty to nine-forty. You said it takes ten minutes to get here, and you got home at nine-fifty . . .''

"Well, if Lois is sure about that. I thought it was closer to eight. When I got home, I mean.''

"That's almost five hours," Annie said. "Takes that long to put a newspaper to bed, does it?''

"Well, the time varies.''

"And you say you were working with the kids all that time?''

"Yes.''

"The kids on the newspaper staff.''

"Yes."

"May I have their names, please, Mr. Haines?"

"What for?"

"I'd like to talk to them."

"Why?"

"I'd like to know if you really *were* where you *say* you were last night."

Haines looked at his wife. He turned back to Annie.

"I . . . don't see why you feel it necessary to check on my whereabouts," he said. "I *still* don't know what you're doing here. As a matter of fact . . ."

"Mr. Haines, were you in Isola last night? In the vicinity of 1840 Laramie Crescent between seven-thirty and . . ."

"I told you I was . . ."

"Were you, more specifically, in an alleyway . . ."

"Don't be absurd."

". . . two doors down from 1840 Laramie Crescent . . ."

"I was . . ."

". . . cutting and raping a woman you thought was Mary Hollings?"

"I don't know anybody named . . ."

"Whom you'd *previously* raped on June tenth, September sixteenth, and October seventh?"

The kitchen was silent. Haines looked at his wife.

"I was at the school last night," he said to her.

"Then give me the names of the kids you were working with," Annie said.

"I was at the goddamn *school!*" Haines shouted.

"I washed your shirt this morning," Lois said softly. She kept staring at him. "There was blood on the cuff." She lowered her eyes. "I had to use cold water to get the blood out."

One of the little girls appeared in the doorway to the kitchen.

"Is something the matter?" she asked, her eyes wide.

"Mr. Haines," Annie said, "I'll have to ask you to come with me."

"Is something the matter?" the little girl asked again.

You want to know why, he said into the tape recorder, I'll *tell* you why. I've got nothing to hide, nothing to be ashamed of. If more people took the kind of stand I took, we wouldn't be overrun by these goddamn groups trying to force their harebrained opinions on others. I didn't hurt anyone by comparison. When you consider all the people *they're* hurting, I'm practically a saint. Who did I hurt, can you tell me? I'm not talking about the two I had to cut, that was protective, that was self-defense in a way. But none of the others got hurt, all I did was try to show them how wrong they are about their position. How sometimes it's *essential* to have an abortion. Something they can't seem to get through their thick heads. I wanted to prove this to them decisively. I wanted them to get pregnant by a rapist. I wanted them to be *forced* into having abortions—would *you* carry a rapist's baby? Would *you* give birth to a rapist's baby? I'm sure you wouldn't. And I was sure *they* wouldn't, either, which is why I worked it out so that they'd *have* to get pregnant sooner or later. If I raped them often enough, they had to get pregnant. The odds were maybe sixty to forty they'd get pregnant. It was as simple as that.

You want to know something? Not any one of my kids was planned. The two little girls you saw? Both accidents. The one my wife's carrying now, an accident. She's Catholic, she won't use anything but the rhythm method. You think she'd know by now that the damn thing doesn't work—a kid sixteen months after we were married, another one two years after that. You're supposed to *learn* from experience, aren't you? I kept trying to tell her. Go on the pill, get a diaphragm, let *me* use a rubber. No, no. Against the rules of the church, you know. The rhythm method, that's it. Or else abstinence.

Great choices, huh? Rhythm or abstinence. I'm thirty-one years old, I've had children since I was twenty-three, that's terrific, isn't it? And now another one on the way. She told me about it in February. We're going to have another baby, darling. Terrific. Really terrific. Just what I needed was another kid. I asked her to get an abortion. You'd think I asked her to drown herself. An abortion? Are you crazy? An *abortion?* Abortions are legal, I told her. This isn't the Middle Ages, I told her. You don't have to go through with a pregnancy if the child will be a burden to you. You just don't have to. She said the church was against abortion. She said even a lot of people who *weren't* Catholics disapproved of abortion and were working hard to change the law. She said the goddamn President of the United *States* disapproved of abortion! I told her the President wasn't earning twenty thousand a year, I told her the President wasn't out there busting his ass trying to clothe and feed and house a family, I told her the President wasn't *me*, Arthur Haines, who didn't *want* any more children! I'm thirty-one years old, I'll be close to fifty when this new one is just starting college. She told me too bad, we're having another baby, so get used to the idea.

I got used to the idea, all right. Not *her* idea, though. *Mine.* An idea I'd been thinking about for a long time. Get those goddamn women out there who are yelling no abortion, no abortion, put them in a position where they *have* to get an abortion, find out how they felt about it when it struck close to home. I wrote to Right to Life, trying to get a mailing list from them, but they told me I had to make my request on organization stationery, and I had to tell them how I planned to use the list. Well, I couldn't do that. I mean, how could I do *that?* So I zeroed in on this local group, A.I.M.—Against Infant Murder, how do you like *that* name?—and I told them I was writing a magazine article in favor of pro-life, and I wanted to contact women supporters of the movement so that I could find out their deepest feelings about the subject, all that bullshit, and they wrote back saying that they could not send the mailing list to anyone who did not first contribute at least a hundred dollars in support of the organization. I figured a hundred dollars was small enough price for what I planned to do, what I knew I *had* to do.

The mailing list didn't tell me anything about their religious affiliations. They had to be Catholics, you see. I mean, if a woman was a Protestant or whatever, she could be supporting a pro-life group and using a diaphragm at the same time, do you understand what I mean. I mean, the idea was to make them *pregnant*. If I went out after a Baptist or whatever, a Hindu, you know what I mean, I'd be spending all my time and energy for nothing if she happened to be on the pill or had an I.U.D. in there, it would just be a waste of time. So I followed them around—I didn't bother with anybody who had a name like Kaplowitz or Cohen, I knew right off they were Jewish—and I found out pretty fast who was going to a Catholic church on Sunday morning and who wasn't. I singled out the Catholics. I singled out all the Catholics who'd made contributions to A.I.M. The Catholics were my targets. I wanted to show them first that you could take the rhythm method and shove it, and I wanted to show them *next* that they were dead wrong when it came to abortion, if they *had* to get an abortion they'd *go* get it, all right, and in a hurry.

It was just coincidence that the first was named Lois.

I mean, my wife's name happens to be Lois, but that wasn't why I chose Lois Carmody. I mean, that was just coincidental. Lois Carmody—that just *happened* to be her name. She lived pretty close by, the first few times out, I didn't want to be away from home too long, I didn't want to have to make a hundred explanations. I mean, I refined it after a while, not everybody on the list lived a half-hour away, I had to find plausible excuses for being away, do you understand? I refined it. So I wouldn't have trouble at home. I got *enough* flak as it was, believe me, but she never really knew what I was doing, my wife—she accused me of having an affair once, can you imagine? That's pretty funny don't you think? An affair? I mean, if you wanted to get technical, I was having a *lot* of affairs. Well, when she accused me that time, there weren't as many then, this was before the summer vacation. I get July and August off, we usually go up to Maine to spend the summer months with her parents up there. I hate it, but what *other* kind of vacation can I afford? Anyway, this was in June when she accused me of having an affair. I didn't do Mary and then Janet until the school term started again.

I nailed one of them the first time out.

She isn't on your list of names, I guess you were just looking for repeaters, huh? I mean, women who were raped more than once. It's amazing how you got to me. Really amazing! You people must work very hard. Anyway, I got this woman—her name was Joanna Little, she's on the mailing list, but not on the list you read to me—I got her for the first time, the *only* time as it turned out, in March, she was one of the early ones. I was planning on getting her again—it doesn't work unless you watch the calendar and get to them on a regular basis—but next thing I knew, I was following her around and she's on the street big as a house! I caught her the first time *out!* That can happen, you know. And then I know she had an abortion because I followed her to the clinic one Saturday, and goodbye belly, all gone. I'd done what I *wanted* to do, do you see? It *worked*. I'd made her pregnant and forced her to have an abortion. Big Catholic! Big pro-life supporter! Got rid of that baby the way she would an old pair of socks. I went out to get drunk that night. Came home stinking drunk, Lois took a fit, well, the *hell* with Lois, popping out babies as if she's an assembly line. But that was just luck, getting Joanna the first time around. I knew that was just luck.

What you have to do, you see, is you make out this calendar, and you keep careful track of each time you get them. I mean, you lay it all out in advance. You have to get them according to the cycle, you see. Listen, I know all *about* the rhythm method, I'm an *expert* on the rhythm method. A woman's menstrual cycle—I don't care if it's twenty-eight days or thirty days or whatever—the woman usually starts ovulating on the twelfth day of her cycle. Those are the crucial days, the twelfth, the thirteenth, and the fourteenth day. You can expand that a bit, you can say the eleventh day to the fifteenth day, or even the sixteenth day in some cases. But I figured the eleventh to the fifteenth were the outer limits. The egg lasts about twelve hours, and the sperm about twenty-four—though some doctors say the sperm can last as long as seventy-two. Still, if you didn't want to take any chances, you had to figure the best time was the eleventh to the fifteenth day of their menstrual cycles. That was when they had the best chance of getting pregnant—when they were ovulating, you see.

Well, I couldn't just go up to these women and ask them when they had their last period, could I? I mean, that was out of the question. These were *strangers*, I didn't *know* them. It wasn't the same as with a wife or a girlfriend, where you're living with them and sleeping with them, and you know when they're about to get their period, it wasn't the same thing at all. These were total *strangers*, do you understand? So I had to figure out for myself when they'd be ripe, and what I did—well, look at the calendar.

Let's take—well, let's take August, for example, which is an easy one because the first happened to fall on a Monday. I was away in August, I was up in Maine. I'm only using this as an example. But . . . well here. In August, the first is a Monday. Let's also say, to make it sim-

ple, that this *also* happens to be the first day of this particular woman's menstrual cycle. Okay, I rape her that
Monday night. The next Monday night is the eighth,
which is the eighth day of her cycle, I'm making this easy
for you so you can follow it. The Monday after that is the
fifteenth. See? I caught her on the fifteenth day, which is
one of the days she's ovulating. Good. In a case like that,
I wouldn't even have to try getting her a fourth or fifth
time. But if you carry it out on the calendar, I mean, it
has to work out that sooner or later you'll catch her.

In August, for example, the twenty-second would
have been the twenty-second day of her cycle. The next
Monday is the twenty-ninth, which with some women
could be the start of a new cycle, it varies. So let's say the
cycle starts all over again on Monday, August twenty-
ninth. If we move into September . . . well, here the
next Monday is the fifth. This, now, is the *eighth* day of
her cycle. The next Monday is the twelfth, which happens to be the *fifteenth* day of her cycle, so there we are
again—bingo! I figured it was fool-proof. I mean, if you
got them on a carefully thought-out schedule, they *had* to
get pregnant sooner or later. And unless they wanted to
be carrying a rapist's baby, they *also* had to get an abortion.

It was as simple as that.

I was doing this to show these people how wrong they
are.

To show them that they cannot simply impose their
will upon others.

To drive home to them the fact that this is a democracy, and in a democracy there is freedom of choice for
one and for all.

Annie read the transcript typed from Haines's confes-
sion.

She read it yet another time.

Haines thought the right was wrong.

The right thought it was right.

Annie thought they were *both* wrong.

She sometimes wondered what would happen if people just left other people alone.

The wind and the rain had stopped.

In Grover Park, across the street from the 87th Precinct, the trees were bare, the ground covered with lifeless leaves.

"Well," Meyer said, "at least the rain's stopped."

They were all thinking that winter was on the way.

The feelings were mixed in the squadroom that Saturday afternoon. They all knew what had happened to Eileen Burke. They further knew that Annie Rawles had collared the rapist. But they didn't know what Kling was feeling, or how carefully they might have to tiptoe around him when the matter of Eileen's rape finally came out into the open. He was at the hospital just now. He'd been there early this morning, and he was there again now, and so there was yet time to explore and consider what their approach might be. You didn't simply go up to somebody whose girl had been raped, and say, "Hi, Bert, rain seems to have stopped, I hear Eileen got raped." There were ways of handling this, they were sure, but they still hadn't figured out how to deal with it.

Until Fat Ollie Weeks called.

"Hey, Steve-a-rino, how you doin'?" he said into the phone.

"Pretty good," Carella said. "How about you?"

"Oh, fine, fine, usual horseshit up here," Ollie said. "I got to tell you buddy, I'm *seriously* thinking of transferring to the Eight-Seven. I really like working with you guys."

Carella said nothing.

"Did you see the papers today?" Ollie asked.

"No," Carella said.

"Full of our Road Runner nut," Ollie said. "All the

headlines yelling 'Lightning Strikes Twice.' I guess he got what he wanted, huh? He's famous all over again."

"If that's fame," Carella said.

"Yeah, well, who knows with these nuts?" Ollie said, and then added, quite casually, "I hear Kling's girl got herself fucked last night."

There was a silence as vast as Siberia on the line.

At last, Carella said, "Ollie, don't ever say that again."

"What?" Ollie said.

"What you just said. Don't ever let those words pass your lips again, Ollie, do you hear me? Don't repeat them to anyone in the world. Not even to your mother. Is that . . . ?"

"My mother's dead," Ollie said.

"Is that clear?" Carella said.

"What's the big deal?" Ollie said.

"The big deal is she's one of *ours*," Carella said.

"So she's a cop, big deal. What's that . . . ?"

"No, Ollie," Carella said. "She's one of *ours*. Have you got that, Ollie?"

"Yeah, yeah, I got it, relax, willya? My lips are sealed."

"I hope so," Carella said.

"Boy, you're some grump today," Ollie said. "Give me a call when you're in a better mood, okay?"

"Sure," Carella said.

"Ciao, paisan," Ollie said, and hung up.

Carella gently replaced the receiver on the cradle.

He was thinking that if Kling was hurting, they were all hurting. It was really as simple as that.

"Best thing about Lightning," Hawes said, "is he wasn't the Deaf Man."

"I was afraid it might be him, too," Meyer said.

"Me, too," Carella said.

"Seemed like the man's style," Brown said.

"Anybody want coffee?" Meyer asked.

"Bad enough as it was," Hawes said.

"Coulda been worse," Brown said.

"Coulda *really* been the Deaf Man," Carella said.

Miscolo came down the hall from the Clerical Office, pushed his way through the slatted rail divider, and walked directly to Carella's desk.

"Just the man we want to see," Meyer said. "You got any coffee brewing in the Clerical Office?"

"I thought you didn't like my coffee," Miscolo said.

"We *love* your coffee," Brown said.

"Go down the street to the diner, you want coffee," Miscolo said.

"Getting cold out there," Hawes said.

"I don't need fair weather coffee drinkers," Miscolo said. "This is for you, Steve. Sergeant sent it up a few minutes ago." He tossed a plain white envelope on the desk. "No return address on it."

Carella looked at the face of the envelope. It was addressed to him at the 87th Precinct. The envelope carried an Isola postmark.

"Open it," Miscolo said. "I'm dying of curiosity."

"Teddy know you got a girlfriend writing to you here?" Hawes asked, and winked at Meyer.

Carella slit open the envelope.

"What'd you do with your rug?" Brown asked Meyer. "You could use it, kind of weather we'll be having."

Carella unfolded the single sheet of paper that had been inside the envelope. He looked at it. Meyer noticed that his face went suddenly white.

"What is it?" he said.

The squadroom was silent all at once. The men crowded around Carella's desk where Carella held the sheet of paper in his hand. It seemed to Hawes that his hand was shaking slightly. They all looked at the sheet of paper·

"Eight black horses," Meyer said.
"The Deaf Man," Brown said.
He was back.